Best Fiction and
Best General Fiction

"…Maitland-Lewis' tale is scrupulously researched, saturated with rich historical detail."

KIRKUS REVIEWS

"…gripping novel of historical fiction."

FOREWORD REVIEWS

"…a fine and recommended read, not to be overlooked."

MIDWEST BOOK REVIEW

"…a thrilling page-turner."

REBECCA'S READS

Praise for Emeralds Never Fade

"Impeccably researched, *Emeralds Never Fade* is a poignant story of two men whose lives, and the lives of their family members, are forever altered by a period of history that should never be forgotten. As Hitler's Nazis march across Europe and the horrors of the Holocaust unfold, Maitland-Lewis delivers a personal account of loss, love, sacrifice and triumph. *Emeralds Never Fade* is hard to close at night and hard to forget."

—*Robert Dugoni, NY Times bestselling author*
Murder One *and* Bodily Harm

"An extremely clever, well-crafted thriller that compels the reader to turn page after page excitedly. The author, Stephen Maitland-Lewis, earnestly informs about an intensely significant historical era which he tautly wraps around with irresistible charm his fascinating tale of mystery and intrigue."

—*Robert K. Tanenbaum*
Bestselling author of the Butch Karp Thriller series

"I started *Emeralds* and couldn't put it down until the end. It is a page turner—greatly enjoyable and informative. Perfecto!"

—*Connie Martinson, nationally syndicated journalist*
and TV host of Connie Martinson Talks Books

"Stephen Maitland-Lewis beautifully crafts a story of intrigue that examines the human condition in all its layers. The fascinating journeys of Leo Bergner and Bruno Franzmann are vividly detailed in a tour de force account of men shaped by their remarkable life experiences. *Emeralds Never Fade* gains power and poignancy with every riveting page."

—*Jim Engster*
NPR host and President of Louisiana Radio Network

"*Emeralds Never Fade* is so compelling that at first I thought I had written it myself. This book is great!"

—*Alan Zweibel*
Thurber prize-winning author of The Other Shulman

"A fascinating combination of thriller and psychodrama of an entire era, *Emeralds Never Fade* is a vivid depiction of two characters in the vortex of the most desperate hour in Jewish history. With echoes of The Chosen, Maitland-Lewis captures the very personal fallout of the Holocaust in a manner that captures events in both their terror and absurdity."

—Eric Dezenhall
Author of THE DEVIL HIMSELF

"*Emeralds Never Fade* is a deftly woven and intriguing tale of two German boys played out against the unspeakable horrors of the Nazi regime and World War II—a page turning thriller that won't disappoint."

—Dr. James Muyskens, President
Queen's College, New York

"Maitland-Lewis is a master storyteller. *Emeralds Never Fade* depicts not only a staggering and grand sweep of history but the fascinating mysteries of the human heart."

—Brad Schreiber
Award-winning journalist and author of BECOMING JIMI HENDRIX

"Stephen Maitland-Lewis deftly guides us through the dark times of Nazi Germany, where birth and circumstance muddy the boundaries of good and evil. We travel the continent and beyond, through the exciting world of international banking, as we follow separate lives that are yet intertwined, with an ending that is completely unexpected."

—Pam Atherton
Award-winning talk show host

"*Emeralds Never Fade* is a major tour-de-force and personal account of one of the most horrifying and compelling eras the world has ever endured. The characters come alive in Stephen Maitland-Lewis' inspiring prose to the point you simply can't put it down or wait to attack the next inspiring, fascinating page."

—John L. Seitz
Senior Editor, The Beverly Hills Courier

"A pulsating story of two boys once joined together by the love of music, then separated by the paths of war. A gripping read with a heart-pounding ending."

—*Monty Hall*
Iconic television personality

"I've been waiting for Stephen Maitland-Lewis to top *Hero on Three Continents* and he has done it with *Emeralds Never Fade*. This compelling story of tragedy and triumph kept me riveted to the very last page."

—*A. C. Lyles*
Producer, Paramount Pictures

"I could not put 'Emeralds' down, and cannot forget the story and the boys whose future was shaped by the Holocaust. It's a thrilling page-turner, believable in its geography and history, and dramatic in every way. It is epic with a powerful ending, and profoundly meaningful."

— *Joseph Benincasa*
President & CEO, The Actors Fund

"A compelling read punctuated with unexpected twists and turns that make it difficult to put the book down."

—*Roger Lefkon*
Former Merv Griffin Entertainment and NBC television executive

"Stephen Maitland-Lewis has crafted an important novel that is an enjoyable and compelling read. An exciting and moving page-turner."

—*Jerry Zeitman*
Hollywood Producer

"Put this marvelous story at the top of your 'must read' list. The characters come alive and will impress you... and haunt you as the story reveals its secrets. A powerful study of behavior patterns as life events unfold. Enjoy it—and take its lessons to heart"

—*Rabbi Dr. Sanford M. Shapero*
Former Regional Director of The Union For Reform Judaism

EMERALDS
NEVER FADE

ALSO BY STEPHEN MAITLAND-LEWIS

Hero on Three Continents

EMERALDS NEVER FADE

STEPHEN MAITLAND-LEWIS

Glyd–Evans Press
Portland Oregon

Glyd–Evans Press
P.O. Box 14946
Portland Oregon 97293-0946 U.S.A.
info@gepress.com

EMERALDS NEVER FADE

by Stephen Maitland-Lewis

ISBN 978-0-9832596-3-3

Library of Congress Control Number: 2011941002

Also available in electronic form for most e-readers.
For more information visit www.gepress.com

3   5   7   9   10   8   6   4   2

IN MEMORIAM

My Father – Philip
(1909–1978)

My Mother – Esther
(1909–1994)

My Brother – Martin
(1936–1974)

My Uncle – Benny
(1908–1980)

My Hero – Louis Armstrong
(1901–1971)

My Mentor – Harold Robbins
(1916–1997)

My Friend – Arthur Marx
(1921–2011)

Once the game is over, the king and the pawn go back in the same box.

Italian Proverb

No man is rich enough to buy back his past.

Oscar Wilde

PROLOGUE

"Avram, it's me, Uri."

Uri Nusbaum spoke firmly, but he was badly shaken. "I'm at the Dorchester. Leo has had a heart attack. He's been taken to the Middlesex Hospital. Danny is with him. I'm coming straight back to the embassy now, and I'll be there in fifteen minutes."

Though officially a senior international banker with the Israeli Bank Leumi, Uri was actually a Mossad operative, and he had known Leo since the two arrived as frightened teenagers in Palestine in 1939. Seeing his friend taken away in an ambulance, lights flashing and sirens wailing, was as if his own heart had stopped beating.

Out of the hotel and onto Park Lane, Uri approached a line of black taxis waiting at the hotel's entrance. Uri told the driver his destination, Palace Gardens Terrace, and sat back. His restless fingers folded and unfolded his wallet until his American Express card fell onto the floor. He realized what he was doing and reached to retrieve it.

How could this be happening? Uri had met Leo in the hotel lobby that evening to join four hundred or more other guests, mostly bankers and financial journalists, at one of the receptions that was taking place during the week of the World Bank's London conference. Leo was still in the midst of a distinguished banking career. Uri knew of no medical problems, at least none that Leo had shared with him. Leo's mood, in spite of everything looking up in his life, had been bleak. Now Uri wondered if that was a sign of the impending attack.

Uri tucked his wallet into a pocket and crossed his legs. Why was he going back to the embassy? Duty? Habit? Certainly, it would have been inappropriate to stay at the cocktail party. But he just as easily could have gone home. Maybe he should have gone with Leo to the hospital instead of his colleague, Danny. No. He had learned during his training as an operative that it was crucial to divert all unnecessary attention. If Danny hadn't been there, of course he would have accompanied Leo. Maybe he should have gone to the hospital anyway.

The cab pulled up outside the embassy, and in a few minutes, Uri sat with the ambassador in his study. The ambassador showed the same anxiety and confusion as Uri felt. Leo was a critical member of their team, a major contributor to their mission. Now what?

"This is bad news, Uri," the ambassador said. "Leo is a good man. Let's hope he'll be okay. As soon as we hear from the hospital, I'll call Geneva and speak with his wife."

Uri nodded. He had been perspiring for some time and his hands were sticky. He wiped them on his trousers.

"You've known Leo for a long time, haven't you?" the ambassador asked.

"Yes." Uri closed his eyes and sighed. "We first met on the way to Palestine in 1939. Nearly thirty-five years ago."

"Given the life he's led," the ambassador said, "I wonder when Leo would say his life really began. With us or earlier."

Uri looked at the man, seeing Leo's dark disposition and questioning eyes superimposed over the ambassador's narrow face and dark beard. Leo had once told Uri of a parting, years before in Nice, France, when he was fourteen. Leo said that he could never erase the memory of that painful farewell on a railroad platform in Nice, when his parents returned to Augsburg, Germany. Within a few short years, Leo had been left an orphan, a man of the world, and a man of his own making.

When Leo had told the story, he kept a palm to his heart, over the very spot where his mother's embrace pressed the family's treasured heirloom against his chest, followed by his father's hand on his shoulder, shaking him. Both of his parents had been uneasy, exhibiting a tension beyond the sadness of separation.

Ulrike, Leo's mother, had been fond of wearing the large emerald pendant on the thick gold chain within the folds of her blouse. She wasn't a woman proud of her riches. Instead, at moments, she was still the beautiful and excited bride who had received the pendant on her wedding day from the matriarch of her husband's family. Leo's eighty-five-year-old grandmother had traveled by train from Hamburg with a widowed sister, and after the wedding, she unhooked the pendant that had for decades bounced upon her formidable chest, waddled across the room, and placed it around Ulrike's neck. The act was a blessing, an acceptance, a dictum to go forward and raise new generations of Bergners.

Each time his mother hugged him tightly, Leo felt the imprint of that pendant, and at the train station, her embrace had been more deliberate than any other in Leo's memory. Then his parents boarded a train back to their family home in Germany, a Germany that would betray them.

All through his life, Leo had often placed his open palm to his chest, many times for Uri and others to see, each time bringing the past into the present. Uri had grown to understand the gesture. Leo's hand to his chest, where his mother's pendant pressed against it, signified his undying love of his family.

1

L EAVING Leo in the safety of Nice with their cousins, Jacques and Karin Kaplan, seemed a wise parental decision in view of the fast-deteriorating situation in Germany. The fear of impending war, and the ever-increasing indignities the Jewish community had to endure, was not an atmosphere in which to raise a child. Leo's parents had planned to reunite the family in Augsburg once the great German nation had finally come to its senses. In the meantime, fourteen-year-old Leopold Bergner would continue his studies in relative safety.

A talented pianist, Leo set about establishing himself in Nice as a professional musician, available for private parties. He averaged three every week—two most weekends and one on a weeknight. He had business cards printed and distributed them at the lycée and among all the caterers in town. With his earnings, he bought himself a smart tuxedo and had a head-shot photograph taken by a professional. He sent two copies of the picture back to Augsburg: one to Professor Hailer and one to his parents with assurances that he was getting on fine and not to worry. And he was doing well.

The best place to play was at the Levys' house. They had an elegant music room, and an ebony concert grand piano imported from Berlin after the Great War. Its polish was so fine it glowed, and Madame Levy made sure the precious instrument was in tune so Leo could play Chopin for her friends. She had a melancholic streak that her friends quietly mocked. Still, they came to her parties and tipped Leo well, especially when he looked tired.

"On time, as usual," Madame Levy said when he arrived.

This particular Sunday evening, the night was clear and breezy. Leo was sorry to step inside the warm house. Still, he had written to Professor Hailer, asking him what to play, and the old man sent him Sonata No. 2. Leo had spent hours practicing to make sure that he would not be a disappointment. Now, when he played a piece he knew well, the music and warmth and background din put him in a trance that felt like the beginning of sleep.

"There's water in the kitchen for your hands," Madame Levy said. "Help yourself to the wine before the guests arrive."

"No thank you, Madame," he said in his German-accented French. "Perhaps after I play."

He soaked his hands and sat down to warm up for a few minutes. He still used the old Czerny exercises Bruno had taught him, long before Professor Hailer took over his instruction. A few of the five-note finger patterns reminded him of a phrase from Schumann, and he played for a while, imagining an orchestra filling out the rest of the score.

While he played, the room filled with guests and he realized he should be playing his Chopin. Once in a while, he answered a question about his studies or nodded in thanks if a few francs found their way into his pocket. As he played, his thoughts remained on the music and his body, a kind of instrument secondary to the piano. He wished he had made time for a nap that afternoon. But his fingers followed a physical pattern of sound in his mind, and if he lost track of the room and people, he doubted he would miss a note.

The guests were usually deep in their conversations about fashion and politics, or in gossip that was just as dull and vicious as what Leo had heard in the streets back home. They never paid him attention for long. Yet through his fatigue and concentration, he noticed the repeated gaze of one of Monsieur Levy's friends.

The man was in his fifties, with a knobby face that was somehow appealing. He also seemed to have spent too much time in the sun. Above his white-as-white collar, his ears were scorched red and looked painful. After the first few guests said their goodnights and how-lovely's, the man appeared at the upper keys. Up close, he was familiar.

"I'm Rabbi Aaron." His smile creased his sunburn. "I shouldn't shake your hand now, should I?"

Leo grinned. The joke was common, and the Rabbi's tip would be higher if Leo acted amused.

"My cousin has mentioned you," Leo answered.

"You're Leo Bergner. Your cousin Jacques is a good man. A bulldog when he is pursuing something he knows is right. In fact, he has reminded me several times to look in on you one of these evenings, and to invite you to my office for coffee."

Jacques wanted Leo to be more religious, but they had avoided discussing the issue at length. To be confronted like this, here, almost caused Leo to miss a note in an easy bass chord.

"It would just be a friendly talk, my boy," the Rabbi said. "I know you're far from home. I'll leave my card here. You may call on me someday after school, if you wish."

"Thank you, sir. Take care of your sunburn."

"And you take care of your studies." The Rabbi slipped his card and a few francs into Leo's jacket pocket, which hung on a chair by the piano. "It's late for a school night."

✳

The next morning, Leo counted his tips from the party and came upon Rabbi Aaron's card. He studied the address and the embossed logo of the Rue De Gustave Deloye Synagogue. It wasn't far from school, but he had no intention of going. He marked his place in his math book with the card and hurried to get dressed for the lycée.

The lycée was hard work. After the informality of sitting around Herr Roitsch's dining room table every afternoon for a couple of hours, it was difficult for him to go back into a structured environment. Leo had to acclimatize himself to the routine of a formal school again, to be in a large institution with hundreds of other pupils spread across many buildings. But he made the adjustment.

His French, good as it was before, was already fluent. He made a few friends, both boys and girls, and through their families, broadened his network of potential clients for his musical soirees. These parties, however, were not the parties of his earlier childhood. He suspected that those days were gone for good with the way the world was changing.

All week long, each time Leo reached in his pocket, he found Rabbi Aaron's card. A few times, Leo thought about throwing it out, but each time he pulled it from his pocket and gazed at the odd logo, he was reminded of his cousin Jacques insisting that he should learn more about his family's Jewish heritage.

On his way home from school, Leo found himself in front of an imposing pair of wooden doors, standing beneath an archway marked with Hebrew letters. He couldn't read them. Inside, the door to Rabbi Aaron's office was propped open with a bronze bust.

"I always thought it was ugly. Some family thing." The way the Rabbi rolled his eyes reminded Leo of his father, particularly his father's attitude toward in-laws. "Please, Leo, sit down. I'm so glad you've come."

The rabbi shook Leo's hand warmly. Leo grudgingly liked him. Over tea, Rabbi Aaron said that he had been living in Nice since 1918.

"How about yourself, Leo? You must come from a musical family."

"Well, sir, it's a rather long story."

"I have time. More tea?"

Rabbi Aaron tilted the pot over the porcelain cup. Leo allowed his thoughts to turn toward home for the first time in months. To his surprise, he spoke about them aloud.

✳

Leopold Bergner was born on April 20, 1922 and started life with a number of disadvantages. First, he was Jewish. He shared the same birthday with Hitler, and he was born in a hospital on Schleissheimerstrasse, not far from the Führer's first home in Munich. Leo was destined to be an only child and couldn't claim kinship with the well-known and wealthy Bergners, the influential and powerful banking family. So he was a Jew without connections in difficult times.

Leo settled into school quickly and was a good student. He outgrew his young friends and became more solitary. He didn't love or despise any particular subject, receiving good marks in all of them. And the classroom taught him apathy.

Then one day his parents, Sigmund and Ulrike, took him to an open-air opera at the Rotes Tor. Each member of the audience came with their own colored cushion to place on the hard seats and listened as the sun went down and the sky sparkled with stars. Leo's eyes glowed with a light his parents had never seen in them before, and he begged to see more concerts.

On Leo's eighth birthday, his parents called him into the kitchen. He threw down his satchel on the bench in the hall and wound his way to the family center.

"Happy birthday!" many voices shouted.

Candles on a cake were ablaze. He looked around the room. His mother beamed, looking very pretty with Grandmama's emerald pendant shining against her white blouse. Papa looked smart in a new suit that he had bought in Munich the week before. Other familiar faces smiled at him—Frau Brindl who came every Tuesday and Friday to clean the house; Hans and Fritz, two of his friends from school; Herr Schultz, the next door neighbor who had retired from the bank the year before and who played chess every Sunday with Papa; and another boy, older than Leo, whom he didn't recognize.

"Leo, come and meet Bruno," Papa said.

Leo walked over to the older boy and they shook hands. The boy was tall, almost as tall as Papa, and had blond hair, a round face and a friendly smile.

"Happy birthday, Leo," he said. "It's good to meet you."

"Leo, Bruno is a pupil at my school," Papa explained. "He's a very good student but needs some extra coaching in algebra and geometry. He is to come here every Tuesday and Thursday at four o'clock, and I will teach him for an hour beginning at five o'clock." His father's hand went to his pocket watch in his vest, but he didn't pull it out. "Well, aren't you going to ask me why he is coming at four, if the lessons aren't due to begin until five o'clock?"

Leo smiled, not knowing what to say. Finally, he shook his head.

"Come with me," Papa said. "Let's go into the living room."

Bruno headed out of the kitchen toward the living room and everyone followed. Leo noticed that Bruno's left shoe didn't match the right one and that he walked with a limp.

"Close your eyes," Papa said quietly.

Leo walked slowly into the room, covering his eyes with both hands. "Now, open them."

A piano of highly polished walnut filled the large bay window. A grand Bechstein. Ulrike had already put some family photographs on it, and it was magnificent.

"Happy birthday, Leo," they all said.

"Now, Bruno is a first-class pianist." Sigmund took Leo by the hand. "He's going to give you lessons every Tuesday and Thursday. Before long, you'll be playing at the best concert halls in Bavaria."

"Please," Ulrike said, "play something for us, Bruno."

Bruno smiled, walked across the room and sat on the piano stool. He looked down at the keys. His fingers slid across the keyboard.

"This is a lovely piano," Bruno said. "It's been a long time since I played on such a beautiful instrument."

Then he sat up straight and played a Chopin piece. Leo stared, mesmerized. Ulrike beckoned everyone to sit.

"Bravo," they all shouted when Bruno finished, Papa the loudest of all.

"This time next year, Leo, I want you to play that too," he said firmly.

And so the routine began. Every Tuesday and Thursday, Bruno arrived at four o'clock to give Leo his piano lessons. For fifteen minutes, Leo would recite what he had practiced since the last lesson. Then for another fifteen minutes, he would perform scales and short drills. The final half hour was devoted to sight-reading and an evaluation of technique. They played Mozart, Beethoven, Schubert, and later Rachmaninoff. Every winter, Bruno added German Christmas carols. There was a dull but pleasant rightness to this hour, a kind of eternity trapped in his mother's living room, in which music notes fluttered at the windows like moths.

Besides the piano lessons, Leo developed a keen interest in military history. He nagged his mother to bring home books from the library on the Napoleonic Wars, the Franco Prussian War of 1870, and the Great War. He badgered his father to talk about life in the trenches. His birthday set so much in motion for him. Leo imagined that his life beyond the living room windows would be an interesting epic full of adventure, and yet in his heart he wanted nothing to change. He thought he was lucky to be born into his family.

After several lessons, Leo and Bruno became more relaxed in each other's company, and one day Leo plucked up enough courage to ask Bruno what was wrong with his foot. Bruno became agitated and was curt for the remainder of the lesson. Leo never approached the subject again.

2

THREE YEARS AFTER COMING TWICE EACH WEEK TO THE Bergners, Bruno disappeared from their lives. Sigmund had less and less time to tutor Bruno, and therefore Bruno could not teach Leo the piano. Something didn't make sense to Leo.

"Why can't we just pay Bruno?" Leo asked. "He is a good teacher for me. You know he is quite good. Even competing in competitions."

"Leo, he comes because he needs my help with his studies," Sigmund explained. "He is not a real piano teacher."

"But I like him. I do so well with him."

"We will find you a real piano teacher," Sigmund declared. "One who is meant to teach. You will see. You will like him much better."

So Leo made peace with his father's decision and took lessons from Professor Hailer. But he often wondered about the young man who limped and played the piano with such ease and happiness. And of course, Leo would remember the things Bruno had taught him. Particularly, as Bruno was a young man whose enthusiasm at the piano made Leo enjoy the lessons so much.

Professor Hailer was a different person altogether, by style and by disposition. Certainly by age. The old man often looked troubled and sometimes lingered on the walkway that he shared with the Bergners, his neighbors. But he rarely shared his thoughts. And if he ever had a passion for the piano or teaching, Leo caught no glimpse of either.

By that time, an ill wind was blowing over the town of Augsburg, over the whole of Bavaria. Jacques had read of troubling times in Germany in the

French newspaper. He and his wife, Karin, wrote to their German relatives to ask what was going on.

"They really do worry, don't they?" Sigmund said with exasperation as he waved Jacques's letter in his clenched fist. "This will pass. It's a temporary aberration. We have nothing to worry about, for God's sake. For how many generations have we been German? Am I not a holder of the Iron Cross and the deputy principal of one of the best schools in the nation? And you, Ulrike, you're now the second highest-ranking person in the town's library department. We have nothing to fear."

Like so many German Jews, Sigmund felt assimilated in the community. They were Jewish and made no attempt to deny their heritage. But they were non-observant, not even joining the local Jewish congregation. Occasionally, Ulrike lit the Sabbath candles on a Friday night. More often than not, she forgot.

"You're right, Sigmund," Ulrike said. "But you can't blame them for worrying about what they read in the French newspapers."

"Jacques hates Germany. Can't you see? He loathes Germans. How he came to marry your cousin remains a mystery to me. Next time you write to Jacques and Karin, kindly remind them about Captain Dreyfus and the French."

"I think you're burying your head in the sand," Ulrike murmured.

"How many thousands of years have Jews had to endure this?" Sigmund said, frustrated, then calmed his voice. "It's a passing phase."

"It's certainly unpleasant," Ulrike said. "You're not going to disagree with me on that, are you?"

"Of course not." Sigmund pursed his lips. "But this will all pass. There is nothing to worry about."

Leo listened at his bedroom door. He heard the note of exhaustion and sadness in his mother's voice. He also knew the frustration that his father felt. At Passover, when they took the train to Munich and the family united for Seder night at Ulrike's parents, Sigmund often confided in Leo that he dreaded these events. Upwards of thirty people sat down for dinner, perched on hard wooden chairs that were either borrowed or rented, cramped together around three rented tables.

Fortunately, the prayers were kept to a minimum, but the food and the conversation were boring. It was always with relief that Sigmund bundled his family into a cab to return to the station and take the last train back to

Augsburg. Sigmund and Leo traded winks and sighs of relief, while Ulrike made herself comfortable in the cab.

"I'd like to go into Munich this coming Sunday," Ulrike said. "It's Freda's birthday. Will you come?"

"No," Sigmund replied. "I think I should stay here. I have to prepare an examination paper for the twelfth grade."

Leo guessed this was a stretch of the truth. Ulrike surely knew that Sigmund would look for any excuse to get out of it.

"I'll take Leo," she said. "I'm sure he would like to go."

✳

Freda's birthday party was a predictably engulfing experience, attended by hordes of relatives seated around tables that groaned with the weight of the platters of food. Leo sat and talked with several young cousins while the adults stuck together and spoke in conspiratorial whispers. Maybe Grandmama was sick? She hadn't stayed long at the party. The men talked among themselves in the hallway while the women congregated in the living room. Something was troubling them. During the cab ride to the station, Ulrike seemed unusually pensive and withdrawn.

"What's the matter, Mami? Is something wrong?"

"No, not really." She picked at lint on her coat. "At least, I don't think so. Why do you ask?"

"Everyone seemed strange today. No one was in a good mood. Is Grandmama all right? She left the party early."

"There's nothing the matter with her. She left because Grandpapa was busy at the office. She worries about him working alone on a Sunday in that large brewery."

"But he does that most Sundays. Why would she be worried about him? Especially today, Aunt Freda's birthday."

"Stop asking questions. Everything is okay." Ulrike caught his chin with her hand and looked into his eyes. "Leo, we're living in difficult times. But there is nothing to worry about. I promise."

These words distressed him, to be brushed off and treated as a child. Her stubbornness was disquieting, as much as her parroting of Sigmund's lines. Leo sensed danger, but knew he held little power as a child to get more from his mother or father than either was willing to tell.

When they arrived at the station, an elderly woman was waiting for a taxi. Leo followed his mother out of their cab, and the woman noticed Ulrike's necklace.

"Oh my, your emerald is stunning," the woman said, unable to look away from the brilliant gem. "It must have cost you a great deal."

Ulrike smiled at the woman and pulled Leo closer. The woman took their vacated cab and it set off.

Leo said to his mother, "Maybe you shouldn't wear that emerald all the time. It attracts unnecessary attention."

"Nonsense," Ulrike said. "I will wear it as often as I want. You're concerned for the wrong reasons over the wrong things."

✳

The next day, after a long lesson with Professor Hailer and a lengthy dinner during which his parents did not speak to one another, Leo stayed awake to eavesdrop on the conversation he knew was waiting beneath their reticence. Shortly after Leo closed his bedroom door, Ulrike reported on her day in Munich. All but Leo's concerns and what had happened at the train station.

"You're listening with only one ear, Sigmund," she said, aggravated with him. "My parents are moving into a small apartment in Eching. There are no Jews there, and they feel they will not attract any attention. Papa has sold his interest in the brewery to his partners. My brothers and sisters and their families have already finalized their plans to leave. People they know are making plans to emigrate, to London, Paris, Amsterdam and New York."

Leo tiptoed from the bedroom and stopped in the hall, near the kitchen door. His father sighed, and his stein rattled as it hit the tabletop. Leo was anxious to hear his father's response, but there was none, only a long silence.

"We're the only ones who have no plans," Ulrike continued. "And we're the ones with the most education, the ones who everyone in the family looks up to as the intellectuals. We haven't a clue of what we're going to do, have we?"

Leo peered around the edge of the slightly ajar door. Sigmund waved her off and went to his study. Leo followed him in stocking feet. The hall light was dark. His father continued undeterred, turned on the dim green lamp at the corner of his blotter, opened a drawer, and took out his Iron Cross. Sigmund held the medal in the palm of his hand, as he often did when something was on his mind. He gazed at it for a minute before putting the distinguished award back in its leather case. His father's dark mood made Leo uneasy.

✳

Six months passed too quickly. The city council was now totally in the hands of the Nazis. Sigmund and Ulrike were fired abruptly from the school and library. The principal was clearly embarrassed and uncomfortable, but like all the others in any position of authority, he explained that he was only acting on orders. So Sigmund took Leo out of the school.

Now every afternoon, Sigmund walked with Leo to the home of Herr Roitsch, a teacher and former colleague. Leo was always alone with his father on these regular walks, but Sigmund was usually too distracted to speak. Sigmund's spirits were low, and he strode quickly along the sidewalk, frequently looking back to see if anyone was following them.

Starting the night he had spied on Sigmund in his study, an unease had settled in Leo and inflamed his fears. Everything became more distressing and shameful. The father he had known had changed. Leo didn't know or understand this man with whom he walked each evening. Then Sigmund decided that Leo should go to stay with their Kaplan cousins in Nice. There, somehow, his father felt Leo would be safe, while he and Ulrike came to terms with what was happening in their Germany.

✳

"There they are," Ulrike said as they disembarked the train in Nice.

She pointed ahead at Karin and Jacques standing on the platform. Leo looked to where his mother was pointing but could not pick out their hosts. He was tired after their long journey, which had involved three changes of train during which Ulrike chattered nonstop about vague childhood memories of her cousin Karin.

Jacques and Karin approached them as the other passengers moved in the opposite direction toward the gate. Leo noticed that Karin was quite a beauty, tall with long black hair, and elegant in fashionable white slacks and a yellow shirt, unbuttoned and revealing her dark tan.

Jacques darted ahead of Karin. "Let me help you with these cases."

He and Karin looked genuinely happy for the opportunity of having houseguests. Jacques was short and plump, and he had a huge moustache. His tight gray suit looked uncomfortable, a relic from more slender days, which had gone, along with his strength for lifting luggage. But he was jocular. Leo knew instinctively that they would get along well.

Within minutes, they had loaded the luggage into the trunk of Jacques's Citroen, and they were on their way to the Kaplan's flat in a street just behind La Promenade des Anglais. While Karin and Ulrike prattled over the top of each other in German, Leo's gaze was fixed on the beach and the calm blue Mediterranean Sea. He couldn't wait to go for a swim and absorb the gaiety of the Riviera while shedding the terror he'd felt so often back in Germany. The difference in ambience was surreal.

"Life is funny, isn't it, Sigmund?" Jacques's German was not as good as his guests' French, so conversation went back and forth between the two languages. "Here we are, friends and relatives by marriage. It wasn't long ago that we faced each other from opposite trenches at the Front."

"Were you in the army too, Cousin Jacques?" Leo asked.

"Certainly I was." He patted Leo on the shoulder, straining the seams of his too-small jacket. "But that is in the past and we should talk about happier things, right, Sigmund?"

"Yes," Sigmund answered. "But be prepared. Leo is a keen student of military history. He will want to talk to you a lot about the war. By the way, do you still have a piano? Leo is quite the pianist and shouldn't fall behind in his practicing."

"Ours may need tuning but you can practice on it," Karin said in German. "Every day you can play for us. How's that?"

"That would be very nice," Leo politely replied.

"Look, there's my shop." Jacques pointed as they approached the Hotel Negresco.

Jacques was successful from the appearance of his pharmacy, practically next door to the famed hotel. The store was double-fronted with a large blue awning and a big sign: J K Pharmacy.

"That's quite a location," Sigmund noted, showing increasing signs of relaxation.

This change might be good for his father, too, Leo thought. His mother was already enjoying herself, chattering with Karin and waving her hand out the window as if her fingers could capture the joy and ease that seemed to ride the air. Later she would share that she expected to be back here in just a few months. Until then, Leo should write every week.

3

THE KAPLANS LIVED IN THE GROUND FLOOR FLAT OF AN impressive building constructed about fifty years earlier. Purple and red bougainvillea wove across the white exterior, giving the building a majestic yet homey appearance. Each apartment had large French doors that opened onto a balcony. Leo would often pause there to breathe in the fresh sea air and watch the seagulls as they flew toward the beach.

The Kaplan flat was luxurious compared to the Bergner home in Augsburg, and it was also much tidier. Yet as much as he liked his new environment, Leo needed no reminders to write his weekly letter to his parents back in Germany, and every other week he wrote to Professor Hailer. Leo's parents wrote every week too, though they feared the Gestapo might read their letters. So they were careful about what they committed to paper. Professor Hailer also responded to Leo's letters and gave him advice on what musical pieces he should study. Leo stored all the correspondence in the sun-bathed desk next to the piano. Jacques and Karin also received letters from Germany and always seemed saddened by them.

On arriving home after another of the Levys' soirees, Leo soaked in the open, quiet night. Though tired from playing and breathing threads of cigarette smoke that caressed his face as he played, he stood in the street for twenty minutes.

Leo patted his pocketful of francs, which he would deposit at Societe Generale the next day. Then he found his key and let himself inside. He took off his jacket, hung it in the closet, and put down the leather attaché case that held his music. He noticed the kitchen light was still on. Jacques and Karin were awake.

"Leo, come have a glass of milk and some apple cake," Karin said. "We need to talk with you."

He rinsed his hands and face at the sink. After drying them, Leo sat at the kitchen table in front of a plate of apple cake.

Jacques looked concerned. "I don't hear of you playing tennis much these days like you used to. Why don't you ever go to the movies with your friends? You're too much alone in your thoughts."

"Is that why you waited up?" A dark thought pierced Leo. "What is it? You both look so serious. Have you had bad news from Germany? Are Mami and Papa okay?"

"No, no, it's nothing like that." Jacques's reassurance was not entirely convincing. He stirred his coffee cup as if he were fishing for the right words. "I want to talk with you about the problem the Jews in Germany are facing. Well, not the whole problem, but one aspect of it."

Leo looked at the apple cake on the plate in front of him. He wasn't hungry and couldn't make himself eat out of politeness. Not until he knew what Jacques had in mind.

"The situation in Germany is terrible for the Jews," Jacques continued. "And so many of them, like your dear father, will still not accept it. They are Germans first and Jews second. They love their country with such fervor that they refuse to admit that what is going on there is anything but a temporary hiccup. Well, from here, we see things differently. It is over for the Jews in Germany. They must get out. I am going to Augsburg next week to plead with your parents to get out while they can."

Leo listened attentively and nodded in agreement to all that Jacques said. He had buried his emotions and his anger for so long. Now, in spite of himself, his eyes filled with tears.

"Can I come, too?" Leo asked.

"I'm afraid not," Jacques answered. "Here you are safe. Who knows what might happen if you go back now. They may prevent you from leaving again. I would never forgive myself for having exposed you to that."

Leo cut a sliver of cake, then laid his fork on his plate. Even a bite of cake in his mouth would have so little flavor in these circumstances.

"The German Jews," Jacques explained, "made the mistake of believing that just because they had assimilated in German society, they would be immune from anti-Semitism. Well, they've been proven wrong. In France, it is different. Here we know our place. There is tolerance and acceptance."

"But we were never practicing Jews," Leo said.

"I know. That is the issue. You were not. Now that you are here in France, you should become part of the Jewish community. We would like you to meet with Rabbi Aaron."

Leo reached in his pocket for the card he'd been given earlier that evening. "He was at the Levy's house tonight."

"Ah, good." Jacques smiled. "I have asked him several times to look in on you one of these evenings and introduce himself. Please, pay him a visit sometime this week. You can stop by his office after school."

Leo put the card back in his pocket. "If that's what you want." Leo had thought this was to be about his parents and their future safety in France. "But I'm not very interested in religion, you know?"

"Leo, I know you aren't religious. This isn't really about religion. It's about identification. Knowing who you are."

Leo felt a rising resentfulness at Jacques's suggestion, but he kept it hidden. He even helped Jacques pack. But his resentment kept him awake that night. And the next evening, Monsieur Levy commented that Leo seemed cross with the guests. Afraid that he'd lose their business, he promised himself to keep his emotions better hidden.

✳

After putting it off for days, the meeting with Rabbi Aaron wasn't as bad as Leo had dreaded it might be. The rabbi was gracious, offered tea, and listened attentively as Leo told the story of his life in Germany, and why his parents had sent him to Nice.

"They were wise to do so," Rabbi Aaron said. "These are troubling times."

Leo got up to stretch after telling his story. The rabbi inquired about Leo's studies, and further offered to take Leo under his wing, give him a crash course in Judaism and Hebrew, even officiate at his bar mitzvah as soon as the rabbi felt Leo would be ready.

As Rabbi Aaron talked, Leo wandered to a bookshelf and browsed through the titles. He was delighted to discover that the rabbi shared his interest in military history.

"I was an army chaplain in the war," Rabbi Aaron explained. "I spent a lot of time with the officers and men in the trenches. It ignited my interest. War is a terrible thing. Let us hope that mankind has learned something from the horrors of the last war."

"Isn't it funny? My father was in the German army at the same time you and Jacques were in the French army. In fact, my father was awarded the Iron Cross."

"This." Rabbi Aaron picked up a framed photograph from his desk. "This photograph is of my late brother. He was killed at the Battle of the Somme. He was only twenty." He put it back. "Life certainly is funny. But now all that is over. European Jews have other problems which we have to confront."

"I'm quite angry with my cousin, Rabbi." Leo stared at the picture. "Jacques has gone to Augsburg to visit my parents. I wanted to go with him. I haven't seen my parents for so long, but he wouldn't take me."

"Leo, Jacques was right." The rabbi laid his hand on Leo's shoulder. "You never know what could happen in Germany. You might be prevented from returning to France. Don't be angry with your cousin. He made the right decision. Now my home is yours. Please come and see me whenever you want. We have so much in common, and I look forward to getting to know you better."

Rabbi Aaron seemed to understand something about Leo, something that Leo didn't. But Leo did understand how it felt to be far from home. Before the turmoil began, Augsburg was full of kind people. People who opened their doors and their hearts to Leo, as Rabbi Aaron had done today. How lonely he had been in Nice until now. This man, this rabbi, Leo would visit him again soon. And next time, he wouldn't go reluctantly.

✳

Jacques sat down at the kitchen table and sighed, exhausted by his trip. Karin poured him a coffee and slid a plate of cookies closer to him. Leo stared at Jacques across the table, his lips pressed into a tight line.

Jacques loosened his tie and ran his fingers through his hair. He looked first at Karin, then at Leo. A deep sigh escaped his lips, deflating him until his shoulders sagged.

"Karin," Jacques began. "You have no idea about the hatred I saw in Germany toward the Jewish community. In shops and restaurants everywhere, I saw placards that read 'Jews not admitted' and 'Jews enter at their own peril.' Jews are even banned from public parks, swimming pools, and public transport. Germans are being encouraged not to use Jewish lawyers and doctors, and there are mass firings of Jewish civil servants and teachers." Jacques took a cookie from the plate on the table, then turned to Leo and softened his voice. "Leo, despite all these indignities and boycotts, and the shameful sight of the Sturm Abteilung picketing Jewish-owned shops, your father remains unmoved." Jacques brushed crumbs from his chin and looked at Karin. "Even after I reminded him that he no longer has German citizenship. The Nuremburg Laws have stripped him of that."

"What about Ulrike?" Karin asked. "She knows they should leave, doesn't she?"

"She said her place was with her husband. She would do whatever he decides. She is a good wife but this is not a good time."

"Mami isn't coming either?" Leo asked.

"I screamed at your parents, they're being stupid, your father is finished in Germany, even told him to throw that damned Iron Cross down the toilet. I shouted at him to get the hell out of that rotten inferno before the Nazis stop them from leaving. But no, they wouldn't listen." Jacques sipped his coffee and reached for another cookie.

Karin asked, "Is there no one who can convince them?"

"I had one ally, Leo's dear friend, Professor Hailer." Jacques shifted to Leo. "He really loves you and your parents." Then Jacques explained to Karin, "This Professor Hailer is a kind man. You would like him. A real mensch. He's a widower and lives alone in an apartment in the building next to Sigmund and Ulrike. Whenever they're away, he waters their plants and takes in the mail. While I was there, he popped in to check on their place. He had received a letter from a friend at the university in Heidelberg informing him that three Jewish professors had left. One went to Paris, another to London, and one to Palestine. He was deeply distressed. He wanted us to understand that not all Germans are Nazis."

"Of course not," Karin said, then looked at Leo. He nodded, thinking he should agree, but unsure of what to say.

"Professor Hailer's first wife was Jewish," Jacques explained. "She died of cancer in 1909 and was buried in a Jewish cemetery in Berlin. The professor had just returned from visiting her grave, and he was horrified by what he saw." Jacques paused as Karin refilled his coffee. "The cemetery had been desecrated," he continued. "Headstones were broken. Swastikas are painted everywhere." Jacques looked at Leo. "Professor Hailer is very worried for your parents. They have a good friend in him."

"Why can't there be more Germans like Professor Hailer?" Leo asked without expecting any answer.

"The professor asked your parents if they had a plan." Jacques looked across at Karin. "It's obvious they have no plan. I couldn't stop myself. I banged my fist on the table and shouted, *For God's sake, isn't it obvious what you must do?*"

This disturbing news should have made Leo sad, to know the separation from his parents would only continue, but all he felt was anger toward his father's refusal to leave Germany. When he grew up and was no longer a child, he would always hold his head up high, show strength and take control of his own destiny, no matter what. And he would not put his faith in such trinkets as an Iron Cross.

As for his mother, of course she would do whatever his father demanded. In that respect, he had to admire her. But at the same time, he loathed his father's stubborn attitude, and wished she would convince him that they both should flee.

Leo stood from the table and walked to his bedroom. At least he had Jacques, Karin, and even Rabbi Aaron. But he wanted his parents.

4

Every Wednesday after school, Leo visited Rabbi Aaron for tutoring. His bar mitzvah was to take place in just under a year, although he didn't remember agreeing to such a schedule. At first, their Wednesday meetings were simply conversations about military history and the lycée, consisting almost wholly of Leo talking and the rabbi at ease in the otherwise uncomfortable chairs, one leg crossed and a hand cradling his chin. After every meeting, Rabbi Aaron would see Leo to the front door, take his shoulder, and look at him from under his whiskery brows.

"You will visit again, no?" the rabbi would ask.

"Next Wednesday as usual would be great," Leo would answer, though he still bore a smudge of guilt. "And would you like me to bring anything from Jacques's pharmacy?"

Rabbi Aaron then began to ask more difficult questions at their meetings. The rabbi was both good-natured and rather sly. Now when Leo left, he promised himself that he would not stay so long the next time. Certainly not let himself be interrogated so easily by the rabbi. But that was the problem. Rabbi Aaron posed his questions as tangents—tangents so interesting that Leo felt compelled to respond.

One time, the rabbi recounted an argument between two medics in a trench. They were trying to decide which one of them should climb out of the trench to retrieve a wounded officer. The older medic argued that he had a wife and two sons at home, so the younger one should do it. The younger argued that the older had already gotten to experience ten more years of life than he had. While they argued, the officer died.

"I often ask myself," Rabbi Aaron said, "what I would have done in their position."

"They're cowards," Leo replied. "Both of them."

"But in the morally cloudy situation of war, who should have gone over the top?"

"Whoever got there first. Helping fallen soldiers is their job."

"Yes, Leo, that's very noble, and I agree. I couldn't agree more, in fact. But imagine yourself exhausted, terrified, starving and sick—your thinking is cloudy. You're tired of risking your life. You've watched your officers and friends lose their sense of decency. It's another day and another battle, and you woke that morning with an uncanny sense that of all days, God would not take your life until next Tuesday. The officer is a stranger to you. The other medic is forever shirking his duties. What would you do?"

Leo would then embark on a crumbling road of arguments, where every step seemed to be the wrong one. But Rabbi Aaron's interest would only encourage him to go further. And Leo would talk and reason and continue.

Their meetings lasted longer each time. Eventually, Leo expressed interest in Hebrew. So their meetings also included casual lessons that somehow became bar mitzvah tutoring appointments. It was during one of these appointments, as Leo chanted shakily from a tikkun, that he felt an illogical tug to return to Jacques's apartment. He looked at the clock. Four o'clock. He often stayed until after five with never a flutter of urgency. Today he stopped chanting.

"Rabbi, I'm sorry," he said, "but all of a sudden, I feel I need to check on my cousins. May I come back later?"

Rabbi Aaron helped him into his coat and offered to phone the pharmacy.

"It's all right," Leo said. "I'll go there if he isn't home by now."

He was already out in the street, jogging through the shadows of buildings, as Rabbi Aaron's concerned voice called after him. The streets and cafes seemed busier this time of day. People were still returning home from work, and a train must have come into the station—a steady press of white-clad travelers moved along Avenue Jean Medicin.

Leo checked the big clock. He was far too early to find Jacques at home, so he diverted his path and went to the pharmacy. Jacques would probably work late anyway, selling aspirin and lotions and toiletries to newly arrived tourists. But when Leo rounded the corner, he could see from across the street that the lights were off. The door was locked, too. Jacques was portly, and sometimes complained of a fast heartbeat. Perhaps the ambulance had already come and gone. Perhaps Leo should stop now and run directly to the hospital. Fearing the worst, Leo turned for home.

His feet carried him all the way to the apartment. He arrived heaving for breath and hot with dread. His key chattered against the lock. He got it in and turned it, but the door was already open. So unlike Jacques and Karin. They never left the door open. Leo rushed into the foyer and hallway. He heard voices in the living room. Familiar voices.

He paused, and it was another moment before he allowed himself to believe what he was hearing. His father and mother had come to Nice. He ran toward his mother who swept him into her arms, her fingers touching and rubbing the muscles of his back, her embrace more a swirl of emotion than the tight hug that he had anticipated. Leo's delight was almost complete. It would have been had his mother not felt somehow distant.

"It's been a year since we have all been together," Ulrike announced, clapping her hands together. "But thank God that we are all safe and united again."

Sigmund was on his feet, and he embraced his son while tears streamed down his face. Jacques and Karin watched from the table, holding hands. No one had ever seen Sigmund display such emotion. He was of the old stoical school that believed showing emotion was a sign of weakness. Ulrike moved to her husband and held him tightly. Leo wrapped his arms around both of his parents, and Sigmund ruffled his son's hair, a gesture that he had never made before.

"We didn't want to tell you we were coming," Sigmund mumbled. "In case our plans changed."

Leo noticed something odd about his mother's face. Around her brow and cheekbone was a greenish haze under the skin. She kept turning away when Leo glanced at her, and she seemed uncomfortable, even guarded, each time Sigmund embraced her. Her hands seemed to move independent of her words, often clapping together or patting her chest just below her throat, her index finger drawing a line at her collarbone.

"Mami, what happened?" Leo asked. "Is something wrong with your eye?"

"It's a long story," Sigmund said, taking his wife's hands and kissing her fingers. "Let's wait and I'll tell you about it later."

*

It wasn't until dinner the next night, when everyone had regained their composure, that Sigmund broached a serious discussion. But he wouldn't address anything about what was happening, or had happened, in Germany. Instead he wanted to discuss his family's plans, how they might survive in Nice. Sigmund talked about how he and Ulrike had handled their finances since the troubles in Germany began, and that their old neighbor, Professor Hailer, was looking after their money now. The professor would send it to them as they asked for it.

"But what I want," he said, "Wish. What I wish is to find some work in the meantime. And somewhere to live."

"Sigmund," Jacques said, "there is no rush. Karin and I have spoken about all this. First, you don't have to find anywhere to live. You are our family. Our apartment is big. There's a bedroom for you and Ulrike, and one for Leo. What more do you need? Why go to the expense of finding an apartment? It's nonsense."

Jacques took a heavy sip of wine. Karin left the table and went to the kitchen, and brought out food. She had cooked a bouillabaisse. Jacques cleared a space on the table for her large blue porcelain bowl. Everyone gathered around.

"Wow, that smells good," Leo said, beaming.

"Jacques, you're very kind," Sigmund said, but the fine meal only made him look more cowed. "But what about work? We need work."

"I can propose this," Jacques said. "I have a lady who works for me at the pharmacy. Pascal. She works with me behind the counter. She is leaving at the end of the month to live in Perpignan. Her husband has a new job there."

Sigmund turned to face Ulrike. Again Ulrike's hand went to her throat. Leo watched her, noticing that she wore a high-necked blouse. And he couldn't see the chain of her pendant.

"Mami..." Leo began.

"Wait." Jacques raised his hand to Leo. "Let me finish. I need to replace Pascal. Ulrike, if you like, you may take over her position, and I will pay you the same as I pay her. Simple. I do not believe there are too many restrictions against me employing a German national, but I will check with my attorney. That would give you a steady income in exchange for forty hours a week."

"That is good," Sigmund said, nodding. "Ulrike will be happy. But, instead of paying her, why not let that be her contribution toward our board and lodging with you?"

"No, no," Karin insisted. "Don't talk about that. It is a mitzvah for us."

"But what about me?" Sigmund asked. "I cannot sit every day gazing at the sea while my wife is on her feet working. What can I do?"

Jacques explained that he knew of a private school, and they could use Sigmund a few hours each week, to give some of the boys extra coaching in mathematics. Also, the Hotel Angleterre needed a nighttime clerk three days a week. The manager was a customer of the pharmacy. The hours were not good, but it was a guaranteed thirty a week. The hotel's owner, Maurice Laidler, was Jewish and sympathetic to the problems Leo and his family faced in Augsburg. As it turned out, Jacques had been making preparations for weeks.

"You have been so kind," Sigmund said. "And I have been very foolish, putting this off for so long." He dropped his forehead into his hands, descending to a new depth of sadness. "You know…" He looked up at Jacques. "The bastards stole Ulrike's emerald. Took it from her. Tore it from her."

Leo sat paralyzed. Mami's emerald? Gone?

"Yes, we noticed." Jacques nodded, finished chewing his food, and frowned. He wiped his mouth. "Karin mentioned that she had never seen Ulrike without it. We wondered what happened. Whether it had been sold or hidden in Germany with the professor, along with your other valuables."

"No, it was stolen." Sigmund reached out to take Ulrike's hand in his. "The same night as the brick hit her on the forehead. Kristallnacht."

"Oh, Mami," Leo mumbled.

Again Jacques raised a hand to him. Leo held his words, but he wanted to scream. His parents should have listened to Jacques and come to Nice sooner, before they became targets. Now every Jew had become a target. Leo wished he were grown, he would go back to Augsburg, find who did this, and punish them. Make all of them stop persecuting the Jews. But they were Germans, the same as his family. Had his father been wrong to fight for Germany? After all, he had been awarded the Iron Cross. Little good it did him now.

"Leo is doing so well, you know," Jacques said in a quiet voice. "He is a wonderful boy. He is earning good money playing piano, and he saves. Why, he has an account at the bank, and every week he makes a deposit.

He has a few friends and everyone likes him."

Leo squirmed, uncomfortable with the praise. Especially in light of the news of the pendant and the bruises that were now obvious on his mother's face.

"Listen," Jacques continued. "There is something else I need to discuss with you, Sigmund. I took the liberty of introducing Leo to a rabbi. I know you have no interest in religion, but I took it upon myself to see that he gets some exposure to Judaism. It cannot hurt." Jacques looked at Sigmund. "Even though you aren't a practicing Jew and were totally assimilated in Germany, and had not one, so I believe, Jewish friend, it didn't help you in the end, did it?"

The news of Leo's meetings with Rabbi Aaron was no surprise. Leo had already written in his letters about the sessions with the rabbi. Still, Leo expected his father to protest, just as Jacques expected. But Sigmund nodded with a look of sadness and resignation.

"Leo sees the rabbi on a regular basis," Jacques explained. "He is teaching him Hebrew. The plan is that in a few months, he would have a bar mitzvah here at the synagogue. But, Sigmund, you and Ulrike are his parents. Now you're here, this is a decision for the two of you. Karin and I will back off. But I have to tell you, Leo likes the rabbi and he enjoys the lessons. He's made some nice friends and contacts through the synagogue."

"No, Jacques," Sigmund replied. "I support this. I will not interfere. Maybe it's a good thing. I don't know. I never had any Jewish schooling in my life, nor did my parents. We were Germans. Nothing else counted for us."

Jacques exhaled with emphasis, hiding his disgust poorly. He had already let his contempt for the German Jews—who put their pride in being Germans above all else—often slip through during his discussions with Leo. In turn, Leo wondered at his own feelings on the subject. Especially as his relationship and respect for Rabbi Aaron grew.

✳

Within a week, the Bergners were established in Nice, both in new jobs and as residents. Sigmund began a habit of writing regularly to Professor Hailer, letters in which he expressed concern about what was happening in Germany. But he was careful not to embarrass Professor Hailer in the event that the Gestapo intercepted the letters. Leo would add an extra page with his news and progress on the piano. He wrote that he felt more relaxed now that he was reunited with his parents.

The professor's replies were guarded. Sigmund guessed that the situation in Germany was fast deteriorating. Any prospects for returning home in the near future were slim. In any event, he didn't want to broach the topic with Ulrike. She had just read a letter from Freda that had spelled out the latest regulations that had been promulgated against the Jewish community.

"Thank God we got out when we did," Ulrike muttered.

She handed the letter to Sigmund. His face froze in anguish as he read his sister-in-law's account of the new restrictions imposed after Kristallnacht. Jews were now required to turn over all precious metals to the government. Pensions for Jews dismissed from civil service jobs were arbitrarily reduced. Jewish-owned bonds, stocks, jewelry and artwork could only be transferred to the German state. Jews were physically segregated in German towns. Jewish driver's licenses were confiscated, along with Jewish-owned radios. A curfew was imposed to keep Jews off the street, and the laws protecting tenants were made non-applicable to them. He said nothing and handed the letter back to Ulrike.

✳

Ulrike enjoyed her work at the pharmacy. She enjoyed seeing so many happy, smiling, fun-loving people. A constant flow of customers, locals and tourists alike, took her mind off concerns about what was happening in Germany. And working with Jacques made her feel safe in this new community.

Sigmund enjoyed his work as well. He hadn't taught for some time, and only when he was teaching was he happy. Monsieur Laidler at the hotel was exceptionally kind, too. He was elderly, and he had owned the hotel for many years. After his wife died in 1910, he had left his two adult children in Paris and moved to the Riviera in pursuit of sea air and a better climate. He already knew of Leo, as he had heard him play at parties, and because Rabbi Aaron had mentioned his name. Soon he offered Sigmund more work and even a promotion.

That night, to celebrate, Sigmund took the whole family, Jacques and Karin included, to dinner at Le Gentilhomme, a new restaurant close to their home. They ate and drank, and for once, even Sigmund looked content. It was the first time in years that Leo had seen him look so relaxed.

✳

Several days later, the doorbell rang at the Kaplan's apartment, at five in the afternoon. Leo had just returned from his Wednesday appointment with Rabbi Aaron, and his mother had just set a plate of cheese and meat on the table for him. He hadn't eaten since lunch. Still he went to the door.

A tall, elderly man stood at the open doorway. He was German, judging by the style of his clothes, which, being made of dark gray winter cloth, were ill-suited to the Riviera. He had a healthy tan and a head of thick white hair. Ulrike showed a flutter of panic. Leo determined to stay near.

"Good afternoon," the man said. "I am sorry to disturb you. My name is Hofmann. Professor Hofmann. I am from Augsburg. Please, may I see Frau Bergner?"

"That is I," Ulrike answered. "How can I help you?"

"Please, Frau Bergner, may I come in? Please do not be nervous. I am a friend of Professor Hailer. He asked me to come and see you."

"Of course, please come in." Ulrike gestured for him to enter the hallway. "I'm sorry if I appeared rude."

"No, not at all," the man said. "It is quite understandable. Certainly these days."

Leo stepped back from the doorway. Karin came into the hall, curious to find out who the unexpected visitor was. After Ulrike made introductions, Karin went back into the kitchen to prepare coffee. Ulrike led the visitor into the living room, and Leo followed.

"How is dear Professor Hailer?" Ulrike asked. "He is a wonderful friend to us."

"He is well, but he is a very sad man," Professor Hofmann answered, then took a seat on the sofa. "I see him twice a week. We play chess together and listen to music. He still goes to all the concerts. But he is revolted, as many of us are, by the Hitler Youth, those uniforms, the ridiculous salutes, the flags and 'Heil Hitler' this and 'Heil Hitler' that. He is deeply depressed."

"The poor man. I am so sorry. My husband told me this morning that he planned on writing to him this evening. We had received a letter only a couple of days ago."

"Frau Bergner. The professor does not want you to write to him anymore."

"Why not?" Ulrike looked up, shocked.

"My wife and I are moving to Nice. She is French and has hated living in Germany for the last three years. So we are moving here, taking an apartment three blocks away from you, on Rue Lafayette."

"But why does the professor no longer wish to communicate with us?" Ulrike's hand reached again for the base of her throat. "Have we offended him in some way? Goodness, he still has all our valuables and money."

"My friend is worried," Professor Hofmann said. "The Gestapo may now, or in the future, intercept all mail that leaves Germany destined for Jews. Also from Jewish people abroad, back to Germany. We have all heard stories about such things happening. The professor is worried this may happen in your case."

The visitor was uneasy in his chair. He leaned forward, clasping his hands and resting his elbows on his knees. Ulrike sat more forward on her chair. Leo felt all the tension between them, and even Karin's, as she stood in the doorway of the kitchen.

"Professor Hailer," the man said. "He tells me that many of the letters between him and your husband contain references to assets he is looking after for you. He would hate for these letters to be read by the Gestapo."

"I see," Ulrike said. "I see."

"The professor proposes that he will write to me in the future. Then I will deliver messages from him to you. Of course, if you wish to write to the professor, from now on you should do that through me, too."

Hoffman rose to leave before Karin returned with the coffee. Ulrike rose too. Leo moved to his mother's side. The man looked into Leo's eyes and conveyed a sadness that Leo felt was increasingly a part of his family's life.

"Thank you, Professor Hofmann," Ulrike said. "I appreciate your help and your visit. I will be sure to tell my husband when he comes home."

✳

Later that evening, Leo sat with his mother and Karin as Ulrike repeated the conversation she'd had with Professor Hofmann to Jacques and Sigmund. Ulrike's voice was calm and confident. But Leo watched his mother's clasped hands grip and relax. She was worried, and Jacques and Sigmund were skeptical.

"Suppose he's not kosher," Jacques said. "How do we know who he is? Maybe he's Gestapo, too, and wishes simply to intercept everything at this end. They do have spies operating on the Riviera. We already know that."

Jacques looked at Karin and she nodded. She stood up and moved to the wall where she crossed her arms and leaned back. Ulrike's expression remained the same, but her eyes seemed to reach out to Sigmund, to somehow make sense of all this.

"I've been told," Jacques continued, "by one of my customers that the concierge at the Negresco is believed to be a German spy. One of the croupiers at the casino may be one, too."

"Well," Sigmund added, "we certainly need to find out before we exchange any more correspondence with Professor Hailer."

The next day was Wednesday. Sigmund had no classes and appeared at Rabbi Aaron's house to pick up Leo from his lesson. And to ask a favor of the rabbi, who had a son in Paris.

"Could your son make inquiries on our behalf in Augsburg?" Sigmund showed his discomfort by clearing his throat. "It would help set our minds at ease. We're fearful of calling Professor Hailer directly."

"Of course, I will call him now." He brought Leo and his father back into the study, and put through the call. "David, it's me, Papa." His son's voice was loud on the line, and Leo heard him start to answer, but Rabbi Aaron charged ahead. "Now I need you to telephone someone in Augsburg. Take a pencil and I'll give you the details in a minute. I want you to say to this person that you are telephoning on behalf of friends in France. He should know it's the Bergner family, but do not mention the name. Make the conversation as short as possible. Tell him that your friends have had a visitor, and ask him to verify the visitor's name. Tell him that the visitor wishes to be in regular contact with them. Verify that that is okay, and it's not a trap."

"Papa, is this very important to you?" David asked.

"Yes, why?"

"I have not mentioned this to you yet," David said. "I am on a committee here in Paris to help our brethren in Germany. One of our people will be in Munich next week. It will be better to deal with this face to face than over the telephone. Can it wait for a couple of weeks?"

Rabbi Aaron looked to Sigmund, who nodded. Rabbi Aaron dictated Professor Hailer's address from Sigmund to David, then he signed off abruptly. Leo was impressed, as though his friend, the Rabbi, had just admitted that he was a successful spy.

"We French Jews are well-organized, Herr Bergner," Rabbi Aaron said. "You will have your answer about Professor Hofmann soon. In the meantime, I would suggest you have no contact with him. Just in case. Be sure to tell your wife, too."

By the end of the month, Sigmund had his answer. Professor Hofmann was clean. There was no reason to doubt him. Everyone felt easier with this news. Especially Ulrike, who worried more and more about what she did, afraid that she might make her family vulnerable in some way that she didn't understand.

Leo discovered her fears one night when Sigmund mentioned something about a cab driver at the hotel. Ulrike tightened up, touched her hand to her chest where the emerald pendant used to hang, and looked to Leo. He remembered the woman who had commented on the jewel when he and his mother were returning from Aunt Freda's birthday in Munich. It was clear to Leo—his mother was remembering that same incident.

✳

The night was especially warm and lush in the fragrances of the purple and red bougainvillea. Leo sat in a corner of the patio reading a Hebrew text loaned to him by Rabbi Aaron. Sigmund was enjoying a rare night off. He stepped out onto the patio to join Jacques for a cognac and a cigar.

"Jacques, I'd like to ask your advice, please." Sigmund sat down next to Jacques and trimmed his cigar. "I am now earning a decent wage, and you have steadfastly refused to take anything from me in addition to the arrangements you have with Ulrike. Leo too is earning money and saving it."

"That's good," Jacques answered. "So what can I do for you?"

"All my capital is in Germany." Sigmund puffed on his cigar. "Who knows if I will ever see it again, or if it is lost forever. I need to make what money I have here work for me here."

"You have an idea about that?" Jacques asked.

Leo put a marker in his book and closed it. He hoped his father wouldn't notice him there. This business about the family's money was of interest to him. With his bar mitzvah coming up, he listened to Rabbi Aaron's lessons about being a man, and he took to heart his advice. Now he wanted to know how his father did things, more than what kind of soldier his father had been, the only stories he had ever shared with Leo.

"There is a piece of land for sale," Sigmund said. "I saw it the other day when I went with Monsieur Laidler to look at some new furniture for the hotel lobby. It's near the railway station. Looks interesting. Maybe you should take a look at it, too."

Within a few months, Sigmund and Jacques had made their first invest-ment, a shop with three apartments above, and the rental income more than covered the outgoings. This initial joint venture ignited a passion for real estate that neither of them had known before. Instead of sitting at home play-ing chess, the two men would take long walks around the city and disappear for hours, looking enthusiastically for properties that were for sale.

"For goodness sake," Karin said, "don't you two have anything to talk about these days other than real estate? You're getting very boring."

Leo agreed, but for another reason. His mother grieved for the loss of her emerald. It was dangerous to put money in objects. What if his father's buildings burned down? Or if there were a flood? From his soirees he had earned a considerable sum in tips, and he also looked forward to some money from his bar mitzvah. After watching the discreet flow of money through Professor Hailer to the stranger in Nice and to his father, he was impressed by its fluidity and speed.

By the end of the year, Sigmund and Jacques had invested in three more properties and had taken in a new partner, Maitre Talais, a lawyer who had been a customer at the pharmacy for many years, buying his catarrh pastilles and medication for his arthritis. Jacques had considerable respect for him, and with great relief, put all the legal work, tenant leases, and bank finance negotiations into Maitre Talais's hands. Sigmund's role was to scour the city for suitable investments, and Jacques was free to use his formidable skill for striking a bargain with the sellers. They made a good team. Prosperity seemed to have returned to the Bergner family. But Ulrike still worried, and Leo watched her.

*

Leo celebrated his bar mitzvah at the Nice synagogue. Afterward, Monsieur Laidler hosted a party at the hotel. Many members of the congregation attended to show their support for the Bergners. Additionally, Leo was an established local musician in great demand, and he had his own circle of friends.

The evening was a blur, but Leo knew he would remember one thing—his father, sitting in complete bewilderment. It was only the second time in Sigmund's life that he had ever been to a synagogue. The Hebrew made no sense, and his total ignorance of the prayers and ritual compounded his discomfort. Nonetheless, tears of happiness slid down his cheeks. His pride in his son was evident and undeniable.

Rabbi Aaron rose to propose a toast. Leo listened attentively and basked, with some measure of modesty, in the lavish praise that the rabbi bestowed on him. Rabbi Aaron glanced at Leo's father and gave him a reassuring smile, as if Sigmund were the shy child and himself the protective parent. The irony didn't escape Leo.

5

"GERMANY HAS INVADED POLAND. GOD HELP US ALL," JACQUES announced. He banged the top of the radio as if to improve the reception. Leo thought he simply wanted better news. His cousin shook his head. "The Germans will push us into war yet again."

"Just wait," Sigmund said. "I am sure that good, sound common sense will prevail. The Americans, the British, and the French will tell Hitler to pull back, and he will."

No one believed Sigmund any more than he believed himself. And his nonsense optimism had begun to embarrass Leo as much as it had once embarrassed Ulrike. Leo was now changing with his bar mitzvah behind him. Rabbi Aaron had challenged Leo to think for himself and to consider his Jewish heritage as part of his personal identity.

Three days later, France and England declared war on Germany. Everything changed, as if it hadn't been changing all along. Leo's family seemed to be dangling in a swirling world. Having felt conspicuous in Germany for being Jewish, Sigmund and Ulrike felt no less so as Germans living in France. Fortunately, finally, Sigmund released his optimism.

"We may be interned as enemies, Ulrike. We should consult with an immigration attorney."

"Karin suggested we talk to Maitre Suchet. Everyone says he's the best in town on advising refugees like us."

Maitre Suchet was helpful. He spoke with the *prefectoire* and the *mairie's* office and had their residency permits extended. The police department issued them the relevant documentation and clearances, exempting them from deportation or internment. But change and challenge were in the air. The family couldn't look at only the short-term. At least Leo could see that, and his mother showed signs of similar concern. That left Sigmund to make changes in his thinking as well.

Rabbi Aaron made an unexpected visit to the Bergner home, asking to speak with Sigmund.

"Herr Bergner," the rabbi began. "There will be a meeting at the synagogue at eight o'clock tomorrow night. We would like you and your wife and your son to attend. Monsieur Albert of Strasbourg will address the meeting."

Sigmund's old resistance to such meetings seemed a long time ago. He was no longer in a position to take a highhanded approach, and he agreed that all would attend.

At the meeting, some three hundred attended to hear the elders of the French Jewish community talk about the impending perils, and to pledge their support for France.

"We must be prepared for a long and hard fight ahead," the most wizened among them said. "There will be much pain and hardship, maybe rationing. Italy is on our doorstep. Maybe they will invade us. The French army is mostly deployed in the North. We have little protection here. I think we should get out now, while we can."

"Nonsense," another answered. "We are French. Vive la France. We will stay and crush the bastard Germans just as we did in '18."

Sigmund fidgeted. Leo knew that even now, his father was proud of his Iron Cross. At least his mother's thinking was on sound ground.

"Don't let any of us forget what our beloved France did to Captain Dreyfus," a woman shouted from the back of the hall. "Have you all forgotten? My father was a cousin of Madame Dreyfus. We must be diligent."

"Where can we go?" a man countered. "Our duty is to stay here and do what we can to win the war. Not to flee like frightened rats. Imagine how the anti-Semitic lobby will react if they see us running away. We must stay."

Rabbi Aaron walked to the podium, cleared his throat, and held up the palm of his hand.

"My friends," he began. "I hear what you all say. But let's be rational, reasonable, and sensible. Of course, we must stay and show our patriotism to France at this time—"

"What good is that?" Monsieur Gilbert shouted. "Just look at Herr Bergner and his wife, sitting here in the front. They behaved like true patriotic Germans. Still they had to run from their beloved fucking fatherland. The same will happen to us. Mark my words."

"Please, Monsieur Gilbert. There are women and children present." The agitated crowd settled, and Rabbi Aaron continued, "What I want to say is this—I believe it will be a major mistake for us to leave France. We will defeat our enemies, I have no doubt of that. But we will have a difficult time, and I am not sure that this will be the right atmosphere in which to bring up children. Monsieur Albert is here to talk about a plan that the Central Committee has, and the French rabbinate unanimously endorses. French children—all those below the age of eighteen—are to be evacuated to Palestine for the duration of the war."

The crowd grew quiet, yet glances between adults, and among children, showed both curiosity and concern. Leo looked to his parents. He was not yet eighteen, and though not born in this country, was now considered a child of France. A Jewish child of France.

"My fellow Jews," Monsieur Albert said. "I have here pamphlets for you all. A number of kibbutzim in Palestine are willing to take in an unlimited number of Jewish children. They will be housed, clothed, educated, and fed at no charge to any of you. And for as long as it takes. Those who need it will receive medical treatment. Ships have been chartered to sail from Marseilles to Cyprus and then to Palestine. They will be met in Haifa on their arrival and taken by bus to their designated kibbutz. Baron Rothschild's committee in Paris is covering the entire cost of transportation. Of course, anyone who wants to make a donation to the committee, or to any particular kibbutz, well, that will be welcome and appreciated. No Jewish child is going to be deprived of this opportunity to get out of Europe on account of shortage of funds."

"What about the British?" a woman shouted. "Will they let our children enter Palestine? After all, they have the League of Nations mandate, and they have been very strict about Jewish immigration into Palestine."

"We have had unofficial meetings with the British," Monsieur Albert explained. "They are sympathetic. We are lucky that Winston Churchill, a fervent Zionist all his life, is interceding with the British government to allow an unlimited number of Jewish children into Palestine."

"When does the first boat leave Marseilles?" a man asked, waving his hand in the air.

"We are hopeful that the first sailing will be in ten days," Monsieur Albert answered. "They will then have sailings every two weeks until all the children are evacuated. Each boat can take up to five hundred. Children will be traveling south from all over France by bus, and we are looking also for homes where they can stay until their departure is arranged from Marseilles."

When the meeting ended, Ulrike picked up several pamphlets and put them in her bag. Neither Sigmund nor Leo said anything during the walk home. Leo suspected that he would soon be traveling again. Certainly his family would send him to Palestine, as they had sent him to Nice not so long ago.

Leo looked around at the faces of his family, his mother and father as well as Jacques and Karin. His father seemed so confused, a proud and troubled German now living in hostile France. His mother only wanted the best for Leo. Even his beloved Jacques and Karin were concerned for his safety. Suddenly, he felt much younger than he was. But he knew the outcome would be for the best. He knew that he was no emerald pendant to be passed on to the next generation. No, he was the next generation, and his survival was far more important.

✳

Each child—Leo bristled at the word—was to take only one valise. He filled his with clothes; a couple of music books in case there was a piano in the kibbutz; a copy of Major Griffith's 1898 classic, *Wellington and Waterloo*; and a new leather writing case that Karin had bought him. She had tucked some family photographs under the first sheets of paper, which he found almost right away.

Leo was apprehensive about leaving Nice, but not as much as he had been a few days earlier. After all, he had been separated from his parents before. He thought back to the first time he had gazed out at the sea from the beach at Nice, and how he had looked forward to his first swim in the Mediterranean. He speculated that he was now stronger. Maybe once he arrived in Palestine, he would swim much further out toward the horizon.

That night he dreamt of a blinding marine glitter, a wall of white fire that called him out further and further from the shore. His body was full of strength. He swam harder and faster without tiring. He was aware that his family waited on the beach for him, but each time he lifted his face from the water, the setting sun called him onward. He needed something in the glare and light, something he needed vitally. So he continued swimming. Finally, he turned around, but he'd gone so far that now the beach was empty. He understood that his family believed he had drowned, that they had searched without success, and finally, they gave him up for dead. Again he tried to swim back, but the current pushed him out to sea.

✳

The day was hot. Blocking traffic, two battered blue buses were out of place with their noisy engines and foul exhaust among the manicured lawns and immaculate homes. After final emotional farewells, Leo took his place on the first bus. Next to him sat a ruddy-faced boy who, in spite of being rather thin, had round cheeks and large, strong-looking shoulders.

"My name is Ulrich," the boy said without a trace of shyness. "My friends call me Uri."

"Okay, Ulrich. My name is Leopold. My friends call me Leo. I'm from Augsburg."

"And I'm from Stuttgart." Uri smiled broadly. "My father is German, my mother from here."

The journey from Nice to Marseilles took longer than expected. The old bus chugged along at a steady thirty miles per hour through small towns, countryside, more towns and further scenic views. Leo and Uri slid down in their seats and talked. Both were bilingual with an acceptable standard of English. Leo's hobbies were music and military history. Uri was a passionate sports fan and knew the names of every major European soccer and tennis player. He poked fun at some of the old men in the towns they passed through, early risers who picked their way along the streets, hailing each other like seagulls.

"We're leaving so much behind," Uri said, gazing out at the passing scenery. "Probably never to return."

"You really think so, Uri?" Leo asked. "I hope to come back someday." Then Leo realized his poor manners. "I mean, Ulrich. Or are we…"

Smiling, Uri planted a hand on Leo's shoulder. "I think we'll be friends for a long time, Leo."

6

"WELCOME, CHILDREN, TO OUR KIBBUTZ." THE ELDERLY WOMAN was plump with snow-white hair and a weather-beaten face that suggested she had spent much time in the sun. "My name is Sarah Almann. My job at the kibbutz is to oversee your welfare. First, I want you all to make a line in front of the desk and pick up your name cards. We want you to wear these for your first few weeks here until we all get to know each other."

Her voice was as sweet as the sun beyond the window, and Leo was already growing enamored. She seemed to have the wisdom and savvy of the women who'd come to the soirées at the Levy home in Nice, and all the warmth of his grandmama in Germany.

"I am from Strasbourg," Sarah continued in French. "I have been here now for several years. Almost the very first thing I had to do when I arrived was to learn Hebrew. And you will do that too. Now, let me see. Today is Sunday. After Wednesday, no one will speak French anymore. Your Hebrew lessons will start tomorrow. I promise you that if you work hard, you will all be fluent in six months."

Leo looked at Uri and then around at the other children. He saw the panic on their faces mingled with an eagerness to prove to Sarah that it could be done—sooner, even.

"Our kibbutz is known throughout Palestine as the Fishing Kibbutz. Of course we grow fruit, delicious oranges and also avocados and other vegetables, but our prime activity here is fishing. We have a fleet of fishing boats that goes out every day on the Sea of Galilee. Some of you will have the opportunity of working on the boats. You will all do a few hours work each day for the kibbutz, either in the kitchen, the laundry, or wherever you are told. That will be after school and after homework. You will have the rest of today to settle in, then class begins tomorrow, starting with a visit from the leader of our kibbutz, Monsieur Lapidus of the executive committee. He is French the same as you, and he is eager to meet you all. He is a good man and regards each of you as one of his children."

She surveyed the room, looking into the eyes and soul of each child. Leo felt swept up in her energy, her sincerity. If this was to be his new world, his new community, his new family, then he was ready.

"We have about one hundred and twenty families. By the end of the month, we expect to have about six hundred French children, like you. You will each be assigned to a family who will be responsible for you. You must look upon every one of us as your extended family." She smiled at the youngest children. "That means cousins, aunts, uncles, grandparents. We are all a big family. We are here for you, and you are here for us. We are a tight and happy community. Welcome."

Leo stayed close to Uri and followed their *metapelet* Rachel, the woman designated by Sarah as their housemother. She, in turn, shepherded them and ten other children to a dorm some distance away. Leo's eyes were wide with curiosity. Clusters of concrete buildings, purely functional and mostly bare, sat together and filled the immediate area. The doors and windows of many stood open. Leo peered inside. Classrooms. Along the path, he passed several adults who smiled and shouted a cheerful *shalom*. He smiled back.

A tall girl with long, black hair walked toward them. She wore a tight-fitting military uniform that accentuated her assertive breasts. Uri stopped, clicked his heels and saluted. Everyone laughed.

"Oh, you have to be French," she said in a calm, Parisian accent, and walked on.

"Children," Rachel announced, stopping outside a hunk of concrete. "This is your dorm. A bedroom and bathroom through that door there for the boys, and another one over there for the girls. Then through that door is your classroom, which doubles as the dining room. Through the door on the left is the kitchen."

Rachel was a bit of a stick in the mud, but the other children seemed to accept her authority. Leo and Uri greeted the other boys, but no one was in a hurry to strike up a conversation. They chose beds near a window and next to each other.

"Okay, Leo," Uri said with a smile. "Let's not fall out over this, but which girl do you fancy?"

"Uri, for goodness sake, we just got here. Give me a chance to get to know a few."

"Good." Uri was serious. "In that case, stay away from Chantal."

Leo spent their first afternoon walking around the kibbutz that spread over several hundred acres of once-barren hillside. Now the landscape was reborn with plantings of palm trees and orange groves. He and Uri strolled along a newly paved path toward the tennis courts and soccer pitch. They looked in at the cold storage and fish-packing room as well as the workshop where the kibbutz trucks went for repairs.

The sense of community and overall friendliness seemed forced at times, but Leo still felt that he belonged. Then his thoughts wandered back to Nice. He wondered about his family and how they were, even worried about them and their safety compared to his here in Palestine. The laughter of a young girl distracted Leo from thoughts of his family. Uri stood ahead, chattering with Chantal and making her laugh. Uri certainly hadn't wasted any time getting into the spirit of things. Leo felt a tinge of jealousy, then a needle of guilt. This new world was *his* new world, though his old one haunted him still.

✳

That evening, after Leo's first communal meal, he joined the other children in clearing the table and washing their dishes. In the midst of this activity, several older boys appeared at the open door. One of them stepped forward, dressed for the hot weather in a thin shirt, shorts, and wearing sandals. He looked athletic and tanned.

"Which one of you is Leo?" the boy asked.

"Me," Leo said, and stood up straight.

"My name is Shimon." He held out his hand. "I'm your new big brother. Welcome to Degani. I'm going to take you over to my parents' place. We'll have some cake and kibitz for an hour or so. That's the routine."

Shimon's parents gave Leo a warm welcome and pulled him into their modest kitchen. Homemade chocolate éclairs were stacked high on a platter. The evening with Shimon and his parents flowed easily as they told how they had all come to Palestine. Mostly Shimon spoke.

He had arrived at the kibbutz a few years earlier as Simon Fabre from Paris. His father had been a dentist there, and in Palestine, he had set up a surgery at the kibbutz and treated everyone from all the neighboring kibbutzim as well. His mother worked in the dining hall. Simon Fabre became Shimon, and within a few months, he was fluent in Hebrew.

Shimon was eighteen and the star of the soccer team. He was also an outstanding tennis player, a weightlifter, and an ace shot. One of his assignments for the kibbutz was to patrol the grounds at night. On several occasions, he had warned off potential troublemakers from the Arab village nearby.

"Now," Shimon continued. "As your big brother, it's my job to see that you get used to life at the kibbutz. Life here is okay. The people are nice. We're all on the same team and playing a part in the development of a new country. I don't miss France at all." Shimon smiled at Leo. "Except for the food. But I shouldn't complain too much since my mother works in the dining room, and I know they do their best with the ingredients they have to work with."

Shimon seemed contained in his own head, where he held a reminder to always speak well of the kibbutz. It gave him an energetic but somewhat recursive way of speaking, and he tended not to meet Leo's eyes. Still Leo felt special to be this young man's new brother.

"I only miss France," Leo said, "when I think about my parents and my family there. You're lucky you have your family here with you. All I have is letters."

A light knock on the door was followed by a girl entering, the beautiful tall girl Uri had saluted earlier that day. Shimon stood and went to her.

"Meet my girlfriend, Yona," Shimon said as he playfully pulled her into the room.

Indeed, she was very beautiful, with pear-shaped eyes, straight black hair, and a perfect figure.

"I've met this young man already today," she said. "Well, sort of. I passed him with Rachel and her new arrivals."

"You have a good memory," Leo said.

"Well, your friend made me laugh."

Leo prickled a little. Uri made friends so easily. And he adapted to these new surroundings seemingly without effort. Leo instead found that he had to think things through and balance the past with the present.

"Are you in the army?" Leo asked. "You were wearing a uniform."

"British army. I am an interpreter." Yona nodded and took an éclair. "I am French, but I also speak German. My mother is German from Berlin. I was brought up bilingual."

She took a bite of the pastry. Leo did the same, struggling to concentrate on what she was saying and not stare at her mouth. Shimon was watching, too.

"The British," she said. "They are not optimistic that they can beat Rommel's troops. Jerusalem might fall to the Nazis, which would be catastrophic for us. They want German-speaking soldiers who can serve behind enemy lines. That's why I'm in the army. But I'm home on leave for the weekend to spend time with my parents." She touched Shimon's shoulder with her long-fingered hand and gave him a radiant but irreproachably polite smile. "And my dear boyfriend, who has not yet sampled one of his mother's famous éclairs. What are you frightened of, Shimon, that we will lose our figures?"

Everyone laughed, including Leo.

＊

August 14, 1940

Dear Mami,

My first year at the kibbutz is passing quickly. Uri and the other boys in the dorm are good friends, and I think Francine might be finally tapping her foot in my direction. She's fifteen and from Bordeaux. We went on a walk the other day. When no one was close enough to hear us talking, we switched to French. It made me homesick.

I think I've mastered Hebrew, and three days of every week I go out with the fishing boats and help unload and weigh the catch. You can't imagine how thrilling it is to sail on the Sea of Galilee and to feel the engine hum to life around you and push the boat free of its moorings. Sometimes, if the catch is small, the captain forgets to speak in Hebrew and curses in French. He is an experienced fisherman and used to own a couple of fishing boats in Toulon before immigrating to Palestine. There is also a rumor that he had left Toulon in a hurry as a result of an argument with another fisherman over a woman. The other man disappeared, and his body was never found. Who knows? There are rumors about everyone.

The kibbutz arranged day trips this month for us to visit Tiberias and Jerusalem. The cities are full of their exotic smells, so many cultures, and so much history. I can't help feeling like we're all getting pulled into it—history—and that every week my life belongs less and less to me. It's harder when your letters don't get through. I feel like I am starting such a new life that I don't remember the past anymore.

Oh, and Shimon has volunteered to join the British army and we only see him once in a while. No one knows exactly where he is serving. He looks good in his uniform, and I can never wait for him to come back with stories. He says the soldiers are a good bunch. Very good men. Their officers are well-trained and the men are tough as granite.

Love, as always,
Leo

*

September 12, 1940

Dear Mami, Father, Jacques, and Karin,

A number of the French children have come down with malaria but they are being treated by the kibbutz's physician and are getting better. It happens a lot and the physician seems to think of it as just a nuisance.

A British officer visited the kibbutz one day a few weeks ago and spoke with the committee. He told us that it would be in everyone's interests to learn German, just in case we find ourselves behind enemy lines. The British officer was friendly and taken on a tour of the kibbutz. He seemed impressed with all our work, and he and his driver were invited to stay for dinner. After dinner, some of the musicians and I went onto the stage and played a medley of British songs. We rounded off with "God Save the King" after Monsieur Lapidus toasted King George and the British army.

Anyway, because of that visit, I'm starting to give German lessons on the days I'm not working on the boats. The pupils are an assortment of members of the kibbutz, some of them a lot older than me. They are having difficulty not only with the grammar but also with the problem of learning a language spoken by our most hated enemies. I wish you were here, Father, to tell them about all the good things Germany is, too.

The kibbutz is growing fast. More and more families and children have arrived and continue to arrive weekly. New buildings shoot up all the time. Now I am a big brother to a couple of twelve-year-olds from Dijon. That was me just yesterday!

Love, as always,
Leo

P.S. Things are going well with Francine. I see her a couple evenings a week. She asks about you often and says to wish you well. Uri says hello, too.

✳

Letters from France arrived less and less. The news of the French surrender shook the camp. And the news of the German occupation of Paris came as a bitter blow to the kibbutz. The war was going badly for the British too. Everyone worried about what would happen next. But Leo felt a glimmer of hope in Mr. Churchill's speeches and of the fortitude and determination of the British.

Finally, Leo received a reply from Ulrike. It was a sad letter and from the postmark, he saw that it had taken weeks to arrive.

My Darling Leo:

I am sorry that you have not heard from us for sometime. We were told not to write for a while in case there was censorship. Anyway, all the parents were contacted last week and told that someone was going to Italy, then taking a boat from Brindisi to Haifa. He would be willing to take letters, but not parcels, with him to mail from there. The poor man. I think he has about a thousand letters to send off as soon as he gets to Haifa.

The news in Europe is bad. I don't know how much you hear. In a nutshell, it is not very good, but happily we are all surviving. Papa, Karin and Jacques send their love and we await your news too. The nice gentleman who has helped in getting this letter to you will be returning in three weeks time and we have been told that the kibbutz will collect letters from you all to bring back. So please make sure to write us a long letter as we have no idea how long this courier service can continue, bearing in mind the present situation.

We haven't heard a word from anyone in Munich for months. Heaven knows where they are and what they are doing. Our dear friend the professor has been in regular contact with his friend here. He sends his best wishes to you and hopes that you are practicing your Chopin.

Papa is working less at the hotel now. The owner, nice Monsieur Laidler, felt that he had to give some hours to other Jewish refugees from Germany too. Papa understood, so there is no problem. He and Jacques have invested in another two properties. Because it is hard to find electricians and plumbers and maintenance people these days, Papa has learned to do some handiwork. It is quite fun to see him go out of the house with his bag of tools.

Karin is working as a volunteer for the rabbi in helping other refugees. Many are arriving also from Paris and the north as the Germans are occupying Paris, as you know. You can well imagine how Jacques feels about that.

We have heard that General de Gaulle is in London and has taken with him a large number of French officers and soldiers who are working, with help from the British, to take back France from the Germans. Jacques knows a few people he thinks will now be in London. Baron Rothschild is there too, we believe.

We are lucky that we are not yet occupied by the Germans and that we are spared the sight of seeing those awful Nazi uniforms all the time. The Germans agreed that the French could set up their own government to administer central and southern France. It sits in Vichy, and we are under their supervision. So far, we have no

*problems, but we worry when we see so many frightened people
arrive here every day from the north.*

*Jacques serves on a committee that looks after them. He goes
two or three nights every week to the railway station to greet the
arriving trains and then takes as many as he can to the synagogue's
community hall. The rabbi and the committee on which Karin serves
take over from there. Papa and I wanted to help on that committee
too, but there is such an intense hatred of Germans right now. We
were told that it would be better if we took a back seat.*

*I am busy at the pharmacy. I enjoy the work, meeting people
and having busy days. The men are really worried and depressed.
Papa had brought his Iron Cross with him from Augsburg, though
he'd kept it hidden. Then he came back the other night after a walk
with tears in his eyes. He told us that he had thrown it into the sea.
I know I shouldn't tell you any of this as I don't want to upset you,
but I can't stop myself now that I am writing.*

*Sometimes I even think of that wonderful pendant given to me
on our wedding day. But I don't mention it to your father, especially
now after he threw away his Iron Cross. I know that they are not
the same, that medal and my emerald, but they were both about
something important in our lives.*

*Do you remember that nice family, the Bernheims? Well, they
have left Nice now altogether. Most of us are content with the Vichy
government although we know they are German puppets. But the
Bernheims were worried and have left for Montreal. I'm not sure
how they managed to get there, but they left a month ago. Someone
said they took a boat from Lisbon, but I'm not sure.*

*Now tell me your news. The last I heard from you was that you
are now fluent in Hebrew and that you give German lessons to some
of your fellow kibbutzniks. You have told me about your work on the
fishing boats. That sounds like a lot of fun. Papa and Jacques were
quite jealous when they read that. And what about your girlfriend?
Is she nice?*

*Now I must stop and let the others write to you. Remember that
we love you and we always want you safe.*

Love,
Mami

*

That night, over dinner, Uri and some of the others seemed sad. They too had received letters and felt homesick and worried. Leo sat with them and felt his own tears. He thought of his father throwing out his medal, and the loss of his mother's pendant. He pressed a fisted hand to his chest, remembering his Mami's embrace when she'd still possessed the pendant. It seemed so long ago.

7

LEO'S MIND WAS IN MANY DIFFERENT PLACES. HE WAS WORRIED about the evening's concert as he had fallen behind in his daily practice. A new group of immigrants had stirred up his anxieties about his family in France. He was now bored with the work on the fishing boats and the stink of the fish. He wanted to volunteer in the British army. And he wanted to spend more time alone with Francine, but either his schedule or hers made it too difficult. And he had grown tired of listening to Uri's exaggerated tales of his sexual adventures.

"No, Leo, please, not yet," Francine pleaded as Leo fumbled to take off her bra.

They had sneaked out during the Friday Shabbat dinner and walked hand-in-hand to one of the garages. They had climbed onto the back of a pickup truck. Leo took off his shirt and rolled it into a small ball to serve as a pillow. He had fallen in love with Francine, and luckily for him, she had reciprocated his feelings. Unlike all the others, he still hadn't lost his virginity. But he was determined to do so before this night was over.

"Come on, Francine, please," he said as his hands explored her soft young body.

"No, Leo, please." She buried her face in his, and he felt her tears against his cheeks. "Let's just lie here together and hold each other. I am so worried about France and everyone there. The time is not right, Leo. Please be patient with me, please."

Leo walked back to the dorm, feeling dejected.

"So where did you and Francine go tonight after dinner?" Uri asked with a grin. "Did you get lucky, finally?"

"Oh, shut up," Leo answered. "It's not just about sex, you know. There are feelings, too."

"Sure, sure," Uri said with a mock serious expression.

Leo thought Uri was laughing at him, but he let it go. Uri had a different idea about girls, and it had little to do with emotion. Unlike Leo, Uri didn't appear bothered by how others felt, nor did he seem very concerned about the war spreading across Europe.

The kibbutz had expanded greatly, and there were new girls all the time. Leo ignored them. If anything, the sight of whole families arriving at the kibbutz made him sad and restless. He would write about that in his next letter and encourage his parents and cousins to come, too, if the situation in Southern France were to deteriorate further. Screw Rabbi Aaron and his good intentions for the Jews of Nice. Jacques and Sigmund had money. They should use it as soon as possible to move eastward.

There was to be a concert that night. Leo turned his mind to the music. Francine's fears and Uri's teasing now faded into other thoughts. Maybe playing tonight would ease his restlessness. He rushed over to the community hall.

"So, you don't say hello to me anymore?" The woman's voice stopped him in the entryway.

"Yona, I'm sorry," Leo said, a blush coming to his face. "I was so immersed in my thoughts, I didn't see you. Forgive me. Shimon is here. I didn't know you were coming this weekend too."

"Well, that's nice, isn't it?" Her face showed a friendly smile. "I'm performing tonight at the concert, dancing with the troupe from Paris. I'll see you there."

✳

The concert was a success. Close to eight hundred attended. Some had even come from neighboring kibbutzim. Many in the audience wore British army uniforms, and Leo envied them. After the music was over, the room filled with conversation and motion. Leo pushed his way through many congratulatory handshakes until he saw a familiar flash of hair swaying and shining like a curtain of dark mercury. He reached for her, and Francine turned around. Her round cheeks were pink in the hot room.

"Francine, let's go and sit down by the lake," Leo said as people began to head back to their dorms and apartments. "It will be cooler there."

"No, Leo," she answered. "I know what you have in mind, and it's late. I have to be up early in the morning."

"Francine, please." He placed a gentle hand on her forearm.

"Leo, no." She pulled away and clutched her purse with both hands.

Her response to his touch brought heat to his face. Enough. He turned and wandered back toward his dorm, wondering why he couldn't persuade her, and cycling arguments through his mind. She wasn't busy. She didn't have to be up early in the morning. What was she up to?

An hour later, Uri entered the dorm. He had a funny expression on his face, then without saying anything, he jumped into bed. Leo watched his friend's broad shoulders rise and fall in a sleep-like rhythm. Uri wouldn't want to hear about Leo's latest frustrations with Francine. He'd probably just laugh and say that Leo wanted sex more that he wanted to admit. Maybe Uri was right.

After breakfast the next morning, Leo grabbed some books and went to the other side of the kibbutz to give a German lesson. But German lessons weren't the answer. They too had become monotonous. And he was now fluent in Hebrew. In fact, he was tired of the constant demands on his time for piano recitals and lessons, his work duties, all of it. It all bored him. And he dreamt about Nice every night. Maybe volunteering for the British army would be his exit out of here.

After the German lesson, Leo ambled aimlessly toward the community hall.

Yona approached. "Leo, what's the matter?" Studying him, she grew more concerned. "You've looked sad for a few days. Come, let's get a coffee and talk."

There was something special about Yona that made it easy for every man to fall in love with her, and for every woman to want her as a friend. Her beauty was undeniable, but so was the warmth of her character, her sense of humor, and her quick mind. Leo accepted her invitation and walked with her. It was a peaceful time of day. School was over, and he had no duties for another hour.

"So tell me, Leo, what's the matter?" Yona sat opposite him at an outdoor cafeteria table. "What's upsetting you?"

"I don't know." He shook his head and squinted at the sunlight, then focused on her. "First, I miss my parents. I've fallen for Francine, but I'm not getting anywhere. And the further away she gets from me, the more I want to see her. She speaks French with me, and it reminds me of home, I suppose. But it's more than that. I'm fed up with working with stinking fish and picking fruit. Uri is acting distant. It's hard work trying to teach middle-aged French people German, a language they hate and don't want to speak anyway. I'm even getting tired of playing the piano."

"Leo, I think you want to join the army like Shimon, don't you?"

"Yes. But Shimon says I may still be too young."

"So, why not lie about your age? It wouldn't be the first time that's been done."

"What if I get caught?"

"I guess they'd kick you out of the army. Then they'd probably take you back when you were old enough."

"But what would they say here?" He waved a hand at the concrete building that had been his home for so long. He felt the irony of his lack of attachment. "Wouldn't they prevent me from leaving?"

"Leo, look around. The place is bursting at the seams with all the new arrivals. They may be pleased to see you go to make room. Look, I didn't mean it to sound that way. Everyone loves you here, but be realistic. Maybe it's just time to move on. Why not get permission to come back with Shimon and me to Jerusalem in a couple of days. I'll take you to the Recruitment Office, and see what they say."

"I'll think about it. Thank you, Yona."

"Leo, just be careful." She leaned across the table and grabbed his hand. "Shimon and I are very fond of you. We don't want you to get hurt. That's all I want to say."

She stood quickly, went to his side of the table, and bent down to kiss him on the cheek. Then she walked away swiftly without looking back. Leo checked his watch. He had another half an hour before reporting for duty at the fish-packing yard. A mountain of wooden crates waited to be repaired. He needed to go to the carpentry shop to pick up a hammer and a box of nails. He rose and set off down the path.

He froze. His heart stopped beating. Seated on a bench a few yards ahead, it was Francine, and her hair cascaded over the arm of another boy. The boy wore a lightweight cream sweater with red cuffs and collar. A second after Leo recognized the sweater, he recognized the tousled blond hair and broad shoulders as Uri's. He and Francine were locked in an embrace. Francine's face was buried in his neck, and she leaned into him more passionately than she'd ever done for Leo. Uri pulled back and turned his head toward her. Their lips touched.

Leo was overwhelmed. Should he turn around and walk back? Or should he continue? If they heard his footsteps approach, they might break from their embrace and see him. He didn't want a confrontation. He felt sick. Anger. Hatred. Hurt. His mind spun in a thousand different directions.

He turned around and walked fast, any faster would be to run, back toward the cafeteria. No, not the cafeteria. The laundry. It was quiet there. No, not the laundry. The library. No, not the library. The greenhouse. Anywhere. Anywhere he could escape from this painful truth he couldn't bear.

The greenhouse was hot and humid. No one was there. He sat down on the gravel floor, wet from the constant watering of the plants. No matter. He felt his body shake, and tears flowed down his face. He had never cried like this before. He had never felt betrayal before either, like this or any other. The minutes ticked by, but he had no reason to get up and leave.

He couldn't decide if he should confront them. Should he say nothing? Maybe talk with someone else about it. Shimon, Yona, or even Rachel? He thought about his parents, and his cousins Jacques and Karin, so far away. He missed them. He needed them. He felt alone.

The tears did not stop, adding to his wet shirt, dripping with perspiration from the humidity. The only sound was of the sprinklers. He put his head down on the ground, stretched out, and turned over on his side. His face pressed against the coarse gravel, but drained of so many tears, there was nothing left to feel, not even the sharp stones biting into his cheek.

✳

"There he is, Arik," Rachel whispered, pointing the flashlight onto the ground. "Thank God, we've found you."

She knelt down and stroked Leo's head. He opened his eyes then shut them tight, blinded by the flashlight. Arik turned it toward the plants.

"What is it, Leo?" Rachel asked. "What's the matter? You missed your German class and dinner. We've been very worried about you. Are you okay?"

Leo stretched his legs and sat up. He raised his hand to wipe the gravel off his face and ran his hands through his hair. He must have fallen asleep, after the shock of today had swallowed him up.

"What time is it?" Leo asked.

"Midnight. Are you okay?"

"I'm fine. I'm sorry I caused you any bother. Let's go back now. To the dorm, please."

He stood and wiped the gravel off his shirt and pants. Back at the dorm, all the lights were out. As he lay down on his bed, he shot a glance at Uri. He was asleep in the next bed, the blanket hooked over his shoulder and bare feet sticking out the bottom. His clothes lay on the floor, his cream and red sweater draped on top of it all. Leo turned over to his other side, his heart beating hotly in his chest.

The next morning after breakfast, without exchanging either a glance or word with Uri, Leo told Rachel that he had to have a quick word with Yona, and that he would be back within fifteen minutes. At her dorm, he asked for Yona and waited in the common room looking at the community board, but was unable to read anything. She appeared, her hair wound up in a towel.

"Leo, you look terrible. Wild. What's the matter?"

"Yona. Please take me with you when you go back to Jerusalem, and set me up a meeting with the recruitment office."

He gave her a weak smile. This was what he wanted, but he never thought it would happen this way. Not this quickly.

*

A few days later, Leo sat in the back of a jeep on his way to the British Army Headquarters in Jerusalem. Shimon had one hand on the steering wheel and the other on Yona's knee. As they drove, they sang a melody of Hebrew and French songs. They tried to include Leo in the songs, but he still hurt from Francine and Uri's betrayal.

"Here we are." Shimon parked the jeep outside the large fortress building. "Tell the corporal at the desk that you are here to see Sergeant Duncan."

Leo waved goodbye to his friends and walked toward the entrance. The building had been constructed at the end of the last century. Solid and formidable. Armed sentries stood at the entranceway to all the outer gates and doors. Jeeps and army vehicles drove in and out, kicking up sheets of sand and dust. Leo was nervous. He stood outside for a long moment to take in the scene, clutching an envelope that Monsieur Lapidus had given him, with his papers and a letter of introduction. Wearing jeans and an open-neck shirt, he felt conspicuous among all the uniformed men in sight.

"Young man, what is your business here?" a stern soldier asked.

"I'm here to volunteer. I was told to ask for Sergeant Duncan."

"The third floor," the soldier answered. The initial severity in his voice became friendlier. "When you go inside, take a right and you'll see the stairs. On the third floor, follow the signs to the recruiting office. Good luck to you."

Inside, Leo scaled the steps, made it to the third floor, and found the recruitment office. At the door, he tapped and waited. The door opened and before him stood a giant of a man with blond hair and a tan.

"Who are you?" the man asked in a strong Scottish accent.

"My name is Leo Bergner. I'm here to see Sergeant Duncan."

"Well, you've found him."

Leo sat down while the sergeant busied himself with sorting papers and finding a blank form that needed to be completed.

"I have my papers here, if you need to see them." Leo handed the envelope to the sergeant, who took it without opening it.

"How old are you?" Duncan asked.

"Eighteen," Leo lied.

"Really?"

"Yes, sir, really."

"I have some information about you already. A telephone call from your Mr. Lapidus. But tell me in one minute about yourself, why you want to join the British army, and why we should have you."

"My name is Leo Bergner. I am German. I speak German, French, Hebrew, English and some Arabic. I am also Jewish, so it should come as no surprise that I hate Nazis. I am in good health and strong. I will do whatever I can to help fight and defeat our common enemy."

"Bergner," Sergeant Duncan answered. "I will recommend your application for approval, but it will need confirmation by the CO. Come back at two o'clock and have your medical examination, complete some forms and collect your uniform. I'll see you back here then."

"Thank you, sir."

Leo walked into the street, nervous and elated. He headed toward a coffee shop. He was hungry and needed to sit and collect his thoughts. At least he now had something other than Uri and Francine to occupy his mind. And it was time to write another letter to France.

✳

Leo returned to the kibbutz on a British military truck. To say goodbye to everyone at the kibbutz was easy—almost bitterly so. Uri and Francine's betrayal had made it that way. He blamed not only them but nearly everyone at the kibbutz. But as he spent time with Rachel, Monsieur Lapidus, some of the fishermen, and Shimon's parents, all of whom hugged him and wished him well, he made some exceptions to his bitter feelings. These were good people here, although none of them was family. Now he was packing to leave the kibbutz. Yes, the kibbutz was easy to leave, and now he doubted he would ever feel at home anywhere.

Leo's belongings fit into a kitbag with room to spare. As he folded the last of his shirts, at the bottom of his drawer he found a too-small red sweater, now with holes in the sleeves and almost threadbare at the elbows. Out of curiosity, he measured the sweater's arm against his. Seam to cuff, it still left four inches of bare wrist. Leo thought about the boy he once was and the young man he had now become. Taller, older, stronger. But still his parents' son.

Then he heard someone behind him. He concentrated on his kitbag. He fiddled with a folded shirt. He'd said his goodbyes, but had avoided Francine and of course Uri.

"Leo," Uri whispered. "I know why you're doing this."

Uri stood in the doorway. Leo looked at him with new eyes. Uri had grown even more than Leo had since they first arrived at the kibbutz, putting on muscle and healthy weight around his face. It made his expression even longer.

"I know it's my fault," Uri continued.

"It doesn't matter." Leo turned back to his kitbag, folded the red sweater, and tossed it into the trash can. "I'm leaving anyway."

Uri shifted from foot to foot, the way he did when he was impatient. Or nervous.

"What?" Leo snapped.

"Leo, look, I shouldn't have done it. Francine shouldn't have done it either. But, we fell in love. It's *beshert.*" His voice was drained of all its strength. "Now, please let's shake hands and not become enemies. After all, you're going into the army. I may do the same thing—join the army. We may get killed. Haven't we been through enough? Can we not be civil to each other?"

Tears streamed down Uri's face. Leo had never seen him so upset before in all the time they'd been friends, all the way back to the bus leaving Nice, which seemed a hundred years ago. And Uri had exhibited such bravado about sex and everything else for that matter. Now none of that was there.

"Uri, you betrayed me. Francine betrayed me. How do you expect me to feel?"

"I don't want you to hate me. Or hate us. I want you to forgive us."

"Maybe I will. But right now, I feel so hurt by what you both did. Behind my back. I feel like an idiot."

"Please." Uri's face softened. His eagerness to engage Leo made the conversation feel a thread of their old connection. "Francine is waiting for us to walk out of here together. She is in the courtyard. I say we go to her and make shalom. I beseech you. We are at war. Leo, the Germans may march into Palestine. Then what? Please."

Leo hesitated. He threw into the kitbag the writing set Karin had given him. He would write as soon as he was at the army barracks and had a quiet hour to himself. With family so far away, there were so few connections to hold on to. Uri was right. Was it worth ignoring their years of friendship? Francine had never been very happy with him anyway. These were hard questions, moral questions, that reminded him of Rabbi Aaron—another friendship Leo had abandoned. Was he willing to do it again, walk away, and swallow even more bitterness over a perceived betrayal? He was still angry at his father for taking so long to bring his mother to Nice. Suddenly Leo felt older.

"Please," Uri said. "The truck will be here in a few minutes."

Leo studied the red sweater in the trash and gathered his courage. He stuck out his hand and walked toward Uri, who moved forward in an instant and pulled Leo into a bear hug. A moment of pause and Leo returned the embrace. Then Uri stepped back, grabbed the bag from Leo's hand, and walked somberly down the path toward the parking lot.

Francine approached Leo. A look of relief crossed her face as her eyes darted from one to the other. She ran to throw her arms around Leo.

"Will you forgive me too, Leo, please?"

"Yes, of course I will," he answered in a choked whisper.

He was full of loss and relief, and never before had he felt so close to Francine. She held him without guardedness—fully, her body against his, and the sensation put a knife in his heart. He'd resolved to say goodbye and forgive, and his resolve made the parting more painful.

Sand and rock crunched beyond the courtyard wall—the British army truck swerved off the road and came to a halt. Many of Leo's friends came forward as he approached the truck.

"Which one of you is Private Bergner?" the driver shouted from the open window.

"That's me."

Familiar faces trailed him to the side of the truck. Monsieur Lapidus made his way to the front of the crowd.

"Get in the truck, Leo, and may God go with you," Lapidus said as he hugged him. "If you're as good a soldier as you were a kibbutznik, we'll all be very proud."

Leo jumped into the truck and waved goodbye. The driver headed out of the gates onto the road to Jerusalem. Leo's last sight was of Uri standing in a haze of yellow dust, several paces out from the rest of the crowd, pumping his arm overhead in a farewell wave Leo would see all the way to England, and for the rest of his days.

8

"PRIVATE BERGNER, YOU HAVE BEEN ATTACHED TO MY UNIT. I'm Captain Talbot." The man was in his early thirties, appeared competent, and was straight to the point. "I'm happy that you have chosen to enlist in the East Kent Regiment. We're known as the 'Buffs' within the military. We comprise three infantry battalions, *The Palestine Regiment*. We are engaged primarily in Egypt, but also in the North."

Leo stood at attention, his focus on the man in front of him. This was what he had wanted. Now he would be a soldier and in the war. But this was only the first moments of that commitment.

"You will receive your initial training here. Then it remains to be seen where we will send you. Most of you Jewish chaps have been given guard duty assignments. But there is a move afoot to create a Jewish brigade under our command. This will ensure that you are fully represented in the fight against Nazi Germany. Anyway, that's a political matter. Right now, we're working with the Palmach. You will be assigned your duties in cooperation with them. What do you know about the Palmach?"

"Actually, sir." Leo struggled with his enthusiasm. "I don't know too much about it. One of my friends, Shimon, is working with the Palmach, maybe."

"We are concerned about a possible German invasion of Palestine. The Germans are now far advanced in Egypt. They need to be stopped. It is our biggest fear that they will prevail. We work with the Palmach in behind-the-lines assaults in Lebanon and Syria, which are dominated by Vichy France. The fact that you speak French and German equips you for service either on the northern front or in Egypt. Understand?"

"Yes, sir."

"I see from your file that you're German but your family lives in France. Well, the sooner this bloody war is over, the sooner you'll be able to rejoin them."

Leo nodded.

"Good luck to you, Bergner, and welcome to the British army. Return to your unit."

Training was brutal but Leo developed muscle and got fit. He adjusted quickly to the routine, the training and discipline, and he relished the respect the officers had for his linguistic talents. His parents would certainly be proud of him. Hell. He still hadn't written to them. He'd been writing mostly to Uri, whose replies surprised Leo with their wit and eloquence. This was an unlikely talent in someone who had been the kibbutz's most dedicated tail-chaser and mischief-maker. Perhaps Francine was good for him.

Leo rarely saw Yona or Shimon. They were assigned to other units and always went back to the kibbutz when they had leave. Leo preferred to stay at the barracks and wander around the old town on his own. Apart from the daily drills on the parade ground, he had a variety of duties at the barracks. Some days he was assigned to the transportation department and worked on trucks. Other times he cleaned rifles in the armory. There were always weekly lectures to attend on tank maintenance and wireless operations as well as rifle practice.

Leo found Jerusalem mystical and unique, a mélange of cultures, Arab merchants with their tarbush and kaffiyeh, the British police with their pith helmets, the Palestinian police with their fur hats, the bearded Orthodox Jews and the monks in an assortment of different colored cassocks. He never tired of exploring, visiting the sights and soaking in the atmosphere of the Old City with its narrow cobblestone lanes, watching the devout Jews scurry through the Damascus Gate toward the Western Wall, and Arab women with food baskets on their heads hurrying toward another gate. The sound of the prayers of the devout at the Western Wall commingled with the piercing call to prayer from the mosques and the bells in the distance from the Christian quarter.

Leo often sat at an outside table at a cafe, admiring the limestone houses and alleyways decorated with bougainvillea, and watched people as they strolled by. Once, he couldn't resist the entreaties of a passing peddler selling jewelry, and he bought a bracelet for his mother and a brooch for Karin. He watched the weavers at work through the open doorways of their ateliers. At sunset, he often went to the Mount of Olives to enjoy the panoramic view of the Old City.

The news from France was mixed. From his mother, Leo received letters telling him how bad conditions were. Karin commented that Vichy French now behaved as badly as the Germans toward the Jews. His father wrote to ask questions about the British army, adding anecdotes about his own experiences in fighting the British during the Great War. Jacques usually confined his letters to a sad account of how the Riviera was bereft of tourists. Each of them would include maybe a twenty or fifty franc bill.

What they didn't relay was how serious it had become for the Jews in Nice. One of the cafes that Leo frequented in the Old City was owned by a Jewish couple from Toulon. The husband told Leo that he had heard through friends that the Italians were in the process of conducting a census of all Jews in Nice as a prelude to introducing Germany's racial policies. There was even talk of transporting the entire Jewish population of the area to specially built camps elsewhere in France.

9

BRUNO FRANZMANN HAD SEEN HIS WORLD DETERIORATE almost at the same rate and in a similar manner to the Bergner family's experience in Augsburg. When he had worked with the son, Leopold, teaching him piano, Bruno had just competed in a recital event in Munich. His careful fingering and intelligent passion had revealed his music selection to be a favorite among the judges. With Herr Bergner coaching him in mathematics and the small amount of money he earned from teaching Leo, Bruno had anticipated a lessening of his fears. But that had not been the case.

At that point in history, what had a German youth to fear? Bruno knew little of the political or artistic opportunities that might have been his. Instead he lived with his mother, father and sister, who for different reasons needed him to support them. His needs were never a priority. For example, he still wore the same shoes he'd worn for five years. Never a new pair to help with his clubfoot. No one was concerned about the teasing and intimidation his peers focused on him. No one noticed that as a disabled youth, he was to be excluded from the German march to perfection.

Then in his own quiet way, Bruno planned an escape from the conditions of his birth. At every opportunity or twist in German politics, he stood back and paid attention. If he were to survive at any level, he would learn from those around him how to profit from a situation. He would learn from the Germans as well as from the Jews, or anyone else who could teach him strategies and tactics, how to deceive and how to take the offensive. He

would make the most of his world, whatever it proved to be. And someday
he would win. Or at least come out ahead of where he'd started.

✳

Eventually Bruno found work in the German bureaucracies. As the war
effort continued, an intelligent, hardworking young man who said little
and caused no one to notice him became noticed. He moved from one
administrative job to another. Each time the pay increase was little but the
work kept him safe. Also, he had found valuables from the raids of Jewish
homes and kept a safe-deposit box out of reach of his grasping mother. So
each day he went to work among people who knew little of him and had
little to do with him.

Today he sat at his desk, shuffling papers and adding numbers. His job
at Dachau included only payroll matters. He went nowhere and sat for long
periods of time. Things were going on outside these walls but that had little
to do with him. His interest remained focused on learning and looking for
opportunities.

The office door swung open. A large man wearing an impressive uniform
strode in and stopped at the center of the room.

"Heil Hitler," Unterscharführer Epp announced.

Bruno and his coworkers pushed back their papers and pens, rose to
their feet, and snapped to attention in front of their guest.

"Following our invasion of Poland today," the officer said, "we can
expect some important changes in the administration of this department.
We anticipate that the British will declare war. All able-bodied men will be
needed for active duty. The others among you will be expected to take on
additional responsibilities, here at Dachau or at other camps. Within the
next few days, you will be receiving your new orders. Heil Hitler."

Epp marched off to deliver the same message in another office. After
the door slammed shut, Bruno's coworkers drifted back to their separate
corners and the whispers of gossip began. Having no friends among them,
Bruno shrugged and remained at his desk, wondering how these new
developments would affect him personally. There might even be some
opportunities for him to realize.

Bruno didn't have to ponder the situation for long. Two days later, on
September 3, 1939, England and France declared war. Bruno had little interest

in the war's progress, and while talk at the camp focused primarily on how the war was proceeding, Bruno searched for ways to make additional money. Sadly, he could find none.

As a result of the reorganization, Bruno's responsibilities were extended to cover the maintenance and upkeep of all personnel records as well as payroll information—meaning more hours and even less leave than before. By then he had accumulated several days of leave, and when he received a letter from his mother complaining that it had been too long since he last visited, and that they were running out of money, he felt no guilt in cashing in some of his leave.

Additionally, his mother wrote that his sister had moved to Munich, where she was working in a munitions factory, and his father had pneumonia. Bruno's visit was overdue, and it would be good to get out of Dachau for a few days. Between his coworkers, who for the most part ignored him, and the Jewish prisoners who disgusted him, he needed a break. But his mother's constant whining grated on him, and his father's weakness within the home shamed him. Regardless, he would visit. At least he wouldn't have to see his tramp of a sister.

Bruno let himself into his parents' flat with his own key, and he was greeted without fanfare or surprise. The house was a mess, dim and dusty, and he found a bare patch of floor to drop his bag. He nodded to his mother and looked around for some beer.

"Come and sit down, Bruno," his mother said from the kitchen table where she sat sewing. "You look tired."

"I am tired. You have no idea how hateful it is at that damned camp. Everything about it stinks. And since September when the war began, I'm working twelve, fourteen hours every day. No time off."

He picked up a last crate, but there was no beer for him. His mother returned to patching a pair of trousers. She either didn't notice or didn't care that he was thirsty.

"Things are bad here, too," she said. "Your sister never sends us any money, and your father lost a few weeks of work because of his pneumonia. He's got a job again. Part-time deliveries for one of the city departments. Barely enough to cover the rent, never mind put any food on the table."

Bruno recognized the hint but said nothing. He'd heard it all for years. And what money he gave her rarely put food on the table as she was more likely to buy clothes for his sister.

"When is Papa home?"

"He'll be back in a couple of hours," she said without looking up.

"Well, I've got an errand I must do. I'll be back soon."

"Poor boy," she murmured, watching him limp to the door. "And you never complain."

Bruno took the tram to the bank. The tellers were unfamiliar now, all older men who had been trotted from their retirement when the younger bankers were called for military duty. He asked for his current balance and showed his identification to one of the tellers, who blinked myopically at the fine print. He waited while the man checked the ledger and copied down the number on a sheet of paper.

"Um, I see." Bruno looked at the figure. It was more than he'd expected. He had lost track of his deposits and total because his pay was sent directly to the bank. He did some quick calculations and told the teller he wanted to withdraw all but five hundred marks in cash. Showing no expression, the teller counted out the money and gave Bruno a slip of paper to sign.

Next, Bruno asked to open his safe-deposit box. Once escorted to the vault and alone with his box, he added half the cash he had withdrawn, and while there, took delight in handling the jewelry and stack of marks already stashed in the box.

On his way home, he purchased some beer. He arrived to find his father at the kitchen table, drinking from a stein. Earlier, his mother was either too self-absorbed to notice that he couldn't find any beer, or she had deliberately hid it for his father. Bruno set down the bottles and wiped a stein clean for himself, then reached in his pocket for a fold of marks he had prepared.

"Here you are, Papa, here's some money."

"Thanks, lad," his father said. "How are you?"

What a pitiful and useless man. Had his father ever had any ambition? Then again, what was the point of ambition? Bruno had always wanted to be a classical pianist, giving recitals in the great European concert halls. Instead, he was obliged to play lousy music in third-rate bars and make a living as an assistant clerk at Dachau.

"I'm okay, thank you," Bruno answered. "But what about you, Papa? You've had pneumonia."

"I'm over it. But it was tough. I had to give up my job after all these years. I'd have probably lost it anyway as business has been going down the toilet. So many of our drivers have been called up for military duty. There's not much business around these days. Business that pays, that is."

"What about for me?" Bruno raised his stein to his father. "Are there any opportunities to make money?"

"No, Bruno." His father laughed. "You're beginning to sound Jewish."

"God forbid."

After a couple of nights, Bruno surprised himself by how glad he was to be back at Dachau. At least away from Augsburg. His mother's whining and complaints got on his nerves, and his father's hollow protestations that he was over his pneumonia saddened Bruno. Fortunately, his sister had not appeared. So the visit had been benign. Still, Dachau was a welcome change.

That week, the monotony of life at Dachau was lessened by visits to Buchenwald and Bergen-Belsen, where he assisted the personnel departments in bringing up their records to conform to those at Dachau. The inmates at these other camps looked more haunted than the ones at Dachau, as they labored under harsher and more savage conditions. There was also the odor of death in the air and constant smoke in the distance. One night over a drink in the mess hall, a Buchenwald guard told Bruno what took place at the far end of the camp.

"Good riddance to the vermin," the guard said. "The more we kill off, the better we'll all be. I saw a lot go today. Hundreds. It was a good day."

Bruno nodded. He thought back to the night he'd been roused by some men at a bar to join in taking back from the Jews. A miserable night it had turned out to be. Of the several houses he broke into that night, one seemed familiar. It reminded him of the house where he taught a young boy piano lessons. But it couldn't have been. He thought then, and still believed, that family wasn't wealthy enough to have owned the gem he found there. In any case, he had taken what he could and now hoarded it in his safe-deposit box.

He knew what he had done was wrong, but he was swept along halfheartedly by the prevailing culture. Because of his foot, he was an outcast, not allowed to join the Hitler Youth. So he went along with the others in a futile attempt to be one of the boys. But he would never be truly accepted. And that's the way it ended. None of the men he had joined that night remembered him or asked him to join in again, either drinking or terrorizing Jews.

He sipped his beer and imagined how it would feel if he were called to shove the Bergners and their ilk into the ovens. He had to admit to himself that it would be hard, perhaps even impossible. But he was accepting of the others who did it. Who was he to judge? These were strange times.

"Tell me, Bruno," the guard said. "How many days' leave am I entitled to? Can you check that when you're next at your desk?"

"Of course." He placed his hands around the stein. "I'll let you know tomorrow. What's your unit number?"

"Four-thirty-six."

The next day, Bruno killed some time by looking up the guard's name in the personnel files. The man was cross-referenced in the Unit 436 file, so Bruno went to the file and looked up the answer to the guard's question. He cast an eye through the rest of the file. Goodness, he thought, look at all these names. Must be a very busy and high-priority unit. Unit 436. He would remember that number. Maybe he could learn some more about it back at Dachau.

Word came through from Berlin that the personnel department at Buchenwald would be transferred to Dachau, and the records would be maintained there. Bruno stayed on for an extra day and supervised the loading of the filing cabinets onto a truck. Now he was going to be tied to Dachau even more firmly. This would be his last trip afield for a while. And there would be no more beers in the evenings. He would be incarcerated within the walls of Dachau, just like the inmates.

He sought out the guard to give him the answer about his leave, then wandered back to his desk. As he passed his coworkers, he felt even more alienated from them. He was unable to share in their camaraderie and banter, or even their concerns about the war. All he knew was that somehow, there had to be a way to profit from all of this.

He wished he could sit and relax at a piano from time to time. Life could have been different had he been just a bit better as a pianist. But could he have been? There was never money for piano lessons. His parents never could afford a piano for him. And he was always bungling the pedals with his clubfoot and mismatched shoes.

✳

A few months after returning from Buchenwald, Bruno received a letter from his mother. She was giving up the home in Augsburg and moving at the end of the month to Munich to live with her daughter. She would try to find a position as a live-in housekeeper because Bruno's father had died. His body was buried in Augsburg.

The news was startling in its content and its delivery. That his mother was moving in with his sister could be foreseen. But only in the event of his father's death. And she relayed that news to him with little sensitivity. So abrupt and so much after the fact. But Bruno knew this was his mother's way.

Regarding the death of his father, Bruno was saddened. He liked his father, even though he hadn't loved him, and he felt closer to him than to his mother whose non-stop complaints over the years had poisoned any filial affection he might have once felt. With his father's death and his mother's departure, all Bruno had left in Augsburg was his box at the bank and his father in a box at the cemetery. Now he could take care of himself and himself alone. He would find an opportunity to collect the contents of his safe-deposit box and then all would be done.

A new directive from Berlin called for the Dachau personnel records to be reorganized by unit and merged with records from Buchenwald. A new master file was to be created that would contain, in alphabetical order, the name, rank, number, date of birth, place of birth, sex and next of kin of each individual, marked with either a "B" or "D" to designate where the individual served. It was a long and boring job with a tight deadline. Again, Bruno proved himself as thorough and focused. After several months of exhausting work, he was ready for a weekend's leave.

He took the camp's bus into Munich and then the train to Augsburg. The town seemed deserted. Most of the people he knew were in the military. He took a tram to the cemetery and bought some flowers from a nearby stall. Then he asked at the office where to look for the grave. He followed the instructions and came to the spot, marked by a simple white stone cross and his father's name painted in black. He stood there expecting to feel some emotion, hoping for tears, or at the very least some feelings. But he felt nothing as he gazed at the headstone.

He looked around. The cemetery was deserted. It was a cold day with a slight drizzle. He looked at his watch, then felt awkward. Checking the time was probably not the appropriate thing to do. Any emotion was lost on him, and when he realized this, he walked away. He went to the bank, checked his balance and drew most of it out in cash, then deposited half in the box.

While waiting for the train back to Munich, he stopped for a beer and some sauerkraut at a cafe. Sitting there, he toyed with the piece of paper on which he'd written his mother's address, twisting it on the bar top while he ate his lunch. No one approached or spoke to him. A few hours later, he stood outside the imposing double-fronted mansion in Regenstrasse. The mansion represented the things Bruno craved most in life: security, absence of hunger, and social acceptance. He stood in awe for a moment, then rang the doorbell.

"Mami, this is very impressive. Is this where you work?"

"Bruno," she admonished. "I told you to come to the servants' entrance in the alley. Come, follow me."

She closed the door behind her and led him around to the back of the mansion. A side door opened to a small hallway that led to a vast kitchen. He had never before seen such a large kitchen, with highly polished tile floor, two large ovens, and a scrubbed pine table that would comfortably seat twenty people.

His mother pulled out a chair at the table. "Sit down and I'll give you some cake."

"Whose house is this, Mami? It's very grand." Bruno approached a window with a view of the walled garden, an immaculate lawn, and flower-beds. "Do they have a piano?"

"This is a guest house," she said, her arms crossed and pride obvious in the tilt of her chin. "For high-ranking people from Berlin. For when they come to Munich. The Führer's house is a couple of hundred yards away. He has been here." She replaced the cover on the cake, retrieved a fork, and set the plate on the table. "No one is in residence at the moment, and the other staff is out until evening. I was lucky to get the job. It pays enough, and I get a room and free meals and my uniform."

"And what about my sister?" Bruno asked. "Do you ever see her?"

"You might as well know." She bit her lip. "Your sister has been a big disappointment to me since she moved here from Augsburg. First, she had to give up her job at the factory when she became pregnant."

"I didn't know about that, but I'm not surprised. She'd been sleeping around since she was fourteen. It was inevitable."

Seated at the table, he put a forkful of cake in his mouth, and was impressed by how sweet and moist it was. He followed it with a second bite.

"She doesn't even know who the father is. Anyway, she gave the child to adoption. It was a girl. I never saw the baby." A look of sadness crossed her face. "Papa was dead by then." Absentmindedly, she brushed at crumbs on the tabletop. "Then she heard about this Lebensborn home in Steinhoring and she volunteered for that. She's been there for months. I never hear from her. Have you heard of that place, Bruno?"

"Yes, I've heard of it." He pushed back the plate and smirked. "In fact, if it weren't for this…" He lifted his foot. "I might have met her there. That would have been interesting."

He laughed, but she didn't share his amusement. After a while, he looked at his watch. The bus was due to leave for the camp in less than an hour. Out of habit, he slipped his mother some money, not as much as he had in the past, and he left.

That night, back in bed at Dachau, he realized why he was different from the others. He had always been different. It was on account of his damned foot. The misshapen foot had probably shaped his misshapen character. He was an outsider at school because he was never involved in sports. His foot had kept him out of the Hitler Youth and then the army. Maybe it was the main reason why he was held back from being the great classical pianist he had always dreamed of becoming.

Bruno looked upon himself as the outsider he was. Germany had made him feel this way—so win or lose, at the bottom of his heart he didn't give a damn about patriotism. He knew he had his fair share of faults and limitations, but one thing was for sure—he was going to make something of himself, outsider or not. He wasn't going to have to live on handouts from anyone. He would find his own way.

10

I N THE SUMMER OF 1942, ALONG WITH MORE THAN TWO HUNDRED other men, Leo was ordered to report to British Army HQ in Cairo. Crammed in the back of an army truck full of men, the journey was long, dusty, and miserable. Most men fell asleep, heads lolling on the shoulder of their neighbor. Leo was no exception. He woke up as the convoy approached the outskirts of Cairo.

Already alive in the early morning, the city was vast, hot and dry, and stank of pollution. Two endless caravans of slow-moving noisy old trucks hogged the road in both directions, emitting poisonous fumes that made Leo and his fellow soldiers nauseous. Smoke from factories on the outskirts of the city only added to the misery. Many trucks had broken down, stalled at the side of the road while their drivers stood by the open hoods, smoking and resigned to their misfortune. Camels and donkeys ambled along the route, oblivious to the noise and commotion. As the convoy pushed deeper into the metropolis, Leo observed sewers that leaked into the street, and increasing piles of garbage stacked against the walls of buildings.

Leo's truck turned onto a road that ran alongside the brown, wide Nile. Two large sailing boats floated by. In the distance, suspended above the gray sand of the desert, he could make out the pyramids. Eventually the sound of bugles and drums indicated their long-awaited arrival at the Abassia Barracks. The troops jumped off the trucks and assembled on the parade ground to be addressed by the regimental sergeant major. Leo was assigned to a tank unit. In addition to studying the mechanics of Sherman tanks, he was also trained to drive them. There was no time for boredom.

Leo formed easy friendships with several of his English comrades. They often went together to the open-air cinemas in town. Cairo was hot and brightly lit. Good food and wine, fresh fruit and steaks were in abundance. The brothels were filled to overflowing. Shepherd's Hotel was one of Leo's favorite venues where uniforms of all ranks filled the bars and lounges. When he wanted to rough it, he spent his evenings frequenting the Birka, the heart of Cairo's red-light district.

Developments on the military front were not going well. By July 1942, the British army had been pushed back almost to Alexandria by Rommel's Deutsches Afrikakorps, which had secured victories at Tobruk in Libya. At any moment, Leo and his comrades could be sent north to stop Rommel's ruthless offensive.

One afternoon, Leo wandered into the mess hall while the mail was distributed, and he was surprised to see a letter addressed to him from the kibbutz. He opened the envelope to find another inside, from France.

July 9, 1942

My Darling Leo:

I am sending you this letter to the kibbutz as I'm not sure where you are. Are you in Jerusalem still or have the British sent you to Syria? Please let us know, as we are so worried about you.

Things are not good here. We do not know how things will work out. Your dear father is suffering from terrible depression as he sees that, just as we had to leave Germany only a short time ago, we may soon have to leave France. Jacques hasn't heard from his family in Paris for a long time. We are concerned because we have heard of deportations from the occupied part of France.

We are now ruled by the Vichy government, which since October 1940 has imposed a great number of restrictions on the Jewish community, similar to those that the Nazis had imposed on us. We also now need to wear the yellow star. Close to seven thousand Jews in the South have been captured and taken to a camp near Aix-en-Provence, Camp des Milles, and put on trains, so we fear, to Drancy in Paris. And then what will happen?

We do not rule out the possibility that the Italians could invade us, too. There have been some very violent anti-Semitic statements made by a number of prominent Italians. We are very afraid. The Italian consul general here in Nice has been very outspoken in his comments about the Jewish community. The pharmacy has some distinguished Jewish customers, the Donati and Vierbo families and Baroness Levy from Florence, and they're all extremely worried.

Anyway, I don't want to pile on you all our fears as I know you must have some very great concerns about the war, too. We're very proud of you. Please write as soon as you can as it's been a long time since we've had any news from you. I hope this letter reaches you quickly.

Also I don't want to appear morbid and gloomy, but should anything happen to us, you should make contact with Maitre Talais, our wonderful friend here in Nice. He has been so helpful and caring to us all. And, talking of friends, we had the sad news that Professor Hailer died in Augsburg. It would have been impossible for anyone to have shown us greater kindness than that very dear man.

Look after yourself, darling Leo.
With all our love,
Mami

Leo lit a cigarette. He read the letter again. The news was indeed bleak. It had taken some weeks to reach him. He picked up a pen and a sheet of paper.

My darling Mother, he began. He found it easy to fill in the basic details, but as his pen moved, he felt his own worries.

We're sitting here in Cairo waiting for fresh supplies and as soon as the big chiefs think we're ready, we are all set to launch an offensive. The Germans could be in difficulties because their supply lines have been cut by the British navy based in Malta. It's a war we have to win here in the desert.

The German goal is to march straight into Egypt, capture the Suez Canal and then march into Palestine. It's scary. If they do that, the Jews in Palestine will be subjected to all the same racial rules that we experienced in Germany and which you now write is happening in France. The Germans would probably, once in Palestine, activate an Arab uprising against the British. The German army would then link up with their German comrades moving south from Southern Russia.

Vichy France controls Algeria to the west of us and also Syria to the north, so all hell will break out if we lose. A number of my friends have been sent to Syria to fight the French.

Isn't it amazing, Mami, that we left Germany to live in France, and now here I am in Egypt, doing my bit to fight both the Germans and the French? Cairo is a bustling city. I have a few good friends, other soldiers, and we often go to the movies here or to the souks, or we just sit and discuss politics and the war. There is entertainment in the barracks two or three nights every week. I play piano, so at least I haven't forgotten Chopin. Hopefully, all this will be behind us before long, and I look forward to our reunion very soon.

Please give my fondest love to Papa and of course to dear Karin and Jacques. I will write more fully within the next days.

With much love,

Leo

He thought it best not to mention the brothels. He placed the letter in an unsealed envelope and left it in a bag against the wall for it to be vetted by the military censor.

*

Within a few days, Leo was transported in a convoy to El Alamein, a mere one hundred and fifty miles from Cairo. That September, Rommel tried to break through the British lines but was unsuccessful. The Eighth Army, of which Leo's regiment formed a part, stopped him and finally, by the end of October 1942, the Germans were forced to retreat westwards toward Libya and Tunisia. The British attacks were relentless, and before long, the Germans had only thirty-five tanks left fit for action. On November 6, thirty thousand German soldiers surrendered.

Leo was exhausted. The dust from the desert and the constant deafening thunder of artillery fire was taking its toll on everyone. But the smell of victory was in the air, and adrenaline ran high. One day Leo saw one of the transportation vehicles departing for Cairo, and he jumped inside. He and his exhausted comrades spent the journey singing cheerful songs and placing bets among themselves as to when the war would be over.

When the convoy of trucks pulled up at the barracks in Cairo, officers went from vehicle to vehicle, congratulating the men. Later that evening, when they assembled in the mess, Brigadier Percy addressed the gathering by quoting a message from Winston Churchill to the troops. "Now this is not the end, it is not even the beginning of the end. But it is, perhaps, the end of the beginning." Notices on the bulletin board listed those men who had been mentioned in dispatches. Leo looked for his name and was pleased to see it included.

One evening, the platoon sergeant went looking for Leo in the barracks.

"Corporal Bergner, Captain Talbot wishes to see you by the squash courts."

Leo got down from the upper bunk and set off for the squash courts. The captain waved and beckoned him to wait. A few minutes later, the captain walked over. Perspiration from the game poured down the man's face.

He patted Leo on the shoulder with a sweaty hand. "You've come a long way since we first met at the barracks in Jerusalem, soldier. Come, let's have a seat in the shade." The captain pointed to chairs under a tree.

Leo followed and waited for Talbot to set down his racket and ease into a chair before taking his own seat.

"Bergner, congratulations on being mentioned in dispatches. And congratulations on your promotion. If you agree, you are about to be commissioned an officer in the British army and to serve with me in the Palestine Regiment. I am being transferred to that regiment, and I'd like you with me." Talbot's eyes were serious and focused. "Our duties will involve work here in Egypt and throughout North Africa. However, as long as there is tension in Lebanon and Syria, you could be posted there. The army has taken careful note of your linguistic abilities, and we want to make the best use of you."

"Thank you, sir." The serious expression on Leo's face was difficult to maintain. This was wonderful news.

"It's always awkward at first when you become a commissioned officer, but you'll adapt quickly. I've been selected as your immediate superior, so if you have any problems, come and see me. We're going to transfer to the Kasr el Nil Barracks tomorrow."

Leo stood, saluted, and walked back to his barracks. That night, he wrote a buoyant letter to France to tell them his news. Leo could hardly contain his delight within the several pages he wrote.

✳

Life as a young lieutenant in the Palestine Regiment in Cairo proved to be anti-climatic. Leo's military service was largely limited to guard duty at strategic installations. After several months in Cairo, he was excited to be selected for retraining in England, at the staff college at Camberley. He completed the intensive course in three months, then transferred to the War Office in London to work in Military Intelligence, where his superiors felt his language skills would be useful. The army put him up in an apartment on George Street, close to Marble Arch, along with four other young officers.

It was Leo's first time in London. In his free time he explored the various neighborhoods—Mayfair, Soho, Knightsbridge and Belgravia. He walked until his shoes were soaking wet, and the winter night crept into his coat sleeves. Blitzkrieg damage was evident the further east he walked, and though over a year had passed since the great fires, blackened shells of buildings and piles of rubble still lurked along the neat rows of history, gaping at him like empty eye sockets. The few Londoners out after dark seemed oblivious to it, but also tired and tempered by the destruction. Leo wondered if everyone in this war looked like them, or just the ones who had lost the most. The ones who had lost something, he decided.

To lift his spirits, he visited the lycée and introduced himself to several of the French staff. It felt good to be with French people again. He went to the headquarters of General de Gaulle's Free French Movement and was given a ticket to see Stefan Grappelli, the French violinist, play at The Victoria Palace.

One night on his way home to George Street, he passed a synagogue on Upper Berkeley Street, a few steps away from his apartment. People were walking in. He looked at his watch. Six o'clock. He was curious.

"Excuse me, sir," he asked one of the congregants. "I am out of touch.

Is it a Jewish festival of some sort?"

"No, young man, not at all. It's just the regular Friday night Sabbath service. Are you Jewish?"

"Yes, I am."

"Well, come in and join us. Take a seat wherever you like."

Leo followed the man into the synagogue and sat near the back. He looked around and saw a few other soldiers in uniform. He picked up a prayer book and turned over the pages. He felt a tap on his shoulder.

Seated behind Leo, a man said, "Excuse me, lieutenant. We haven't seen you here before. Are you away from home?"

Leo hung his head.

The man reached again and touched Leo's shoulder. "We are proud of our troops, and thankful to you for serving. Please, it would be our honor if you would join my family for the Sabbath dinner. We live nearby in Connaught Square, a short walk only minutes from here."

Leo looked into the eyes of the distinguished gentlemen, and while he had relished the idea of a quiet evening at home, listening to the radio, he was flattered to be invited. And he could tell that this man would be disappointed if he declined. In his best manners, learned an epoch ago in Nice and that felt as remote as his childhood home in Augsburg, Leo accepted.

During the service, Leo was moved when the rabbi spoke a prayer in English for the safety of the Allied troops and for the British Royal Family. Leo felt, in so many respects, stateless. No longer German or French. Certainly not English, despite the uniform on his back. Still the prayer included him, and placed him as appropriate in this world.

Once the service ended, Leo stood at the back of the synagogue, waiting for the older man, who had moved closer to the front. The congregants meandered their way toward the door. Like the tide, they carried the man who had sat behind Leo closer, and Leo got his first good look at him. He could not have been younger than sixty, but his body was wiry and quick and his back was straight. He wore an impeccable suit, and his yellow-white hair was perfectly groomed, as if the Blitz and its mess had not settled on him. When the older man reached Leo, he in turn inspected his guest with slightly protuberant black eyes.

"I am Oliver De Sola," the man said. "And you, what is your name?"

"Leo Bergner, sir."

"Well, come with me." He rested a hand on Leo's back and steered him through the knots of worshippers. "I want to hear all about you on the way home, so I can introduce you properly to my wife and family."

By the time they approached the house, Leo recognized that he was in the company of a distinguished, wealthy member of the British Jewish aristocracy. A butler opened the door and took his employer's coat. Leo handed him his cap.

"Tell Cook we have a guest for dinner," Mr. De Sola said to his butler, then he quietly explained to Leo, "Tonight is my wife's birthday, so you'll forgive us if we seem overdressed. Please, you should feel comfortable in your uniform. Our drawing room is upstairs, this way."

Climbing the stairs, Leo recognized a Poussin, a Breughel and a Degas. Mr. De Sola led the way into a large square room, with casement windows that faced a courtyard, and with a log burning in the fireplace. Before it, a pair of sofas faced each other, and there, four people were enjoying the fire's ambiance.

Mrs. De Sola was the first to turn around. She wore her hair in an elegant chignon, at her temples a shade of dark iron. The knot of longer hair was black, like her dress. In profile, her face was not what Leo expected. Her features were small, innocuous, and motherly.

"You've brought me a guest," she exclaimed, and stood. "How wonderful. I was just saying that this birthday seemed too quiet."

A man stood. Leo estimated him to be near his own age. He had the bearing of an adult but a certain young freshness around his eyes and cheeks.

"This is my son-in-law, Anthony," Mr. De Sola said. "I've mentioned my wife, Florence, but not my two daughters, Holly and Elizabeth."

Leo smiled and thanked them all for their hospitality. His impression of the daughters was favorable, but he found himself inexplicably nervous, and he noticed only their general friendliness.

"I'm afraid with food rationing," Mrs. De Sola said with a broad smile, "tonight's meal will not be an event of gastronomic importance, Lieutenant Bergner. But I hope you will enjoy it."

As she came close to offer her hand, Leo noticed her sapphire and diamond necklace. The memory of his mother's emerald became vivid, and Leo found his breath catch. A spectacular jewel made more important by his grandmother passing it down at his mother's wedding. He thought of the pendant rarely now. Did his mother still think of that emerald?

"But," Mr. De Sola said, "at least we still have a well-stocked cellar. So you won't go short of good wine. Thank God I stocked my wine cellar before the war."

They sat at a polished mahogany table, set with sparkling silver and crystal, around a centerpiece of fragrant pink roses. It had been a long time since Leo had dined by candlelight in so formal a setting. He paused to enjoy his glass of Chambertin while Mr. De Sola gave them a quick account of Leo's life and his experiences. Leo answered their questions at length, and each seemed to be interested in his answers.

As the Chambertin seeped into his blood, he directed more of his answers to the younger daughter, Elizabeth. She had a smile that lingered around her eyes even when she spoke. Her eyes were green and held mischief. Her skin glowed with the candlelight, and the soft light reflected from the rose petals. Everything about her bearing—from her questions to the way she held the wine glass to her lips—suggested patience and refinement.

"I was injured at El Alamein," Anthony said. "I was in a tank division and oil leaked. Got into my eyes. So that put me out of commission, and they shipped me back here. Now I have a desk job in Whitehall at the Ministry of Defense."

"Well, our paths have crossed then," Leo replied. "I was at El Alamein. Now I'm working for a short time in Military Intelligence."

"What an amazing coincidence," Elizabeth said with a friendly smile. "I hope you'll come for dinner with us again."

He realized what appealed to him about her bearing. It was the same as his—a comfort with formality, even though it was not her chosen mode of existence. Leo had grown up with manners, of course, but not until Nice had he learned how to be charming. Elizabeth used charm like a weapon, a subtle one. Still, he understood and appreciated her the more for it.

As the plates were cleared from the table, Leo looked around the room, discreetly, to see if he could recognize any more of the artwork. He spotted a Renoir and a Modigliani. Then in the far corner, he saw an ebony grand piano, a startling surprise.

"Do you play?" Elizabeth asked, having noticed Leo's interest. "I do hope so, as some music would do us all a lot of good. None of us play, I'm afraid."

"I used to a little," Leo replied. "But I haven't played much recently."

"It's a pity that none of us do," Mrs. De Sola said. "We've had it since the children were small. But they showed no interest in practicing after the first week. Funnily enough, our butler's brother is a piano tuner. He came over a couple of weeks ago to tune it."

"I don't know why we don't sell it," Mr. De Sola said under his breath.

"Would you play for us after dinner, Lieutenant Bergner?" Elizabeth asked. "It would be wonderful to hear that piano come to life again."

"Well, I haven't played in some time," he said, then lied, "and I wasn't very good."

Embarrassed, Leo blushed beyond all reason.

"Please, you must play for us," Mrs. De Sola urged. "The first time I heard a note from it in years was when it was tuned two weeks ago. I thought then how wonderful it would be if someone would actually sit down and play it."

Leo walked to the piano. It had been a few years since he had played a Steinway. That had been in Nice. Pangs of nostalgia stirred within him as he sat and touched the keys. As his fingers spread across the keys, he thought of the Levys and all the others who had enjoyed his playing before the war. How kind they had all been to him. He recalled the summer nights when the Levys had their piano moved outside onto the patio, and he played under the stars well into the night. Well, tonight he would play for them too, wherever they were, as well as for his parents and Jacques and Karin. How would the music sound? He nervously looked up at the chandelier, as if for inspiration.

He tested the ivory keys with a few bars of Mozart to warm up, then paused to stretch his fingers. He looked at the heavy blue silk curtains and nodded in appreciation of the room's fine acoustics. How he wished his parents were there, but he knew that they were in spirit. A few seconds passed in silence as he sat motionless. He stared down at the keyboard and then, like a racehorse taking off, he hit the keys. He played his beloved Chopin and some Mozart pieces as well as popular songs by Gershwin and Noel Coward. Then he let his hands drop to his lap.

"I think you've had enough of me now," he said. "I will stop."

He rose from the piano, feeling good. He had lost himself and had no idea how long he had been playing. When the grandfather clock downstairs in the entrance hall declared midnight, he realized that he would have continued playing into the early morning. He looked up again at the chandelier. If only everyone he loved in Nice could have heard him tonight. Maybe they had.

"Leo," Elizabeth said. "Please play more."

Her attention was riveted to him, as if she were trying to pierce him with a message. It filled his loneliness and old fears, patching them over. He would play all night if she would keep looking at him like that.

"Pay no attention, Leo," Mr. De Sola said. "Come and have a brandy. You've played nonstop for well over an hour. You must be exhausted."

"Thank you." Leo stroked the piano respectfully and moved away from it. "But I must decline the brandy. I should go back to my apartment on George Street. I need to be at my desk tomorrow at seven o'clock to prepare for an important meeting. Thank you so much for inviting me into your home. I have had a lovely evening."

He took his leave as politely as he could, given the comfort and warmth of the De Sola home. He heard himself promise too eagerly to return the next Friday night. Their parting at the door was genuine, though. As he walked home, he chuckled at himself, remembering his morose stateless feeling in the synagogue. Now he felt quite well.

Over the next few weeks, Leo spent every available free hour with the De Sola family. He developed affection and respect for them that bordered on familial. He learned that the De Sola name was one of the most distinguished in Jewish history, and that it could be traced to the tenth century. The family had produced many talented rabbis and scholars in Spain, Portugal, England, Holland, Latin America and the United States. Oliver De Sola was a partner in a prominent merchant bank in the City. His interest and affection seemed mutual and grew at each meeting.

Leo felt at home—so much that he worried. A feeling of falseness invaded his level of comfort there, an elation at creating a new family to replace the old. His fear for his parents resided now within a weird numbness, almost forgetfulness. He feared what it meant, and what the war had done to his spirit. What had it done to love, and the role of family? Could all things be replaced? He hoped that what he felt for his family was not replaceable. There was terror in that thought.

And there was Elizabeth, the younger and unmarried daughter. He'd become enchanted by her, and she with him. Or so he prayed. She was tall and blond. Her long straight hair rested sensually on her shoulders. Her bright green eyes lit up whenever she was in his company. She didn't chatter like her mother and sister did. When she spoke, she was clear and precise and always with a spark of humor.

She had graduated from Oxford with a degree in German, and within three months of her graduation, England was at war. She had become an interpreter at the Foreign Office, working long hours and sometimes throughout the night. But when her mother criticized her for the long hours, she would answer that exhaustion satisfied her, like the periods of solitude she seemed to require. Her work ethic was as strong as her father's, yet also somehow self-punishing.

Leo was always included in family gatherings and at their dinner parties, when he was often entreated to play the piano. After especially long shifts, too, she'd ask him to play. She would sit in a shaft of morning sunlight, listening, a mug of tea between her hands. She would nod along to the music like an old woman remembering better times. The tea and his playing seemed to revive her enough for a stroll in the city, or to Lyons Corner House for a meal.

"How long will it be before they send you back to Egypt, or wherever?" Elizabeth asked one Friday afternoon.

They strolled hand-in-hand through Hyde Park. Leo noticed how the damp spring light called out the fatigue in her face. He never knew if she asked questions out of curiosity, or to keep herself awake.

"It could be a week, a month, two months, I don't know," he replied.

"I'm going to miss you terribly, you know."

"And I'm going to miss you too." He was surprised to hear himself say it.

"What time is it, Leo?"

"Two o'clock. Why? Do you need a rest?"

"We're not due home for dinner until half past seven." She looked him directly in the eye. "Let's be naughty."

Now when she smiled, he noticed her twinkle. The feeling of precipitousness startled him. He was in love.

"Are you sure?" he asked.

"I've never been so sure of anything in all my life," she replied. "Take me back to your apartment. You said your roommates were gone this weekend."

"Apart from Josh. He'll be home around nine."

"Come on, let's not waste a moment."

He led the way to George Street, awkwardly. He didn't know whether to talk or not talk. He commented on a store window they passed, a hatter with a new display. Elizabeth squeezed his hand tighter and did not answer. The air seemed too warm, and he glanced at her to see if she thought so, too. Her face, usually pale from lack of sleep, was flushed. He fumbled with the key and held the door open. They climbed the two flights of stairs to his apartment and to his bedroom. He had dressed carelessly that morning. A basket of laundry sat on the bed, another was spilled by the radiator. Heat ticked from its coils, shimmering in front of the open window.

"I'll just turn this off," he said, fiddling with the knob.

His fingers felt like rubber. She pulled his hand away and turned him to face her. She wrapped her arms around his neck.

"Come closer, my love," she whispered.

Her lips felt like rose petals. She reached up to undo his tie, and pulled it free. She shrugged off her coat and let it fall. He felt himself harden as his arms wrapped around her, and for a moment he was back in Palestine, sixteen years old, fearing that his arousal would show and in another moment, Elizabeth would be gone. But Elizabeth forced her body even closer and ground against him.

She unbuttoned her blouse and took off her skirt and shoes. He quickly undressed and moved back toward her, taking her by the shoulders and guiding her to the unmade bed. Her skin under his hands sent shivers along his belly and to his groin. He lowered himself next to her, aroused nearly to the verge of being lightheaded. He removed her bra, cupped her breast, and fondled her nipple as their tongues played. She arched her back, pushed her torso into his, and slid her leg between his. He deftly removed her panties and felt her heat against his leg.

He positioned himself on top of her, admiring her, kissing her, whispering that he loved her. She nodded and pulled her fingers along his back. Some native mischief rose to the surface of her face, and with a purr of satisfaction, she wrapped one leg around his waist. He could no longer hold back, and entered her.

Leo was oblivious to the small cramped and untidy room with its dowdy furniture, dirty windows, and flickering light bulb. They lay entwined, her head nestled on his shoulder. With each new lovemaking, they had come closer to each other's rhythm, then found one of their own. Leo started to feel the nuances of her body, the way she tilted her hips, the meaning of her breaths, and the minute pressure changes of her hands on his back. Now he tried to memorize them all.

Spent and sweaty, they snuggled side by side. After a time, she looked at him with a small degree of mischief in her green eyes.

"You never speak about your family in Nice, Leo. What do you hear?"

"I hear nothing." Reminded of the world outside, he sighed. "I worry so much. The Jews in France are in the same situation as in Germany. In fact, I've heard the Vichy government has gone over and beyond even what the Germans asked them to do about the Jews."

"But what have you heard about your family?"

"Really, nothing. My father never wanted to leave Germany. He was so loyal that he thought all this was just a temporary abomination. And my cousin Jacques in France, he never thought they would go that way. So there you have two extremely disillusioned men. And my mother and her cousin Karin, God alone knows what's happened to their families in Germany."

"Don't you feel lonely?"

"Not as long as I have you and your family in my life." He ran his fingers through her hair. "Your family has been wonderful to me. Of course I miss my family, though. There is no replacing kin."

He wondered if he believed it anymore. Everything beyond this moment and place seemed distant. Even fantastic. No, what was real was right here.

"We feel that destiny brought you into our lives," she said. "You're a wonderful distraction for us."

"What on earth do you mean?" he asked.

"Poor Holly has been so worried about Anthony since his injury at El Alamein. Anthony is distressed because as much as he likes being back home, he feels he should be overseas at the front with his regiment. My mother is worried that my father is working far too hard at the bank on account of all the younger men serving in the forces, and my father is having sleepless nights about the war, the economy, and what will happen to all of us if the Germans win."

A faint note of mocking threaded her words, as if her family's worries were amusements to her. Her face, though, wore an expression of contentment.

Leo rose up on one elbow. "The anxiety is enough to drive anyone stark, raving mad," he began. "Let's pray that the war ends quickly and the Nazis are destroyed."

He got up from the bed, went to the window, and looked out onto the street. There was some noise from the pub at the corner as several of its customers were leaving for home, much the worse for wear. One man stumbled on the curb and braced himself on the side of a moving car. A horn sounded. It was the times. People drank themselves to oblivion because they had to. Leo felt the stress. Elizabeth must also.

"Leo, come here."

He turned his back to the window, sat beside her, and held her hand. The mischief was gone from her face, and the fatigue had returned. He pushed her hair back and kissed the bridge of her nose.

"I have a question and I want an honest answer," she said. "Are we just having a wartime romance, or is this for real?"

He had come to expect her sudden clear-eyed questions. Still, this one caught him.

"How can you ask such a question, darling?"

"I don't want to end up as some lovesick, used and abandoned London bird."

"That won't happen. I mean, I don't think it will, or want it to, but—"

"Have you had lots of girlfriends, Leo?"

"No," he answered honestly.

Apart from Francine, there hadn't been anyone with whom he'd felt an attachment during all those years since adolescence. Sometimes he wished there had been someone to erase his memory of Francine.

"And you?" A smile crept into his voice. "Lots of boyfriends?"

"No, silly."

He moved closer, kissed her cheek, her neck, nuzzling his face in the warmth of her skin, and within minutes they were making love again. Until Elizabeth noticed the time—six o'clock. She scrambled from the bed and gathered her clothes.

"I have to get home," she said. "We should be naughty more often."

He smiled as she walked toward the door.

The bed was rumpled, and the room was even darker than it had been. But he had no wish to turn on the light and disturb its sanctity, or to do anything but breathe the lingering fragrance of her perfume. He stretched his naked body and wallowed in the joy of those special, intimate hours when their relationship had crossed into a new world. It was as though he had fully participated in humanity for the first time since childhood. Always his allegiance to others, his parents, cousins, friends in the Kibbutz and the army, were dictated by others or by circumstances. But this was different. This was his own choice.

✳

Three weeks later, Leo received official notification that he was to return to active duty. In seventy-two hours he'd be leaving on a flight from RAF Benson in Oxfordshire for Cairo. He also learned that he had been promoted to captain. He spent the evening with the De Solas, knowing that if the war had not brought them together, he would not now be feeling the weight of the coming farewell. In a moment alone with Mr. De Sola, Leo assured her father of his love and commitment to Elizabeth. But he could do no more until he felt his world was safe enough to propose matrimony.

"Sir," Leo explained, "I am very much in love with Elizabeth. I had intended to ask your permission for her hand in marriage, but not while the war is raging. I am going back in three days to a theater of war, where there is intense fighting. There is the very great risk that I might be killed or severely injured. Neither of us would want Elizabeth to be a war widow at such a young age, or to be married to someone who might be a burden on her. When the war is over, then I will come to you and ask for your consent. But not now."

"Does Elizabeth know?" her father asked.

"No, I haven't confided in her. Let's just wait and see this war out, sir."

Mr. De Sola nodded. On impulse, he held out his hand, then he withdrew it. Instead he patted Leo affectionately on the shoulder. The mood was gloomy. Leo knew what he'd said was right and respectful. Things needed to be resolved with Elizabeth when the world had better to offer a young couple.

11

CAIRO LOOKED THE SAME TO LEO. ON HIS ARRIVAL BACK AT Kasr El Nil Barracks, Leo ran into Major Talbot in the mess. Leo congratulated the major on his promotion, then smiled when the major congratulated him.

"You're going to spend a month here in Cairo," Talbot began. "Then we have a unit conducting covert operations in Damascus, in dire need of someone with your linguistic skill."

"Will I be able to spend any time in Jerusalem, sir?"

"I don't know." Major Talbot shook his head. "The British army had been working with the Jewish underground fighters, Haganah. Since El Alamein, there has been less cooperation, but you may be useful to them."

"I think so, too, sir." His promotion to captain gave Leo more confidence to offer his opinions and knowledge. "The Haganah has had a countrywide force of full-time soldiers to protect the Jewish settlements from Arab attacks."

"Yes," Major Talbot added, "and it also served, thankfully, as a reserve force for the British army. It's now known as Palmach. Its senior officer, Yitzhak Sadeh, is a good man. I met him last month in Jerusalem."

"Can you arrange for me to meet with him, sir?"

Talbot promised that he would try. Leo's one month in Cairo turned out to be three, and he no longer had any interest in strolling around sampling the delights of the red-light district. He spent many hours writing letters to Elizabeth and her parents as well as to his own family in Nice. Away from both families, he felt oddly better. He was reminded of the kibbutz, where he had lived in comfortable independence.

He received letters back from London and an occasional package—a cake, some magazines, and pullovers that the De Sola's cook had knitted. As more of these packages arrived, bouts of lovesickness afflicted him, at first one every week or so, then every few days.

Leo would wake at three in the morning, and the horrible loneliness of his single bed would weigh on him like a lead blanket. The less he slept, the more he missed Elizabeth, and he would rise before dawn and write her letters that later embarrassed him, as if they came from someone else whose constitution was far weaker than his own. Reading the letters over afternoon coffee, and their passages of terrible writing—*you are a morning star that lights my being*—he'd tear them up in disgust. Then he'd post short, upbeat missives about his explorations of the ancient city. Often these were near-duplicates of letters to his mother. But his letters to France went unanswered, while his letters to the De Sola family brought ever more communications.

As he walked toward the parade ground one morning, after a night of terrible sleep, a private rushed toward him and saluted. Leo still found it uncomfortable to be the recipient of such formality.

"Captain Bergner, sir, Major Talbot would like to see you."

He thanked the private and made his way to Talbot's office. Talbot was at his desk, shuffling papers. He looked more tanned and relaxed than when Leo had last seen him.

"Captain Bergner, good morning. I don't suppose you've brought me back some Stilton, have you?" he said jokingly. "I'd give my right hand for some and a glass of port. Anyway, it's not going to be Damascus or Beirut. You are to set off immediately by jeep with Corporal Houston to Jerusalem. When you get to the barracks, report to Brigadier Hallock. The army has an interesting mission for you. And incidentally, you'll meet Yitzhak Sadeh. He has asked to see you."

The announcement puzzled Leo more than anything else, and with his mind in a fog, he returned to his room. He quickly packed his belongings, including the battered writing kit, and decided to wait until he was stationed in Jerusalem before attempting another letter to his family. He didn't know what to say about anything yet.

The journey back to Jerusalem passed quickly, and Corporal Houston was an amusing travel companion. Houston had served for a number of years in Jerusalem and skillfully maneuvered the jeep around the narrow streets toward the barracks. Leo studied the familiar sights, looking for any changes since he last visited. It all looked the same, but of course, it probably had for the past thousand years.

They passed a coffee shop that Leo used to frequent. A few old-timers were seated at outside tables, some playing backgammon, others engaged in a heated conversation, Leo guessed about religion. That's all they talked about in Jerusalem. A young Greek Orthodox priest with a long black beard appeared from an alleyway and held up his hand, forcing the corporal to stop the jeep, all so that the priest could cross the road.

"Some of these fucking bastards think because they have a direct line to God Almighty that they can cross the road whenever they want." Corporal Houston waved his fist at the priest. The priest smiled back.

Upon arrival, Leo was instructed to report at once to the office of Yitzak Sadeh. Sadeh had been born in Poland at the end of the nineteenth century, became a sergeant in the Czar's army during the First World War, and before emigrating to Palestine, he had commanded a company in Petrograd. Once in Palestine, he organized a mobile unit of volunteers whose mission was to track down and ambush Arab guerilla gangs on the outskirts of Jerusalem. In time he became the commander-in-chief of the Haganah, whose doctrine was "Go after your attacker, don't wait to be attacked." He was encouraged and supported by the British officer, Orde Wingate. Leo's heart skipped a beat, to imagine he would soon meet such a renowned man.

Leo tapped on Colonel Sadeh's door and entered. His office was in the basement of the building. Others might have taken this as an insult, but Sadeh didn't care. The room wasn't much bigger than a walk-in closet, had no window, and one corner of his desk was propped up with a book. Sadeh was on the telephone and beckoned Leo to take a seat.

Sadeh had a reputation of having no time for the inspection parades, polished boots, and impeccable uniforms demanded by the British. He considered all that useless when fighting Arabs and the Germans. Leo tended to agree with him, but his German background, with its inherent respect for order and discipline, caused him sometimes to raise an eyebrow when he heard examples of Sadeh's informality.

"We've heard good things about you," Sadeh said.

"Thank you, sir."

Sadeh grasped the desk and looked into Leo's eyes. Leo felt the man's passion invade him, like a welcome breath. His vitality filled the small room.

"The Palmach was established in 1941," Sadeh explained, "and very soon I anticipate we'll have three fighting brigades. We worked in total harmony with the British. They helped us to get established so that we could protect Palestine from the Nazi threat. We worked with the Allies to consolidate our positions in French-dominated Syria and Lebanon. However, since El Alamein, the Palmach has been largely dismantled, and to some extent we are forced to operate underground."

Sadeh took a deep breath. His hands now flattened on the desk, and his eyes took in Leo in a questioning manner.

"The British don't need us so much anymore," Sadeh continued. "Nevertheless, as you can see, I still have an office here, and for the present, I enjoy excellent relations with them. How long that will last, God knows. We must not forget that the British, for some unknown reason, have this romantic notion about the Arabs."

"Yes, sir."

"Brigadier Hallock, who you were supposed to see, cannot see you. He has left it for me to discuss your mission with you. The British have a convoy of buses that will leave tomorrow for Baghdad. The British have chartered the buses to take an Indian battalion to Baghdad, then return here with an English unit. Your mission is to travel on that convoy and take with you approximately twenty suitcases that contain small arms. These are to be delivered to our people in Baghdad to help them defend themselves against local Arabs."

"Are the British aware of this, sir?"

"Put it this way," he said. "Brigadier Hallock is a friend of ours. Draw your own conclusions about his absence from this meeting."

Leo was flattered to be trusted with this mission. Yet if he dismissed his sense of flattery and looked at the facts, he confronted the larger question of why. How did he look to Sadeh? Young, still. Strong, but on the lean side. Perhaps a sort of non-entity, stateless, speaking many languages, but ashamed of his mother tongue. Someone with an acute sense of duty, but who was important mostly for his unremarkableness to everyone but those who knew him well. He shouldn't flatter himself. He was here because of his unremarkableness and his penchant for following orders.

12

DURING 1942 AND 1943, NOTWITHSTANDING CENSORSHIP, news reached Dachau that the Russians were doing well. Bruno listened and watched the men in the office take in the news. The German army on the Eastern Front had been encircled and obliged to surrender at Stalingrad, its first major military disaster. Work at the camp went on as usual, but amid the routine, the staff raised quiet questions about the invincibility of the German military.

One night in the mess, Bruno overheard a few of the men in Unit 436 whispering among themselves, concerned they might be targets for revenge squads after the war in the event of a German surrender. Some even questioned whether the victors would put them on trial. In 1943, the Americans and the British invaded Italy, and talk of German failure became more frequent despite Berlin's deluge of propaganda. The northern border of Italy was not that far away from Dachau.

The war posed no problems for his mother. One day, Bruno received a postcard from her to say that one of the high-ranking Germans had offered her a job at his estate near Berlin and that she would be leaving Munich at the end of the month. She said she would write again once she was there and let him have her new address. He looked at the front of the card, a well-known Leni Riefenstahl photograph from the 1936 Olympics, then tossed it into the wastepaper basket. She wasn't his responsibility any more.

In June of 1944, word quickly spread around the camp that the British had landed on the Normandy beaches. A German defeat now looked more likely than not. One night in the mess, Bruno listened carefully while a steward from the officer's mess told a group of his friends what he had over-heard earlier that evening. Two high-ranking camp deputy commandants had whispered about a plan to escape from Germany because there would be *big trouble for them* if the Allies arrived in Dachau.

Bruno didn't wait to hear more. In the first weeks of 1945, news reached the camp that the Allies had crossed the Rhine and that the American forces had advanced northward from Italy. Bruno had already taken a lesson from what he'd heard about plans to escape Germany. The first step in his plan was a visit to his superior.

After the required salute to Hitler, Bruno pleaded with the officer, "May I have your permission to go to Augsburg this weekend, sir? My father died some time ago, and there are some issues that need to be taken care of. Especially now that my mother is working in Berlin for Herr General von Kluge."

Hearing the general's name, the officer narrowed his eyes. A wave of the man's hand told Bruno that he was free to go. When Bruno arrived in Augsburg, his first stop was a tailor he had passed scores of times over the years.

"Grüss Gott," the old man said. "How can I help you?"

"I need something done in a hurry," Bruno replied. "You see this overcoat I'm wearing." Bruno took it off and spread it across the tailor's front counter. "I want you to put in a new lining. I want some secret pockets inserted in the sleeves and armpits and wherever else you can suggest. I want it let out, too, so that it won't look bulky when I fill up the new pockets."

The tailor's eyes lingered a bit too long on Bruno's face, but he said nothing.

"And you see this suit I'm wearing? I want the same thing done to that. Both the jacket and the trousers as well as the waistcoat. Let out and new secret pockets."

The tailor flipped the coat to and fro, but he didn't seem to be paying attention to it.

"Can you do that, yes or no?" Bruno asked.

"Yes," he said after a long time. "But it will take a lot of work. A lot of hours. And it's an expensive job."

"How much? And how long will it take?"

"Two weeks, and it will cost maybe three thousand marks."

"I want everything back tomorrow night," Bruno said. "I will pay you five thousand marks for your work. Is that agreed?"

For a moment, the tailor wore a blank expression. Then he said, "Nine o'clock tomorrow night. But I want half the money now."

"I have some other clothes with me." Bruno eyed the man and counted out the money. "Let me go and change out of this suit so I can leave this one with you."

A few minutes later, he stepped back into the street wearing another jacket and trousers. His next stop was a shoemaker.

Bruno bought a pair of shoes and explained that he wanted hidden hollow heels. The shoemaker agreed to have them ready the next day.

At the bank, he emptied the contents of his safe-deposit box into his black leather overnight bag and withdrew all but five hundred marks in cash from his account. He had accumulated a sizeable sum that weighed a few pounds. He gazed down inside the bag at the tall stacks of neatly bundled marks. After snapping it shut, he opened it again to savor the satisfaction of having all that money. It spelled independence and hopefully security.

On his way back to the hotel, Bruno stopped to buy a few more items. The first, a map, which he picked up at a bookstore. Then at a pawnbroker's shop, he pushed the door open and breathed the damp, musty air. A heavyset blond woman stood behind the counter, writing prices on tags.

"I need to buy some binoculars. They must be good but also small so I can keep them in my coat pocket. Also a handgun. What have you got?"

"Why do you want a gun?" She looked at him suspiciously.

"For self-protection. You see I have a clubfoot. I cannot run. I have been attacked from time to time, and these attacks are becoming more frequent."

She studied his foot, thought about it for a moment, then nodded. "Follow me." Through a doorway behind the counter, she led Bruno into a living room. Boxes were piled up between too many pieces of furniture and towers of suitcases. She unlocked a desk drawer and produced a small handgun.

"It's in good working condition," she said. "A Luger 9mm. The best. But you know I'd be breaking the law if I sold it to you. Civilians aren't allowed to have guns."

"I know, but I must have something to protect myself. These attacks are terrible. I can hardly walk down the street without being accosted." He pointed again to his foot. "How much is it?"

"It's not cheap. A thousand marks," she answered.

"Do you have ammunition?"

"Some. But that's separate. I can let you have fifty cartridges for a hundred and fifty."

He nodded. She peered at him again, and a flush had crept into her face.

"You're not from the police, I hope." she said. "I'm not sure I should be selling you this."

"Don't worry." Having recognized her fear, he gently tapped her hand and smiled. The gesture felt unnatural for him, but it worked. He settled up and took the tram back to the hotel.

That night he lay on the bed and contemplated his next move. He was still young, had a sharp brain, and some capital, but he was clearly on the losing side. At least his foot had kept him out of the army where he might have been killed on the Eastern Front. He thought for one split second about sending his mother some money, but she hadn't given him her address in Berlin. There was no point in sending any to his sister, as she was probably doing well as a state-approved prostitute.

The night before he left Augsburg, Bruno emptied the contents of his bag onto the bed and methodically placed the money and the jewelry into the secret pockets and heels of his shoes. He then dressed and looked at himself in the mirror. The tailor had done well, sewing hidden pockets within a second lining that was impossible to see, and which could only be accessed from certain regular pockets.

Back at Dachau, he hung the coat and suit in his locker, turned the key, then checked the latch and checked it again, leaving no question about it being secure. Satisfied, he reported to work.

Bruno liked money, and he liked how the tailor, shoemaker, and pawn-broker had treated him when they saw he had a lot of it. Money had its advantages, especially for him. He was not charming, or attractive, or even very smart. He'd always believed that those who focused hardest got ahead the soonest. Now he'd keep his money for himself and himself alone.

✳

The war was going badly for the Germans. The enemy was closing in from all directions and advancing toward Berlin. A few days after Bruno returned from Augsburg, he decided it was time to act. There was only one more piece of his plan and he'd need to take care of that as soon as possible.

Bruno waited until his coworkers had left their desks, and he was alone in the office. From his shirt pocket, he took out the razor blade he had put there that morning. He walked to the filing cabinet and removed the personnel file for Unit 436. Eighteen pages of confidential records, each containing the names of twenty-five individuals, four hundred and fifty names in total. Within minutes, he had neatly removed the pages from the ledger, folded them in half, and put them in his back pocket.

By the time he returned the file to the cabinet, he had convinced himself that he'd done them all a big favor. The file was not going to be one that anyone here wanted the enemy to find.

He left the office and walked across the camp to the transportation unit. He faced a familiar blast of stale air and followed it to its locus around Sergeant Müller's desk. The man was smoking, and his butts were piled high on a dinner plate.

Bruno plopped down on the edge of Müller's desk. They had enjoyed beers together in the mess a few times, and in Müller's drunken honesty he had mentioned that many guards turned a blind eye to most nocturnal visits to the women's barracks, and that Müller earned a few extra marks by occasionally letting the men take out a military vehicle for quick trips into Munich.

"This is one of those evenings when I'd kill for a vehicle." Bruno leaned in closer, pitching his voice in a friendly whisper—experimenting with the distance he kept between his body and his fellow man. "Say I wanted to drive to Munich, see my mother and sister, and hopefully have a little fun afterward. Is there anything you can do for me?"

"Maybe." Müller regarded him carelessly. His eyes were the color of cigarette ash. "When will you be back?"

"Maybe between two and three in the morning."

"Be back by midnight. I go off duty at twelve, and I need the vehicle back before my shift ends."

"That should be okay." Bruno looked at his watch. "But I'll need to set off in half an hour."

"It'll cost you five hundred marks. And you'll get four gallons of gas. No more. The money before you get the keys."

"I'll be back with your money," Bruno said, and gave him a friendly pat on the shoulder. He went to his locker and quickly changed. Half an hour later, he was on the road to freedom.

13

BRUNO DROVE SLOWLY TOWARD THE CAMP GATES AND WAVED to the guard. It had been some time since he sat behind the wheel, and his heart was beating fast. Four gallons of gas was enough to get to Munich and back, but it certainly wasn't enough to get to Innsbruck.

The guard waved him through. In a few minutes, he discovered there was little traffic headed toward Munich, and it was a clear night. The heavy rain of the previous few days had eased off, leaving puddles on the road and the depression of gloomy clouds. On the outskirts of Munich, he pulled up at a truck stop. A driver was leaning against his vehicle, smoking a cigarette.

"Good evening," Bruno said, and got out of the driver's seat. "I wonder if you can help me. I have left without my petrol coupons, and I need to visit my mother in the hospital in Salzburg. If there is any way you could assist me, I would very much appreciate it."

The truck driver surely had heard stories like this time and time again, and like most, he was quick to see a way to make some extra money. He looked suspiciously at the military vehicle and then at Bruno's civilian clothes, but swept his concerns aside.

"I can give you a few gallons for a hundred."

Within a few minutes, with a short rubber hose, the driver siphoned some gas from the truck's gas tank into Bruno's vehicle, and Bruno was back on the road headed toward Rosenheim and Chiemsee. More vehicles, mostly military trucks, headed toward Munich than toward Salzburg. He glanced at his watch. Nine o'clock. He parked and relieved himself by the lake and felt hungry. There was nothing he could do about that.

He got back in the truck and drove a few miles south to Kufstein, just inside the Austrian border. This was as far as Bruno thought it wise to drive. To venture deeper into Austria could be problematic. He parked in a side street to avoid attention and left the keys on the front seat, hoping that someone might steal the truck before the police found it.

The well-ordered street with freshly painted wooden frames—Tyrolean houses on both sides, their wooden shutters mostly closed—seemed untouched by the war. He looked for a hotel or inn but there was none. His next stop was Innsbruck, twenty-five miles away. There was no way he could walk that far without rest. He saw a church a few hundred yards away and approached in hopes that it would be unlocked. He was lucky.

The church was old but immaculate, small compared to churches that Bruno had known in Augsburg. He hadn't been inside a church for many years. The dark brown pews smelled as if they had just been polished. A few candles burned in the vestibules. On busy days like Christmas and Easter, the sanctuary would barely hold three hundred worshippers.

Bruno found a pew, picked up a couple of kneeling cushions, and made a pillow. He lay down and closed his eyes. So far, so good. He pondered his inability to feel any emotion about being in such a meditative and spiritual place, and how any feelings he did have were subordinated by fears for his safety and his constant calculations with money.

"Who are you?"

Bruno awoke to an aging priest, well into his seventies, staring down on him.

"What are you doing in my church?"

"Good morning, Father." Bruno sat up and then stood. "I needed somewhere to sleep. I arrived last night and I couldn't find anywhere to stay in town. I'll leave now."

"No, wait. Where have you come from?"

Bruno hesitated.

"Well?" the priest asked. "You can trust me. I may be able to help. You must be hungry. Come, let us get you breakfast."

The growling of his empty stomach told Bruno he should trust this man, at least long enough to have a meal. Bruno nodded, and the priest led him from the church. They walked down the street where Bruno had parked the truck the night before. The vehicle was still there, hunkering and sticking out like an ugly lump of green steel in the picturesque residential neighborhood. Bruno kept his eyes forward.

The priest pushed open the wide wooden door to his small house that faced the street. Window boxes bloomed with geraniums on each window ledge. Bruno followed the priest into a narrow hallway with polished hardwood floors and white painted walls on which were hung two large crucifixes and a painting of the Madonna with the infant Jesus.

"Sister Gertrude, we have a breakfast guest."

"You're back early, Father." A middle-aged nun appeared from the kitchen. "I'll have breakfast ready in ten minutes." She studied Bruno. "You look as if you could eat a good breakfast, young man." She smiled and returned to the kitchen.

"I'm sure you have a lot to tell me," the priest said in a knowing voice. "Save it until after breakfast. Meanwhile, if you wish to use the bathroom, it's at the end of the hall."

"Thank you, Father."

The nun served muesli, newly laid eggs, smoked ham, a variety of cheese, bread, fruit and good coffee, not like the piss they brewed at Dachau. Bruno had not eaten so well in a long time. Nor had he eaten before at such a fine table, in a formal dining room, with a freshly laundered white linen napkin next to a setting of fine Meissen china. The priest watched Bruno devour the food. Being a priest had its advantages, Bruno noted. Unlike his parishioners, this priest didn't experience any wartime shortage of food.

"Now, tell me your story, young man."

"Well." Bruno chuckled. "I suppose if I can't trust a priest, who can I trust?" Bruno took another sip of coffee. "Father, for the duration of the war, I have been working at Dachau, a camp near Munich."

"Yes, I am familiar with that place. It's a camp where we detain those individuals who pose a threat to society. You have been doing God's work, my son."

"Thank you, Father. I've also worked at other camps, but now the war is going badly for Germany. The British and the Americans are closing in on us. The work we have been doing will, I am sure, result in recriminations. Revenge squads, lynchings, and maybe prosecutions. Who knows? I am trying to escape. I left Dachau last night and got as far as here. I need to get to Italy and from there, I don't know."

"My son." The priest sipped his coffee and returned the cup to its saucer. "You are blessed that our Lord guided you toward our church. God has given me the responsibility of comforting people like you who are indeed the true victims of this war." His eyes grew sad. "The war against Germany is not a crusade, as our enemies maintain. No. It is a result of rivalry in economic matters. Pure business. But what can you expect? The Jews are the warmongers. Churchill and Roosevelt, they use meaningless catchwords like democracy, race, and religious liberty. Such nonsense. You are not the first National Socialist I have helped since the British landed at Normandy and the Americans advanced into Italy."

Bruno had not anticipated that his request would be considered patriotic. The priest and his politics surprised him. Thinking it was the appropriate thing to do, Bruno crossed himself.

The priest continued, "I want you to stay here for a couple of days while I make arrangements for you. You will be quite safe in this house. Sister Gertrude and I will look after you." He pushed himself to his feet. "Now, follow me, I will take you upstairs to a bedroom and show you the bathroom, and make sure you get some proper sleep."

Bruno threw himself onto the bed and stared at the ceiling. He fell asleep thinking about how lucky he was to have a warm place to rest and warm food in his stomach. He woke up at the sound of knocking. He rose and found himself still in a full outfit of clothes. His reflex to answer the door conflicted for a moment with his love of the privacy, and he called out that he was getting dressed.

"Don't rush, my son." The priest's answer was muffled and patient. "It's seven o'clock and I thought you might like some dinner. Sister Gertrude has made us a pork and vegetable stew."

"Yes, I can smell it. It's making me hungry. I'll be right downstairs."

The priest's footsteps retreated.

Downstairs, Bruno ate stew at the dining room table in near silence for several minutes. Another large crucifix stared down from the wall. Bruno mopped the plate with a piece of bread and smacked his lips.

"That was good, Father, thank you."

"My son, I work closely with our Croatian brethren, they are Franciscans. Father Krunoslav Draganovic leads this blessed order from Rome. Many of the Franciscan brothers are working to assist young men such as you in escaping to Italy. Friar Cecelja reports directly to Father Draganovic, and Friar Cecelja is here in Austria. I have been in contact with him today." The priest folded his hands together. "Tomorrow morning a farm truck will come here at five o'clock to take you to Innsbruck where you will spend a few days in lodgings at a friendly farm there."

"That is most kind, Father."

The comprehensiveness of the priest's plans startled Bruno. This all had been done before, for others. But those others really were a part of the Nazi movement. They really had reason to be fearful of the Allies. Bruno sensed a turning point in his understanding of how things worked. How he should think about opportunities in the future.

"You will then be taken to a small town on the border, Lientz. You will remain in lodgings there until a mountain guide can escort you over the Karnische Alps into Italy."

"Is part of the journey on foot, Father?"

"Yes, it will be. I have noticed that you have a problem with your foot. I have informed Friar Cecelja, and the guide will be aware of it. He will take you through easy passes and not rush you. When you get into Italy, you will be driven to a monastery in Bolzano. At that time, your destiny will be decided by Father Draganovic in Rome."

The priest filled Bruno's glass and watched as he brought it to his lips. Bruno suddenly felt ill at ease, wondering whether his host had another agenda and how he should respond.

He went to his room and lay awake, fearful that he might have an unwanted visitor to whom he owed a great debt of gratitude. But how much was his freedom worth?

*

Bruno's fears were unfounded. At a quarter to five, he arose from a needlessly fitful night's sleep, dressed, and went downstairs. The priest opened the door to a man in his forties, whom he introduced as Fritz.

"It's important you get on the road straight away, before sunrise," the priest said. "Do what Fritz tells you. He will drive you to Innsbruck where you will stay with his parents at their farm. May God bless you, my son. Hurry."

"Get in." Fritz hopped onto the truck's running board and leaned across to unlock the door. "It's best that we arrive before seven o'clock, when there'll be more workers out on the road."

Within the hour, they arrived in Innsbruck. Bruno was relieved to get out of the old truck. It was noisy and stank of fuel and manure. Fritz led him inside a house and into the kitchen, where an elderly couple was seated and drinking tea. The old man waved at an empty chair.

"We are delighted to assist you," Fritz's father said. "We have heard from Friar Cecelja that he is making arrangements for you. In a few days, someone will come for you and take you to Lientz, where you will wait until a guide comes to fetch you and take you over the Alps into Italy." The old man's long eyebrows drew together sternly. "We want you to remain in your room at all times. Workers come in and out all day as well as some of our neighbors. We don't want to give anyone reason to talk if we can avoid it. So we will bring you your meals."

A few hours later, after Bruno had settled in his room, there was a knock on the door. The old farmer came in with a tray of coffee and a piece of cake.

"There is a change of plan. You will be leaving for Lientz very early tomorrow morning. The military police are looking for you. It appears that they found a parked vehicle in Kufstein that was reported missing from Dachau. It had apparently been stolen by you."

That night, he lay down expecting another bad sleep. The walls were thin. He heard Fritz's parents speaking in the next room, but he couldn't make out the words. Everything felt alien. He was no more uneasy than he had been anywhere else in his life—this house was another setting in which he didn't quite belong.

The adventure in front of him did not excite him, nor did his escape from Dachau. He searched himself for the impulse to steal something from the old couple, but dismissed the idea as impractical—nowhere to hide much, and he didn't want to poison his luck. Instead, he listened to the aged woman's voice rising and falling on the other side of the wall, and tried to imagine himself in a marriage bed of his own. All that came to him was a memory of a toothless gypsy prisoner at Dachau and her frightening, beautiful eyes full of mockery.

At five o'clock the next morning, Fritz knocked on Bruno's door.

"We're leaving for Lientz now. I've put some bales of hay in the back of the truck. I want you to lie there. If you hear me call to you, cover yourself with the hay. You must keep your head down all the way. You got it?"

Bruno met him outside and got into the back of the truck. It was cold. He was thankful he had his heavy coat, not just for what was hidden within it, but also for the warmth. Lientz was a short distance away, and within an hour, Bruno was dropped off, shivering, at a church in the center of town. A priest stood in the doorway.

"I'm Father Mandic. Come inside. You are to stay here in my study until one of the guides returns. He will then escort you over the mountains."

"When will that be, Father?"

"I am hopeful he will be back this afternoon. Then you will set off tomorrow morning."

An uneventful night passed and the morning came. Outside the door to his study, the priest knocked lightly then whispered, "Giuseppe is here. Get dressed."

The priest knocked again and repeated his message. Bruno grunted. So far, the price of this journey was privacy, and he was sick of being shaken and startled and prodded awake. Even so, he was away from Dachau. He dressed and went to meet his guide. Giuseppe, a strong fellow in his prime, shook Bruno's hand hard.

"We will walk as quickly as we can," Giuseppe said, pointing to Bruno's foot. "You will follow me. We will walk in silence as voices carry. When you are too tired to continue, you will attract my attention as quietly as you can and we will stop for a rest. We will pass a few cabins. I have in my backpack bread and some cognac. After we reach Italy, one of my colleagues will take you to a village on the outskirts of Bressanone. Then to the monastery in Bolzano."

"How long will it take to reach the other side?"

"It's about thirteen miles. But it's a strenuous pass. I'd like to think that you could do it in a day, but that may be too hard for you. Rain is expected in a few days so we should take advantage of the good dry weather. Are you ready? The priest will drive us to the foot of the mountain where we start."

"Let's go."

Daybreak had not cut through the chill in the air when Bruno and Giuseppe got out of the car. They turned up their coat collars and put on gloves. The priest drove off without a word or a wave.

"If I'm walking too fast, tell me," Giuseppe said softly. "Now remember, no talking."

It was said that the Tyrol was a walker's paradise. Bruno never antici-pated that he would experience it firsthand. He did his best to keep up with his guide and now and again paused to take in the beauty of the mountain huts, the woodlands, the wildflowers, the blue and green lakes, and the many streams they passed. Bruno had never walked in nature before, or felt the sky's light and splendor pushing through him as if he were a being made of paper and silk. The breeze carried the scent of pines, unstained by exhaust and waste. His lungs expanded. He was taking his first breath and felt weightless. For the first time in his life, he was awed.

"Are you okay?" Giuseppe whispered.

"I have never seen such beautiful scenery before."

"I know. But we have no time to be tourists. Keep going."

Bruno walked on, relieved that his foot wasn't giving him too much trouble, and he took in as much of the experience as he could. The lush mountains and bare slopes gripped him and left him feeling new. He wished that he could have seen them under different conditions, when he really could have been a tourist. Maybe someday, in the future, when he was established and could live openly and be someone. Maybe even fall in love and bring his wife to see these mountaintops in peace. He tried to imagine his wife. He dwelled on her minute features—fingernails, eyelashes, waist—without ever seeing an actual woman.

"There's a hut," Giuseppe whispered, "about half a mile from here. We can rest there."

Bruno roused himself from his thoughts and looked around. The trail had closed in a bit. The smell of pines was thicker.

"How far have we gone?"

"About eight miles. You're holding up well."

Bruno looked at his watch. They'd been walking for four hours.

The hut was simple: a small table and two benches. Giuseppe pulled a flask from his pocket and sat down. He took a large gulp, wiped the top with his sleeve, and passed it to Bruno.

"Here's bread to go with it." Giuseppe took a couple of slices from another pocket. "You're a lucky man to have stumbled onto that old church in Kufstein. What would you have done if the priest there had turned you in?"

Bruno accepted the bread and took an unmannerly large bite. "I had intended the next day to make my way somehow to Innsbruck. I never considered the possibility of being turned in." He shook his head. He hardly recognized the energy in his own voice. "After all, this part of the country is still true to the Führer, isn't it?"

"Let me tell you," Giuseppe said. "The war is over for all practical purposes. Germany has lost. It's every man for himself now, and you know that."

Bruno nodded. The man was speaking Bruno's language. Giuseppe's forthrightness made him feel pleasantly uncomfortable. Perhaps this was what friendship should feel like.

"Has anyone told you how much all this is going to cost you?" Giuseppe asked.

Indeed, it had crossed Bruno's mind on several occasions that perhaps he should offer to pay or at least leave some money behind at each place he had been given refuge. One of the reasons he hesitated about doing so was the fear of revealing that he had a stash concealed in his clothing. The other reason, he admitted to himself, was simply that he found it difficult to part with money.

"No, not yet," Bruno replied. "I haven't asked but I expect to have to pay someone at some point for all the help I've been given."

"Believe me." Giuseppe grinned. "They will present you with a bill for services rendered. Don't forget the Vatican is behind all this, and the Vatican is some business. They're bigger than Fiat and probably better businessmen." He looked at his watch. "Come on. We better get moving."

They continued in silence. Their pace quickened, and pain developed in Bruno's foot. He felt it best to say nothing for as long as he could hold up. He had lived with pain from the foot all his life, and it was as if they were bonded like dog and master. It burrowed in his bones and sawed at the ligaments—a dog, then, that was getting the best of its master.

"Another hour and we should be in Italy. My cousin Antonio will meet us there. I'm not sure what is planned."

Since waving to the priest earlier in the day, they hadn't seen anyone. The only sound was the twittering of birds. It was almost sunset. Through the trees, a distant church steeple glowed a burnt orange in the day's last light. Then a cluster of houses and chimneys emerged from behind the dusky trees.

"That's our destination over there," Giuseppe said. "You've done well. It will be dark in an hour."

Bruno looked down at the village. Italy. Thank God, he found himself repeating.

✳

They approached the outskirts of a clean and orderly village. A few people walked from the town's central marketplace, and Giuseppe and Bruno fell in with them. Some greeted Giuseppe with a wave, and he waved back. Talk was of prices and comparison of the goods to what they'd bought before the war. One woman advised another about how to make the most of vegetable broth. It was the same story, probably, everywhere in the world.

"I do this twice a week," Giuseppe explained. "The villagers are very helpful. There's Antonio over there, on the corner."

At the top of a rise in the street was an angular intersection and a burly man with gray hair. He waved and walked down to them. Giuseppe touched his forehead as if tipping an imaginary cap.

"Our friend must be very tired," Giuseppe said. "He has been walking all day and has a bad foot."

"I'm okay." Bruno shuffled. "I was in good hands."

"We'll take you to Sofia's now for some food and a good night's sleep," Antonio said. "And tomorrow morning I'll take you on my motorbike to the monastery in Bolzano. Father Angotti will look after you. And you, Giuseppe, will you stay for something to eat? Or will you be going, as usual, to your girlfriend?"

Giuseppe smiled and nodded.

"You see, Bruno," Antonio explained, "your mountain guide is very hardworking and energetic. More energetic than his wife in Austria may realize. Crossing the mountains twice a week gives him time to spend with his Italian girlfriend."

Giuseppe turned to the darkened avenue and seemed wanting to throw himself into it. Bruno distracted him with an offer to shake hands, and he thanked his guide. Bruno wondered if he should do more. After all, his coat was full of money, but public displays of gratitude would expose his secret. Giuseppe tipped his imaginary cap again and hurried into the darkening evening. Antonio led the way in the other direction, to the far side of the square, to a simple inn. A few locals sat outside sipping wine and talking softly among themselves. War had made people lower their voices to barely a whisper.

"Sofia, we're here," Antonio said as they walked through the front door. His voice seemed too loud for the small common room. A moment later, a middle-aged woman appeared, overweight and wearing an apron. She looked Bruno up and down, said nothing, and nodded.

"Have you some food for our friend here?" Antonio asked. "He has had a long journey."

She looked sullen. She shrugged and turned toward the kitchen, waving for her husband to take Bruno to an upstairs room.

"What's the matter with her?" Bruno asked. Pain gnawed at his heel as he climbed the stairs. "She doesn't seem very friendly."

"She doesn't approve of the work I'm doing." Antonio shrugged. "And she hasn't seen much money yet for all the people who've passed through her place. The Church keeps promising she'll be looked after, but so far, she's received very little. Here's your room." Antonio opened the door and brightened a lantern. "Stay here. Sofia will bring you a tray. I'll be back tomorrow morning. The bathroom is at the end of the corridor. You should bathe that foot if it hurts you so much."

A few minutes later, Sofia tapped on the door with a tray. Pasta, bread and a carafe of wine. She set it down on the table and left, ignoring Bruno's murmured thanks. He took off his shoes and socks and threw his coat and jacket onto the bed. He was almost too tired to eat. He gazed at the tray and slowly got up from the bed to sit at the table. He picked up a piece of bread as if to weigh it.

The food was freshly cooked, and the wine tasted good. Luck had again been on his side. He threw his coat under the bed and went to the bathroom, where he rolled up his trousers and plunged his feet into the bath. The hot water soothed his aching ankle.

That night he dreamt of arriving at his final destination, wherever that might be, and making a new life for himself free of the burdens of war and family. A solid roof over his head, a full pantry overflowing with only the best, and a bed with the softest linen. Maybe there would be some friends, a handful of Giuseppes, with whom he could share some simple pleasures, like a meal, a drink and a few laughs. People who wouldn't consider him an outcast. And a prosperous business of his own, too. Maybe a woman.

He turned over in his sleep and opened one eye. The room was bright. He closed his eyes and dozed off.

A sharp knock awoke him. Bruno dragged his watch to his face. Eight o'clock. He had slept for close to ten hours.

"Good morning, friend. Are you ready for your ride to Bolzano?" Antonio chuckled. "Well, when you are, Sofia is at the market so we'll have to stop for coffee in Bressanone. It's five minutes away, en route to Bolzano. Looks like you need it."

Bruno made his way downstairs and found Antonio in the street, waiting on his motorbike. Bruno hadn't ridden one since before the war.

"C'mon, jump on," Antonio called.

Bruno still felt half asleep, but the sound of the revving engine woke him and vibrated in his bones. He climbed on and grabbed Antonio around the waist just in time. The bike moved swiftly into the cobbled square toward Bressanone.

Bruno was too concerned about Antonio's maneuvering through winding narrow streets to take in the uniqueness of the beautifully preserved historic town with its colorful houses and medieval bridges. Finally, Antonio pulled up beside a cafe, and the engine cut out with a bang.

"Bolzano is about forty kilometers from here. Father Angotti is expecting us at around half past nine, so we can relax for a while."

Relax might have been an overstatement. Bruno stood up and waited for something in his body to break or collapse. Nothing happened. Perhaps the ride had not been as assaulting as it had felt.

"What happens after Bolzano?" Bruno asked.

"I have no idea. That is for Father Angotti and Bishop Hudal to decide. We have time to go and visit the cathedral here if you want. Very important thirteenth-century frescoes."

"I think I'd rather stay here for a while. I'm going to get more than my share of cathedrals and churches while at the monastery, don't you think?"

Antonio smiled. He lit a cigarette, then offered one to Bruno.

"You don't smoke?" Antonio asked.

"No. I don't drink much either."

"So what do you do?" Antonio drew on his cigarette.

"I think a lot. And play the piano whenever I can."

The ride to Bolzano was uneventful. Fortunately, Antonio drove slowly to preserve fuel, and Bruno was able to admire the castles that dotted the landscape and breathe the fresh air of the Italian Tyrol.

"Bolzano is the capital of this province, Alto Adige," Antonio explained. "Do you see the cathedral over there with its green and yellow mosaic roof? Just look at the Italian-Austrian mix of the city. Do you see the narrow cobblestone streets, my friend, and did you notice that all the signs are in both German and Italian?"

Bruno looked but felt little enthusiasm for being Antonio's tourist. Antonio continued regardless.

"We're passing the main street, which you will see is lined by the famous arcaded walkways. If they ever let you out of the monastery," Antonio joked, "you should take a walk up the mountains. Fantastic views of the Dolomites. Try to visit the vineyards too, or even borrow a bicycle. You can ride for hours on the pathways by the river." He pointed to the snowcapped mountains. "Just look over there. Before the war, that was a major ski center. Do you ski? Ah, sorry, not with that foot I expect."

Antonio revved up the engine. Ten minutes later, they crossed a bridge and approached Piazza della Erbe. The fruit and vegetable market was busy. They passed the famous Neptune Fountain.

"Do you see that plaque over there?" Antonio asked. "That marks where the old Hotel Sonne stood. It was one of Goethe's favorite places."

All Bruno wanted was to arrive at the monastery. He'd had enough of Antonio. Finally, at the end of the street, they arrived at the twelfth-century monastery, an appealing baroque building set in the middle of a small park and next to the old Gothic St. George's Church of the Teutonic Order with its many flags flying in the breeze.

"This is it," Antonio said. "I'll come with you to the gate."

He led the way up the gravel path toward a pair of huge double doors that were closed. Antonio knocked hard. A minute or so later, footsteps scuffed to a halt on the other side.

"Who is there?"

"Antonio Carrera and a passenger. Father Angotti is expecting us."

Metal clanked and one of the doors creaked open. A young priest stood in the gap.

"This is my passenger," Antonio said. "Bruno Franzmann."

Bruno thanked Antonio and waved goodbye with relief. Then he followed the priest into a large quadrangle, through an archway, and up a stone staircase. His foot was being ornery today and throbbed all the way to the top. There was no handrail, and Bruno imagined himself falling to the bottom and breaking his neck after having survived the whole journey from Dachau.

"Father Angotti's study is at the far end of this corridor."

"Where is everyone?" Bruno stopped to rest and disguised his hesitation as mere curiosity. "It's so quiet."

"Our many brothers are either in church praying, working in the fields, or studying in the library. My name is Father Silvano. I'm Father Angotti's secretary."

Father Silvano paused, tapped the door, and opened it for Bruno. Seated behind a large desk was Father Angotti, dressed in a brown cassock and skullcap. Glass-fronted bookcases lined the somber room, which smelled of dust, oiled leather, and something else—like the liniment his mother used on her knees before the war.

Father Angotti did not rise. He looked at Bruno and said nothing. For the first time, Bruno's self-confidence disappeared. The austere man was more than three times Bruno's age, but his penetrating stare was equal to a wildcat in its prime. Bruno felt trapped.

"Sit down, Herr Franzmann," the elder priest said. "Father Silvano, bring us coffee."

Bruno sat down in a cushioned armchair facing the desk. The young priest went to a table at the back of the room and poured coffee for each of them from a silver pot. The scent of the beans dispelled some of the room's fug. Silvano handed them their coffee, then Father Angotti waved a hand, shooing the younger priest, who stepped out to stand in the hallway like a sentry taking his station.

"You've had a busy few days, I hear," Angotti began. "Why did you run away from Germany? Are you a criminal?"

"No, sir," Bruno replied. "I think we all know that Germany will lose the war. The enemy is closing in on Berlin from all sides. It's only a question of time."

"But why did you feel the need to escape?"

Bruno looked at the priest. This priest was weighing more than Bruno's soul. More likely his worth.

"The Germans established camps," Bruno explained. "Things happened at those camps. I worked there, but I didn't do anything wrong. I worked in the administrative department. But I know things happened, and when the Americans and British arrive and find out what some Germans have done, there will be trouble. There could even be revenge squads out to get Germans who belonged to the SS."

"What sort of things went on?"

"Medical experiments. Beatings, slave labor." Bruno shifted in his seat and avoided eye contact. "People were... I mean, the Jews, they were..." He knew the word the officers had used, but it was stuck in his swelling throat. "Exterminated."

"Yes, I know." Father Angotti stared at Bruno with less warmth than a praying mantis. "I am well acquainted with what went on at the camps, but you must not feel guilt. You did God's work in helping society rid itself of the vermin there. It is you who are a victim."

Relief steadied Bruno. He allowed himself to take a sip of coffee, and managed to do so without spilling any on himself.

"We have helped many like you over the last few weeks," Angotti explained. "And more of your comrades will be coming here over the next several months. We are here to help you."

Bruno wanted to ask how many others at the monastery were Nazi deserters. But the past felt like a taboo subject. Father Angotti's gaze pushed the question even further from the realm of what was acceptable, and Bruno settled for an awkward "Thank you, Father."

"You're welcome," he said with a touch of sarcasm. "I suppose you want to know who we are. My colleague in Rome is Bishop Hudal. A great man, much loved in the Austrian and German communities. He is Rector of the Pontificio Istituto Teutonico Santa Maria dell'Anima, a seminary for Austrian and German priests. He has set up an organization to assist men such as you. Many Germans have been helped and will continue to be helped by him. Now, my immediate superior, who works alongside Bishop Hudal, is Father Draganovic, who is also in Rome at the San Girolamo Degli Illirici Seminary College. We have very good connections in Genoa."

"And these gentlemen," Bruno dared to ask, "oversee the organizations that help people such as myself?"

"Correct. Now all this costs a great deal of money. But I will come to that later. Our belief is that for the next few years, Europe will not offer a comfortable environment in which people such as you can live and work. The solution is to get you a berth on a vessel going to South America."

"I can't speak Spanish."

"You will learn." Father Angotti sipped his coffee. "You can expect to remain here for six months or so. During that time, you will work for a few hours each day. Use your free time wisely, to study in the library and learn about Argentina and Buenos Aires. We are also fortunate that three of our brothers here are from Spain. One of them, maybe Father Fernando, will help you learn Spanish. Buenos Aires has a growing German population. You will be welcomed into it. Learning Italian would also be helpful. Father Silvano can take care of that."

"Thank you, Father."

"The formalities are very straightforward. The Vatican, namely the Ponteficia Commissione di Assistenza, the Vatican Refugee Organization, will provide you with papers and identity documents. With those papers, we will arrange for the International Red Cross to issue you a displaced persons passport, which will enable you to apply for a visa for Argentina. The Red Cross will issue the papers according to our specifications. You will appreci- ate that we take care of people in the Red Cross. Another expense."

And another hint for money, Bruno thought. But he did not speak. Instead he cast his eyes down at his coffee cup and hoped to appear humble. Maybe even poor.

"We will then make contact with our man in Genoa, Monsignor Karlo Petranovic. He is a good friend of Alberto Dodero and often spends week- ends at his villa in Rapallo. Señor Dodero is the owner of an Argentinean shipping fleet. Through him we will arrange for you to get a berth on a crossing."

"Thank you, Father. And once I arrive in Argentina?"

"We will give you a letter of introduction to a gentleman by the name of Wolfgang Fischer, the managing director of Banco Altman Transeuropeas in Buenos Aires. He will help you at that end."

"How long will it take before I can sail to Argentina?"

"Maybe six months. It takes us time to prepare the paperwork."

"Father, you have mentioned the cost. I have no money."

"We understand that. You will work for a few hours each day and that will go toward the cost. You will be provided with food and a bed, so you will have no need for money. When you arrive in Buenos Aires, Herr Fischer will find employment for you. Out of your wages you will pay something each week to the organization, to reimburse the expense of your relocation."

"How much will that be, Father?"

"I don't know exactly. But you should think roughly five to six thousand American dollars."

"That's a lot of money."

Father Angotti sharply answered, "You're a young man, able to make good money in Buenos Aires. Payment for our services should be no problem for you."

Bruno nodded. Of course, he could pay that sum immediately. But that would be risky. Even in a monastery, to admit he was carrying a great deal of cash and valuable jewelry would surely lead to its loss.

"Now I'm going to place you in the care of Father Silvano. He will show you to your quarters. He will provide you with work clothes and introduce you to Father Fernando and Father Erich, our librarian. We must also determine what work is available for you. Do you know anything about vehicle repairs?"

"A little, Father. Why?"

"Good. We have recently been given two trucks in need of repair. Father Gustavo is a trained mechanic but he could use some help. Father Silvano will take you to the workshop now." Father Angotti stood and indicated the open doorway.

Bruno got up from his seat, not knowing whether to extend his hand or to bow.

Father Angotti turned his gaze to a file on his desk, and the meeting ended.

14

By the end of his first week, Bruno had acclimatized himself to his new existence. He took in all the restrictions and expectations without question or reaction. But inside he chafed at the idea of being incarcerated, yet again, in another work mill. He had exchanged the harsh severity of his former German SS officers for the rigidity of monastic life. But Dachau and Augsburg were behind him. The day would come, and he would make it to Argentina. Until that day, the wealth concealed in his clothing was at risk of being discovered, leaving him a penniless soul, lost in a country a world apart from his own.

After a couple of months, Bruno proved to the fathers that he was a quick study. Besides assimilating the fundamentals of automobile mechanics, he absorbed elementary Spanish and some Italian, as well as knowledge of Argentinean history. And though talking was not forbidden at mealtime, conversations on secular matters were frowned upon.

The other Germans had schedules that differed from Bruno's. He didn't know whether by design or by chance. Some worked in the fields, others in the garden, and some on repairing the large roof. An unspoken protocol dictated that no questions be asked. Especially where anyone was from, or what type of work they had done during the war. Bruno could not ask nor answer. So he kept to himself among the monks and had little opportunity to fraternize with other Germans.

The silence was abrasive. Bruno felt the other men's curiosity between the lines of every *good morning*, every *how are you*, and every *Hail Mary* in between. The discretion felt false and awkward, pushing him back into his old manner of loneliness and annoyance. Sometimes, when he was sure he was alone, he pilfered what valuable trinkets he could find—a golden candlesnuffer, a silver rosary, pieces of copper from the scrap metal shed, a few bills and coins lost in the automobiles he repaired. He'd become carried away with the earlier hope for friends and a pleasant future. Now, as always, he remembered there was nothing to do with his time except patient hoarding.

✴

On May Day, during Bruno's third month at the monastery, Father Silvano left his table during lunch and walked to the back of the refectory, where the Germans were seated.

"After lunch, you are all to report to Father Angotti's office," Silvano said.

Half an hour later, they assembled in silence outside Father Angotti's chamber. Father Silvano opened the door to let them in. They stood before the desk, where Father Angotti was seated, reading a newspaper. After a minute's silence, he folded the paper in half and looked up at his visitors.

"It is my duty to inform you that your Führer committed suicide yesterday in Berlin. May God rest his soul. Berlin is in a state of chaos. We must expedite your departure to make room for the many Germans who will be fleeing their country after this news."

The men looked at each other in silence, with haunted and surprised expressions. As they returned to their quarters, each looked dour and pale. Though it was nothing Bruno had ever hoped for, the death of his Führer was confirmation that escaping his homeland was the right choice. The Germany Bruno had known was now dead. Now more than ever, it was each man for himself.

15

BRUNO WAS IN A PIT BENEATH ONE OF THE MONASTERY'S OLD trucks, repairing a damaged axle, when Father Silvano summoned him to see Father Angotti. The priest was at the workshop's open door. Bruno climbed the ladder out of the pit and wiped his greasy hands on his coveralls.

"That's okay," Father Gustavo said. "I can finish it."

"I should wash first." Bruno raised his greasy hands.

"Yes," Silvano said. "But hurry."

After waiting outside the washroom, Father Silvano escorted Bruno to the older priest's study. Bruno hadn't seen Father Angotti since the news of the Führer's death three months earlier. As usual, the old priest did not look up from his sheaf of papers. After a while, he gestured to Bruno to sit down. Bruno pointed to his greasy coveralls and remained standing.

"We've arranged for your exit papers. In fact, you're jumping the queue. Some of your comrades have not learned Spanish as well as you, and based on your knowledge of administration and also mechanics, your chances of finding employment in Argentina are excellent."

"Thank you, Father."

The prospect of leaving was dizzying. Bruno had been one of the last to arrive at the monastery. Now he was the first to leave. Did any German deserve such luck, Bruno wondered.

"I have your papers here," Angotti said. "Father Silvano will give you your file this evening. Study it before leaving tomorrow. Within it, you will find your ticket, a letter of introduction to the secretary of The German Club, your Red Cross passport, your visa for Argentina, and a letter of introduction to Herr Fischer in Buenos Aires. He expects to hear from you as soon as you arrive. The file also contains identity documents provided by the Ponteficia Assistenza and some pesos in an envelope for you, a sum roughly equal to fifty marks. That will be included in the final cost of arranging your exit from Europe."

God, freedom. Bruno had spent six months in virtual isolation. Even the kind Father Gutstavo limited his conversation purely to instructions on mechanics. But now change decreed he'd be back out in the world again.

Father Angotti continued, "A car will come for you at six tomorrow morning. Its license plates will bear the initials *CD*: Corpo Diplomatico. The car is protected by diplomatic immunity. No one will stop you on your way to Genoa. The chauffeur will drive you straight to the harbor, to where your ship is moored. The ship is the *Giovanna*. Stay in the car until one of the ship's crew returns with the chauffeur. He'll take you aboard. Expect to see on board many victims such as yourself. Maybe you will meet some of your former colleagues," he added.

"How long is the voyage to Argentina?"

"Normally twenty-one days. It depends on the weather, and the ports en route can vary, to deliver or take on cargo. You should arrive in Buenos Aires around the third or fourth week of September. Good luck, young man, and may God be with you."

Bruno extended his hand, but seeing that his fingernails were cracked and blackened with grease, he withdrew it and nodded his head awkwardly. But the old priest had already turned his attention to papers on his desk.

✳

At eight o'clock that night, Bruno heard a tap on his door. It was Father Silvano. Silvano closed the door behind him and sat down on the bed.

"Here are your papers, Herr Franzmann. I've also put in the file a couple of addresses of other people we've helped and who have written to us to give us their news. One man is now working for Mercedes in Buenos Aires and the other for Compagnia Technica Internazionale, an engineering company that is very active in Latin America."

"Thank you, Father Silvano. You have been very helpful to me."

Bruno took the file and checked its contents. There was his new Red

Cross passport, which looked as if it had just come off the printing press. The type was too small for Bruno to read so he passed on to the next item, in Spanish, his Argentinean visa document, stamped with the seal of the consulate in Rome. His ticket for the voyage was printed on a dirty-brown card. Bruno glanced at the letters of introduction that Father Angotti had mentioned, and which Father Silvano had typed on the heavy monastery letterhead engraved with a gold crucifix on the left side of the paper.

Bruno narrowed his eyes to try to decipher the identity document provided by the Ponteficia Assistenza. It was incomprehensible. But his eyes widened when he saw the pesos, a good number of bills, and he couldn't resist a grin. When he looked up, Father Silvano had not moved, and he was smiling, too—but his smile was oddly shy.

"It is very lonely sometimes here at the monastery," Silvano said. "I was wondering if, before you leave, we might get to know each other a little better."

Silvano cocked his head to one side, gazing at Bruno as he awaited a response. Bruno ignored him as best he could and closed the file. Silvano, misreading Bruno's silence, softened his posture. His pale hands moved to the belt around his cassock, and his fingers worked the knot.

"Father, no." Bruno drew back. "I know I owe you a great debt of gratitude for all your help, but I'm not going to repay it like that."

"But let me kiss you, before you leave," Silvano pleaded.

"No, Father," Bruno said firmly. "Thank you for everything, but no."

Silvano scowled. "You Germans are all the same." He stood and put the belt back around his cassock. "Ungrateful swine."

The priest hurried out the door and slammed it shut behind him. Bruno moved the bed against the door. As was his nightly habit, he felt for the secret pockets in his coat and suit, and satisfied himself that everything was still in place, along with his Luger and Unit 436's personnel records. Tomorrow this monastery would be as much a part of his history as his parents and Dachau.

✳

At six o'clock the next morning, one of the friars tapped on his door—a car was waiting at the outer gate. Bruno lifted his battered valise and followed the friar through the long corridors and across the quadrangle. He came to a door in the thick and ancient wall. The friar was bereft of any social skills and said nothing as he opened the door and pointed to the waiting car. A loose iron hinge clanked, and the door thudded shut.

The uniformed chauffeur got out of the car, an old Mercedes. He took Bruno's case and placed it in the trunk. Bruno looked around and realized this was the first time in six months that he had left the monastery. He could not hide his relief.

"We have a long journey to Genoa," the chauffeur said. "We need to arrive before seven o'clock this evening."

Bruno got in the car and noticed a map on the seat beside him. He wasn't in the mood to look at it. In any event, it was too dark. There was also a leather-bound bible. He wasn't in the mood to look at that, either. He closed his eyes. There was no point in staying awake. Outside, it was pitch-black early morning.

Would he ever see Europe again? He wondered if he would ever see his mother again and how she was. She was his last link to Europe. And what lay ahead for him in Argentina? He also asked himself why he was fleeing. After all, he hadn't done anything in the camps of which to be ashamed. He'd basically been doing the same sort of work that he'd been doing in Augsburg before the war, handling personnel and payroll records for city workers. But after the war, when the enemy entered the camps, found the crematorium, and saw the surviving Yids—skin hanging from their bony frames—all personnel staffing the camps would be held responsible whether they operated the crematorium or not, and that included Bruno.

Yes, a new life on another continent was preferable. Also, in Argentina, he wouldn't have to account for the money and jewelry he had on him. Who knew what he might have to face in Germany with such a hoard. And look at all the others who had been at Dachau. He could easily be grouped with them and their deeds. Who was there who would say different?

And for the first time, he wondered about the other things stolen in Europe. His small hoard of treasures was truly minute—a mere skim off the vast wealth of European Jews. What about the rest—the art, the wealth, the estates and antiques, the jewels? Where had it all gone? Many must have been smarter than Bruno. If even a portion of Germans had his skill for money, those few must be making a killing. And then there were those who aided him and others to escape.

"Father Angotti, you old hog," he murmured.

Giuseppe had said it himself—the Vatican was the biggest business in Europe. There was another reason Bruno was better off on the other side of the world. He wouldn't have to work so much in its shadow. And he would pay his debt as soon as he could without raising suspicions. Then Bruno would be on his own and truly free.

*

The chauffeur drove at a steady pace. Bruno skipped in and out of sleep like a stone across water, until he finally sank into its depths. He awoke with a start as the chauffeur brought the car to a stop and turned off the engine.

"We are on the outskirts of Verona," the chauffeur said. "I am going to get gas. I need to fill up everywhere we can, as there is a shortage. You must stay in the car. As long as you remain inside the car, you are protected by diplomatic immunity."

"And you? How are you protected?"

"I have two passports, one Croatian, the other a diplomatic passport. In the trunk I have some food for you. Fruit, eggs, bread and water. I will get it now."

A few minutes later, they were back on the road. Bruno absent-mindedly picked up the map on the seat beside him.

"So, Parma is the next place?"

"Yes, we'll stop for gas there too," the chauffeur said." We have about another hundred miles to go."

Bruno felt the stubble on his face, days old. He was hot in his suit and overcoat, but he was reluctant to shed either. He opened the window and was grateful for the breeze, but more than fresh air, he wanted to stretch his legs.

The car pulled to the side of the road. They were in the countryside, far from any town. The chauffeur said he'd warn Bruno if a vehicle approached. Bruno walked for a few minutes, then returned to lean against the car and absorb the scenery. Fields stretched far to the horizon, ablaze with white, red, pink, lavender and blue flowering kale.

"I wonder when I'll see Europe again," he said quietly. "I'll miss kale. It was the one thing my mother cooked well."

"Don't be sad," the chauffeur said. "Europe is going to be hell for a few years. With Hitler and Il Duce gone, the Russians in Germany, and the communists taking over Italy, Europe is finished. You're lucky to be getting out."

"If you feel like that, why don't you go too?"

"I can't. I have a big family here. It's not easy. But believe me, I would if I could."

Bruno nodded. Despite the suit of armor that shielded him from emotion, in which he'd wrapped himself all his life, he felt some sympathy for the chauffeur.

"Listen," the chauffeur said, cupping one hand to his ear, "I hear a truck in the distance. Get back in the car."

Bruno climbed in and shut the door, and the chauffeur was in the driver's seat just as quickly. He started the engine and steered the car back onto the road. The fields of kale were soon behind them.

Next they passed miles of wheat ready to harvest, then cattle and pig farms. There were few vehicles on the road, just the occasional tractor and cyclist. They stopped again for gas. Bruno stayed in the car.

"We've made good time," the chauffeur said. "We will be at the docks in half an hour. Don't go back to sleep."

Genoa was in the distance. As they approached the outskirts of the city, Bruno made out the fortified hill and the Cathedral of San Lorenzo. Small groups of people scurried about, others occupied outdoor tables at several of the bars that lined the street. As they drove closer, he saw mules laden with goods and the funicular railways that climbed the hillsides. The city looked inviting. Maybe someday he'd return.

They reached the port by sunset, ending their day of travel with a view of the Mediterranean reflecting the red and purple sky. A guard at the harbor gate beckoned them to stop, but once seeing the diplomatic plates, he waved them through. The car accelerated again, through a complicated maze that ended at the far end of the port.

The chauffeur turned around in his seat and whispered, "Stay in the car. Under no circumstances get out. This place is infested with Italian police and secret police and God knows who. We don't want any trouble." He pushed his hand around the edge of the seat. "I need your file."

Bruno passed the file to the chauffeur. What's the worst that could happen? The Germans, having surrendered, would hardly be pursuing him as a deserter or for not returning an army truck. He had never killed anyone at the camps, let alone ever laid a hand on any of the prisoners.

To the right lay the *Giovanna*. To the left, another vessel of the same fleet, the *Santa Fe*. Nighttime settled along the poorly lit docks. A few sailors and port workers approached, looked at the car, waved at Bruno and walked on. After about fifteen minutes, the chauffeur came back down the gangway with a man in naval uniform. They were two shadows, and the one belonging to the chauffeur signaled Bruno to lower the window.

"This is one of the ship's officers, Second Officer Rodriguez. He will take you aboard now. I will get your case from the trunk."

Out of the car, Bruno took his case from the chauffeur and shook his hand. The chauffeur lingered a moment, and when it became obvious that there would be no tip, he shrugged irritably and returned to the driver's seat. Again, Bruno was mindful of his failure to reward a man for his work. Friendliness could only be sustained, it seemed, with a little cash. He followed Rodriguez up the gangway, turning for a moment to see the Mercedes coast back toward the main gate.

"Welcome aboard, Herr Fernandez. I will take you to your berth. You may be lucky. You were due to share your cabin with another passenger, but he has not arrived yet. If he is not here within the next hour, we will sail without him."

"Excuse me, my name is Franzmann. Bruno Franzmann." Panic struck. "Has there been a mistake?"

"Well, according to your file, you're Bruno Fernandez." Rodriguez smiled. "You better get used to that from now on. You're not the first who couldn't remember his own name."

Maybe the new name was a boon. No one cared who Bruno was. His name meant nothing to anyone. His only true identifiers were his wealth, which was secret, and his lame foot. He would have both no matter where he went, and no matter what he was called. And being called Fernandez would improve the odds of keeping his hoard. Perhaps as his fortune grew, people would forget about his foot.

16

Bruno's home for the next several weeks was minuscule, maybe ten feet by seven with bunk beds and a small closet, a narrow table affixed to the wall, and a stool. There was a communal bathroom somewhere along the corridor. Rodriguez hadn't mentioned it. Locking his cabin door made Bruno feel more at ease. He sat down for a long minute to catch his breath. Somehow, he felt as though he'd taken a shot to the stomach.

His practicality, as usual, brought him around again. Time to unpack. One metal coat hanger, barely strong enough to bear the weight of his heavy overcoat, hung on a peg, but Bruno took a chance. He had few clothes, and there was more than enough room for them. His case took up much of the space in the closet, but the door closed. The bunk wasn't made—there was a pillow, a blanket, and a sheet neatly folded on each of the two berths. He opted for the lower one, and set himself the task of making it. He looked at his watch. If no one else arrived within the next twenty minutes, he'd have the cabin to himself.

He wiped the perspiration from his brow. It was hot. There was no air in the cabin, and no porthole to open. He heard the loud clanking of machinery, maybe a generator or the engines warming up. Then noises in the corridor, footsteps. Was this his cabin mate? The footsteps continued past his door. Relief.

"Bruno Fernandez. Bruno Fernandez. Bruno Fernandez," he repeated to himself.

Maybe he should have given the chauffeur a tip. When he handed Bruno his case, he'd also given him the bag of leftover food stowed in the car's trunk. The noise became greater. He looked at his watch. It was already eight o'clock. No need to stay in his cabin until nine. On the other hand, he didn't want to leave until he knew whether or not he would have a traveling companion.

Movement. The noise of the engines became louder. Maybe the journey had begun. Bruno left his cabin and retraced his steps. The stairway ended at a steel door that opened to the outer deck. Several other men stood at the railing, watching in silence as the ship pulled away from its moorings. They stared out at Genoa and waved their goodbyes to Europe as the shoreline grew smaller in the distance. Bruno rested his arms on the railing and gazed at the receding land, his mind a blank as he focused on the light of the cathedral's steeple.

That light spelled Europe to him, and with his gaze fixed on the sight, the moaning and clanging of the ship faded into the background. The light grew smaller and smaller until he could no longer make it out among the smattering of lights on the horizon. After a while, an announcement in German came through on the ship's loudspeaker system: All passengers were to assemble immediately in the main saloon.

Bruno followed the others into a large saloon with tables and chairs and portholes all around. There were only men, and they sat down wherever they found a spare place. No one had instructed them to remain silent, but no one spoke. The only sound was the clanking of the ship's engines. Three more men in naval uniform entered the saloon from behind Bruno and walked to the front. One of them was Rodriguez.

"Good evening," a man in the center said. Bruno guessed him to be in his early forties. "Welcome aboard the *Giovanna*," the man continued. "I am Captain Schneider. This is First Officer Mendoza, and Second Officer Rodriguez. The *Giovanna* is an Italian freighter of the Dodero Shipping line, a joint venture of the Dodero family in Rapello and the Lopez family in Buenos Aires."

Bruno studied his fellow passengers. Where had they come from? He could only imagine what they had done to prompt their escape. He felt them staring, probably wondering the same about him.

"This is not a cruise ship," the captain continued. "We can only offer you the basics. Normally, we only carry a maximum of eighteen passengers, but on this crossing we have forty-six. We were supposed to have fifty. Maybe the others were arrested on the way here—that happens all the time. You are fortunate." The officer folded his arms across his chest. "The Vatican is one of our best clients, and that means you are our prized cargo. There will be three meals every day. Breakfast at eight, lunch at noon, and supper at six. The meals take place here in this saloon, cafeteria style. You will be expected to clean up behind yourselves after each meal. Likewise, there is no one to clean your cabins. We have no entertainment to offer you, but there are a few books over there." He pointed to a bookcase behind him. "There're some playing cards and dominoes, too, but gambling is not allowed. I suggest you take the time to speak Spanish among yourselves."

Bruno looked around to see if he could identify someone who might be a good conversationalist. No one appeared friendly. He sat through the rest of an information-dense orientation with his eyes focused on the naval officers.

✳

The passengers kept mostly to themselves and rarely left their cabins. A few played cards for matchsticks. Bruno looked around for a piano without success. At mealtimes, he took any place available, nodded to his table companions, and ate in silence. The food was basic and certainly not as good as at the monastery, where he'd even put on a few pounds. When the weather was bad, he sat at a table in the saloon and studied an atlas and books about Argentina. He scribbled facts into a notebook that he had taken from the monastery. He had written his name, Bruno Franzmann, in the inside cover but decided he should scratch that out and use Fernandez instead.

When the weather was good, Bruno passed several hours outdoors each day. The deckhands, like the passengers, were rough and unfriendly. They were forever painting some part of the ship, and there was a constant smell of paint, seawater, and disinfectant used to cleanse away the salt. When the ship docked at the various ports en route, Bruno stood by the railing, watching the activity of loading and unloading, more envious than ever of the crew. They were allowed to go ashore for a few hours of pleasure, and often returned with newspapers, which they dropped off in the saloon. The passengers would rush for the papers as if they were gold.

The news was depressing. Germany, since the surrender, was now occupied. The victors had carved up Berlin between them, and the highways of

Europe were congested both with military vehicles and refugees on foot. The camps had been liberated, and Germans working at them had been arrested.

"Thank God I got out in time," Bruno said aloud.

None of his fellow passengers at the table answered. Only the man holding the newspaper nodded, surrounded by Bruno and others reading over his shoulder.

After the newspapers had been picked apart and distributed among the passengers, conversations sometimes opened up, although as reluctantly as oysters. The overall consensus was relief—they had managed to escape. None of them said if they were married or whether they had left any children behind. Bruno thought about his mother, and whether the victors would come down heavily on her on account of her employer, a senior German general. As for his sister, she'd soon be sleeping with an American GI, he speculated, if it meant she'd get a few pairs of stockings or a pack of Pall Malls.

✳

Montevideo looked interesting from the ship's railing, but Bruno pushed aside the strong temptation to go ashore. A fellow passenger had attempted going ashore in Rio and was taken below deck, placed in solitary confinement in a practically airless cell next to the engine room. There he stayed for nearly a week.

"Next and final stop, Buenos Aires." The captain drew in the salty air and gazed at the open sea. He smiled, and the *Giovanna* pulled away from its berth.

The River Plate was wide, muddy, and disappointing. The next day as they approached the port, Puerto Madero, Bruno looked out toward the city, expecting to see some edifice that would tug at his emotions, something like a Statue of Liberty, but there was none. A few hours later, he stood in line with his fellow passengers, preparing to disembark the ship and begin a new life. He felt conspicuous wearing his suit and heavy overcoat in the midday heat. His first steps on Argentinean soil were unsteady due to his extended time at sea. He showed his passport and entry visa to the immigration officer. Then he ambled through the gates of the port, into the slums of La Boca.

17

IT TOOK LEO FOUR DAYS TO REACH BAGHDAD. WHEN THE CONVOY arrived at the British camp some thirty miles beyond the city, Leo received his orders. He was to remain at the camp, but he managed to sneak out at night and drive to the Hotel Umayyad in central Baghdad, where he met his contact. It wasn't easy to smuggle twenty-plus suitcases of small arms out of the military camp. But with bribes, the mission was accomplished. As the English unit boarded the buses going back to Jerusalem, Leo smuggled twelve young Iraqi Jews aboard dressed as British officers, and with more bribery, arranged for them to be dropped off at a kibbutz close to Jerusalem.

Leo participated in four similar missions over the next couple of months. But once again Leo felt bored and underemployed. He heard a rumor that Winston Churchill had sent a telegram to President Roosevelt, suggesting that "the Jews, of all races, have the right to strike at the Germans as a recognizable body." A short time later, on July 3, 1944, the British government consented to the establishment of a Jewish brigade with handpicked Jewish and non-Jewish senior officers. Soon after, the British army gained a new fighting force: The Jewish Brigade Group.

The brigade included several thousand Jewish volunteers organized into three infantry battalions commanded by Brigadier Ernest Benjamin. Through Yitzhak Sadeh, Benjamin had heard of Leo and put in a special request that Leo be transferred to serve under his command. Upon acceptance, Leo was promoted with immediate effect to the rank of major, becoming one of the youngest majors in the British army.

Stunned by his unexpected promotion, Leo burned to tell someone about his news, particularly Elizabeth, but that was impossible. At the officer's mess, Leo checked the mail and sat alone at a corner table to contemplate this latest development.

Since the beginning of the war, the Jews had been clamoring for the chance to fight the Nazis as a separate unit within the British army. For the duration of the war, the British had always hesitated about establishing such a unit. However, as the defeat of Germany became more a reality with the fall of Berlin, and as the extent of the Nazi atrocities had begun to be uncovered, Churchill decided to push through, over the objections of others, the establishment of the Jewish Brigade.

A new army was forming, with the clear goal of defeating the Nazis, but in the long term it could mean far more. Organized militarily, the Zionists could realize their wish—the formation of a new state. Leo didn't know how to feel about this. He sipped his coffee and closed his eyes. He remembered living alone on the kibbutz, watching whole families arrive together. Then, for the first time, his old feelings of resentment and loss unclenched. He felt renewed hope, the hope of seeing his family again. This time, in Palestine. In peace.

Within a few days, Major Leo Bergner was back in Egypt, this time at Burg-el-Arab, between El Alamein and Alexandria, where he joined five thousand other officers and men for training in the combat-ready Jewish Brigade. Leo stood proudly with his golden Star of David on his blue shoulder patch as Brigadier Benjamin, in a speech to the officers, announced, "This is the first official Jewish fighting force since the fall of Judea to the Roman legions."

On October 31st, 1944, the ships left Alexandria. Its passengers were on their way to take on an enemy that had as one of its prime policies the destruction of their people. The crossing was rough, interrupted by heavy storms and harsh winds that tossed Leo and his fellow fighters around their cabins. No one ate, but almost everyone reported to the mess for meals, just to get out of their cabins when the captain said it was safe. A few tried to eat hunched over their plates, holding it steady between their elbows, and clutching cups of coffee that were at best one-quarter full.

"How are the eggs?" Leo asked one of the privates, who in spite of being pale with seasickness scooped a forkful of scrambled egg toward his mouth.

"Fucking awful," the young man replied, his eyes half-closed.

"And the coffee?"

"Fucking shit-colored piss," he answered.

The private looked up and saw that he was talking to an officer. His face went paler, and he stood upright, letting his plate and mug slide off the end of the mess table. He saluted.

"Sir."

Leo picked up the spilled plate and cup, staggered across the 45-degree floor to the mess line, and got the private some more eggs.

"Here," Leo said. He sat down across from the man with his own partial cup of coffee. "You're braver than I am. Are you eager to fight the Nazis?"

"I'm going to be two-stone lighter when we get where we're going. But I'll still put a bullet between the eyes of the first German bastard I see."

"If I don't beat you to it." Leo realized he was mashing his teeth so tight his molars ached.

It was a relief to finally reach Taranto, Italy. From Taranto, the brigade traveled north in convoy to Fiuggi, a liberated town fifty miles south of Rome, where they established a base. Before the war Fiuggi had been a spa, but now it was deserted, and the town's many hotels served as barracks for the troops. A bottling plant nearby became headquarters. It was winter, and the Italian front was quiet.

Near a window looking out on the growing snowdrifts, Leo sat down to write a letter.

Dear E.,

The training camp is a two-hour march from Fiuggi, but there the British are teaching the brigade about house-to-house and street fighting, platoon attacks, river crossings, signaling, decoding and mine laying. The courses are rigorous. So rigorous that Brigadier Benjamin has been admonished by the War Office for being too tough on us. But I'm holding up—the brigadier's ruthlessness is a necessity of wartime, even though I wonder if he's as tough in civvy street and whether I'd want to spend any time with him when the war is over. Probably not.

Anyway, my love, Fiuggi is a Jewish enclave now, and the brigade's blue and white flag flies daily over the town's main square.

Trucks with the Star of David fill the narrow streets. Nevertheless,
the novelty is wearing off—being holed up for endless weeks in
a remote muddy Italian resort without you is beginning to grate
on my nerves. I am also aware of being close to Nice, with all the
dreaded uncertainty that it invokes, and I find I cannot think
about it too much or I will never sleep.
    Love,
    Leo

❋

Military strategy finally decreed that the British Eighth Army, of which the Jewish Brigade was a part, should make a series of thrusts to confront the German Army under Field Marshall Kesselring. The Brigade was given the task of crossing the Senio River. The men bid farewell to Fiuggi and traveled northward in convoy, enthusiastic about finally having an opportunity to face the enemy. In March of 1945, the brigade took up their positions outside Ravenna and at the front. Leo's chance of seeing combat duty had arrived.

The war was soon coming to a close. Both sides were tired, and the German army could smell defeat with the arrival of the Allies on European soil, Allies who came in large numbers. Rumors of massive desertions and the hysterical German military propaganda, intercepted by British intelligence, indicated a breakdown in the enemy's control of the situation. A German surrender was imminent.

Leo weathered the convoy and new encampment with patient resolve. He understood that he was a soldier now. He accepted a soldier's distance from his own self when fulfilling orders. Days slipped by in which he reflected upon almost nothing, and instead passed the hours talking to the other officers about nothing or anything. War stories followed the personal ones. Leo felt that he had fought on every front of every battle, and that at night, his dreams were the dreams of other men. Perhaps they were all the same dream.

The Germans shelled them often. They were no more than a half-mile or so across the Senio River. The air was always misty from smoke, and the grating whistle of incoming shells and subsequent blasts became almost routine. Or the men had numbed themselves to it. Their hearing dulled. They sat around playing cards and retelling endless war stories, perspiring in their winter uniforms, and waiting for the signal to begin the final offensive of the Italian campaign. The wait seemed never-ending.

One afternoon, a soldier drove a three-ton truck into the makeshift workshop for urgent repairs. Leo walked over to him.

"What's the matter with it?" Leo asked

"The clutch, the brakes, the electrics. It's in a mess, sir. We need to get it repaired quickly. We're using it to pick up Jewish refugees along the roadside and drive them to the coast for transportation to Palestine. They need to get the hell out of here."

Leo got behind the wheel, reversed the truck out of the shop, and parked it in the camp's driveway. It stank of leaking fuel, and he saw for himself that the clutch and brakes were in poor shape. He felt as though he ought to know more about car maintenance, then he could contribute, in at least some small way, to the evacuation of Jewish refugees. Then he told himself it wasn't his purview, and he shouldn't feel guilt. He returned the truck to the soldier and gave the order to have it fixed and to make it a priority.

Stories of the cruelties began to circulate, about the extermination camps and the sheer numbers massacred. Stories of the gas ovens into which men and women, even children, had been herded. Stories of dead bodies piled high like mountains of garbage, of crying babies thrown into the air and used as target practice by bored German soldiers, the mothers held at gunpoint, forced to watch. Stories of women raped by camp guards and of men and women falling dead on the ground from malnutrition, disease, or exhaustion. The men listened to these accounts, stunned and horrified. They sat in despondent, angry silence. And just half a mile away were the perpetrators.

Wireless Officer Goodman walked into the room, clearly rattled.

"What's the matter?" Leo asked.

"You may want to hear this. I've just taken it down." He read from a pad he was carrying. "This is what we've just picked up on the wireless. German propaganda. *It is sad to see how much the English people have deteriorated that they have sent a Jewish flatfoot brigade to fight in Italy against an Aryan army. The German people can be assured that the Jews will never fight. They will run at the sight of our Aryan Wehrmacht.*"

This outrage—this insult—was too much. Leo's thoughts focused on action. There had to be more to do than deal with broken trucks and trading stories. He pushed past Wireless Officer Goodman and went to find his superior, Colonel Travers.

The colonel was leaning against a truck, smoking his pipe. A career officer, he'd been seconded to the brigade and was popular among the men. He'd earned the Military Cross earlier in the war for defusing unexploded bombs during the Battle of Britain. The wife he'd left behind in England was Jewish, so he had considerable empathy for the men in his unit.

As Leo approached, the colonel took the pipe from his mouth. The two men exchanged salutes.

"Sir, I have a request," Leo began. "The Germans will never expect us to mount a daytime raid. Let me take a few men to the German encampment. It's chancy, but there's no shortage of soldiers here who want to get at the Nazis."

"Major Bergner," Travers said. "I can sympathize with your men's restlessness, and how you must feel toward our enemy. In all honesty, I share those feelings. But you are asking to do something quite irregular. And something you know I cannot approve. In any official capacity, that is." His stern face began to loosen, and he winked. "Of course, when attacked, any of us are compelled to fight back."

"I'll be the one who decides when we're attacked," Leo muttered.

"Proceed as you choose," Travers said, resuming the staunch persona of a colonel. "But understand—this conversation never took place."

Leo approached each of the men assigned to his unit and in turn described his idea. The response was overwhelming. Within a couple of hours, he had assembled two dozen volunteers. Leo sat up through the night and talked with his men, discussing every aspect of the plan. Like Leo, they were all determined to get revenge.

✳

The next morning before sunrise, three of Leo's recruits left camp on patrol to establish a myth that they were attacked. Fifteen minutes later, the rest of the squad followed the agreed route, with bayonets fixed and ready, into the woods toward the German encampment. They crossed the river where it had become a shallow ditch, then approached a clearing. A light drizzle floated down from the morning's gray mist.

As the enemy camp came into view, Leo was surprised to see it so peaceful. The squad halted and surveyed the scene ahead. A couple of outdoor lanterns flickered, casting eerie glows across the quiet and seemingly empty farmyard. No sign of any German soldiers. The enemy was still asleep.

"We should toss grenades," Corporal Cohen said. "Then fire through the smoke."

"No." Leo put out his hand to hold back the troops. "We have the advantage of surprise." Motioning to the rest, he urged everyone to stay low in the tall grass. "Creep in quickly, but carefully, and get as many as we can before more are alarmed. Don't fire until absolutely necessary. Then throw grenades all you want."

His men silently nodded, and Leo gave the order to move out. Crouched and clutching their rifles, the squad scurried across the clearing and hopped over a fence. The horizon glowed orange as the day's first light approached.

They made the final dash, around one side, and clung to the farmhouse. Leo noticed an open window and silently motioned to it, calling for two others to join him, and for the rest to gather near the front door and wait. Leo climbed in through the open window.

On the floor, three German soldiers were sprawled out on their field blankets. Two never woke beyond their dying moans of bayonet wounds, but the third scrambled to his feet.

"Scheisse!" He lunged to the baluster of a staircase and shouted, "Wacht auf! Engländer sind hier."

The front door burst open and Corporal Freedman plunged his bayonet into the noisy swine.

A clatter of boot steps scattered across the upstairs floor.

Leo looked to Cohen and nodded, giving the okay for grenades. Cohen had already pulled the pin. He tossed his grenade up the stairs and the old house rocked from the blast. Half the squad stormed upward and a volley of gunshots followed.

More Germans flowed from the kitchen, half-dressed and scrambling to reach their rifles. Leo and his men cut them down with bayonets, not once, not twice, but stabbing the bastards six or more times, erasing any chance of surviving their wounds. In minutes, ten Nazis were dead on the floor.

Glass shattered and the zing of a bullet passed Leo, striking Corporal Jacobs. He cried out and dropped to one knee, clutching his shoulder.

Freedman rushed to his aid while Leo and others hurried to one side of the broken window, out of the sniper's aim.

Cohen, brave as he was, peered out and spotted the sniper in the window of a shack across the farmyard. "I got him." He crouched and used the lower window frame to steady his rifle, patiently sighting down the barrel, waiting for the German bastard to pop up and take another shot. The only shot was the bullet the Nazi took in the head.

Leo gathered the troops and they advanced into the farmyard. They showered the shack with grenades and exchanged fire with the few remaining Germans. The squad checked the shack, then back at the farmhouse, they checked closets and the cellar for any further resistance and reported back to Leo that all was clear. Their operation was complete inside an hour, and they had wiped out eighteen Nazis with only Corporal Jacob's injury to his shoulder, which he would survive.

The Jews had killed the Germans. And Leo enjoyed it. Killing anything, even an annoying fly buzzing around his face, was something Leo could not bring himself to do, and to harm another person was unthinkable. But not with these vermin. Staring down into the open eyes of his dead enemy, Leo felt only hatred. Certainly no shame for his violent acts done that day. No shame for ignoring their howls of innocence, no shame in denying their pleas for mercy.

"Should we bury them?" one of the men asked.

"No." Leo felt the full force of his contempt. "Leave them to rot."

Corporal Cohen reached into his pocket. He pulled out a square of white cloth cut from a bedsheet. Several of the men broke into smiles.

"What is it?" Leo asked.

"Our flag, sir." Cohen held up the piece of cloth by two of its edges.

The Star of David was crudely painted in blue on the cloth. A flag. Their flag.

"Attach it to a German rifle," Leo said. "Then get on the roof and tie it to the chimney."

The men poured out of the farmhouse to watch Cohen climb ivy clinging to the stone chimney and reach the roof. He cinched a rope around the rifle and their little flag fluttered in the wind. The squad faced it, stood at attention, and saluted.

*

"Major Bergner," Colonel Stanton said. "I need to talk with you urgently."

Leo sprang up from his cot where he had immediately collapsed upon returning from the German attack two hours earlier. Depending on the outcome, the possibility of reprimand was a calculated risk, so it was not a complete surprise, but he had not expected a visit from Colonel Stanton, the one officer he feared most, and the one hardest to read.

Stanton was a loner. He was rarely seen socializing with fellow officers, and when addressing troops, all exchanges were limited to official business only. He remained strangely remote from the shared hardships of wartime, leaving that burden for the men he commanded.

"Major Bergner." The man's voice was steady and calm. "What you and your men did this morning, unofficially, was brilliant. But I'm here in an official capacity. There can be no repeat of what happened today. We are part of the Eighth Army and we must conduct ourselves accordingly. Your conduct was, by the book, disgraceful."

"Yes, sir, I understand." Leo stood with great care not to seem arrogant. "However, you should know that even if I'm not personally involved, others will continue similar attacks. The men are restless and angry. Less than half a mile away were men who worshipped a manifesto targeted to annihilate us. What can you expect of us, sir?"

"Major Bergner, I'm well aware that there will be revenge squads, and to the best of my ability, I'm going to look the other way." He pulled a stool closer and sat down. "My thinking is that you could become involved in more useful efforts on behalf of the European Jews."

"What is that, sir?"

"Instead of seeking revenge," he said, then lowered his voice to a whisper, "why not work for Berihah?"

Leo was surprised at the suggestion. Berihah was the organized effort to help Jews escape from Europe to Palestine.

"These poor people." Colonel Stanton lit a cigarette and then, as an afterthought, offered one to Leo. "These people who have suffered so much cannot leave legally. They need to be helped. Again, we'll turn a blind eye and the Americans will help."

"I don't know, sir." Leo accepted the colonel's lighter. When the colonel waved for him to sit, Leo obeyed. "Of course, it sounds important and obviously I want it to succeed, but—"

"Listen, Major, the war is about to end. We have received word that after the enemy surrenders, which should be any day now, we will be stationed in Tarviso, near the borders of Italy, Yugoslavia and Austria. Believe me, our boys are going to play a key role in the work of Berihah."

"Sir, please understand, I've just had a taste of killing our enemies firsthand. Not from a tank, in the distance, against another tank. I've come face to face with these swine. I've seen the color of their eyes. I've watched them piss in their pants. I've heard them howl that they weren't Nazis, that the Jews were never their enemies. I've heard them scream about their wives and children back home. I've heard them beg for their lives. And, sir, I liked it."

Colonel Stanton nodded sympathetically. Leo tapped ash from his cigarette.

"We have to do something, sir," Leo continued. "Can't you understand? It's impossible for us to sit, day after day, awaiting some development, with these scum so close and knowing what they've done to innocent women, children, and men. I never thought I could kill anyone. I never thought that I was capable of such intense hatred. Believe me, sir, my behavior has shaken me too. Now it is our turn, sir."

"But," Stanton countered, "you're a commissioned officer in the British army. If you receive an order forbidding you to take part in any more of these revenge expeditions, you must obey it."

"Sir, I hear what you say, but please understand, I'm also a Jew. And something else, sir. I have deliberately kept my private life to myself. Right now I have no idea about my own family in Europe. I don't know whether they're dead or alive. How many miles am I from Nice, my home? Or was it my home? Where do I belong?"

"Major." Colonel Stanton crossed his legs and looked around the room. "I sympathize with you. But we are in the military. We have to obey orders and live by the book. There can be no more killing sprees like today."

Staring at the dusty floor, Leo muttered the only acceptable response. "Yes, sir."

"I'm sorry about your family," Stanton said, his tone softer. "It is true, these are difficult times for us Jews."

Leo studied the colonel's face. "You're Jewish? But then you should understand, of all people."

"I realized long ago, to have a successful career in the military, it was best not to wear my Jewishness on my sleeve. So I buried my background, up until the formation of the Jewish Brigade. If it was good enough for Major Edmund de Rothschild to serve with us, believe me, it was good enough for Maurice Steinberg, now Stanton, to come out into the open. Still you must ask yourself what it means for you, having chosen to serve in the British military. I wouldn't deny you or myself our heritage, but I would counsel you to make the best use of these opportunities. Right or wrong, a revenge squad is a bold move that is sure to draw attention. And more importantly, and give this some thought—does it really serve any useful purpose to dwell on your need for revenge?"

✳

Early the next morning, Leo was awakened by a corporal and escorted— practically frog-marched while still half-asleep—to see Brigadier Benjamin. He'd had limited contact with the brigade's commander. From what he had observed, the brigadier was the quintessential British army officer. He was also known to be tyrannical, and prone to temper tantrums.

"Sit down, Major."

Leo sat and looked straight across at his commanding officer. Behind Brigadier Benjamin's desk, a map of Europe was taped to the wall. Leo resigned himself to a court-martial. He expected it now, but to a large extent, he was beyond caring. His only regret was that the news would reach the De Solas.

"Major Bergner, I'm very concerned. You're a good officer and a credit to the Brigade. But what you did, and from your discussion with Colonel Stanton, I'm afraid that you've become a loose cannon."

Leo looked directly into the eyes of his commander. He had nothing to say and was certain the Brigadier expected no response.

"Colonel Stanton and I have serious doubts as to whether you're going to restrain yourself from any more of these foolish and irresponsible exercises. They're dangerous. We may lose men, and achieve what? Nothing, that is, other than a temporary feeling of exhilaration and gratification. I'm going to ask you one straight question. Can you give me your word that you will not embark on any more of these sorties?"

"No, sir," Leo answered without pausing to consider the question. "I cannot, in all good faith, give you that assurance."

"Well, thank you for such a candid answer." The Brigadier's expression showed no reaction. "It was, of course, the answer I expected. I'm afraid I cannot have you serve here any longer. I do not wish to see you, one of our most talented and distinguished officers, end up doing something that could get you court-martialed. Nor do I want the responsibility of worrying about what you're up to when we have more important matters to confront. I've spoken with the War Office. You're being transferred to the 32nd Guards Brigade in the Guards Armored Division in Holland. Your language skills and combat experience are needed there."

"Are you serious, sir? Is this an order?"

"Yes, it is. You are needed there, and frankly, I can't take the risk of having you here."

Leo took a deep breath and closed his eyes for a moment.

"And when am I to report to the Guards Brigade in Holland, sir?"

"You will take a jeep and are expected there in one week. You will have to take a circuitous route that's been mapped out for you, and you'll have supplies for the journey."

"When do I leave, sir?" Leo looked down at the floor.

"Within the hour."

"Sir, may I ask a favor of you? The route that I'm to take to Holland, can I go via Nice? I'd like to see what I can find out about my family there."

"Colonel Stanton told me of your family situation. I'm sympathetic. Talk to him before you leave and if your wish can be accommodated, then you have my consent. I will arrange for you to have an additional three days to make it to Holland. But it all depends on the logistics of the route you need to take. Bear in mind that sporadic fighting is still taking place. I have no desire to lose you in that way to the war effort."

"Thank you, sir." Leo stood and saluted.

18

Nice looked desolate. Shops and restaurants were boarded up, and few people were out and about. The sky was gray, and the sea looked forbidding. A youth on a cycle rode by and nodded, but there were no other people to be seen. Leo drove to the apartment building where he had lived just a few years earlier and parked the jeep.

Leo nervously approached the familiar door and looked at the names next to the doorbells. Kaplan was still there. He looked at the other names. Most of them were familiar. He rang the doorbell, firmly. No reply. He waited and rang it a second time. The same result. He rang the bell of a neighbor. No reply. After a few more attempts, he gave up and walked back to the jeep.

He headed toward La Promenade des Anglais and to Jacques's pharmacy. The building was boarded up. Then he drove to the synagogue and saw that it was in ruins, burned down. Leo pulled up at a brasserie in the army jeep. As he entered, customers stopped talking and stared at him. He walked to the telephone on the wall and dialed his family's attorney, Maitre Talais, who managed his father's and cousin's real estate investments, and the one person his mother had instructed Leo to contact were he to fear the worst.

"He is a friend of my family," Leo explained to the receptionist. "I will come straight to your office."

When Leo arrived, Maitre Talais greeted him at the door. He was an aged man, short, and dressed in a gray three-piece suit with cigarette ash all over the lapels. His fingers were brown with nicotine. He stood back to admire Leo and beamed with joy.

"Leo Bergner, how wonderful to see you." Maitre Talais invited Leo inside. "My, you look handsome in that British uniform. A major, too. I am still the old man who attended parties at the Levy home, though you probably do not remember me. Mon Dieu. Come into my office."

Leo sat as Maitre Talais cleared away some papers on his chair before sitting at his desk. Leo felt good to be in the glow of the old man's warmth. And the old man must have news of his family.

"These have been terrible years, Leo. Terrible." Maitre Talais sighed. "Between the Germans, the Italians, and the Vichy government, we have had a miserable existence."

"The last letter from my mother was a considerable time ago." Leo hoped he did not sound as paper-thin as he was feeling. "She told me to be in contact with you. I have just come from the apartment. It seems as if the whole building has been abandoned."

"Leo, can I offer you a cigarette or a drink? A cognac, perhaps?"

Maitre Talais's eyes danced around the room, seeming to be embarrassed. The look of dread in Leo's face must have been plain. Or maybe it was the knowledge that the man held. Leo shook his head. Maitre Talais poured himself a drink and rubbed his lips.

"Leo, I have some bad news for you. The police rounded up most of the Jews in Nice and took them to a holding camp near Aix. From there they went by train to Paris, to Drancy. And from there it is believed they were put on trains and sent to the East. I'm afraid that we must expect the worst."

Leo felt a sickness in his stomach, and his vision turned blurry. He said nothing. He was not surprised.

"And Jacques and Karin too," he whispered.

"I'm afraid so."

"And Rabbi Aaron, the Bernheims and Monsieur Laidler from the hotel and Monsieur Levy?" Leo asked, his voice rising in a crescendo of ever more horrified whispers.

"All of them, I'm so sorry. They were all my friends. My wife and I begged your parents and Jacques and Karin to leave."

Without asking again, Maitre Talais poured Leo a drink. He pushed the tumbler toward Leo and nodded in encouragement. Leo emptied the tumbler and sat clutching it in bewilderment.

"How long will you be in Nice, Leo?"

"I have to report to my new unit in Holland in five days."

"The last time I saw your parents." The old man leaned forward, rested his face on his folded hands, and looked straight ahead at Leo. "And Jacques and Karin, was when my wife and I went to their apartment for dinner. We discussed much that night. They made me promise I would look after everything for you. That I should treat you, in the event of them not returning, as my own son."

Leo bit his lip and nodded. Tears ran over his face. He made no attempt to conceal or wipe them away.

"That was what they demanded of me. And I will not let them down," Maitre Talais said gently. "My wife is Jewish, you know. Italian. Some of her family also, we fear, perished in Auschwitz. I will explain everything to you." Maitre Talais handed Leo a pad and pen. "You may want to take some notes."

In an office that was chaotic with books and piled papers, the man quickly put his desktop into a marvelous display of order. He seated himself on Leo's side of the desk and placed his hands on his knees. Leo squared the pad on his knee. He saw the man's point. Writing would be easier. He could react with his hand and pen rather than his heart.

"Leo, your parents, Jacques, and Karin all made wills. You are their sole beneficiary. If we are to assume that they have perished, you will inherit a reasonable sum. The apartment will be yours, too. I visit it every so often to see that it is okay and that no one has broken in. I have had additional locks put on all the doors. I can take you there tomorrow, if you would like, before you leave."

Leo nodded, scribbling now some of the things he wanted to know. Then he looked up at the man. Maitre Talais smiled.

"The pharmacy has been closed for some time. So there is no business anymore. But as you know, Jacques and your father and I were partners in a number of properties. We each owned a third. There were nine properties in total, including the pharmacy and the apartments above. We were lucky to have been able to buy that building."

He plucked a cigarette from a wooden box by the lamp, and with a precise flick of his wrist, removed his lighter from his vest pocket and produced a flame in one gesture. Leo declined the offer to join him in the smoke.

"In my other office, I have the files of all the properties, the bank statements, and the rent books. You are welcome to see whatever you wish."

"Thank you, Maitre Talais. I trust you totally."

"Thank you." He drew on his cigarette, as if he needed the smoke to permeate his brain for clearer thought. He exhaled, nodding. "Some of our tenants have not been able to pay, on account of the war, but I took no action. They are all good people. As soon as circumstances change, they will resume their rents. We may have to forego the back rent, but we were lucky to have covered all the mortgages with the rents we did receive. So we are not in any danger of losing properties."

"That is good." Leo's notes were a block of neatly written but unintelligible text. "It is so much for me to absorb, Maitre Talais."

"I understand. Of course." He took another drag and set himself on track again. "Karin and your mother had some jewelry. That is in the safe in this office, in an envelope identifying it as theirs."

"The only piece of jewelry my mother had that would still interest me is an emerald pendant that she loved. My grandmother gave it to her. Anyway, that went years ago."

"Well, there are a few pieces."

"Maitre Talais." Leo thought of Elizabeth and the jewels her mother had worn that first dinner. "Once the war is finally over, I may want to marry, then of course I would like my wife to have that jewelry."

"Naturally. Next, there are some bank balances. When it looked as if the authorities would place a freeze on Jewish bank accounts, your father and Jacques transferred their money to Switzerland, to a bank in Zurich. They were lucky to do that. I have the details. When you can, you should go to Zurich and see the bank there. Of course, it is a numbered account. I have power of attorney on the account, and you are a named beneficiary."

"Yes, I will go."

"Now, about the properties. Assuming the worst, you and I are now partners, with you owning two-thirds." He stubbed the cigarette out in a discreet ashtray by the chair. "What would you like to do with the properties? My advice is that we should keep them. Once the war is finally over, the Riviera will return to its former glory, and we will see them appreciate greatly in value. Their value now, given the war, is rock bottom. Now is not the time to sell, now is the time to buy, but alas…"

"Whatever you advise, Maitre Talais. You have been so kind and a wonderful friend to my family. Thank you."

Leo felt a moment of embarrassment. Try as he might, though, Leo simply could not convey his sincerity. He only felt self-conscious and wished to be alone. He slapped the pad on the desk and stood up. Maitre Talais rose and offered his hand.

"I gave your parents my word. And besides, Leo, we will be friends. Your young life has seen too many upheavals, and despite it all, you are as good a man as both your father and cousin. And we will hope to be reunited with them, if that is God's will."

✳

At six o'clock the next morning, Leo met Maitre Talais at the apartment building. Leo stood on the deserted sidewalk while the old man struggled to find the correct key. A riot of emotions stirred within Leo as they crossed the threshold and climbed the stairs. The interior was dark with no light bulbs in the hallways.

"The caretaker comes to the building once every two weeks," Maitre Talais explained, "and, as all the occupants have left the Riviera, the light bulbs haven't been replaced. They're very hard to find these days."

Leo stood outside the door of the apartment for an awkward moment. Then Maitre Talais offered Leo the keys.

"Lock up when you leave. I shall go to the cafe on the corner for a coffee and a brioche. Come whenever you're ready."

Leo waited until the man's footsteps had receded down the stairs, then he pushed the door open. The lights in the apartment still worked. The drawing room, with the family photographs on the piano, and the familiar paintings on the wall, looked the same as the day Leo had left. He sat at the piano and let his hands stroke the keys. He rose and went into the kitchen and dining room. Nothing had changed. How long had it been empty? It seemed as if he had been there just the day before.

Where next, his bedroom, his parents' bedroom, or Jacques and Karin's? His feet made the decision for him. He looked at his books, still neatly positioned on the bookshelves, books on military history, on music, and a few comics. He opened the doors of his parents' clothes closet. All still hanging there, his father's suits and his mother's dresses and shoes. Part of him felt that he was intruding.

As he turned to leave, he glanced down at the nightstand and saw his father's gold pocket watch. He picked it up and looked at it, wondering whether to take it with him or put it back. He put it in his pocket and walked toward Jacques and Karin's room. He stood by her dressing table and looked around the room, at the paintings and the Oriental rug that Jacques had bought in Istanbul, and had convinced himself but no one else, that it had been a great bargain.

He went back to the drawing room, sat on a sofa, and stared at the fireplace with the large ornate mirror over the mantelpiece and the onyx and ormolu clock in the middle. He wondered if the key to the clock was still behind it. He could see that it was. He stood and walked over to wind it up, then listened to its familiar ticks, the only sound in the room. He thought of his old metronome. Yes, it was still there, on a table next to the piano.

There was a stillness and sanctity, almost holiness, in the room. He closed his eyes. He could hear his mother's voice, his father talking to Jacques about a tenant, Jacques telling Karin about his day at the pharmacy, and Karin asking what everyone wanted for dinner the next day. Their voices were so clear, and their laughter so present. Where were they now?

✳

The journey from Nice to Holland was arduous. Many of the roads had been badly damaged. Leo stuck to the route given him by Colonel Stanton and managed to avoid crossing too close to enemy lines. The hours spent on the road should have given him time to think, to consider his future, and to make decisions. While these topics crossed his mind, he couldn't focus enough to make any meaningful conclusions.

Leo's arrival in Holland was on schedule. The 32nd Guards Brigade was placed under the command of the First Canadian Army. Their mission was to break through into Germany and destroy all German forces between the Rhine and the Meuse. The roads were heavily mined, and buildings along the frontier had been fortified in preparation for battle, their windows reduced to narrow slits from which to fire at invading enemy troops.

Military intelligence had learned, through interrogation of prisoners taken, that German morale had plummeted. The German army was about to fight, for the first time, on its own soil. Even the lowliest of ranks could smell impending defeat. At the beginning of the onslaught into Germany, the ground was frozen, which made progress easier. But as the days dragged on, the ice began to thaw. The Germans breached the banks of the Rhine, and the whole area flooded, making further progress practically impossible with troops, tanks, and trucks bogged down. The battle continued for several weeks until the US Ninth Army crossed the Ruhr River and advanced to the Rhine, gaining fresh momentum.

Within days, two Allied airborne divisions were dropped behind the German lines and the army crossed the Rhine. Leo gazed at the destroyed buildings and watched townspeople walk the streets in shock. He saw members of the Dutch underground pointing their rifles at German soldiers with hands tied behind their backs. Women had shaved the heads of others suspected of sleeping with German troops. Thousands of German refugees thronged in the streets, and when Leo paused to talk with them in his native tongue, their cringing denials made him want to throw up. He remembered the instructions Colonel Stanton and Brigadier Benjamin had given—abandon any idea of revenge squads. Now would have been a good time for one.

The German port of Bremen still had to be taken. White cloths appeared on almost every building as a sign of surrender, but still many soldiers continued the battle. Leo was summoned to join General Horrocks, the corps commander, and his adjutants in a convoy that sped through the streets to a suburb of Bremen. They arrived at a camp just outside the city. There they discovered an overflowing population of emaciated figures clad in filthy striped pajamas. Most lay about without the energy to move, though some retained the strength to stand, barely, as their haunted stares from sunken eyes focused on the troops entering the camp. The stench of death was overwhelming.

Bewildered by the spectacle, Leo could only stare at the inmates, slowly panning as he took in one anguished face after another, and another. Their eyes told of the horrors of which they could not speak. He wondered if they could comprehend that it was finally over, but their senses had been shattered after years of torture, deprivation, humiliation, and starvation. Leo wanted them to know, to celebrate, there would be no more shrieking of orders, clicking of polished jackboots, work squads, slaps and punches to the face and body. And the most horrifying, the daily march to the crematorium. No longer would they inhale the smoke and fumes from the bodies of their friends and loved ones.

"Major Bergner." General Horrocks came from around the side of a building, wiping his mouth with a handkerchief. "You speak German. You are to take as many men as you need to round up every man, woman and child in the immediate area. Have the men clean and take care of these prisoners, give them food, clothes, and whatever medical supplies they need."

"Yes, sir." The task helped him overcome his own growing sense of nausea.

Hours later, he watched in disgust and also amazement as civilians joined the troops, going about the job of cleaning up and attending to the prisoners mechanically, without any expression of human horror. It was as though they were tending to stray dogs.

Leo walked among the inmates and told them in German that he had served in the Jewish Brigade and had lived in Palestine. Their tears were overwhelming and contagious.

An elderly man was leaning against the wooden barracks. Leo approached and asked his name.

"Maurice Goldfarb, from Berlin, sir," the man answered.

The man's gaze was confused. Leo studied him closely. He had been mistaken. The man was not elderly, perhaps no more than forty.

"I am German, too, Herr Goldfarb. From Augsburg. Shalom."

Goldfarb burst into tears and covered his eyes with both hands. His body shook and his cries were loud. He slipped to his knees. Leo knelt beside him and put his hand on the man's shoulder.

"Herr Goldfarb. It's over now. We will soon have you out of here." Leo observed that the man had difficulty breathing. "The doctor will examine you. You will receive whatever treatment you need." He took his arm and helped him back onto his feet. "What did you do in Berlin before the war, Herr Goldfarb?"

"I was a musician. I played cello with the Berlin Philharmonic. But then, the war." He looked at his hands and slowly stroked each of his fingers, bending them one at a time. "I'll never be able to play again."

"I'm a musician too, of sorts. I play the piano."

Goldfarb did not react. He turned to face the now idle crematorium a few hundred yards away, and stared at it.

"Emile Pearlman, my cousin," he whispered, "was a pianist too. Also with the Berlin Philharmonic." He closed his eyes. "May he rest in peace. May they all rest in peace."

"Amen," Leo answered softly. "Would you like to see the military chaplain, Herr Goldfarb? The British rabbi?"

"No, thank you. I don't need to see the rabbi, or any damned rabbi. What for? Where was God when all this happened? Where was he? How could he?"

"I understand." Leo returned his hand to Goldfarb's shoulder. He shared in the man's fury and confusion. "How could it have happened? Never again, Herr Goldfarb. Never again."

"Please, please, whatever you do in life after all this is over," Herr Goldfarb said, fixing Leo with a stare and beckoning with his hand, "make sure that no people ever have to suffer like this again."

✳

A few days later, Leo received a summons to report immediately to corps headquarters. He was advised of the impending German surrender and that he was to attend in case there was a need for an interpreter. By afternoon, the German officers arrived. They were marched and ordered to stand in front of Horrocks' makeshift quarters.

"I will not have them inside this building," Horrocks ordered his adjutant. "They can stand out in the open air, in a downpour of flaming oil for all I care."

Horrocks stood from his desk and tugged his hat firmly down on his brow. He walked out to face the group, twenty strong, of various ages and ranks. With a corps commander like this, Leo felt proud to be a British officer.

"You are to surrender immediately," General Horrocks announced in a loud voice that left no doubt as to his authority. "Our orders are to be followed meticulously. We shall have no mercy if they are not. I have seen your camps and your bestiality, and neither I nor the Allies have any moral responsibility for you German soldiers. The world will never forgive you for what has happened here."

The German officers stood in silence before him, their faces bearing expressions neither of remorse nor compassion.

Three weeks later, Leo decided it was time to put in for home leave. Approval was given, and he was driven to Celle Airfield, near Bergen-Belsen, and secured a seat on a military plane to an RAF base in Swindon. He was dropped off in town and wasted no time reconnecting with normality.

Leo wandered down a busy street and saw a double-fronted stone building with red geraniums in window boxes. He pushed the door open. The pungent ambience of a typical British pub was unique, a mixture of freshly poured draught beer, cigarette smoke, and the clatter of new barrels being delivered and wheeled in through the tap room and into the back. A few locals sat around a corner table, a solitary man played darts, and a couple of privates stood at the bar exchanging jokes. The elderly landlady smiled at Leo as he approached. A photograph of Winston Churchill was pinned onto the wall behind her.

"What will it be, love?"

"I'll have a pint, thank you. But first, where's your telephone?"

She pointed to a doorway in a far-off corner. He exchanged a cordial nod with the men at the bar as he went to seek out the phone. The contrast with what he had witnessed at Bergen-Belsen and all this normalcy hit him as he dialed the number. The line connected and a female answered. Leo plugged his other ear.

"Mrs. De Sola, it's Leo. How are you?"

"Leo!" she exclaimed. "How are you? Where are you? We've been so worried about you."

"I've written a number of times but it takes forever for letters to get past the censor, so heaven knows how long it takes for them to get to England."

"Where are you?"

"I'm calling from a pub in Swindon. I've been in Germany. I arrived here on an RAF plane two hours ago. How are you all? And how's Elizabeth?"

"She's well. She'll be overjoyed. We all will be to see you."

"Mrs. De Sola, this is awkward. I'm dying to see her, but I've been away for so long. Do you think she will still want to see me? I mean, has anything happened?"

"If you mean has she met anyone else—don't be silly. She's very much in love with you, and you're to get here as quickly as you can."

"Well, that's a relief." He broke out in a broad smile. He'd feared hearing a very different answer. "I was really worried that she might have met someone. After all, I've lost track of how long I've been away. I've missed you all. Very much."

"Will you please tell me when you're coming to London?"

"There's a train leaving in an hour and a half. I should be at your doorstep by half past six."

"We can't wait."

Leo picked up his duffel bag and walked toward the station. It was a sunny afternoon, all blue skies. He admitted to himself that if Elizabeth had in fact moved on with her life, he would have been devastated. He would probably have taken the next available military flight back to Germany.

Leo found it a joy to walk down a civilized high street, without the noise of gunshots and bombs, and be confronted only with smiling faces. He looked in the window of a newsagent and saw the familiar poster of Winston Churchill, sporting his hat and displaying the V-for-Victory sign. On the opposite corner of the street was a florist and he thought of flowers to bring to Elizabeth. Enamored with the idea, he moved to cross the street.

"Look out, sir, look out!" a stranger shouted.

19

THE AMBULANCE ARRIVED QUICKLY AND WITHIN HALF AN HOUR, Leo was in the emergency wing of Swindon General Hospital. The smells and lights accosted him, disturbed him. He moved to rise.

"Stop," a man demanded. "You were knocked down by a truck. You have a slight concussion and a leg injury. Until we x-ray the leg, it's not possible to give you an accurate prognosis. The x-ray will be in a few minutes."

The doctor was well past normal retirement age. He seemed rushed. Leo looked around the ward. Every bed was taken by an injured soldier, with nurses darting back and forth from one to the other.

"Christ. I was on my way to London. I'm on home leave."

"I know," the doctor said. "We checked your papers and notified the 32nd Guards Brigade."

"What happened?"

"Witnesses said that when you crossed the road, instead of looking right, you looked left."

"It was my fault?" Leo asked in disbelief.

"Yes, it appears so." The doctor put his hand on Leo's shoulder and shrugged awkwardly.

"Will I be able to walk?"

"You may have a limp. We'll know more after surgery."

"Doctor, I was due to visit friends in London this evening. They're expecting me."

"Give me their name and number, and I'll call them." He took a pen from his white coat and scribbled down the number on the back of a prescription pad. He shook the pen, irritated that it wouldn't work. "These bloody pens," he muttered. "I haven't had a decent pen since the war broke out."

Later, the doctor returned with news of the x-ray. Leo had suffered a compound fracture of the right tibia and fibula. Leo frowned and looked puzzled.

"The surgeon will insert a titanium nail into your tibia and then it will be screwed in place. The fibula will align itself on its own and will heal in due course. But you'll be here for a week. Then on crutches for a while."

"How long?" Leo winced at the prospect.

"Maybe six to eight weeks. Then you may limp for about three months, but that should clear up. And I called your friends in London to give them the news. They're very worried."

"Thank you, Doctor."

When the doctor left, Leo closed his eyes. It was his first real downtime since he'd been in Nice and then at the concentration camp in Germany with the survivors. Being in a hospital bed, under a white sheet, made him check and recheck his waking state. He lay still and stared at the pale gap around the shade. Slowly, the longer he gazed at it, the more it seemed to produce a sound. He listened past the silence around him. The sound was like a whisper, but he couldn't make out the words.

"Mother?" he said. The cadence of the faint sound certainly could be Ulrike. He smelled something, too, like the smoke of a crematorium.

The voice said something.

"Mother, I don't understand. Where are we?"

"Hello, darling," the voice said.

A cool weight touched his forehead. He continued to stare at the light beyond the shade, but it lost some of its brightness.

"Darling, it's me."

The voice was Elizabeth's. Leo opened his eyes slowly and looked up. She leaned over the bed to kiss him on the forehead, her hair brushing against his cheek. He took in her fragrance, Guerlain. It had been so long.

"And how are you feeling today?" another female asked from the other side of the bed. He turned, but felt a pain shoot up the side of his leg.

"Mrs. De Sola. This is such a wonderful surprise to see you both." He shuddered to rid himself of the image of Herr Goldfarb standing, with a haunted look, staring at the crematorium with Ulrike standing next to him.

"Thank you for coming. I am thrilled to see you again. Forgive me. I was having troubling dreams."

"We came down on the train, and we have to go back in a couple of hours. We've brought you a few things." Elizabeth pointed to a parcel. "We wanted to bring you some fruit and chocolate, but it's quite impossible with food rationing to do anything spontaneously. We either have to accumulate coupons or get them on the black market, and Daddy is so strict about that sort of thing." She picked her bag up from the floor. "Still we've brought you some magazines and two slices of cake."

"How do you feel?" Mrs. De Sola asked.

"To tell you the truth, I feel like a damned fool. I survived El Alamein and the invasion of Holland and Germany, only to be knocked down by a bloody van here in Swindon. I guess I'd forgotten that you British drive on the wrong side of the road."

"Well, that's proof that you've been away far too long," Elizabeth said with a smile. "You're going to have to get used to our British ways again, Major."

"I've spoken with the doctor here," Mrs. De Sola added. "We wanted you transferred to a hospital in London, but that's not possible. They need to keep you here. However, they will release you next week. Your therapy and weekly checkups over the next couple of months, that you can do in London. So we want you to come and live with us in Connaught Square. We'll come and collect you next week. How's that?"

"Mrs. De Sola, you're very kind. That would be wonderful."

The hour passed quickly. Mostly, Leo listened to their chatter about London, Mr. De Sola's colleagues at the bank, Holly, Mr. Churchill, and the horrors of wartime rationing. He basked in their concern for his wellbeing, and throughout their visit, never let go of Elizabeth's hand.

✳

A week later, Leo hobbled on crutches up the steps to the De Sola's front door. It was a crisp afternoon, chilly but with clear blue skies. It felt good to be back in London and crossing the threshold into Elizabeth's home. She helped him out of his scarf and coat, and let him steady himself on her shoulder. The house was not much warmer than outside, but the effort to climb the stairs quickly overheated him.

In the drawing room, Mr. De Sola pointed to a decanter of cognac on a side table and invited Leo to have a glass.

"No thank you, not just yet." Leo smiled. "I'm wobbly enough already on these damned crutches."

He looked over at the piano. Elizabeth noticed.

"There'll be plenty of time for you to catch up," she said and smiled. "I bet you haven't played in a long time."

"You're right. I haven't."

"Well, we're going to have plenty of musical soirees now that you're back, my darling. Lots of bright and cheerful music, that's what we all need." She kissed him on the cheek, then giggled as one of his crutches fell to the floor.

That evening over dinner, Mr. De Sola pressed Leo to talk about the war, and of how he had spent the time since they were last all together.

"And your family in France, what news?" Mr. De Sola asked.

"I have no definite news as to whether they are dead or alive." Leo felt a burning around his eyes and closed them for a moment. "It doesn't look good. The Jewish community in Nice was taken to camps inland, then put on trains to Drancy, and from there transported east to labor camps. From what we are hearing, most did not survive."

He didn't elaborate on the camps, and the others did not probe. Elizabeth moved her chair closer and held his hand. He squeezed it for confidence.

"When I left Italy, en route to Holland, I spent a night in Nice and met with our family attorney there. He was also a partner with my father and cousin in a number of real estate investments. We discussed everything, but pretty much on the basis that my family perished."

The image of his parents' apartment in Nice came back into view. Everything there was still in place. Just as they must have left it. An empty silent neatness.

"Well, we're your family, Leo," Mrs. De Sola said. "Never forget that."

"Would you excuse me if I went to bed?" Leo struggled to stand. "I'm very tired," he said, but it was not his only reason to leave the table. He didn't want to become overly emotional in their presence.

Elizabeth helped Leo up, handed him his crutches, and took him upstairs to his bedroom.

"Good night, darling. Sleep well."

She hesitated at the doorway. Leo, too, was unclear whether he really wanted to be alone. His eyes searched hers. Her gaze was firm and brave.

Under her delicate features, she was still tireless and dedicated and deeply in love with him. She kissed him on the lips and wished him goodnight.

✳

The next two months passed quickly. Elizabeth still worked in Whitehall, and Mr. De Sola kept busy at his city office. Leo spent his time at the house, playing the piano, reading, and talking with Mrs. De Sola. He often walked with her in Hyde Park, stopping for coffee at the quaint little shop on Connaught Street still run by the Belgian lady. He would listen to Mrs. De Sola as she chatted with her neighbors, and other women who had sons and husbands serving overseas.

Sometimes Leo would take out his father's pocket watch and daydream until either the waitress or Mrs. De Sola said something to get his attention. As well, the watch would sometimes remind him of his father's Iron Cross. When he thought of his mother's pendant, he would squeeze the watch in his hand and startle himself out of his memories.

One afternoon, he had a visit from his colonel, and Mrs. De Sola served tea in the drawing room. The colonel told him that in view of the final German surrender, and the fact that Leo was still considered unfit to resume military duty, he was to be honorably discharged and once more a civilian. Several weeks later, he received an official thank you from "The King and the Country" for his service.

Leo had mixed feelings. The army had given him security, self-confidence, and pride. He was ill-prepared for civilian life and worried about the adjustment. Soon the crutches were gone, and Leo managed with a cane, then without one, and finally without even a limp. Now healed and a civilian, Leo was restless. He had no idea of what to do with himself.

"Leo," Mr. De Sola said one day at breakfast. "I'm leaving the office early today. Would you like to join me for lunch at my club?"

A few hours later, after an adequate if not particularly delicious meal, Leo walked into the austere reading room with Mr. De Sola and made himself comfortable in a large leather armchair.

"Leo, the war is over and thank God, you've survived. So, do you remember a conversation that we had a long time ago in my study?"

"Mr. De Sola. I would very much like to marry your daughter. I am in love with her, as you know. But I have no job. No career. I have just been

discharged from the army, and whatever capital I have is tied up in France."
Leo gazed at the fire, his eyes fixed on a large log that was about to break in
half. "Until Maitre Talais obtains the appropriate documentation from the
French authorities to confirm the deaths of my family, he can do nothing
with their estates. So, I am penniless, though I intend to look into the
accounts in Zurich."

"Leo, my bank has connections throughout Europe. In fact, we have an
investment in a bank in Geneva. We expect that now the war is over, the
bank will expand. I can arrange for you to spend a year or so there and
receive training. Then you could come back to London or go anywhere.
With your language skills, there are many doors that would open for you.
Could you be interested in banking?"

"It has crossed my mind. I've had a lot of time to think these last few
weeks. I also thought of going to a university. Would I be paid sufficiently
by the bank in Geneva to support your daughter?"

"Well." Mr. De Sola stroked his chin. "You would be paid, but it would
not be enough for a married man, I'm afraid. Elizabeth would have to work."
He grunted. "She should be able to get a job in Geneva, though. And we
would not let either of you go hungry. My wife and I would very much like
to call you a son, you know. My God, what am I saying, Leo? Forgive me,
I'm somewhat jumping the gun, aren't I?"

He smiled mischievously, raising his eyebrows. Leo smiled back and
felt a boundless delight in the sudden possibilities in his life.

✳

After a small and simple family wedding, Leo took Elizabeth by train to
Dover, then by ferry across the English Channel to Calais, and then another
train to Paris. It seemed years since Leo had been to Paris. The last time
had been a quick trip when he was immersed in military history, and he
had nagged to be taken to Les Invalides to see Napoleon's tomb.

Elizabeth, however, had spent many vacations and long weekends in
Paris, and she knew it well. She charged ahead, taking delight in introducing
Leo to Monmartre, Les Halles, Montparnasse, and the Bois de Boulogne.
She planned a mind-boggling number of trips to Versailles and on the Seine.
Despite being almost constantly on his feet, he was happy to be a tourist
and above all in her care, all hours of the day and night, walking the streets

hand-in-hand and very much in love.

The scars and skeletons of war were all around, not quite surprising Leo, but taking him off guard, as had the bombed-out buildings in London the first time he visited. His heart fell every time their journeys took them over railways. His thoughts turned to death trains full of Jews and the barren yards of dirt and human waste. After more than a week, he struggled to hide his sullenness, afraid of hurting Elizabeth's feelings. But he could not take his mind off his family. During these moods, she remained stubbornly bright.

"Darling," he finally said, and as gently as he could, "I know this may seem dour, but perhaps we could cancel tomorrow's plans and make another trip instead."

An injured look crossed her eyes, but she agreed to go with him. The next afternoon, they took a bus to Drancy, seven miles north. They wandered into the camp, deserted except for an office manned by volunteers whose job was to assist prisoners who had survived, and to comfort the friends and families of those who had not.

"I'm sorry, sir," a lady from the Red Cross said after flipping through pages of records. "I cannot be certain, but I do see that a Monsieur and Madame Kaplan were transported to Auschwitz from here and that they were from Nice. And on the same date, also from Nice, a Monsieur and Madame Bergner. That is all the information I have."

"Thank you, Madame." He felt helpless as he stood before her, staring at the pile of papers on the woman's desk, so full of facts yet so barren of answers.

Leo held Elizabeth's hand as they left the office and walked into the open air. He felt sick. He stopped and gazed off at nothing, unable to speak. Then he saw the empty railway track leading into the distance, to a place of no return. Elizabeth stood back. Leo glanced at her, gauging whether there was something he should do or say to stave off her impatience. But, like him, she stared at the railway track that for so many was their final journey. She stood with arms folded as blond strands danced across her face, tossed by a breeze, and she made no effort to clear the hair from her view.

After several minutes, an elderly man approached, short and well dressed. Leo waited, watching, unsure if he wanted to welcome an intrusion. The man held out his hand and smiled.

"Forgive me, monsieur. I am a rabbi from Paris. I come every day to help comfort those who visit here hoping for the best, but leave in despair. If there is anything I can say or do, please, let me."

He took Leo by the arm and led him toward a bench. The rabbi listened as Leo spoke, his chest heavy and face wet with tears, while Elizabeth stood somewhere behind them. He could not remember what he said, or what the rabbi told him, but after some time, the two men sat together in silence.

"Please wait here," the rabbi said. "I'll be back in a minute. Don't go anywhere."

Leo turned around to look for Elizabeth. She was seated alone on a bench on the station platform. He wiped his face and struggled to his feet. When he went to her, he could not tell if she was lost in her thoughts or simply bored.

"I'm sorry, darling. I didn't mean to be rude, but I had to talk with him. He has, I'm afraid, convinced me that the chances of my parents and cousins being alive are very remote. He has helped me pull my head from out of the sand." He looked down at the ground. "After all, I had seen a camp in Germany just a few months ago. I know what they were like."

"How do you feel?" She reached for his hand and pulled him near.

"So sad and numb it is hard to describe. It is difficult for me to accept."

Leo turned at the sound of footsteps. The man approached from another building, leading a group of men closer, and their footfalls made a hollow sound under the platform pavilion.

"Major Bergner. I am afraid that it is time for you to recite the Kaddish, the mourner's prayer. According to our custom in the mainstream of Judaism, a minyan, a quorum of ten adults, is needed to recite this prayer. Come, let us go over there and face east, and recite it together."

Leo followed them. One handed Leo a sheet of paper on which the prayer was written. Another handed him a skullcap. He stood, almost at attention, as the rabbi solemnly recited the ancient prayer. Tears streamed down his cheeks as his turn arrived to read aloud from the paper in front of him. His head became a confusion of memories—the laughter and gaiety of that sunny apartment in Nice, its balcony aflame with bright red roses, geraniums, and bougainvillea. He remembered the aroma of fresh coffee and his mother's strudel, which lay in sharp contrast to the inferno of inhumanity, and the spectacle of frightened, humiliated, and hungry masses.

He had no family to write to anymore. Now his family was only Elizabeth.

20

Bruno and his fellow immigrants walked silently toward the harbor gates. Those who had formed friendships during the voyage walked in small groups, others walked alone, keeping themselves at a distance. Bruno walked apart from the others, as was his choice and his situation.

Everyone stopped at the gates. Beyond, the street was dirty and noisy with the constant passing of heavy trucks entering and leaving the docks. The air stank from the fumes. The men looked unsure as to the direction they should walk. Bruno made up his mind—whichever way the rest of them went, he would go the opposite. They moved off like sheep, crossing the road.

From the maps he had studied, Bruno headed in the direction of La Boca, one of the industrial areas. He passed meat-packing plants and warehouses. Strains of tango music meandered through the alleyways. He paused to listen. It had been a long time since he played the piano. Maybe he could find a job playing, he pondered, then shrugged and walked on, keeping his eyes open for any sign of a rooming house.

He read the sign, El Obrero, and looked through the window. The place appeared a colorful and seemingly well-established restaurant. He checked his watch. By Argentinean standards, it was still early, and apart from a couple of occupied tables, the place was empty. He took a stool at the bar and ordered a glass of red wine.

"Malbec, some call this our national wine," the barman said. "I see you're studying a map. Where are you from?"

"Europe. I'm looking for somewhere to stay for a few days, until I find my feet. I need a room, inexpensive. Do you know any?"

"Wait a moment." He walked toward the kitchen and returned with one of the waiters. "This is Ricardo. His mother works at a hotel a few blocks from here. It is not fancy, but it will be cheap. If you like, he will telephone and ask if they have a room."

"Thank you. I would appreciate that."

Ricardo went behind the bar and dialed the hotel while the barman filled Bruno's glass. Bruno took another sip of wine, so dark it was more black than red.

"They have a room," Ricardo called. "It is small. I don't think there's a window. It may suit you."

"Did she say how much it is?" Bruno asked.

"I think you can have it for ten pesos a night." Ricardo handed him a piece of paper with the address. "You may get it for less if you take it for the month and pay in advance."

* * *

The room turned out to be small, at the front of the building, with a window and even a ceiling fan. Probably because of the wine, Bruno realized he was tired. Or maybe it was the long walk from the docks in the midday heat. He unpacked his few clothes, hung his coat in the closet, and lay down on the bed.

He couldn't sleep. The room was hot. The fan clanked. The noise of traffic in the street never abated. The music, at full volume from the bar next to the hotel, began at midnight and did not end until seven in the morning. So much for cheap hotels.

The next day, Bruno's first order of business was to buy new clothes. The guidebooks advised that Buenos Aires was a city where it was important always to look one's best, and he was, after all, seeking employment. The woman at the front desk suggested that he take a bus to the Once train station where he would find inexpensive clothing stores close by on Avenida Pueyrredon. Within a few hours, he had kitted himself out with a new wardrobe, and as soon as he could afford it, he'd order new shoes too. His old clothes would go to the secondhand store down the street from his hotel. Perhaps get him a few pesos.

There was no telephone in his room. The woman at the front desk graciously allowed him to make a local call from the office. "Herr Fischer, please."

"This is Fischer," he said in a thick Bavarian accent. "Who is this?"

"Bruno Franzmann. I have a letter of introduction to you. I was told to contact you when I arrived in Buenos Aires."

"Do you mean Bruno Fernandez?"

"Yes, I'm sorry. It will take me time to get used to my new name. I arrived just yesterday."

"You had better get used to your new name. That's very important. Come to my office at eleven o'clock tomorrow morning and bring all your papers."

The next morning, immaculately dressed and having stopped for a haircut, Bruno presented himself at the downtown office of Banco Altman Transeuropeas. He felt confident in his new double-breasted dark suit, white shirt and blue silk tie. A few customers stood at the counter. He sat in an armchair and waited. To his side were some newspapers including the German paper, *Argentinisches Tageblatt*. But he had no time to read any before being ushered into Herr Fischer's office.

"Show me your papers." Herr Fischer remained seated behind his desk and projected an aging stare past his thick glasses. His suit was better than average, but not fitted recently, as the growth of his rotund middle prevented its buttoning.

Bruno handed him the letter of introduction, his Red Cross Passport, and his Argentinean visa. While Fischer looked through them, Bruno wondered whether he should take a seat. He took a chance and sat.

"Everything is in order. The organization has found a job for you. It is as bookkeeper at a tire importing company. How's your Spanish?"

"It's improving. I had lessons in the monastery and practiced as much as I could by reading Spanish books and newspapers."

"Can you count in Spanish? That is important."

"Yes, of course."

"The company, Trautman Tire Import and Export Company, is owned by a German family. They have been here since 1906. It is a medium-sized company with maybe sixty employees. The owner, Señor Alfredo Trautman, is the son of the founder. He is a sick man. I don't know how long he will keep the business. But in the meantime, he has agreed to hire you. He knows of the work you did in Augsburg and during the war. You seem to have the qualifications. He is also a religious man and was impressed by the letter of recommendation we received from the monastery."

"Thank you, sir." Bruno nodded to the note of polite praise.

Herr Fischer tented his hands and leaned back in his heavy chair. "The business is located in the San Telmo area, on Balcarce. I will give you the address and telephone number, but first I will call on your behalf to inform Señor Trautman of your arrival, and to discuss your start date."

"Thank you."

"From whatever he agrees to pay you, he will deduct a sum of money that he and I will decide. He will send that to me to go toward reducing your debt to the Organization. Was that explained to you?"

"Yes. I also have a letter of introduction to The German Club. Is that nearby?"

"About a ten minute walk. You will find it useful to join."

"There is one other thing. I would like to open a bank account, and also, because I'm staying in a bad area, I'd like to rent a safe-deposit box. Somewhere to keep my papers. Is that something I could do with your bank?"

"No, Herr Fernandez." He then smugly explained, "We only take customers with substantial accounts, not newly arrived penniless refugees."

Bruno flinched. He felt an instant dislike for this man. One day, he'd show him.

"Go to Banco de la Provincia," Fischer continued, "a few blocks from The German Club, and ask for Señor Varela. My secretary will telephone him to introduce you." Herr Fischer picked up the phone and dialed. "Señor Trautman, this is Fischer. I have your new bookkeeper in my office. I am sure he will be satisfactory."

On the phone, Fischer continued in short replies that left Bruno guessing at what Trautman might be saying.

Fischer covered the phone with his hand. "He wants you to start on Monday. He will pay you four hundred a month, a very generous salary, in my opinion. Of that, you will remit eighty to us each month, leaving you with more than enough."

Bruno nodded and made a smile for the benefit of Herr Fischer. The job and the pay mentioned would be a start. But Bruno would find ways to supplement his income, and without Fischer or the Catholic Church taking a cut. After all, he was in Argentina. His escape was complete.

"Señor Trautman, Fernandez accepts. He will be at your office at nine o'clock next Monday morning." Fischer ended his call and said to Bruno, "Everything is arranged."

"Thank you, Herr Fischer. You have been very kind. There is one thing. As today is only Thursday, and I won't be starting the job for a few days, maybe if you would agree to advance me a loan, it would be helpful."

Fischer looked Bruno up and down, taking in the elegance of his new clothes. "You appear better off than many of the new arrivals. It doesn't look as if we need to lend you any money."

"You were right about penniless, Herr Fischer." Bruno used the earlier insult to fuel his blatant lie. "The fact is, I spent my last dime on this outfit. I thought it was the right thing to do. You know, look good and all, to improve my chances of getting hired."

Fischer scoffed, almost chuckling. "You have much to learn about managing money."

Pompous ass. First insulted, then spoken down to as if he were a child, Bruno determined that he would show Herr Fischer who manages money better. But to expose his secret wealth would not help his current situation, other than the satisfaction of putting Fischer in his place. Not now. Someday.

"So where are you living?" Fischer asked.

"At a small hotel in La Boca."

"No wonder you want a safe-deposit box. That is not a good area. You should find somewhere closer to your new workplace in San Telmo. There must be some inexpensive apartments or hotels on Balcarce and Defensa. You have time to check them out before Monday."

Herr Fischer called out to Señora Cervantes. An attractive secretary in her early thirties came into the room and gave Bruno a pleasant smile. She held a notebook and pen at the ready.

"Telephone Señor Varela at Banco de la Provincia," Fischer instructed his secretary, "and tell him to expect Señor Fernandez within the next couple of days to open an account. His initial deposit will be two hundred American dollars. Then arrange for our cashier to issue a check to Señor Fernandez for that amount and have him sign a receipt for it, and place that receipt on his file. Get him to sign a one-year promissory note for the two hundred at an interest rate of nine percent. Also, type out the address of Trautman Tire Company for him."

"Thank you again, Herr Fischer," Bruno said.

Nine percent. The man was a thief. Still, Bruno smiled, stood, and extended his hand. Herr Fischer ignored him and picked up another file. Bruno followed Señora Cervantes back into the banking hall where she told him to take a seat while she arranged his loan.

By late afternoon and after a good lunch, Bruno had his new bank account, a safe-deposit box, and he had become a member of The German Club. By lunchtime the next day, he had removed the jewelry and money from the secret pockets and heels of his shoes, and placed the valuables in the box at the bank. He counted the money he had brought from Germany, took it to Señor Valera, and had it converted into American dollars. He looked with satisfaction at the receipt, showing his balance at the bank was not the two hundred dollars that he had deposited the day before, but in fact, six thousand, one hundred and ninety. It was a relief to no longer live in fear of that damned overcoat being stolen. And of course, to have money available when he chose to use it.

A bus ride took him to the Trautman Tire Company. The stop was practically at the door of the two-story building with a large warehouse on the ground floor and offices upstairs. Outside, large trucks parked along-side rows of tires stacked high. A German shepherd snarled at Bruno as he approached the gate. Apart from the dog, there was no sign of life. The office was closed over the weekend.

Walking back along Balcarce, Bruno passed a few small bars and restaurants. He headed toward Plaza Dorrego and discovered narrow cobbled streets lined with two-story colonial houses, several of them converted into small apartments. He saw a 'To Rent' sign outside one building and rang the bell.

A caretaker escorted him to an upstairs furnished apartment, consisting of a bedroom, bathroom, and small living room. Perfect for his immediate needs and having the advantage of being just a ten-minute walk to his new job. And at one-sixty a month, the place was affordable. For the first time in his life, he would have a home of his own.

His only surprise—he could not bring himself to visit the secondhand store to sell his overcoat. It had served him well. And a lingering notion surfaced whenever he heard the sound of music. His thoughts turned to his one-time ambition of becoming a great classical pianist and performing at an important concert hall. Perhaps here in Buenos Aires, praised by the press and Argentinean society. Just like that Jew, Arthur Rubinstein.

21

BRUNO FOUND WORK AT THE TIRE COMPANY INTERESTING. The company had been established forty years earlier by Trautman's father, and imported heavy-duty tires for trucks and bulldozers. Sales representatives served throughout Argentina as well as in Brazil and Paraguay. Business was steady, but Bruno soon discovered a decline due to Trautman's general lack of interest.

When Herr Fischer referred to Trautman as a *sick man,* he had understated the situation. Trautman's illness had begun as a heart problem diagnosed two years earlier, which he might have overcome, but his poor health was exacerbated by his wife's open affair with a local politician. Furthermore, Trautman had no heirs and derived most of his income from real estate investments. So day-to-day involvement in the tire business grated on his nerves.

"Herr Fernandez, come in and close the door," Trautman called as Bruno passed his office one morning. Trautman gave Bruno one of his usual, inscrutable looks. He had a face as plain and thick as the tires he sold. "Herr Fernandez, how do you like working here?"

"Very much. I enjoy the work and I see that business is steady." He hesitated, then decided to finish the thought. "But we might do better if we had a more aggressive sales force."

"I'm pleased with your work." Trautman interlaced his meaty fingers. "I want to take it easy over the next few months. Spend some time in Patagonia." His plain face betrayed a slight improvement, perhaps swooning anticipation. "How would you like it if I promoted you to general manager? Gonzales wants to retire, and I admire your good European work ethic."

"I'd be pleased to take on additional responsibility." This development was not expected, but Bruno welcomed it. "Will I be paid more?"

"I see we're paying you four hundred a month. I'd increase that to six hundred."

"Herr Trautman," Bruno said evenly, "if I am to take on Señor Gonzalez's position, with all due respect, I should be paid at least the same that he's getting paid. I do the payroll. I know he's earning seven hundred and fifty, and has the use of a company vehicle."

"Seven hundred and fifty it is and we'll get you a car." Trautman gazed out the window. "Now, I'm honor-bound to call Herr Fischer at the bank. In all probability, he will want to increase the amount of your monthly repayment to the Organization."

Trautman turned back to Bruno with a smile. Gonzalez could bring forward his retirement date, Trautman could go to his home in Patagonia, and Bruno, after barely a year in Buenos Aires, would be the general manager of the company. Everyone was a winner.

Trautman would call each week to check on Bruno and was always pleased to hear that things were going well. Then Trautman surprised Bruno when he brought up an interesting subject during one of their calls. He thought it was time to sell the company.

"I'm coming to Buenos Aires at the end of the month." Trautman cleared his throat wetly. "To meet with my attorney and locate a buyer. I want you to know that your position is secure, and in the event of a sale, I will encourage the new owner to keep you on."

Bruno didn't care what Trautman might encourage, too consumed with calculating the potential of this opportunity and the money required to seize it.

"Herr Trautman," Bruno said. "Suppose I have a buyer."

"You?"

"I may know of one," Bruno lied. "How much would you want for the company?"

"I'll have to speak with my accountant and ask his opinion. Of course, we're only talking about the business. I own the property, too. I don't know whether I want to include it."

"When will you know your asking price, Herr Trautman?"

"I'll let you know next week."

Bruno hadn't felt this excited in years. He was in no position to buy the company, but he did have a few assets, namely around ten thousand American dollars in his bank account. He continued to live frugally, and there were earnings from playing piano at the Europa three nights each week. But he had something more. Something he had known might prove valuable when he'd taken the files at Dachau. Then he hadn't known how. Today, the Unit 436 payroll records were a means to realize his scheme and potentially others.

✳

"Herr Stichler, please," Bruno said into the telephone.

"This is Stichler. Who is this?"

"Bruno Fernandez, a fellow member of The German Club. They gave me your number."

"Oh, I see. What can I do for you?"

"I would like to meet with you as soon as possible. It's about a very important matter."

"Well." The man's voice had aged since Dachau. "Can we speak about it on the phone?"

"No," Bruno said. "It needs to be in person."

"What is it about?"

"Unit 436."

The phone went dead.

Bruno waited for half an hour, then he called Stichler back.

"That was a mistake, Herr Stichler." Bruno realized that if this plan were to work, he'd have to appear more threatening, and make it believable. "You shouldn't have put the phone down on me."

"What is it you want?" Stichler sounded impatient, but also worried. "I know nothing of what you mentioned before."

"Let's meet this evening for a drink at The Alvear. Six o'clock. I suggest you be there. Then we can see what we both know or not."

Now it was Bruno's turn to put down the phone. By the fear in Herr Stichler's voice, Bruno knew he was onto something. He made a star next to the man's name and noted the meeting time and place in his ledger. He turned the page and dialed the next number.

"Herr Gleixner. My name is Bruno Fernandez. I'd like to set up a time to meet with you."

"What is it about? Who are you?"

"Let's just say it's about Unit 436."

"Oh. What would you want to discuss about that?"

"Why don't we meet at seven o'clock tonight. At The Alvear. I'll tell you then."

Herr Gleixner reluctantly agreed, and their call ended.

Over the next few hours, Bruno set up nine appointments. No one declined to meet with him. And he still had plenty more pages of payroll records to sort through. He turned out the lights and stood for a moment at his door, polished his shoes on his calves, and went out.

Herr Stichler came into the bar. Bruno recognized him, not only from the nervous manner in which he looked around to identify a Herr Fernandez, but also from his memory of Stichler strutting around the camp at Dachau in his highly polished boots. Herr Stichler had barked instructions at whoever passed by—Jews, subordinates, even Bruno one time, when he had knocked over a tin of pencils on his secretary's desk. Stichler had always made his point by waving his swagger stick up and down forcibly in the air, like he was leading a parade. Here in the bar, amid the smells of alcohol and rich cigars, he looked out of place and certainly older. Bruno beckoned him over to his corner table.

"Do I know you?" Stichler sat down stiffly.

"I doubt that you'd recall. Let's just say, I know you, Herr Stichler." Bruno sat back in his chair and crossed his legs. His slacks, perfectly pressed and creased, gave his action a certain elegance. "I worked at Dachau in administration and know exactly what you did there, and that you were stationed there right through until the end. I know what you did very well. There's a lot of blood on your hands."

"Who do you work for, the Jews?"

"I work for the new authorities in Germany," Bruno said.

He waved for the waiter, then mulled over the drink menu for several minutes, asking as many trifling questions as he could, aware of Stichler squirming in the chair across from him. Finally, Bruno ordered a cheap glass of Malbec and an even cheaper one for his guest. The waiter left. Bruno tented his fingers on the table and sighed.

"The question of your extradition is being considered right now."

"That's nonsense," Stichler snapped. "I have friends here and in Germany. That would never happen. I'm already established here."

"Well, if that's your position, you and I have nothing further to discuss." Bruno swallowed the last of his Malbec and stood to leave. "I'll notify my colleagues in Germany accordingly."

Stichler grabbed Bruno's arm. "Herr Fernandez, I don't want any trouble." His haunted stare was like that of the Jews he had beaten at Dachau. "I just want to get on with my life. Let's talk about this."

Bruno sat down again. An hour later, he had extracted from Herr Stichler a promise to return the next morning with a cashier's check for ten thousand dollars. The once pompous SS officer left with hunched shoulders and furtive glances.

Bruno looked at his watch. Herr Gleixner was due to arrive any minute. No doubt, the next conversation would go well. All of them would. Around midnight, Bruno went back to his apartment to pore over the payroll records.

✳

Early the next week, a call was put through to Bruno in his office at the tire factory. Trautman was on the line. Bruno had all the papers for his weekly meeting in order. He adjusted his cufflink and reached for the phone.

"Good morning, Herr Fernandez." It sounded like Trautman was calling from a phone box in Antarctica. "I've spoken with my accountant. He believes the correct price for the business without the property is five hundred thousand American dollars. With the property, seven hundred thousand. Do you think you have someone?"

"It's possible. Would there be a commission, sir?"

"Five percent."

"Plus my bonus for finding a buyer," Bruno added.

"Well, wouldn't the commission take care of that?"

"Not really. But why don't we just call it a six percent commission. And I would like an exclusive on this for a month."

"What do you mean an *exclusive?*" Trautman questioned.

"That you won't offer it to anyone else for a month."

"Do you think you can wrap this up in a month?" Trautman's voice filled with optimism. "That would be wonderful."

"I'll do my best, sir."

Their call ended, then Bruno searched his wallet for the card he had picked up at Banco de la Provincia long ago. He dialed the number and asked for Señor Valera.

"Bruno Fernandez here. May I invite you for lunch tomorrow at The German Club?"

*

Bruno sat comfortably at a table laid out with china, fine linen, and silverware. He glanced at the menu while Señor Valera pointed to an item on his, and the waiter made notes. Then Bruno waved the waiter away.

"According to my records, Señor Valera, I have on deposit with you approximately two hundred and forty thousand American dollars. I expect to increase that to three hundred thousand by the end of the week."

"That is most impressive, Señor Fernandez. You're now one of my most important clients. And imagine, you only opened the account with us less than a year ago."

"I was with my attorney this morning," Bruno explained. "We have set up a corporation, Telmo Investment Corporation—TIC. The attorney's name is Salvador Mares. Our accountant is Tomás Esquival. I want you to set up an account at Banco de la Provincia in the name of the corporation. Señor Mares and I will be signatories on the account. Once the new account is set up, transfer two hundred thousand from my account to the new company account. When I make more deposits, part will also go into TIC's account."

"Yes," Señor Valera answered. "I'll take care of it by this afternoon. There will be papers for you to sign."

Valera seemed a bit nervous, as though certain that his client—whose notes were written in a cheap notebook with a chintzy pen—was either too good to be true or simply off his rocker. Bruno smiled. At that point, being underestimated worked to his advantage, as it gave time to better initiate his plans. Time would pass, and these same people would have their own agendas.

"Now," Bruno said, "TIC will be making an offer to buy the Trautman Tire Company and also its property. Señor Mares will discuss this with you, as we will need financing. If you will provide it, you will have Trautman's business. The company does a significant volume of letter of credit transactions. You will earn good fees. You understand, Señor Valera, this will make you a star at the bank."

"I do. Thank you. I look forward to speaking with Señor Mares."

"And if you do not provide the finance," Bruno added, "then the Trautman account will stay with Herr Fischer's bank."

Señor Valera nodded and took great care to remain composed. Any earlier judgment he had of Bruno needed quick revision. This promising opportunity, if all could be achieved, would bring both men tremendous gains.

22

THE REVENUE STREAM FROM UNIT 436 CONTINUED TO GROW, and by the end of the month, another hundred thousand had been deposited into his account. Being the chairman of Telmo Investment Corporation suited Bruno well. He was no longer a man of little consequence, and more and more people were working for him, by choice or not. Bruno felt the power of his position grow not only with his bank account, but with his increased adeptness at manipulating people.

When Herr Fischer called, asking for a meeting at his bank, Bruno was delighted. He was entering into the final moves of another excellent checkmate.

"Herr Fernandez, this is Fischer. I need to see you. It's important. Can you come to my office this afternoon?"

"No. You will come to my office, Herr Fischer. You know where I am."

"Then…" Fischer stopped himself. "Of course. Yes. I will be there in half an hour."

"Make it two hours, Herr Fischer." Bruno dropped his polite tone and became firm. "I'm very busy."

Through the phone, Bruno could hear the snap of a lighter and a sigh of smoke. Herr Fischer's blood pressure must be climbing through the roof. Señora Cervantes had probably turned in her resignation that morning. Bruno had several plays in motion now.

Two hours later, Fischer burst into Bruno's office, wearing his tailored gray suit that barely buttoned around his middle. He looked forlorn without his desk and office around him. He took in Trautman's old office and its refurbishments. Bruno sat behind the new desk and smiled, enjoying Fischer's discomfort.

"What is it you want to see me about?" Bruno asked.

"Herr Fernandez," Fischer began a bit breathlessly. "I don't know who the hell you think you are, but you're making a very big mistake. You've been in this country for only a year, and you're already making a lot of enemies. I'm here to give it to you straight. We need to discuss a few things."

"So, let's discuss." Bruno sipped his coffee. "May I offer you a coffee?"

Herr Fischer ignored the offer and clenched his hands into fists resting on his knees.

"First, my bank has handled the Trautman Company's accounts since 1906. How dare you take the account away from me. What can Banco de la Provincia do for you that we can't? Don't you consider that you owe us something? After all, if it hadn't been for the Organization, where would you be now? Being prosecuted for war crimes, very likely. Don't you know that the Organization owns my bank? They deserve better treatment than this, Herr Fernandez."

Bruno opened his eyes and tilted his head as if to show interest and concern. But he was truly enjoying the moment and would have preferred to smile at his opponent, who was railing against an impenetrable defense.

"Is there anything else that is upsetting you?" Bruno asked.

"Yes, there is. I had a call from the chairman of The German Club. There have been complaints that you have been blackmailing a large number of the members. The club insists that this practice cease forthwith. Members will be advised about you."

"Anything else, Herr Fischer?"

"No, but take heed. You have accumulated many enemies. You'd better watch your back from now on."

"I have a few questions of my own. According to my records, I still owe your bank two hundred dollars, and I owe the Organization a remaining balance of about eighteen hundred. Is that right?"

"I don't have the exact figure." Fischer looked unsure whether to storm out or to answer the question. "Something like that. What is the meaning of your question?"

"According to my records, your cousin, Fritz Ganzler, works at your bank in the accounts department, and he has a shady history. I was about to telephone him today anyway. I suggest you ask him to redeem these obligations totaling around two thousand."

"You bastard."

"Next, please don't accuse me of blackmail. I have investors. Their loans have been converted into bonds issued by TIC Corporation. All very up-and-up. They will each have received a bond certificate from my lawyer. Your cousin Herr Ganzler will be receiving his, too."

"An investment?" Herr Fischer's voice rose in a crescendo. "A bond that has a redemption date of thirty years forward at an interest rate of two percent. You call that an investment?"

"Of course it's an investment. If any investor wishes to redeem, they can contact me. At the moment, it would be around twelve cents on the dollar."

"Are you crazy?"

"Never felt better."

Fischer got up from his chair. "There's talk at The German Club." He gathered his coat over his arm and shook his hat at Bruno. "You will be thrown out."

"I'll survive. And just one other thing before you leave, Herr Fischer. Please tell Señora Cervantes not to be late for work when she starts here in a couple of weeks."

*

Bruno didn't have to spend too long in Veronica. The small town had a population of less than six thousand, a number of whom were former members of Unit 436. With two hundred thousand dollars committed, his next stop was Bariloche, where he had set up a meeting with a former Nazi surgeon at Buchenwald. The good doctor had conducted experiments on homosexuals, castrating them and then inserting metal sex glands that caused their agonizing deaths. At their meeting, the man was cool to the point of being deranged. Bruno was glad when their meeting ended. He had another group of Unit 436 men to meet.

Now armed bodyguards accompanied him to every meeting and never left his side. They felt like an extra pair of arms—thick with a kind of brute strength that he had always admired and maybe envied. At the hotel, Bruno stepped out of his limousine and walked briskly through the revolving doors into the opulent lobby, followed by his bodyguards. He collected his key from the front desk and took the elevator to his room.

Bruno's room was not the biggest or the most luxurious that the hotel had to offer. He couldn't bring himself to that level of extravagance. Still, he was staying at the best address in town, and that was all that mattered. And he could afford to dress even better now—custom-made suits, shirts and even shoes. Bruno threw his jacket on the bed, sat at his desk, and pulled the phone closer. He dialed his accountant, with whom he felt a growing attachment.

"Tomás, it's Bruno. I'm back."

"How was your trip?"

"I sold seven hundred thousand worth of bonds. The money will be coming in over the next few days. Alert the bank. Tomorrow, I'll have my driver bring you the list of investors."

"Good work."

"Now, I think we should go into the air charter business. Contact the owners of the charter company I've just used and set up a meeting. This is going to be a growth industry."

✳

A few days later, Herr Rothmund of The German Club called Bruno's office. Bruno recognized the voice immediately, a braying that was never far from the maitre'd's booth at the Club. Today, the man's tone on the telephone asserted his authority.

"Your membership here has become a problem. You have already been warned by Herr Fischer to cease this blackmailing of our members."

"I blackmail no one." Bruno remained calm. "I don't hold a gun to anyone's head. I sell bonds in my company. These bonds are investments. Good investments for these people."

"Herr Fernandez, don't be surprised if someone holds a gun to your head and pulls the trigger."

"You threaten me?" he replied with false innocence. "I'm not afraid."

"We do not want trouble within the German community," Rothmund said. "We have friends in high places. We have practically a direct line to General Perón and the First Lady. It would take one telephone call for you to be eliminated."

"Maybe yes, maybe no. But will killing me protect men with bloody hands?"

"Do not underestimate the Organisation der ehemaligen SS-Angehörigen." Herr Rothmund spoke as if through clenched teeth. "Don't you feel that you owe us something?"

"I am most grateful to them. If it hadn't been for Odessa, God knows where I would be now. And, Herr Rothmund, I've paid what I owe. Herr Fischer will confirm that."

All Bruno could hear was soft breathing. He knew that his simple answers would only serve to ignite this man's anger. Especially as Rothmund had been obviously pushed into making this call. What else would drive him to confront Bruno? His name didn't appear on any of Bruno's lists.

"Your records, Herr Fernandez." Rothmund spoke slowly. "Let's make a deal. You will cease and desist selling any more of your bogus bonds. And we will buy your records at a reasonable price. How's that?"

"How much?"

"Two hundred thousand dollars."

"Go to hell," Bruno shouted and banged down the phone.

An hour later, after a shower and a change of clothes, Bruno left his room. The thought of living at a luxury hotel brought a smile to his face. His bodyguards fell silent when he appeared at the door, then they followed him to the elevator.

"I'm going downstairs to the bar," Bruno said to the biggest of the men. "Sit at a table close to me, but not with me."

In the bar, Bruno was greeted by the head waiter. "Good evening, Señor Fernandez. Your usual table by the piano?"

"Yes, and a table close by for my two friends."

Bruno ordered a cocktail and stretched his legs under the table. The new handmade orthopedic shoes were a godsend. The best he'd ever had. He shifted a few thoughts and reactions around in his head, looking forward to the next sally.

Two tall men, tough looking and determined, walked into the bar, passed the head waiter, and marched directly to Bruno's table. His bodyguards stood up. The cocktail pianist missed a few notes of "The Nearness of You." Conversation around the room came to a halt.

"Herr Fernandez," one of the men said, "we have come to see you on behalf of Herr Kommandant Joseph Schwamberger."

"Oh, yes, the good commandant. I have an appointment with him tomorrow afternoon."

"No, you don't. Herr Schwamberger will not receive you. He will not meet with you here or anywhere else."

"Gentlemen, please inform Herr Schwamberger that the meeting between us will take place tomorrow at six o'clock in the evening. He will meet me at this table right here. Please tell him that it is in his best interest to attend. Many people are looking for him right now. In addition to the massacres he ordered as camp commander, he was also directly responsible for the murder of several hundred Italians. Did you know that?"

"That is not our business."

"It could well be your business. Many Italians now live in Buenos Aires. It's not just the Jews here who want to get their hands on the commandant."

"Herr Schwamberger will not come. In fact, he's flying out tonight to Patagonia. He tells us to ask you your price. How much do you want, Herr Fernandez?"

"I would like the good commandant to make an investment in TIC bonds in the amount of one hundred and fifty thousand American dollars."

"He has authorized us to pay up to one hundred thousand."

"You asked me what his investment must be. I told you. Do not try to bargain with me."

"We will be back tomorrow at six."

The men turned and left. Bruno's bodyguards resumed their seats. Conversations opened up again around the room and the pianist went back to playing. All seemed calm, and Bruno scanned the restaurant.

A man approached Bruno's table, wearing a military uniform, medals pinned to his chest, and carrying an officer's hat.

"Señor Fernandez?"

"Who wants to know?" Bruno asked.

The man put out his hand to shake. "I am Colonel Francisco Manzano." Bruno did not accept his hand, and the colonel let it drop. "You do not know me, Señor Fernandez, but I know of you. I have for some time. May I join you?"

One of Bruno's bodyguards stood. Bruno beckoned him not to worry.

"Is there something I could do for you, Colonel?"

Manzano pulled out a chair and sat across from Bruno. "I am well aware of your activities recently." He said no more and his smile began to grow.

"Are you threatening me?"

Manzano laughed out loud but cut it short. "I wouldn't dream of it, Señor Fernandez. No, I have much bigger goals. I am with the Government Procurement Office. We ensure that government departments are properly equipped, and we oversee the accountability of vendors providing those needs."

A waiter stopped, inquiringly, at the table in front of Colonel Manzano, who waved him away.

Manzano continued, "I must say, Señor Fernandez, your sale of bonds is a clever approach to…" He paused to clear his throat. "Opportunities, shall we say. And we must all take advantage of business opportunities when they arise. It would be a shame to pass up any clear chance to gain a profit."

Bruno smelled a rat. But just the kind of rat that could make TIC a preferred government vendor. Of course, provided Manzano received regular kickbacks. His motives were becoming clear to Bruno. Considering the potential gains, diverting a cut to the colonel was a price worth paying. Exclusive government contracts, Bruno imagined. The profits could be fabulous, and better still, guaranteed. But it also worried Bruno, not having initiated the idea himself. Though it was to their mutual benefit, Bruno was still being played. And Manzano, the sleazy rat that he was, could double-cross Bruno on a whim. The opportunity was too good to pass up, but he would need to be careful.

Manzano glanced over his shoulder to view a table across the room. "You see, Señor Fernandez, my presence here is not a coincidence. My wife and daughter thought dinner here tonight was a surprise, but they needn't know. I have tracked your routine, and I chose this evening to dine at your hotel."

"So we could talk," Bruno suggested, "about future opportunities that might profit both of us." He followed the colonel's gaze across the room to the table where Manzano's wife and daughter were sitting. His daughter was striking—straight black hair almost to her waist, olive skin, and a certain vivaciousness that made it impossible for Bruno to avert his eyes. She smiled back. His face heated. He felt like he was looking into the eyes of a queen—powerful, dangerous, and beautiful.

"Ah," the colonel said, delighted to notice, "it is clear that you fancy Elena."

"Elena?" Bruno could not take his eyes off her. "Every man in Buenos Aires must fancy her. All of Argentina, even."

"Señor Fernandez, you are dining alone," Colonel Manzano said, glancing at Bruno's bodyguards sitting a few tables away, then back to him. "Perhaps not alone, but the social equivalent. Please do join us at our table, as our guest, and I will introduce you to Elena."

They stood to approach the colonel's table, but he reached to Bruno, urging him to pause before they were in earshot.

"One thing." Manzano kept his voice low. "The ladies are under the impression that you are one of our government suppliers." He grinned. "Which of course, most likely, you will be soon. My wife and daughter understand the duties of my office, in keeping good relations with our suppliers. How rude it would have been of me, to ignore you dining all by yourself. You do understand."

They continued toward the colonel's table. Bruno bowed to the ladies as he was introduced.

"Good evening, ladies. Please forgive me for staring, but you're both so beautiful."

"Thank you," Señora Manzano replied with a practiced smile.

"Why do you need bodyguards, Señor Fernandez?" Elena asked.

"I haven't been in this country for very long, and I have been quite successful. There are some who are jealous. Business can do that to people."

"I would be afraid too," Elena said.

"Not afraid, just cautious."

Bruno watched her every glance.

"You are safe with us," she said. "My father has served in the military for many years."

The colonel focused on Bruno. "Yes, the military, though assigned to our government's Procurement Office, of course, as Señor Fernandez well knows." Bruno didn't seem to hear him. Manzano studied his wife and daughter for their reaction.

Elena turned away from her father and frowned, then she glanced at Bruno, and her smile returned.

"That's interesting work, Colonel," Bruno said without looking at him, too captivated by Elena. There was much to consider between what was being said and what Bruno noticed in the young woman's expressions. While he marveled at her skin, her lips, her eyes, and how her shiny black hair flowed past her shoulders, his mind wanted to concentrate on the business potential of partnering with her father. But all he could do was stare at her, enchanted by her beauty.

After dinner, Elena excused herself to use the ladies' room. Bruno seized the opportunity.

"Colonel and Señora," he began. "Would you raise any objection if I were to invite your daughter to dinner?"

"We have no objection," the colonel said. "But please remember, she's only nineteen. Very innocent. And you, Señor Fernandez, are so mature and such a man of the world."

"Believe me, I'm not so much older than your daughter. But I have lived through some tough years, which have made me appear older than I am."

Colonel Manzano studied Bruno's face. "I must say, Señor Fernandez, after learning of your accomplishments, I had thought of you as an older man."

"Twenty-nine is not a child, Colonel."

"You are certainly clever beyond your years."

Elena returned to her seat, smiling flirtatiously at Bruno. Embarking on a new business alliance had become a part of everyday life for Bruno, but now he was in uncharted territory. The longer he sat facing her, the more foreign the emotions were that stirred within him, feelings that he had never experienced before. Could it be true? So this is how it feels, he thought, and everyone talks about. He could hardly believe it. He might be falling in love.

"I have to make an early start in the morning," the colonel said abruptly, glancing at his watch. They stood and walked toward the door, accompanied by Bruno. Señora Manzano held out her hand and Bruno raised it to his lips. He turned toward Elena and they exchanged a sultry glance that suggested it would not be long before they would meet again. He watched the Manzanos as they walked through the lobby and to their car.

He turned to summon his bodyguards and was escorted upstairs. Upon entering his room, Bruno noticed an envelope had been slipped under the door. It was a message from The German Club.

I am sorry you rejected our offer. There is the possibility that we might be able to increase it. We should meet tomorrow to discuss. I will telephone you at nine.

Rothmund

Bruno put the note on the desk and smiled. He had them on the run. Little did they realize, after their first refusal to pay, his price to hand over the payroll records had increased. Now they owed him one million.

✳

Bruno spent most of the morning thinking about Elena, with a few interludes of business. The tire business was booming, especially after he had taken on a new sales team. The Perón administration was proceeding at full speed with the industrialization of the country. That meant new roads, new factories, and heavy construction projects as well as a major reservoir development in the north. That in turn spelled trucks, bulldozers, cranes and backhoe diggers. In other words, tires. Then he could contain himself no longer.

"Señora Cervantes, would you find out the address of Colonel and Señora Manzano. I have their telephone number. Send them some flowers and include a note. Make it impressive."

"Yes, of course. You have three calls waiting. The German Embassy, The German Club, and a Señor Schwamberger. Who would you like to take first?"

"None of them. Tell them I'm in a meeting. Tell Herr Schwamberger I'm looking forward to seeing his men at six this evening at the Alvear, and with a check for one hundred and fifty thousand."

Besides the booming tire business, Bruno's new company demanded his attention as well. The air charter business was expanding, mostly cargo, but some passenger routes had been negotiated with the aviation authorities. He considered the acquisition of a construction company, a bank, and a newspaper. But any further expansion was unlikely in the short term unless he could sell more bonds.

"Señor Fernandez, there are two men here from the German Embassy," Señora Cervantes announced over the private intercom. "They insist on—"

The door opened, and Bruno looked up. Two tall men, dressed identically in light gray suits and brown shoes, walked into Bruno's office. For a moment, fear overtook Bruno. He felt like a child, when he was vulnerable, crippled.

"I'm sure," he said quickly and stood, "you have no appointment. I'm very busy, so please make an appointment with Señora Cervantes."

"Herr Fernandez," one of the men said. "We are from the German Embassy. We demand to converse with you immediately. You would be well-advised to give us fifteen minutes now."

Bruno looked at Señora Cervantes and nodded. She backed out of the room and the door clicked shut. He felt a flash of annoyance that her obvious trepidation might betray his own.

"I am not usually honored by members of the corps diplomatique," Bruno said. "Sit down, gentlemen. What is it you want of me?"

They took seats and looked at him squarely. He in turn took his seat behind the desk, hands clasped in front of him on the polished wood.

"We're here to warn you," the other man said. "Your practice of blackmailing your fellow Germans here in Argentina is criminal. Furthermore, we have heard that you tell your victims that you are representing the German government in relation to extradition matters. Anything to do with extradition is handled by our embassy. Unless you refrain immediately, you will be silenced."

"Are you threatening me, gentlemen, with my life?"

"You will be silenced," one of them replied.

Bruno looked around the room for a few seconds. This confrontation required some thought. He needed to find his confidence. He needed to show his power.

"First, gentlemen, I have very close connections with the highest echelons of the Argentinean regime. I am protected by them. Even though I am a member of The German Club, I am technically no longer a German citizen. I am here under an International Red Cross passport. So, I would respectfully suggest that you have no authority to tell me what I should or should not do."

Bruno felt his strength returning. He also realized that what he had said was not a bluff, but true. Some of it yet to be maximized, but all of it available to him.

"If anything should happen to me," Bruno continued, "a complete dossier of my investors and potential investors is in the hands of a third party. That dossier will be made available to the German government, the United States government, and any Jew who wants to review it. Any attempt to silence me is the last thing you or your constituents should want to see happen." He shooed them like a mosquito. "Now I must ask you to leave. I'm a busy man."

After they left, Señora Cervantes tapped on the door and looked sternly at Bruno.

"What kind of risk are you taking?" she asked. "You've changed since those first meetings at the bank. At thirty you are wealthy, certainly. But must you also put yourself in danger?"

"Sit down, Señora. Yes, I have changed. When I was in Germany, I was a nobody, no friends, no life. I was nothing. Yet I craved to walk into the grandest restaurants and sit at the best tables, to have a fine home, and to be accepted. Now, I'm beginning, at last, to be somebody, and I like it." He looked down at his desk. "But I never got to be the great concert pianist I always wanted to be. And there's more I want now. Particularly, as I can afford it."

"Yes." She gave him a scolding look. "But I heard what you said to those men. These men are diplomats. They're important. They have close relations with the military, all the way to the top. They mean business. They can have you killed."

"I know, but they won't." His chest felt light, as if full of champagne bubbles. "I meant what I told them. If they have me killed, my files will become public. They're better keeping me alive even though that irks them." He tapped some papers into a pile. Another thought crossed his mind. Now he imagined yet another way to make money, and be safer by doing so. "Señora, I have a question. How long had you worked for Herr Fischer at the bank?"

"Fifteen years."

"Did Herr Fischer manage only high net worth individuals as he mentioned at our first meeting, when he humiliated me?"

"Yes. There were many Germans who came here after the war, assisted by Odessa. And others who came before the war and have been clients for many years."

"Señora, do you still have good friends at the bank?"

He loved the suspense, the deepening question in her face. He could make her wait all day for his point, and she would.

"Of course," she said. "My cousin Jaime is in the accounting department, and my sister-in-law works in the investment department. Why?"

"Señora, if you and your sister-in-law let me have a list of all the Germans who came here, assisted by Odessa, and who have accounts at the bank, it would be very helpful." He leaned forward on his elbows. "I will need their addresses and telephone numbers and their last account balance. I'll give you ten percent of whatever they invest in TIC. How you split it with your sister-in-law or cousin, that's your business. No one will suspect you. For every million, there'll be one hundred thousand for you. That's a big multiple of your salary, isn't it?"

She sighed and scratched her neck, seeming for a moment to be tired of him, tired of her job. But when she looked back at him, there was a touch of humor in her weariness.

"I suppose I should tell you to go to hell, but I won't. Herr Fischer was a pig. What he made me do sometimes was humiliating. And my family could certainly use the money." She held her notepad and pen in a neat pile on her knees, and leaned forward. "But you must give me your word not to expose any member of my family or me to any danger."

"You have my word, Señora. Take your time about the list. We won't talk about this again until you get it to me. Now can you get me Colonel Manzano, please?"

"Flowers, phone calls." She stood. Her humor came out in a smile. "Who is this man? What is he to you?"

"With good fortune, he may be both my business partner and my father-in-law."

"Ah." She gave him one of her more mysterious smiles and left the room. He picked up the phone and waited to be connected, still watching her through the glass. Her body language betrayed nothing as she dialed the number. He stood to shut the blinds.

"Colonel," he said energetically, "it's Bruno Fernandez. Are you free for lunch today?"

"I am. What time suits you?"

"How about one o'clock at The German Club?"

"I can manage that," Manzano said.

"Perfect. Also, please let me know when I can take you and your wife and Elena out for dinner."

The conversation over, Bruno straightened his tie and took in a deep breath. This was going to be an interesting lunch. And of course, his thoughts turned to Elena and when he might see her next.

∗

The lobby of The German Club was busy. The members who recognized Bruno either ignored him or turned their backs. He smiled at everyone and called out "Guten Tag" to whoever passed by. He made sure his smile told them how broadly he didn't give a damn.

"Herr Fernandez, you have a lot of nerve coming here. I have the power to have you thrown out, you know."

Bruno turned quickly. The voice belonged to the club's president, Herr Rothmund. Bruno kept his face neutral.

"What the hell are you talking about?" Bruno answered. "I'm a member in good standing. My dues are up to date."

"You are not wanted here." Herr Rothmund turned to the doorman. "Get security. I want this man thrown out. Fernandez, you're a disgrace. You are banned from the club."

At that moment, Colonel Manzano entered the lobby through the revolving doors. He looked particularly elegant in his immaculate military uniform. In the doorway light, his medals sparkled against his jacket.

"Señor Fernandez, how good to see you."

"And you too, Colonel. Herr Rothmund, I don't know whether you know my lunch guest, Colonel Manzano. He's a very close friend of mine. In fact, a cousin of our president. Now, if you'll excuse us, we're going into the dining room for lunch."

Rothmund turned on his heels, livid with humiliation. He crossed the lobby to his office and slammed the door so loudly that a few heads turned in the dining room. Bruno clasped his hands behind his back and peeled out his best smile for the maitre'd.

"Ricardo, I want the best table in the house. One in the middle of the room where everyone can see us."

"Certainly, Señor. Come this way. It's fortunate you are early. Another ten minutes and this table would not be available."

Bruno waited until they were seated and their drinks ordered before he would begin. Their menus lay in front of them, unopened. Bruno smiled at the Colonel, who looked pleasantly amused.

"Thank you, Colonel, for joining me on such short notice. You saw the slight problem I had in the bar of the hotel last night with those two men. Well, I had it here at the club a few minutes ago. Earlier this morning, I had a similar visit at my office, and on it goes. I have round-the-clock security but it may not be enough. To be seen with you, a high-ranking military officer, is extremely helpful."

"I guessed as much. Especially when you mentioned I was a cousin of the president. Very naughty of you."

"Ah, one look at your uniform and medals is enough to silence them."

"But, Señor Fernandez, they too have friends in high places. Do not underestimate that. Many of them have direct lines of communication to the president. His private secretary is German and a member here."

"Really?" Bruno paused. "The first topic I want to discuss is that you and I should have lunch here every week. Bring as many high-ranking fellow officers as you want. I want to be seen with the right people. Let's make it a weekly fixture. I'll arrange with Ricardo that he keep this table for us every week. How's that?"

"Señor Fernandez, I'm certain your company is excellent, and the food good. But I'm unsure that I can commit to every week. I have other responsibilities."

"You wanted in on my action and this is part of it. And I'm sure your wife, already accustomed to a lifestyle exceeding an Argentinean military salary, would only like further luxuries."

Manzano gave it some thought and began nodding slowly.

Bruno continued, "What did you imagine our association was going to get you?"

"I think you know the answer to that as well as I do, Señor Fernandez. I can see to it that your company wins certain bids for products that you can provide. I only ask to be rewarded for my, shall we say, promotion of your products as the superior choice."

"Colonel, this country is in the midst of a construction boom. We all know that. We can see it everywhere. My main business is tires, but there is more. Far more."

The colonel put down his glass and twisted it irritably on the tablecloth. It was time for Bruno to close the deal.

"I'll give you five percent commission of everything the military buys from us, Colonel. You'll get it monthly. It could make you a very wealthy man. And that's just the beginning."

"What else have you got in mind, Señor?"

"I want you to arrange that my competitors lose the right to import tires from the United States. I want to be the exclusive importer of tires from North America. They can still import from Europe, but they won't be competitive. The costs of transportation will kill them. Can you arrange that?"

"Maybe." A muscle in the colonel's face twitched.

"Think of what that will do to your five percent commissions, Colonel." Bruno allowed himself a touch of showmanship, and paused for the numbers to sink in. He was getting closer. "And, Colonel, my company, TIC, is looking to acquire a construction firm, a bank, a newspaper and a radio station. All these acquisitions will require government approval. I want you to arrange for us to get approval and for all other bidders to be denied. I'll give you the details on another occasion. Can you do that?"

"Yes, but not on my own." The colonel leaned closer. "Several others will have to be involved."

"I'll take care of everyone, don't worry. Now, that's enough business." Bruno sat back. The air lightened immediately. "Just remember, I'm going to make you a millionaire very quickly. We'll make a killing."

"I have a question, Señor Fernandez." The colonel folded his hands on the table. "Seeing that I am going to be involved with you in business, and that you will also be seeing my daughter, shouldn't I now be free to address you as Bruno? I am of course Francisco, and my wife is Dolores."

"Of course. Francisco." Bruno spread his hands. "I would like to telephone Elena tomorrow and invite her for dinner, but I am unsure of the protocol here in Argentina. If you and your wife would like to chaperone Elena, I understand. Believe me, I only want to do the correct thing. While some may criticize my business methods, I never want it said that I behaved in a less than totally respectful manner toward your family."

"I appreciate that, Bruno. No, Elena will not need a chaperone. We trust you. And in any case, it is you with your two bodyguards who has the chaperones." The colonel laughed and lifted his glass. "Let's drink a toast before we leave, Bruno, to our new friendship and our new business relationship, and who knows what else."

On the way out, Bruno slipped Ricardo fifty pesos and promised another fifty every week the same table was reserved for him. Outside, Francisco got into the back of his waiting limousine, the Argentinean flag fluttering from the company's hood. Bruno dared to wave from the curb, and Francisco's pale hand lifted to the window for a moment and dropped. The car turned the corner and was gone.

As Bruno stood alone on the sidewalk—it must have been his imag-ination—he could smell her. That sweet perfume she wore. He must be hallucinating, he thought, so he drew in a deep breath, chilling his nostrils as he searched for her fragrance. It was as clear as if she were standing before him. No one ever explained to Bruno about the strange things that love can do.

He knew what he would do. He would have her. She will be mine, he kept telling himself, she will be mine.

✳

His bodyguard, Alfredo, rang Bruno a few minutes after six. His guests had arrived in the bar. Two of them, not three. Bruno smoothed his hair in the mirror, washed his face, straightened his tie, and put on his jacket. A sixth sense told him to retrieve the handgun from his old overcoat. He had never thought it necessary to carry it around in Buenos Aires, but the mounting hostility toward him made him tuck it into his jacket pocket.

Bruno squared his shoulders in the elevator. When the door slid open, he walked smoothly into the bar and nodded to the two men from the night before. They were seated at a table at the far end. Alfredo sat at an adjoining table.

"Good evening, gentlemen," Bruno said, and sat down in the empty chair. "I knew you would be here. I'm only sorry that Herr Schwamberger declined, as I would have liked to have met him. Well, we can make this meeting very short. What do you have for me?"

"Herr Schwamberger agrees to invest in your corporation, TIC." The man who spoke was ugly. He had the pockmarked face of a peasant, and his lips seemed to get in the way of his words. "He will invest one hundred and fifty thousand American dollars. We have brought a check for that amount."

"I am glad he saw the wisdom of making such a sound investment."

Bruno opened the envelope and stifled a smile when he saw that the check had been issued by Herr Fischer's Bank. Bruno tucked it away in his suit jacket.

"Herr Schwamberger wants your confirmation that you will never attempt to make contact with him again."

"I can confirm that, except in the case of matters that relate to his invest-ment. We keep all our investors fully informed about our activities. That is standard practice." He patted the check through the fabric of his suit. "Gentlemen, I believe we have concluded our business. I wish you a good night."

Bruno stood and gestured to Alfredo that they should return to the room. They traveled in the elevator in silence. Bruno felt the unfamiliar weight of the gun in his inside jacket pocket. He tugged his coat square again.

As he fished out his room key, Bruno thought about calling his secretary and telling her to expect him later than usual in the morning. He deserved a good sleep. The lock clacked, and he pushed the door open, expecting to see the bedside light glowing softly and the sheet still rumpled from his nap. Instead, the room looked like a battleground. Pepe, one of his bodyguards, was on the floor gagged and bound.

"Jesus Christ, what the hell happened? Alfredo, help me untie him."

Pepe had been clubbed on the head. Blood still flowed from the wound, staining the carpet. Alfredo walked past him with his gun drawn and checked every shadow in the room. He holstered his gun, pulled out a knife, and knelt to help his friend.

"There's no one else here, boss," he said and sliced through the rope around Pepe's wrists. "Looks like whoever broke in went through all your drawers. You better check if anything's missing."

"Screw that." Bruno marched to his desk phone and stated a terse request to be put through to the colonel. It was late, and the man's voice sounded roughened by a few drinks.

"I need your help urgently," Bruno said. "I'm at the hotel. Someone broke into my room while I was at a meeting downstairs. They've beaten one of my bodyguards. I don't want to involve the hotel. I need a military doctor as quickly as possible. There's five thousand dollars in it to attend to him, and to get him out of the hotel without anyone noticing. He's to get the best medical treatment." When he hung up, Bruno turned back to Alfredo. "They'll be here in twenty minutes."

The phone rang seconds later. Bruno grabbed the receiver and waited for someone to speak.

"Rothmund here. I suppose you thought you scored a big victory over me at the Club today. You thought you'd humiliated and embarrassed me, didn't you?"

"Your emotional state does not concern me one iota, Herr Rothmund." Bruno forced himself to smile. "What does concern me is whether we have a deal or not."

"You have the Club's message, Herr Fernandez?"

"Which is?"

"Why don't you ask your bodyguard?"

"Herr Rothmund," Bruno said. "I suggest you get on the telephone straight away to your friends at Mercedes, Siemens, I.G. Farben, Krupp, and Thyssen, because the required investment is now two million and one hundred thousand, with some minor additions."

"Are you mad?"

"Now write these additional items down, Herr Rothmund, because I am not going to repeat them. First, I want Mercedes to provide my tire company with ten trucks. Second, between the Krupp and Thyssen subsidiaries here in Argentina, I want twenty tons of steel held to my order. I will let you have the exact specifications. Got it? Two million dollars, ten heavy-duty trucks, and twenty tons of steel, and one hundred thousand for Pepe.

"You are insane."

"I may well be, but I'll tell you what I am not, and that is patient. One week from today, I want your answer in the positive. A week is more than generous. Good night, Herr Rothmund."

23

"Bruno," Elena purred. "I need to ask you a question." She sat up in bed and let the sheet fall behind her. The warmth trapped in the bed escaped, and his skin prickled in the air. The linens smelled of sex and perfume. He marveled at her beauty, her lithe, tanned body, and the way her black hair fanned across her smooth shoulders. She sat astride him and he stretched out his arms to stroke her.

"Ask, my darling." Bruno felt so different when he was with her, tender, caring, compassionate and gentle. His hands shook sometimes when he went to touch her, as if she would crumble, and he'd find himself in love with an illusion. He held her face in his hands and pulled her down toward him.

"Bruno." Her arms stiffened. So did her voice. "We have been seeing each other now for six months. And I still thank God you moved into a suite. We can really play at having a home here—but, my love, I'm worried."

"Elena, what is it?" His stomach flipped. "What's bothering you?"

She lowered her chin and stared hard into his eyes. She seemed to know that this particular expression left him powerless. His body felt weak under her hands.

"Do you really love me?" Elena asked. "Or are you just using me to cement a business relationship with my father?"

Bruno nodded at this confirmation that his early speculation was correct. Elena didn't notice. She was getting worked up.

"My parents are talking about buying a place at The Falls or in Patagonia, and evidently you've even promised my father a seat on the board of the bank you want to buy. Bruno, look at me, are you using me?"

"Is that a serious question?"

"Yes. And I want a straight answer." The skin around her eyes looked delicate, as if it were about to tear.

"Elena, I adore you," Bruno said. "You're the most important part of my life, the love of my life. Nothing else matters but you."

"Then why don't you ask me to marry you?"

The question was more angry than tender, but the scrap of tenderness made Bruno's heart cramp. He swallowed to clear his throat. He didn't meet her eyes.

"Maybe I'm afraid of rejection." He cleared his throat again. "After all, you should know that what I have accomplished here hasn't been through brilliance. I've done things to achieve my objectives that haven't been above board. We don't need to talk about it any more, but..."

He made himself look at her. Some of the anger had left her eyes. He couldn't tell if she was bored or genuinely waiting to hear him finish.

"My darling," he said, "I'm not really a decent person. I try to be with you and your parents and with those who are in my inner circle, but other than that..."

"Well, I love you." She leaned harder on his chest. "You should have more self-esteem. You have so much to be proud of."

"Only an idiot could fail to build up a business with almost interest-free loans that don't mature until God knows when." Bruno sat up in the bed. "And what if it all should crumble? A deformed German immigrant without any real training other than as a payroll clerk and cocktail lounge pianist. And it could crumble. I lived in Europe, don't forget. Hitler and Mussolini were the all-powerful super-gods. Look how it ended, one was assassinated and the other poisoned himself. Do you believe Perón can last forever? Be realistic. His turn will come. Then where will that leave us?"

"Shh... Shh..." She put a finger to his lips then pointed around the room. There had been rumors that the administration had bugged certain rooms at the major hotels. Bruno nodded. He had gotten himself as worked up as Elena.

"Okay," she said. "I hear what you say but it doesn't make sense. Do you think I would reject you?"

"I don't know," he said softly.

"Why don't you ask and find out?"

He looked at her and smiled. His eyes were moist and he heard himself speaking the question he had been afraid to ask.

"Elena, will you marry me?"

"Yes, my darling Bruno, yes."

She straddled him and pushed his lips open with her tongue. He felt himself harden and she reached down to guide him into her. The warm room glowed softly, like the inside of an egg, and he was holding the only woman he had ever loved.

Elena ceased her affections and leaned back to stare down at him. Something was wrong. "Bruno, I adore you. I want to be your wife, but I'm worried."

"What are you worried about?" he nervously asked.

"You may not like to hear this, but I hate my father. He is a crude, corrupt bully. God only knows why my mother married him. I'm frightened about your association with him. Sometimes I see many similarities between the two of you." Elena's eyes were sad. "Bruno, hear me well. I want my children to have an honorable man as their father, someone they can look up to. I don't want my children to have the sort of father I have. Understand?"

"I understand," Bruno said and gently wiped away her tears.

✳

A week later, Bruno got a call at his office.

"Bruno, we have something to celebrate," Francisco said. He spoke quickly and without elaboration, his usual style. "Dolores would like you and Elena to come for dinner tonight."

Bruno and Elena, with two bodyguards in the car behind them, drove to the Manzanos' new apartment in Recoleta. To Bruno, it seemed strangely liberal that the Manzanos would allow their daughter to spend every night with him at the Alvear. He and Elena would still dine at least twice every week with the Manzanos at their apartment.

Over dinner, he listened to Francisco's account of discussions with the Finance Ministry and with the Central Bank. He had pulled it off. TIC had been given the approval for the purchase of a majority interest in Banco de Financiación e Inversión, an old bank headquartered in Buenos Aires, with representative offices in Rio de Janeiro, São Paulo, Miami and New York. It was a coup to the order of eight million dollars. The business potential was significant, not only for the tire company's activities throughout Latin

America, where Brazil was in the midst of a major industrial revolution, but because of BFI's controlling interest in two Argentinean newspapers and several radio stations.

They raised their glasses high above the table. The candlelight shone in the wine and made deep purple splashes of light dance across the walls. The colonel's face was flushed. The wine colored it quickly and made his close-set eyes shine. He would never be an independent thinker, but he was loyal. The tight curls of his hair reminded Bruno of a spaniel.

"Francisco," Bruno announced, "there is a seat on the bank's board for you whenever you want. And, Dolores too, maybe you would like to be involved in the newspaper or radio stations."

That night they would have agreed to anything, and toasted everything. But it was Elena whose excitement drew a sudden quiet around the table.

"Mamá, Papá, listen," she said. Her eyes sparkled in the dim light. "There's some good news that we have, too, don't we, Bruno? Or do I have to kick you hard under the table?"

Bruno reddened and shuffled in his seat. All eyes were on him. He played with the stem of his glass.

"Dolores, Francisco," he began. "Surely, I am not doing this correctly, in that I should have discussed it with you in private. But I didn't, and I apologize. I did not intend to be discourteous." Elena reached out and grabbed his hand, and he cleared his throat before continuing. "I am very much in love with Elena. I have asked her to marry me and she has accepted. Please," he said, and his voice broke into a whisper, choked with emotion, "may we have your consent and your blessing?"

Elena squeezed his hand tightly. Her parents laughed and jumped to their feet. They embraced their daughter and her future husband.

*

The next morning, Pepe drove Bruno to his office. Bruno had chosen to keep TIC at the Trautman Tire Company rather than move it to a new office in the skyscrapers downtown. As the car pulled to the curb, he realized how much like a home his office had become. He had his staff, his routine, and his unshakable sense of being in charge. Buzzing with optimism and a second cup of coffee, he called his secretary in for their Monday meeting an hour early.

"Please sit down, Señora Cervantes. I have a lot to discuss. First, I am getting married to Señorita Elena."

"Don Bruno, that is wonderful news." Her expression said she'd seen it coming. "I imagine you'd like my help."

"I want you to work with Dolores Manzano to arrange the wedding, yes. It should take place as quickly as possible. Elena is pregnant, and only you know, Señora. Please keep it that way. The Manzanos will arrange for us to be married in the cathedral, and I am going to pull off a coup." Señora Cervantes looked up from her notepad. "I am going to arrange for the reception at The German Club."

"Is that wise?"

"It most assuredly is. I'm going to invite Herr Rothmund and all the other board members."

"Ah, but they won't come, you know that. Right?" Señora Cervantes looked worried about his mental state.

"I promise you they will not only attend but they will outdo themselves in sending the most lavish presents."

"Now I know you're joking." She smirked.

"I'm absolutely serious. They will be there and so will Herr Fischer. I'll invite him too."

"How can you be sure they won't toss the invitations into the trash?"

"Because they wouldn't dare." Bruno tugged his shirt cuffs even with his wrists. "You see, Señora, President Perón and First Lady Eva will be coming to our wedding. How could those bastards at The German Club snub our President?"

His face broke into a huge smile. She began to chuckle and then laugh aloud. She clapped her hands and shouted, "Bravo, bravo!" He allowed himself another moment of self-satisfaction, and then tapped his pen on his list of tasks.

"Now, Señora Cervantes. I want to talk to you about the list you gave me a few weeks ago." Her smile still danced in her eyes, but her face became more serious. "We have made and are continuing to make good progress," he said. "Your commission is approaching one hundred and seventy thousand, and we're not ready to close the books yet on that list, so you should see more soon. I will need to make another trip to Bariloche, for sure. But there is something else we may be able to do to keep the revenue stream flowing."

Her arms were crossed, and she was smiling. It flattered him that she enjoyed watching him work. Bruno smiled back.

"Several months ago when Herr Fischer came to my office fuming and screaming, he stated categorically that Banco Transeuropeas is owned by the Odessa. What do you know about that?"

"Nothing," his secretary replied. "After all, the ownership of the bank is a matter of public record. That information is readily available at the Central Bank, I believe."

"Yes, that's for sure. But whom did Herr Fischer report to? Were there regular board meetings? Did you ever see minutes or agendas of meetings, and did you ever see to whom they were sent?

"Hmmm." She gazed at the ceiling, remembering. "Actually, Don Bruno, the only person Herr Fischer was in regular contact with was a German attorney, a Señor Sachs. He rarely came to the bank, but Herr Fischer would visit him every Thursday morning. They would have lunch together."

"What sort of law practice does Herr Sachs have?"

"I don't know. I assume he has a number of German clients."

"Do you know anyone who works for him?"

"Well." She considered the question, and lifted her hand in a half-shrug. "I had regular contact with one of his secretaries. Her name was Astrid. I haven't spoken with her since I left the bank and came to work for you."

"Señora, we're going to need to do some more prospecting for gold. Everyone on your old list was a client of the bank. Now let's see if we can penetrate the bank's ownership. Plan on getting together with this Astrid to do some probing. See how receptive she is. If she cooperates, she could make a lot of money, too."

"Good." She nodded and made a note for herself. "I'll get on it straight away."

He watched her as she wrote and he smiled, congratulating himself on what a good little accomplice he had made of her. This Astrid could be useful too. But first things first.

"No," he told her. "Call Dolores Manzano and Elena about the wedding first. I'm going to see Herr Rothmund at The German Club."

"I know you're going to enjoy that meeting," Señora Cervantes said. "I will relish hearing about it."

✳

Within an hour, Bruno was ushered into the club president's office. Herr Rothmund sat behind his desk. He sneered over the entries in his ledger, refusing to look Bruno in the eye. The picture window behind him overlooked a burned-out shell of a building, and beyond that, a bare tree. Among the building's charred beams, a couple of mangy dogs were rummaging for scraps of food, and if they were lucky, maybe a dead rat.

"What do you want?" Rothmund said. "Isn't it enough that you've practically bankrupted the club? You come here for lunch every week with your high-ranking friends in the military, flaunting your so-called immunity. You've been paid your money, you've been supplied with the trucks, and all that remains is your delivery instructions on the steel. So what else is there to discuss?"

"Herr Rothmund, enough of the pleasantries, thank you," Bruno said with a grin. "First the steel. Expect to hear from my accountant sometime during the next week. Don Tomás will give you delivery instructions. I thank you for taking care of that."

"Good, so if there is nothing else, please would you now leave?"

Bruno leaned on the chair-back. Taking the weight off his foot was a relief. Besides, leaning removed the feeling of standing before the club's president like a disobedient schoolboy.

"There is something else, Herr Rothmund. I am pleased to inform you that I am about to be married to Señorita Elena Manzano. I want to discuss the wedding arrangements. I want the wedding reception here at the club."

"You must be joking." Herr Rothmund laughed. "It is quite out of the question. The committee would never allow you, after all you have done, to have your wedding celebrations here." He made a shooing motion. "Now please leave."

"I would like to take over the club for the wedding party on May 31st, four weeks from now." Bruno pretended to look at Rothmund's desk calendar. "Of course, I shall be inviting you and all your fellow officers of the club. My future mother-in-law, my fiancée, and my secretary will be in contact with you to discuss all the arrangements. Expense is no object."

"You obviously didn't hear me, Herr Fernandez," Rothmund said. "You will not be celebrating your wedding at this club."

"And I want it to be especially decorative." Bruno smiled. "The floral displays must be particularly sensational. Please bring in your best floral designers."

"Herr Fernandez, I've already told you..."

"Our first lady, Eva Perón, particularly likes white flowers, so we must have plenty of those. And I want the lighting and microphones to be of the utmost quality when President Perón stands to toast the health and happiness of the bride and groom." Bruno stood up and inspected his fingernails. "Can you ensure that? It would be embarrassing if I had to tell the president's secretary that the club needs to borrow equipment from the Presidential Palace."

"Herr Fernandez." Rothmund's eyes widened in their fleshy wet lids. He slowly sat up at his desk and become rigid, like a man about to die in an electric chair. "Are you telling me that the President and the First Lady will be attending your wedding here?"

"Yes, unless you want me to go back to them to say you are refusing to allow our celebration at the club."

"Get out of this office."

"Auf Wiedersehen, Herr Rothmund."

Bruno exited the club with a lighter step and took a seat in his car. As Pepe maneuvered into the flow of traffic, Bruno looked out over the burnt ruins of the Jockey Club. It had been burned to the ground one night, the arson rumored to have been triggered by an insult allegedly hurled by a member at the First Lady.

"Pepe, back to my office, please."

✳

Señora Cervantes took his coat. "Don Bruno. Your visitor, Señor Vetter has arrived. He is accompanied by another gentleman, a Señor Ginsberg. They are in the conference room."

Ginsberg. This should be interesting, Bruno thought. He stood to the side of the conference room door and observed them through the blinds. Vetter was thin for a middle-aged man, making his ordinary gray suit a baggy fit to his small body. His companion, Ginsberg, was younger—he had wavy black hair and a more heroic build than his companion. They were chatting across the table but stopped abruptly when Bruno seized the door handle.

"Gentlemen, good morning. I hope I haven't kept you long." Bruno drew the door closed behind him. "What can I do for you?" He sat at the head of the table and poured himself a cup of coffee.

"Señor Fernandez, thank you for receiving us," Vetter began as they settled themselves around their subject. He had a dry voice that suited his gray clothing. "The reason for our visit is unusual and even unique. I live in Brazil. I left Germany in 1945 for all the obvious reasons. I have heard of your activities in Argentina and how you have built up a huge business conglomerate here as a result of interesting and advantageous bonds." He raised a brow. "Soon, I would suggest, you will run out of potential investors in Argentina. The good times won't last forever here. I can help you in Brazil and maybe other countries like Chile, Bolivia and Paraguay, where I have similar connections to those that you have here. In Brazil, we may have some very big fish—Borman, for instance, and Rauff in Chile. Mengele is floating around, too."

"Herr Vetter, if you have these leads, why would you wish to share them with me? I don't quite understand your rationale of wanting to discuss this with me."

"In Germany, before the war," Vetter explained, "I was a detective in the Berlin police department, dealing mainly with homicide and missing persons. During the war, well, I don't wish to discuss what I did. I am now living a quiet life in Brazil. I have no business experience. I am not aggressive enough to convert the information I have into hard cash as you have done. That is why I need you, and if you wish to break into more markets such as Brazil and other countries, you need me."

Bruno paused to sip his coffee. He saw that his visitors' cups were still full.

"And you, Señor Ginsberg. What is your involvement in this?"

"Señor Fernandez. My position is unique. I am an Italian Jew. I served with the Italian resistance during the last days of the war in Europe. Our unit subsequently attached itself to The Jewish Brigade in Northern Italy. I then became involved in Berihah, a movement to smuggle Jews out of Europe and into Palestine. I am now active in seeking out Nazis in Latin America and bringing them to justice."

Though difficult, Bruno forced himself to make eye contact. "Señor Ginsberg, I simply do not understand why you would wish to sit at the same table with men like Herr Vetter and me. Equally, why you would expect us to want to sit with you. I am very confused."

"Yes, I accept that this is unusual." He did not share Bruno's difficulty with eye contact. He sat comfortably in his chair, suit jacket unbuttoned. In his eyes was a faint look of disgust for the two other men. "Bottom line, we are all, the three of us, involved in tracing former Nazis. So it is probably beneficial if we were to cooperate. We also have different agendas. You and Herr Vetter wish to locate them, blackmail them, and in your case, force them to invest in your company. My organization's goal is to find and kill them in the name of justice for the Jewish people."

"Well, that doesn't suit me. I cannot milk a dead cow."

"You can provide me with a list of your investors, and I will see that they are taken care of. They will never be a threat to you in the future. Likewise, I will provide you with a list of our targets and their addresses, and you will have a window of opportunity to establish contact with them to extract what you can, before we eliminate them. We will be giving you a source of funds, and we will also be removing them as potential threats down the road, to the benefit of you and your family's physical well-being."

Bruno chewed on this, and receiving no immediate relief from his confusion, he shifted his gaze to the older man. "Herr Vetter, what do you have to say in response to Herr Ginsberg's suggestions?"

"On the one hand, I do not like it. After all, you and I are both German." His heavier eyebrow sunk lower over one eye. His tone excluded his colleague. "It is one thing to take money from these people, who upon paying it expect to be spared exposure to danger—and it is another to cooperate in their assassinations. However, I see the obvious logic. You and I would be provided with leads, and Herr Ginsberg..." He waved at the younger man without looking at him. "After an agreed period in which to extract our funds, the Jewish revenge would then reduce the risk of future reprisals. I see, for instance, that you are always accompanied by bodyguards. You must already be mindful of the danger you face."

Bruno twisted his cup delicately on the table. "Herr Ginsberg. If I give you a list of names, how do I know you won't eliminate those individuals before I've had the opportunity of persuading them to invest?" He looked up and met the Jew's eyes. "These names are my assets, you understand."

"How much time would you need in each case?"

"Maybe three months."

"You would have it."

Bruno halted the conversation and stood. "Gentlemen, let's meet again in a couple of days. I need to consider this carefully. The idea of spreading our business activities more aggressively outside Argentina is appealing, given the uncertain political climate, but wholesale assassinations are not part of my philosophy. I also need to consider whether I wish to be involved in such an activity with a Jew."

✳

Two nights before the wedding, Bruno surprised Elena during dinner at her parents' home. While they were all sitting at the table, he rose and told her to close her eyes. He moved behind her chair, and from his jacket pocket, he took out the emerald pendant that had been languishing in his safe-deposit box at Banco de la Provincia.

For her birthday, he had given her a piece of jewelry and another at Christmas, but he had kept back the pendant with this night in mind. It hadn't been cleaned in years, and when he unwrapped it from its velvet cloth and showed it to Señora Cervantes, she recommended that he have it professionally cleaned. The emerald shone in the light and he was pleased that he had listened to her advice. The jeweler had been jealous of it, and gave Bruno several opportunities to consider an offer for it. Bruno had ignored them and felt his heart swell now as Elena's mother moved her hand over her mouth to stifle a gasp, and she and Francisco stared in awe at the precious emerald pendant.

"Can I open my eyes now, darling?"

"Not yet." He fiddled with the clasp and positioned the pendant so that it hung on her tanned cleavage.

"Now you can open your eyes."

She slowly let them open, and looked down.

"My God," she gasped. "I have never seen any emerald so beautiful. So bright... so perfect." It burned with light as she lifted it on her fingertips. "My darling, this is wonderful. I love this piece. I will cherish it forever. Darling... thank you." She held it in front of her eyes, and the sparkling gem caught the candlelight and threw green sparks across the walls.

The Cardinal Archbishop officiated the ceremony at the cathedral, and the reception afterward at The German Club was considered the highlight of the social calendar. Bruno tried hard not to smirk as he led the First Lady past Herr Rothmund's table on his way to the dance floor.

*

Seven months later, the press reported on the birth of Carlos and Isabella, saying, "Though premature, the twins are blessedly in boisterous and robust health."

*

Bruno and Elena moved out of his suite and into their own mansion in Recoleta, a villa set in a two-acre walled garden, with a gatekeeper on duty at all times.

TIC's business grew beyond Bruno's expectations. In Argentina, the tire business, the bank, newspaper, radio stations, air charter subsidiary, and construction company all reported steadily growing profits. The recently acquired grain exporting business had secured some significant orders, too. In Brazil, as a result of Herr Vetter's efforts, investments had been made in a bank and a hotel chain. Now and again, Bruno read small items in the paper about the mysterious death of a member of the German community, and smiled to himself. The Jew had kept his word. And in truth, Bruno was glad to be done with that business. His chess set languished under a layer of dust in the back bedroom.

One morning, after putting aside the paper, Bruno dialed a number he knew by heart. "Francisco, we need to talk. Can you come over to the house, please?"

Within an hour, his father-in-law arrived. He had become used to responding immediately to Bruno's requests.

"Let's sit in the garden," Bruno suggested, after taking his father-in-law's hat and coat. It was important not to treat the older man as a minion. "One never knows how loyal the servants are these days. I don't want anyone listening at the door."

The children were at school and Elena was visiting friends in New York. They walked outside and toward the pool, its glassy surface gleaming in the morning sun.

"I am very worried about the political situation," Bruno said and flagged the servant for coffee. While the boy set up their table and brought an ashtray,

Francisco engaged himself with his long cigar-lighting ritual.

When the servant was done, the colonel said around puffs of rich smoke, "We're all very worried, Bruno."

There were now frequent riots against the administration. Perón was hated by as many as once worshipped him. Bruno believed it was time to begin distancing themselves from Perón, and the colonel agreed that the president would be deposed within a few months. Perón had alienated the Church over the Divorce Law, and the economic downturn was a strain on everyone. Thank God, Bruno was diversified enough to dodge that bullet. And then there were the damned riots.

"Only a few weeks ago," Francisco said, "three hundred and sixty four civilians were killed at the Plaza de Mayo. And here we are, very much identified with the Perónists."

"Who do you see as possible leaders of a coup?"

"There is General Onardi, General Aramburu, and Admiral Rojas. They are most widely spoken of as being behind a possible coup." Francisco pushed his coffee toward Bruno. He said the smell interfered with his cigar.

"This is what we need to do," Bruno said. "Make contact with them. Do not pledge support, just establish a friendly relationship. If they ask for anything, say that you will get back to them after you have discussed it with me. Also, make an appointment to meet confidentially with Perón and ask him what his thoughts are, should he be deposed in a coup. Draw him out. Find out if there is anything we can do to assist him. Meanwhile, I want to move aggressively to develop our business interests outside Latin America. I have an ambitious plan."

Francisco lifted his eyebrows but did not ask the obvious question. He was used to Bruno's showmanship by now—but if there was tension between them, he diffused it by relighting his cigar.

"There is a bank for sale in New York," Bruno explained. "The Pillsbury Bank & Trust, well-established, in business since 1874. It's largely family owned and apparently has a sleepy management. The bank has rested on its laurels since the end of the First World War. They have no significant commercial customers, but within New York society, the name counts for something. I think if we acquired the bank we could use it as a springboard to shift the future growth of TIC to the more economically stable North America, as opposed to what I see as potential chaos here in South America. I can be more objective than you, Francisco. I'm European and I saw what happened to Hitler and Mussolini. The same can happen here."

Francisco exhaled a stream of acrid smoke into the morning air, and looked through it toward the garden wall and vista beyond. "So how do you propose buying into one of the old New York private banks?"

"I'm flying to New York next week. Elena and I will spend some time looking for an apartment there, and I will instruct attorneys to look into the possibility of TIC, together with our banks in Rio and here, buying it either outright or buying into it. I'm also open to discussing a possible merger of TIC with a US company, or maybe a flotation on the New York Stock Exchange. That way we would, as best we can, protect ourselves should our world turn upside down here in Argentina."

✳

And the world did turn upside down.

Perón was deposed in a military coup and went into exile. Perónists were persecuted. The Manzanos were unaffected and TIC managed to survive, thanks to Bruno's diversified investments. He and Elena made New York their primary residence, and they bought a house in the Hamptons. The children were sent to boarding schools on the East Coast and became Americanized.

Then Perón returned to Argentina, and in 1973 was elected to a third term. At the Manzano's behest, Bruno and Elena flew to Buenos Aires with the twins, now in their early twenties, to pay their respects to the aged general and his new wife, Isabel.

The investment in the Pillsbury Bank turned out to be successful. The bank's connections with TIC resulted in a stream of new business, and soon it attracted the accounts of multinational corporations eager to expand their commerce in Latin America. Bruno was appointed vice-chairman.

One morning, while shaving, Bruno had an idea. It came to him in a flash. He wiped the shaving cream from his face, wrapped a towel around his waist, and walked onto the patio. Elena was already there, lounging in her silk robe and sipping coffee while reading the morning paper. She looked up at him and smiled. She could see that he had something on his mind, and she raised her eyebrows, inviting him to share his thoughts.

Bruno sat in a patio chair across from her. "Darling, I have an idea. Neither you nor I have ever been to London. In fact, I haven't been to

Europe since the end of the war. Next month is a big international banking conference in London. I think as vice-chairman and the largest stock-holder in the Pillsbury Bank, we should go. What do you say?"

24

LEO WOKE UP THE NEXT MORNING IN A SOMBER MOOD. THE trip to Drancy had left him drained. Perhaps it was the prayer that had drained him. Or knowing that, for many, the only exit from the camp at Drancy was a train to their death. All of life was draining, to imagine his family was gone, and he would never see them again. Elizabeth showed the same expression and fatigue.

In the kitchen, Leo sat across the table from Elizabeth.

"Darling, I have an idea," he said while pouring coffee. "Why don't we postpone going to Nice for a few weeks until my emotions settle? After all, this is our honeymoon, a new beginning. Let's just continue on to Geneva now. Our apartment is ready and I have another week before starting at the bank. You have two weeks before you begin at the International Labor Office. We can settle in, explore the city, go out on the lake and relax."

She hesitated, and Leo studied her. Had he misjudged her? Perhaps she'd been looking forward to a few days on the Riviera. He loved her so but still was unsure if he understood her.

She smiled. "Okay. I think that's a very good idea. Nice isn't going away."

They took the train that afternoon and arrived in Geneva at six o'clock. The apartment provided by the bank was a short ride from the station. A double bed filled the bedroom, and the tiny bathroom had only a shower. Two people couldn't fit in the kitchen at the same time, and the narrow living room, consumed by a sofa and coffee table, was no less claustrophobic. The place hadn't seen a coat of paint in years and had a musty feel, but it would work.

"Let's open all the windows," Elizabeth said, sniffing. "I think I smell gas." She rushed around the apartment, wrestling with the windows to let in fresh air.

"Well, the price is right," Leo offered.

"Is Banque Lapis providing us with accommodations, or an early death?" she asked with a sigh, then laughed. "Why don't we leave the unpacking until tomorrow and go out and have something to eat. Toast our new lives in Geneva." She turned around in the empty kitchen, opening and closing the few cabinets and drawers. "After all, there's no food in the bloody place."

"Good idea." Leo swept her along and straight out the door to better air.

They spent the next few days as tourists. They took walks along the waterfront and marveled at the Jet d'Eau, the swans, and the flowers in bloom. They window-shopped along the Rues-Basses and explored the Old Town with its cluster of small shops, sidewalk cafes, and street musicians. They stopped to feast on raclettes and fondue. Another day they traveled by water taxi to dine on trout at La Perle du Lac, housed in a chalet in a park overlooking the waterfront.

"Let's check out where I'll be working today," Elizabeth said enthusiastically over breakfast one morning.

Leo felt a touch of resentment that it was the brightest she'd sounded since they'd arrived. But he was eager to humor her. So they walked to the international zone, several long blocks from their apartment, to the Palais des Nations, and made their way between the embassies, villas, and museums. They sat and held hands, relaxed in the Jardin Botanique, and gazed at three-hundred-year-old trees and the mountain views.

Geneva was a beautiful place. And it was a fresh start. There was much he and Elizabeth could do together in this wonderful new city. So much to plan, to discover, and to enjoy. So much to talk about with his loving wife. Elizabeth only wanted to talk about her job.

✳

Monsieur Hug had a flat, bald head and colorless eyebrows, and he was very short. He sat on an artificially high chair behind his desk that brought his bottle-cap spectacles to the level of Leo's gaze.

"Good morning, Mr. Bergner. Welcome to Banque Lapis. Your father-in-law has spoken very highly of you. We're delighted to have you join us for a two-year training program. Your language skills are impressive and will be useful. Your stay with us will be divided into specific programs. You will spend time, and in this sequence, in our four principal departments— bullion, foreign exchange, investments, and banking. I will oversee your training."

Leo observed the bank's managing director carefully as he spoke. Monsieur Hug did not appear delighted to have Leo at the bank and clearly, he had agreed under duress.

"First," Hug continued, "you need to report to our personnel department and complete the usual forms, especially those that relate to Swiss bank secrecy. You must be very careful not to violate any of our secrecy laws, as it will get you into deep trouble, not only with us but with the Swiss National Bank, and maybe even the police."

The work in the bullion department was interesting. Leo monitored the daily fluctuations in the price of gold, kept the bank's clients informed of trends, and took their instructions for sales and purchases. To improve his knowledge, he read up on the economics and history of gold and attended a number of seminars on bullion. Leo settled into the routine of conventional office hours and followed his interests when he could.

At the end of each day, Leo enjoyed the pleasant commute by streetcar to the Boulevard du Theatre. He often stopped at a boulangerie to buy fresh bread and croissants for the next morning. Lunchtimes, he wandered around the Old City and had a sandwich and a glass of wine, usually alone. His past connections seemed hopelessly distant, which made everything around him seem arbitrary and uncertain. He felt both settled and at the same time uncomfortable.

Sometimes he complained to Elizabeth. She blamed the wine for these thoughts and told him to stop drinking alone. Meanwhile, she had settled into her job at the International Labor Office. She had her own office, small but with a magnificent view of the lake. She liked the work and spoke highly of her manager, Signor Ramati, an Italian attorney. Her frequent remarks about his immaculately tailored suits, custom-made shoes and shirts, and dark ties made it clear that she admired the way he dressed. She began dressing better too, with the added flair of a bold-colored Chanel scarf around her neck.

After a few weeks, and one of his forbidden glasses of wine, Leo came home with an announcement. "Darling, next Monday is a public holiday.

Let's each take Friday off and go to Nice on Thursday evening." He moved closer and wrapped her in his arms. "I'm ready to face it finally."

"Of course, Leo." She kissed his ear tenderly. "Of course."

✳

The train pulled into Nice's main station at close to eleven o'clock. The station evoked those summers when he and his parents would arrive from Augsburg, with Karin and Jacques standing at the barrier waving vigorously. It made him angry, that everything could look so much the same. He put such thoughts to the back of his mind. This was a time to be happy.

The next morning, Maitre Talais beamed as he welcomed them into his home. "Well, it is very nice to meet you, Elizabeth. I have heard so much about you from Leo. Welcome to Nice. Sadly, my wife is away, visiting her relatives." He was a rush of energy and words, as if trying to fill the empty space in Leo's chest with his own brisk enthusiasm. "When we have finished, I will take you to the apartment. Better still, I have the keys here. You can go on your own. Afterward, Leo, I need you to come to my office. There is much we need to discuss."

Elizabeth offered to stay behind, but Leo wanted her with him. He struggled with the key, then managed to open the door. Leo wandered into the large apartment in silence, moving slowly and scanning from side to side. Elizabeth paused to look at each of the photographs. It was the first time she had seen pictures of his family, and she seemed reluctant to comment on them. He came up from behind her and stood at her shoulder. He studied the framed shot of his mother and Karin standing in front of the pharmacy.

"Which is your mother and which is Karin?" she asked.

"That's my mother, and that's Karin. She always smiled like she was the happiest she'd ever been. Always. And this is my father, and that one is Cousin Jacques."

"They all seem so happy." She touched the glass. "Your mother was very beautiful. Such lovely hair. And just look at that pendant."

"That would have been yours one day, but God knows where it is now."

"It's spectacular."

Leo looked at his mother with her hand on the pendant. What would that amazing stone look like on Elizabeth? He would never know.

"Is this you?" she asked, looking at a photograph of when he advertised his piano services.

"That's me," he said.

The boy in the picture was just fourteen. Or maybe thirteen. Just looking at the picture made Leo feel ancient.

They sat for a while. The sofa felt different under his weight—more spongy, less natural. He held Elizabeth's hand and wanted to speak. The only sound was the birds chirping on the balcony.

"Leo," she said at last, "while you go and see Maitre Talais, why don't I go and buy a suitcase, and I'll meet you back here. I can pack all the photographs and other mementos, and we'll take them back to Geneva. Better we have them there. And all this beautiful porcelain and silver. We can't just leave it here indefinitely."

"I know, darling. The photographs, and also that old metronome. It brings back so many memories."

✳

Maitre Talais escorted Leo into his office. There were papers to sign—many of them—which Talais would file in court the next week.

The man was wreathed in his eternal ring of cigarette smoke. "First, we have proceeded on the basis that you are the sole heir of your parents and cousins, in accordance with the terms of all four wills, and that they are all now presumed dead. Net after taxes, this means that you have inherited close to two hundred thousand, which can be transferred to you next week, wherever you want it."

Talais opened another file with details of the Nice real estate and other salable goods. Leo could gain another fourteen thousand for the fixtures and fittings at the pharmacy. Then there was the jewelry and contents of the apartment.

"I advise you to sell the apartment," Talais added. "You will also receive one hundred and fifty thousand from the life insurance company, once they accept the premise that all four policyholders have perished. In the meantime, you remember the rabbi here before the war?"

"Rabbi Aaron," Leo said.

"He also perished at Auschwitz."

Both men sat in silence, downcast with their eyes closed.

Maitre Talais looked up. "The rabbi's son-in-law, Andre, is a local developer and partner in a real estate investment firm. He has close ties to the Nice community. He has expressed an interest in your properties."

The words passed through Leo like a ghost. So Rabbi Aaron was dead, too. Leo could not fathom his old anger, or his conviction that the rabbi had deliberately kept his family in France. The man had done all he could to save the children. The adults, however, all died together.

"It would be good to sell," Talais said. "Pass the burden to another."

Leo nodded, and kept nodding. He simply could not care what became of such an inheritance.

*

A couple of days after returning to Geneva, Monsieur Hug summoned Leo to his office.

"Mr. Bergner, we have a new weekly assignment, and I have chosen you and Monsieur Fabre for it."

In a chair to one side sat Fabre. They exchanged nods. Fabre had worked at the bank for several years and was considered a rising star in the bullion department. His hair was combed and waxed in a moderately high bouffant. He too, it seemed, resented Leo's presence at Banque Lapis.

Monsieur Hug continued, "One of our important clients is the Pontificio Istituto Teutonico in Rome, a seminary located close to the Vatican. Many of their wealthy benefactors remit funds to them via their account here with us. The Istituto has a need for gold. It is not for us to question their reasons, it is our duty as one of their bankers to be of service to them, you understand?"

Leo and Fabre nodded.

"Every Thursday afternoon," Hug continued, "a priest from the cathedral here will come to the bank. One of you, together with one of our security guards, will leave by car to the railway station and take the train to Rome. You will take two suitcases on each trip."

Hug pulled a handkerchief from his coat pocket and held it to his lips. Leo remained attentive. His military training served him well during these long discourses on duties.

"The train," Hug said, "unfortunately, is not a direct route. You will make two changes, one at Brig, and the other in Milan. The train arrives very late in Rome. A car will meet you at the station and take you to the Istituto where you will hand over the cases to Bishop Hudal, who will be waiting up for you. He will sign a receipt for the gold and give you back the two empty suitcases. The car will then take you to a small hotel near the station where we will make arrangements for you to stay."

Courier services. This must be a regular part of banking. Leo never imagined his job would include such responsibilities. Especially with the commodity being gold.

Hug continued, "You will have Friday free in Rome to do as you please. As long as you are back at nine o'clock on Monday morning, Banque Lapis does not care what you do. The bank will give you a per diem allowance, for the Friday, Saturday, and Sunday. It will be a good opportunity to see Rome."

"And we are to take turns doing this, Monsieur Hug?" Fabre asked. There was a note of resentment again.

"Yes, so create your own schedules."

"How long will this go on?" Leo asked.

"Until the client says so, Mr. Bergner."

On his way back to the apartment, Leo thought about his new assignment. What would Elizabeth have to say about it? Perhaps she'd enjoy spending every other weekend in Rome. Yes, it might be fun.

"I think you'll just have to see how it works out." Elizabeth stood at the stove, stirring a pan of onions. "After all, you're traveling with a priest and a security guard. It may not be appropriate to take a wife."

It was her practical side emerging again. With a pang in his heart, Leo realized how much she could remind him of his mother. How Ulrike had argued with his father to leave Germany. They'd be alive today if he would have listened to her.

"Let's see," Leo said, and left it at that.

The bullion department was busy and understaffed. The bank had purchased large volumes of gold during the war, much of it from Germany, and was sitting on significant stockpiles. It was an interesting activity but not one that Leo found sufficiently absorbing to consider making it his life's vocation, so the diversion of spending regular weekends in Rome was welcome, especially if Elizabeth kept him company.

"I really do hate this damned apartment, Leo," Elizabeth said one evening. "It's dark, it's depressing, and it stinks. I don't know what we could do to brighten it up. What do you think?"

"I guess some fresh paint, a few plants and brighter light bulbs would be a good start," he replied. "But remember, it's rent-free, and we're only here for a short time."

"But it's so depressing. I don't even like making love here. It almost makes it seem seedy, as if we're renting it by the hour." She laughed.

"You have a point."

"When is your first trip to Rome?" Laughter still sparked in her eyes.

"Fabre goes this week, then I'll be going the following Thursday. The last time I was in Rome was during the war, when sometimes I would hitch a ride from our base. I'm looking forward to it. But I wish you were coming."

"Maybe on another trip." She sighed. "I have so much work at the office. I am so lucky to have this job. The work is interesting, the pay is good, and the benefits are marvelous. I have a diplomatic passport, a great office and fun colleagues. I'm happy, Leo."

"What about a wonderful husband?" he joked.

"Yes, he's okay, too." She smirked.

The twice-monthly trips to Rome soon lost their appeal. Long waits at the stations in Brig and Milan, surly traveling companions, a disgruntled security guard whose breath stank of garlic, and a priest who discouraged any attempt at polite conversation—all made Leo long for his seedy apartment with Elizabeth.

Then there were the suitcases, always heavy and cumbersome. And the reception upon arrival at the Pontificio Istituto was unfriendly. The per diem allowance proved barely enough to buy a slice of pizza and a glass of the least expensive Chianti. Leo wandered the city and spent hours sitting at a cafe on the Via Veneto, watching postwar Rome come alive again. More often than not, he did not wait until Sunday to return to Geneva.

Then Leo was transferred to the foreign exchange department. But there was no letup in his trips to Rome. The new job was hectic, and Leo enjoyed the excitement of telephones ringing nonstop and dealers shouting rates across the room. Also, a greater camaraderie occurred among the dealers than had existed in the bullion department. They invited him out for drinks many nights, and he learned more than he'd wanted to know about the new Europe that was growing up around him.

The postwar monetary world developed a confusing and sinister side, as a shady world of barter and countertrade sprung up between the Soviet block and its satellites—Hungary, Poland, Bulgaria, Rumania and so forth—and the West. The Soviets had little hard currency, but they had product. They exchanged, for example, Polish hams for trucks and tires from the West. A whole cadre of countertrade and barter specialists grew up within the cracks of this business, many of them dubious characters, and Vienna seemed to be the unofficial center.

More than ever, the world around Leo looked like nothing he recognized. Each day, he wondered if he even knew himself anymore. He was no banker at heart, but he lived like one, worked like one, and saw no one but other bankers. He seemed to enjoy their company. He wondered if this was the rest of his life, and what good any of it was.

✳

"Hello, darling." Elizabeth lay on the couch, reading. "How are you? Did you have a good day at the office? I had to stay on an extra couple of hours and go through a memorandum with Signor Ramati. He has to make a presentation tomorrow." Her eyes stayed on her book, but finally she frowned and shut it on her chest. "And you?"

"I met with Andre today, Rabbi Aaron's son-in-law. He gave me a lot of details about his company." Leo set his briefcase on the floor and tapped it. "I'll read the papers later, but I'll probably sell him the Nice properties. Shall we go round the corner for a bite, or do you want to have dinner at home?"

"Oh, let's go round the corner and have a pizza or something. This apartment really depresses me."

"I know, darling, but it's the best we can do at the moment."

"But I'm saving nearly all my salary. I could put something toward a better and brighter place." She looked up at the ceiling, then at the miserable gray burned lampshade and the depressing mustard-colored drapes. "I really can't stand it here. I feel miserable in this hole."

"It wouldn't look right at Banque Lapis. It's an apartment they're renting for us. Let's just grin and bear it. It's not forever."

During dinner, he looked at her across the table. She didn't look happy—she looked nervous. Leo put down his fork.

"You look troubled, Elizabeth. What's the matter?"

"Darling, I love my work and I love you, but we have a few problems.

I hate our apartment. It's so damned drab. Can't you see it for yourself?"
Her stare defied him to defend it. "And you work so hard at the bank that
by the time you come home, you're dead. Then every other weekend you're
away. And we don't seem to spend much time together. There's something
else, too. Not that I'm anxious to have children, but why am I not getting
pregnant? We make love often enough."

"If you're not eager to have children, what are you worried about?"

"I'd like the option." Anger showed in her eyes. "I'd like to know that
I'm normal."

"Then let's make an appointment to see a doctor."

✳

Andre's company made an offer Leo couldn't refuse—three hundred
thousand shares in their real estate venture in trade for the Nice properties.
Two hundred thousand for Leo, and one hundred thousand for Maitre
Talais. Leo accepted and became a stockholder in a dynamic French
enterprise.

Then Leo's term in the foreign exchange department came to an end,
and he was transferred to the investment department under the supervision of Dr. Breitman, considered one of Geneva's most brilliant portfolio
managers. Dr. Breitman's specialty was the American stock market. He
insisted on compulsory daily reading of the *Wall Street Journal* and *Barron's*.
Every morning he required a two-page typed summary of highlights in the
financial world.

"Mr. Bergner, I also want you to take a course in financial accounting.
It is very important that you understand the rudiments of how to read and
analyze a balance sheet. It will help you in determining what stocks are to be
bought and which are to be avoided. Also, when you are transferred to the
banking department, you will be much more useful to my colleagues there
in putting together loan requests to the board. My secretary is telephoning
the University of Geneva. They usually have classes two nights every week
for people who have day jobs. Banque Lapis will pay. My secretary will give
you the details."

"Thank you, sir," Leo mumbled, apprehensive of how Elizabeth would
react to yet another pair of late nights with him away from home.

He needn't have worried. She took it. Only he seemed taken aback by the amount of work that would now be his. And all the time he'd be away from Elizabeth.

"Are you off to Rome tomorrow, darling?" she asked. She was refilling her diffuser of perfume.

"Yes. I'm trying to persuade Monsieur Hug to relieve me of this duty, now that I have these two classes every week, but I'm not optimistic."

"My appointment with the gynecologist is tomorrow." She capped the bottle.

"Would you like me to come?" Leo asked.

She tested the perfume and placed it on the bathroom shelf just so. Then she looked around at the tiled walls and sighed. Her eyes never turned his way.

"That won't be necessary. But if I need to go back, maybe."

✳

"Mr. Bergner, come and see me, please," Dr. Breitman said in his usual autocratic manner.

Leo put down the telephone and started into the corridor, wondering what this might be about. He was surprised to find Monsieur Hug and Monsieur Fabre standing in the doorway of Breitman's office.

Dr. Breitman was behind his desk. "Mr. Bergner, I'm afraid we are going to have to prevail on you and Monsieur Fabre further with regard to these weekly trips to Rome. For the next four weeks, you are each going to make one trip every week. I'm sorry about this, but we have to accommodate our client's requests."

Fabre looked at Leo and shrugged. They had both grown tired of these trips and formed some kind of unspoken camaraderie over it. Sometimes Leo felt like an accomplice-in-crime with Fabre.

"You will each make a weekly trip," Breitman continued. "One week by train, as before, and one week by road. The trips by road will be in a vehicle provided by the client, Pontificio Istituto. The vans will leave every Monday and return every Wednesday. The empty van will arrive here every Monday morning at nine o'clock, with the priest and a driver, and as soon as it is loaded, you will be on your way." Dr. Breitman's demeanor reminded Leo of one of his old army commanders. "Bergner, smile. You will be spending so much time with the priest, he may convert you to Catholicism."

Leo bristled. The trips to Rome were tiring enough. Dr. Breitman's frequent inappropriate attempts at humor only made the assignment worse.

"What is the cargo, sir?" Fabre asked. "Am I permitted to inquire?"

"I am coming to that. Monsieur Hug is going to treat you to something very special. He is going to take you down to the vaults, to one particular area that very few of our employees, let alone managers, have ever seen. I must remind you of the confidentiality agreements you have signed. You are not at liberty to discuss this with any other employee of the bank or with anyone outside the bank, and that includes your families. Do you understand?"

Leo looked at Fabre and nodded. Fabre answered more with a shrug than any affirmative answer.

"Come with me," Hug said.

Leo followed Fabre, then Monsieur Hug out of the office and toward the elevator. Hug entered a security code on a panel inside the elevator, fearful of making a mistake and setting off the bank's alarms. As they descended, Leo watched the display above the door counting down the level and was surprised to see it stop at 'B' though the elevator continued to drop.

"Yes, Mr. Bergner," Monsieur Hug said, "we have several floors beneath the basement level, all unmarked."

Once the elevator stopped, they exited into a small carpeted area, brightly lit, with two security guards seated behind steel desks. The cramped space for visitors wasn't much bigger than the elevator car.

"Good morning, Schmidt," Hug said. "We need to open Vault 39."

Schmidt stood and led the way to a tall iron door. He turned various dials and waited for Monsieur Hug to provide a code. The gate opened electronically to reveal a long, carpeted corridor, along which they were forced to walk single file. On both sides were solid steel doors, each with two dials and a keyhole.

They stopped at a door, and Leo saw that it was marked Number 39. Hug stepped forward to unlock the door with a key, then each of them spun a dial to enter a combination and the door swung open. Monsieur Hug turned on a light. Paintings hung on all four walls from the ceiling to the floor. No furniture, just a few bronzes in neat lines. The room was laid out like an art gallery.

"Goodness, this is quite a museum here," Fabre remarked. "Can we have time to look at these paintings? Just magnificent. Isn't that a Van Gogh over there?"

"And look at this," Leo said. "This has to be a Renoir and, God, look at that, I bet that's a Gauguin."

Leo approached the Gauguin and had to resist stroking the canvas with his fingers. The primitive figures stared back at him, in sharp contrast to the femininity, diffidence, elegance, and sophistication of the Renoir. This was Aladdin's cave. And knowing what he did about Europe's shady new banking world, he wondered where the evil genie was hiding. Monsieur Hug allowed them another moment of unprofessional wonder and then raised his hands.

"Gentlemen, two men will be coming every day for a few weeks. They will crate these paintings, and you will each be responsible for seeing that they reach their destination in Rome. And remember, this is confidential."

"Is the Istituto planning to display these paintings in Rome?" Leo asked.

"That, Mr. Bergner, is not our business. We are here to act on their instructions, not to ask their plans. Now, let's return to our desks."

✳

Leo put down the newspaper and looked out of his living room window. The news from Palestine did not look good. If the Jews took the next logical step of declaring statehood, now that the United Nations had approved partition, there would be a war. December in Geneva was bleak. Such news about Palestine made the weather more burdensome.

Also, Elizabeth was not able to have children. They resigned themselves to the fact, though now and again Leo brought up the possibility of adoption. Elizabeth was in no hurry to discuss it. Instead she focused on her job and had recently accepted a promotion. Now she worked late at the office more than before and had occasional weekend conferences to attend in Paris, Brussels and Vienna, where the International Labor Office had sister departments.

Leo found it tedious that some weekends when he was not in Rome, he would be alone in Geneva as she would be away. It was on one of those weekends that Mr. and Mrs. De Sola arrived in Geneva.

At the station, his mother-in-law rushed to greet him. "How wonderful to see you again, Leo. We couldn't bring ourselves to go back to London without seeing you. How are you?"

He escorted them to their hotel and waited in the lobby while they freshened up, then took them around the corner to a neighborhood restaurant for dinner. They had already seen Elizabeth in Paris. She seemed well, they reported, although she was unhappy about not being able to have children.

"She may change her mind about adoption in a year or two," Mrs. De Sola said. "But she's very committed to her work, isn't she?"

"Yes, she is," Leo acknowledged. "Unfortunately, we're not able to spend as much time together as we would both like. I now have weekly trips to Rome, and twice-every-week classes at the university. She is working late at the office most nights. Then she also has these weekend trips. I'm glad you were able to see her."

"Banque Lapis is very pleased with your progress, from what I hear," Mr. De Sola said, smiling with pride. "They think you'll make a very good banker."

"That's good to hear." Leo hoped he sounded sincere.

"We have been talking," Mr. De Sola said. "When you finish in Geneva, there's a place for you in the investment department of my bank. It would be good for you and Elizabeth to come back to London. She would find an acceptable position, and we would help you establish yourselves in a comfortable home. You'd have a secure future. It would be good for you and good for your marriage. What do you think?"

Mr. De Sola held the door for his wife, and got her settled in the cab. Leo looked up at the sky. The engines of a passing plane were deafening.

"I'm not so sure that Elizabeth is ready. She adores her job, quite likes Geneva, but hates our apartment. Once I leave Banque Lapis, if we chose to stay in Geneva, we would need to find another apartment anyway."

"You're right. She is not too keen on the idea." Mrs. De Sola looked sad. "Elizabeth said that if you wanted to work in London, she would have no problem with that. Maybe you and she could alternate. She could come to London for a few days, and the next month, you would come to Geneva for a few. It's not ideal, but what do you think about such an arrangement?"

"Frankly," Leo said, "I would hate it. We are already separated far too much."

It angered Leo that his wife and father-in-law were negotiating his marriage for him. Elizabeth was growing away from him but not from her family. But wasn't he her family too?

"If you were to come to London, which is what we would want, and she wants to stay in Geneva, then I don't know how we can get around that."

"Is Banque Lapis going to kick me out when the anniversary of my starting date comes up?"

"Pretty much, I'm afraid." Mr. De Sola patted him on the arm. "They have no suitable position for you right now. It was always the agreement that they would take you for two years, then you'd come and work for us in London, or in another job altogether."

✳

It was a damp spring evening when Leo learned that an old friend was in town. For reasons he could not understand, he lied to Elizabeth about his destination. He told her that he had promised to have drinks with his colleagues. His last view was of the back of her head, a blond knot of hair that shone in the lamplight. As always in those days, she was indifferent to his departure.

Uri was in Geneva on business. They had kept in touch by letter, and when Leo learned that his friend would be in the city, his heart lightened. Uri was the only person Leo felt he could talk to about his problems with Elizabeth.

They met in a noisy pub. After waiting to order drinks, they found a table in a far corner where the chatter of surrounding conversation was slightly less intrusive.

As Leo talked about his marriage, Uri hunched forward over his cognac, bulky shoulders bulging against his shirt. Uri's face had grown thicker and squarer, like a bulldog's. His blond hair was now a dry, dusty color, seeming to match the color of his skin. He still worked in Palestine, and from the looks of him, spent a lot of time outdoors.

"She's cheating on you," Uri said.

"To hell with you." Leo hit Uri on the shoulder. "Should I order us another round?"

"I'm not kidding, old friend. Your wife is cheating on you."

"Oh, come on. I haven't seen you in how long, and this is what you tell me? Have some respect for my marriage."

"I have plenty of respect," Uri said, "having been through two of them already. I should have taken a hint when Francine cheated on you." He extinguished his cigarette with a single jab and twist, and shook his head. "I hate to break it to you, but it's how you pick them. You scent them out. Women who will grind a mensch into a pile of ashes."

"Elizabeth loves me," Leo said, and took a long draught of his cognac. He sounded weak even to himself.

"I never said she didn't." Uri shrugged as if to discard the topic. "How've you been otherwise?"

Leo was eager to reconnect, and while catching up with his old friend, he drank more than he should. Uri had developed a liver of iron, and Leo struggled to keep up. His friend had found work with the developing Jewish bureaucracy in Palestine, which made him thicker with news than the Sunday paper.

"There is something I need to discuss with you," Uri said. The crowd had thinned, and Uri pitched his voice lower. "I don't know your politics. I've never asked. But I am passionate about Zionism. After all, it was because of Zionism that, unlike our parents and cousins, we are here now. We owe a lot to that little country. They took us in, gave us a home, an education, and made men of us."

"I am a Zionist," Leo said. "More than you realize. I saw what happened to my own family. I was also at the camps at the end of the war. I have been affected ever since by that experience. You don't know this, but I was so angry, the real reason they transferred me out of the Jewish Brigade was because I led a small unit of men on a revenge raid. I personally killed a number of German soldiers. The Brigade moved me out fast—they considered I might do it again. And I may well have."

Uri listened and the waiter brought another round of cognacs. Leo awaited his friend's reaction. Uri didn't appear too surprised, as if he already knew why Leo was elbowed out of the Jewish Brigade. Uri seemed to know everything.

"On November 29th," Uri said, "just a few days ago, the United Nations approved partition. There will be a hard war, mark my words. What will you do?"

"Anything I can," Leo said promptly.

"Good. How do you feel about your marriage?"

The cognac tasted unusually strong, and Leo pushed it away. He'd definitely had enough to drink.

"I'm done." He shook his head. "Not with my marriage. I want that to work. What do you think?"

"Speak with Elizabeth," Uri said. "Then, in a couple of months, come to Palestine and see if the Palmach can use you. After all, you are a decorated British army officer, a trained soldier with combat experience. I think you can be useful." He picked up Leo's cognac without asking and quaffed it. "It could turn into a bloody war, not just Jews against Palestinian Arabs, but Jews against all the neighboring Arab states. If you come back and Elizabeth is still around, you'll know whether to stay in the marriage. Sorry to be so blunt, but you're not going to find out any other way."

Leo felt naive. He was at a loss with Elizabeth. Maybe Uri was right.

"The problem is serious," Uri continued. "It's not just a shortage of manpower, there's also a shortage of equipment. There is only one weapon for every three fighters. Think about it."

"How much of this should I tell Elizabeth?"

"All of it," he said, throwing his hands in the air. "Except that you think she's cheating."

Uri smiled. Leo nodded slowly. He didn't know what to think. Uri's perspective was so different, Uri being so different from Leo.

"I'm going to talk with her some more when she gets back from Paris, next week. I'll see you in Palestine."

✳

Leo's head still throbbed faintly from the cognac, which had intoxicated him until almost noon the following day. He'd taken a rare sick day from work and remained in his dressing gown, examining his options for the future. Shortly after two, Elizabeth came in the door and dropped her case onto the floor. She sat down and lit a cigarette. Leo welcomed her with a kiss.

"I was thrilled to see your parents last week, darling," Leo said with some enthusiasm. "I hope you had a fun time with them in Paris."

"Yes, I did." She took off her shoes, her cigarette dangling from her lips. "So busy, and hardly any time for fun. It was good to see my parents though, and how they enjoyed Paris. It was their first trip overseas since 1938."

She worked her fingers through her toes, massaging her arch and then heel. Leo watched her, aware that she hadn't yet really looked up at him.

"You do know," he said, "in a few weeks, I'll be unemployed. I need to discuss that with you."

"I know," Elizabeth answered. "We talked about it in Paris."

"Your parents want me to go to London. I don't think I have anything to offer another Swiss bank yet, and I would like to have some experience of working in the City. So, I'm in favor of us doing that. Of moving to London, that is. After a few months of doing what I have to do first."

She shrugged through the cigarette smoke. "I am not moving to London. My career is taking off here. I could end up being promoted to a department head before too long. My work is important to me. I am not going to move. We will have to work it out and spend long weekends together, one month in London, one month here. Absence makes the heart grow fonder, you know."

"Or go yonder," he muttered.

She stared at him in silence.

He spent the next few minutes explaining his compulsion to travel to Palestine and play a role, however minimal, in what he perceived as being an imminent military confrontation. Again, he did not mention his conversation with Uri.

Elizabeth ground out her cigarette. "I want no part of that. On that you're on your own. It doesn't even enter my mind to accompany you and volunteer at a kibbutz or school. No discussion, Leo. I'm staying in Geneva. The first thing I do on your last day at the bank is to start packing up this shithole."

He had anticipated her response and looked down at his hands. Had this small apartment been such a terrible place? Maybe there had just not been enough love between them to overcome even simple challenges.

"I'm planning to see a real estate broker that Signor Ramati recommended," she said. "We'll go and see what's available, within my budget. After all, you'll need to find somewhere to live in London on whatever Daddy's bank pays you. So I'll take care of the costs of an apartment here."

Elizabeth was so definite. Her plans all made. Every reason now for him to go to Palestine. But could Uri be right? Could she also be having an affair?

*

Leo's last day at the bank passed smoothly. Dr. Breitman and Monsieur Hug took him for lunch at the Hotel des Bergues, wished him well, and expressed the hope that they would stay in touch. He felt, inexplicably, that he had been used.

That evening, over dinner at a local bistro, he listened attentively while Elizabeth described the apartment that she had found. A corner apartment on the fourth floor of a building that had a view of the lake from the living room. Tall ceilings, an elegant fireplace, and one large bedroom. She was confident that she could manage the rent. Other people at the International Labor Office lived in the building, she added. He ordered a second glass of wine and drank it sullenly. Again, he felt used.

"I wish you well, darling," she said as she watched him pack. "I will miss you. And I will take good care of all your photographs. You will be thrilled when you come back and see our new apartment."

The next morning, Leo hugged and kissed Elizabeth. She did seem sentimental and affectionate. But as he sat in the train compartment and looked at the scenery, he wondered about the state of his marriage. He was slightly envious of her career, her fast track.

Stuck on a train, Leo had plenty of time to second-guess himself. Going to Palestine might not have been the practical thing to do, considering his trouble with Elizabeth. Perhaps he should have settled into a new job at her father's bank. He had a short time in Lyons to wait for the Marseilles train, so he read a letter from Maitre Talais. His old friend congratulated him on deciding to spend some time in Palestine before moving to London. That made him feel a little better.

Maitre Talais also wrote about the successes of Andre's real estate business, pleased that the investment proved to be a sound decision, and that the insurance company had recognized Leo's claims that his parents and cousins had perished in the Holocaust. They intended to release the funds within the month. A chapter closed.

25

THE LAST TIME LEO SAILED FROM MARSEILLES TO PALESTINE, he was only a boy. The voyage aboard the *Victor Hugo* had been miserable, the ship overflowing with French children like a good season's catch of sardines. Now a grown man, he could actually enjoy a trip across the Mediterranean. No sleeping on the deck this time, and his meals were no longer just stale sandwiches. Once arriving in Palestine, there was a normal disembarkation process, no wading through water in darkness to reach the shore, as he had done so many years before.

Leo decided to travel first to Degani, the kibbutz. This involved several different changes of bus, and the thrill of passing through familiar countryside, breathing in the air, and savoring the feeling of coming home.

As the bus approached the village, Leo was surprised and delighted to see how it had grown. The bus came to a halt, Leo picked up his duffel bag, and he said farewell to the driver. He waved at the bus as it drove off to the next village, then he approached the gate, closed even though it was broad daylight. He felt the desert dust on his shoes and perspiration streaming from his forehead. A lone guard dressed in khaki fatigues was on duty, armed with a rifle slung over his shoulder.

"Who are you?" the guard demanded. "What do you want here?"

"Shalom," Leo called out, startled by the unfriendly welcome. "My name is Leo Bergner. I am a former resident of the kibbutz, before the war, when I was brought here with other children from France. Then I was in the Jewish Brigade during the war, and I have come back to volunteer for the Palmach. Is Monsieur Lapidus still in charge here?"

"Wait where you are. I will tell him you are here."

"I guess this is what happens when you're under constant threat of attack."

The soldier didn't answer. Leo wiped his brow and turned away to absorb the landscape. He noticed newly planted orange groves. Long ago that had been a soccer pitch. Footsteps over gravel quickly approached and Leo turned back to the gate.

"Leo, Leo." Monsieur Lapidus rushed toward him, his arms extended. "Welcome home, Leo, welcome home."

Leo ran to Lapidus and embraced him. His frame was smaller than Leo remembered, but there was a rangy strength in his hug. A lump of emotion rose in Leo's throat.

"How are you, Monsieur Lapidus?" Tears blurred Leo's vision and the verge of crying strained his words. "You remembered me, after all these years. I am touched."

Lapidus remained joyful. "Of course. How could I forget any of my children? Come, you look so well. I want to hear all your news."

He led Leo through the gate and along the familiar turns of the kibbutz. In his office, nothing had changed, either. The constancy of this place reassured Leo. Somehow this made his decision to come here feel like the right thing to do.

"You will have a few happy surprises here. You could not have arrived at a better time. Believe me, it is very emotionally moving for us old people here, to see so many of our children come back to us, now that we are facing the prospects of a war. Forgive me—I call you children. You will always be one of my children, even though you became an officer in the British army. Thank God you survived that."

"What surprises have you for me, Monsieur Lapidus?"

"Your friend Uri is here. He came back, just like you, by bus, last week. He has been living in Jerusalem and decided to pay us a visit tonight." He quietly added, "He is no longer with Francine. But they are still friends. She is coming with him."

"I look forward so much to seeing them." Leo smiled.

"And Sarah is here, and Rachel. Shimon is now a colonel in the Palmach. Yona is with military intelligence based in Haifa. But she is here on leave. They got married, too. Shimon's parents still bake the best éclairs east of Paris, and I should know." He patted his belly. "Tell me, do you still play the piano?"

"Not for some months."

"Ach." Lapidus waved the answer away. "This evening, we have a concert. Everyone will be here. I want you to make a surprise appearance. Everyone is working now, but at six this evening, the bus from Jerusalem will be back. At seven is the show. I don't want anyone to know you are here until then, when I will introduce you." He looked at his watch. "Come, I'll take you to my apartment, you can rest there. Eat something. At seven o'clock I am going to take you and surprise everyone. But don't go wandering off. Let this be my bit of fun."

Leo grinned as Lapidus furtively led him to his small apartment a few yards down a path behind the office. He was welcome to help himself to whatever food and drink he could find and to rest until seven. Leo was glad for it. He was tired. He looked around the room. Every inch of wall space had been filled with a photograph, postcard or letter from one of Monsieur Lapidus's children. Leo tried to read some of them, then looked to see if he could find one from himself.

At a quarter after seven, Monsieur Lapidus summoned Leo. He got up from the bed, straightened his hair and quickly splashed water on his face. He followed the old man through a maze of paths, some of which he remembered, others were newly created. He went past buildings that he didn't recognize, to the back of the school's auditorium, which was used for plays and concerts. Leo climbed a few steps to the stage. Then Lapidus beckoned Leo to remain hidden in the wings.

"Ladies and gentlemen, our concert is about to begin." Monsieur Lapidus took out a piece of paper with the program. "Our first act is a clarinet concerto played by Sigmund Cohen, aged fourteen, but before Sigmund mounts the stage, I want to present a member of our kibbutz family who came back to visit us this afternoon. A complete surprise. He was with us before the war, then he served in the British army and fought at El Alemein, then with the Jewish Brigade. He is one of our heroes. He came back from his home in Switzerland, leaving his wife there, to come and stand shoulder to shoulder with us while we prepare to face whatever challenges lie ahead. Everyone, please stand and welcome Leo Bergner."

He waved for Leo to take the stage. Everyone stood and applauded. Handkerchiefs appeared from nowhere as row upon row of men and women cried with joy. Leo stood motionless at first, then his shoulders shook as he too was unable to control himself, and tears wet his cheeks. From the side of the room, a caravan of people ran down the aisle to mount the steps to the stage—Shimon, Yona, Uri, Francine, Sarah, Rachel, Chantal, Yves, Nicole, Charles. He found himself enveloped in the warmth of their embraces.

After a few moments, he composed himself, and they stood back as he went to the front of the stage. He didn't know whether to cry or laugh, to be sad or overjoyed, or if he could even play. He sat down at the piano, but the keys looked strange to him. He turned to the quiet hall.

"I guess I could say a lot, or say nothing. All I can say is thank you. Thank you for giving me a home and a family."

✳

On May 14, 1948, the State of Israel declared itself an independent nation, and within a few days, was invaded by Lebanon, Syria, Iraq, Egypt, and Transjordan, as well as by volunteers from Saudi Arabia, Libya, and Yemen. Leo and Uri were caught in Jerusalem, having gone there for an overnight trip. Now heavy fighting broke out on Tel Aviv Road, between Transjordan's Arab Legion and the Israeli forces that were grouped together into an official Israeli army.

Within days of leaving the serenity of Geneva, Leo found himself embroiled in heavy house-to-house fighting within the Jewish Quarter of the Old City. Residents barricaded themselves in their homes and avoided the windows for fear of snipers. There was a constant noise of bullets and scampering of the assailants down narrow alleyways. The coffee shop that Leo had frequented years before had long been boarded up. Food and water were in short supply, and the shrill crying of hungry infants was heard throughout the area.

Leo's unit was charged with the task of protecting the Jewish residents of the quarter. It was dangerous work, patrolling the narrow streets with a rifle, just a few bullets, and a couple of hand grenades in his shoulder bag. Ammunition was in short supply.

Hearing a truck approach from beyond a street corner, Leo ran to an apartment building and pushed past the heavy wooden door, then pulled it shut, all but a sliver—just enough to spy outside. The truck turned into the street. Leo held his position in the doorway. Four men jumped from the truck, brandishing rifles, and fired into the air, then shot out windows across the street. Leo nudged the door for a clear aim. He shifted to center his first target in the crude sights when a rooftop sniper put a bullet deep into Leo's shoulder.

Hours later, the fighting had died down. Jewish refugees swamped the streets, made their way out of the Old City, and down the hill to a safer area where the Arab Legion had less of a grip. People moved with frantic urgency, frightened and panicked. Anyone with a spare hand helped a neighbor, clutched a child, carried a case or assisted the elderly.

Leo remembered enough to navigate the narrow streets and back alleys, after wrapping the wound with his shirt. He blended with others moving along an avenue but had trouble keeping up. His legs felt disconnected from his body, unable to receive commands correctly.

"A soldier's injured here," a voice called out. "He's bleeding. Help."

In seconds a crowd surrounded him. One man removed Leo's blood-soaked shirt and replaced it with his own shirt. The commotion sapped Leo of his last strength, and his legs went weary as two men dragged him onward. Others passed. All stopped to look and offer to help.

"How do we know he's one of us?" someone said.

"I am, I'm…" Leo mumbled.

"Take him to Shaare Zedek," another said.

The thickening crowd hoisted his limp body onto the back of an open truck.

*

Leo woke a few hours later. The space was big like an aircraft hanger, but stuffed full of hospital beds, one of which was his. A man in the next bed was asleep, with rubber tubes taped to his arm. Leo tried turning to the other side but his shoulder exploded with pain. He did not try again.

Nurses were moving quickly through the aisles. Volunteers of all ages stopped at beds to chat with wounded men in various languages. Squads of white-coated doctors, stethoscopes around their necks and charts in hand, talked with patients and recorded details on their pads.

"Nurse, where am I?" Leo whispered in Hebrew.

"I am sorry," she said in German. "I don't speak Hebrew. I'll get someone who does."

Leo grabbed her arm to keep her from leaving. "I speak German."

"You are in the hospital at Shaare Zedek. One of the oldest in Israel, now a military hospital."

"How? I was…"

"Civilians found you wounded."

The sniper, his shoulder, and all the blood. Leo scanned the overcrowded room, loaded with wounded. "The war must be going badly for us."

"We have repelled Syria in the North and Egypt in the South. The Arab League, having been trained and armed by the damned British, have given us a tough fight in Jerusalem. We've lost the Jewish Quarter of the Old City, but the war is not over. Not by a long way."

The nurse took a pen from her pocket and scribbled notes on a pad, glancing every few seconds at Leo.

"What happened to me?" Leo asked. "My shoulder hurts and I'm burning up."

"You have a fever, and you were shot in the shoulder. You lost a lot of blood. There's quite a line for the operating theater. When your turn comes, we'll get you in and remove the bullet. Meanwhile, try to relax."

Leo closed his eyes. Back in 1945, within an hour of arriving in England he had been run down by a van. And now, on his second day at the front, he'd been shot.

"Bonjour, mon ami." A doctor approached. "Forgive me, I struggle with Hebrew. You understand French, no?"

"Bien sûr. Tell me, please, what is my situation?"

"The bullet penetrated mostly soft tissue, and there is no clear sign of nerve damage. So far, that is. I am hopeful, but I would recommend that you remain cautious. At worst, you may have limited use of the arm. At best, you should recover after a few months of physical therapy. We'll know more once the bullet is removed."

"When?"

"I'm afraid you're well down the list. We'll get it out as quickly as possible. In the meantime, get some rest."

Two weeks later, Leo took the bus back to the kibbutz. The bullet had been removed and saved. He wore it around his neck, threaded on a string. The truce allowed him a few days of relaxation while awaiting his next military orders. But that was short-lived.

The mood back at the kibbutz was dispiriting. The loss of the Old City had been devastating, notwithstanding the good news from other fronts. Immediately upon his arrival, Leo received a communiqué to report back for duty, despite his incomplete recovery and lack of time for any therapy. The Israelis were about to launch a large-scale offensive, Operation Dani, to secure and enlarge the corridor between Tel Aviv and Jerusalem by capturing the roadside cities of Lydda and Ramle.

The Transjordanian army, together with Palestinian militias and the Arab Liberation army, defended Lydda, but to no avail. The Israeli Defense Forces attacked the city from the north and east, and finally captured it on July 11. The next day, Ramle fell.

A second truce was declared on July 18, and by the end of August, it looked as though it would stick. Leo decided it was now time to return to Europe.

He stepped off the train in Geneva and walked slowly toward the gate. Carrying his case in his left hand was a strain. Frequently he lost control and bumped into a passerby. Still he searched the crowds for Elizabeth. She was at the barrier, waiting for him.

"My darling, welcome home." She put her arms around him and hugged him tight. It hurt a little, but he was laughing.

"I did it again," he said. "This time it wasn't a van, but a sniper's bullet."

"Come on. Let me carry that, you poor darling. I saw you struggling with it. Signor Ramati has allowed me to use one of the office cars and a driver to pick you up. I can't wait to show you the apartment."

Her new apartment was everything that their previous home had not been. Slightly larger, airy, and with a view of the lake. Polished wood floors, newly painted walls, a glass dining table and brown leather sofa. Elizabeth had hung a few paintings that she had picked up from a gallery in Lausanne. Leo smiled. One of them looked like a Magritte, another a copy of a Mondrian.

"What do you think of it?" she asked, her gloved hands clasped together.

"It's lovely. I like it a lot," he admitted. "It's a wee bit on the small side, though, isn't it? It doesn't seem much bigger than our old place."

"You'll be in London on alternate months, so it's big enough the rest of the time."

"I like the way you've furnished it." He sat down in an armchair and beckoned her to sit on his lap. "Very cheerful compared to where we were before."

"Signor Ramati gave me the address of an Italian furniture store where he knows the owners." She reclined against him and worked a cigarette out of a tortoise-shell case. "I got some fabulous discounts."

"When am I going to meet this Signor Ramati of yours?"

"Oh, he's away at the moment," she answered, "but he should be back at the end of the month."

"If I'm still around, we could have dinner with him one night, maybe."

"When do you think you'll be starting in London?"

"I think your father wants me there next week."

Her lighter snapped. She turned away and exhaled slowly. The smoke drifted toward Leo anyway.

A week later, during the train ride to London, he wondered about Elizabeth. He detected a measure of relief in her when she learned that he was going away so soon. She seemed preoccupied, tense. Even after he had been home for days, she showed no degree of warmth. He had just returned wounded from a theater of war. Was her full attention, even for five minutes, too much to expect? Should he have chosen to remain in Geneva and seek a job in banking there? After all, it was a banking center. All these thoughts drifted in and out of his mind until he arrived back in London, and his cab pulled up outside the De Sola residence.

"Welcome home, Leo," Mr. De Sola said with warmth and affection as he poured Leo a drink. "We would have loved it if Elizabeth came with you. But she's so gung-ho about her job. In some ways that's good, but in other ways, we just don't know."

Within a couple of weeks, Leo settled into his job as a portfolio manager at the bank. He liked the work and his colleagues. He welcomed the daily routine of traveling to the City office every morning on the underground train from Marble Arch, the walk to the office on Throgmorton Avenue, and stopping for breakfast at a cafe on the way.

Now and again, he heard whispered comments about nepotism—his father-in-law was the vice-chairman of the bank. But he dealt with that by arriving before everyone else and leaving later, ensuring that his clients were well satisfied with his performance. He made it a point to meet with them on a regular basis, and soon enough, through word of mouth, he picked up a number of new clients.

Every other month, he flew to Geneva for a long weekend. Elizabeth's visits to London, although originally planned to take place on alternate months, were inconsistent. The nature of her work, she explained, was that often things cropped up at the last minute—presentations, seminars, conferences. She just could not always get away.

Finally Elizabeth did come to London, to her parents' home, to see Leo. But he recognized that she had come on a mission. Everyone felt it, the tension of knowing that Elizabeth had something to say, something she was committed to do.

"We need to talk about our marriage," she said to Leo in the professional voice she used with her clients. "It's not working. Your life is here in London, mine is in Geneva." She lit a cigarette and watched the smoke at the tip. "I am not in love with you, Leo. I like you. I respect you. But I'm not in love with you. It's not your fault. Maybe we were, after all, the subjects of just a wartime romance."

Leo picked up his glass of cognac and took a quick gulp. His face had turned splotchy. No surprises in anything that she said. She didn't love him, hadn't loved him, and he had known it.

"Elizabeth, I've feared as much. I know that it's a strain living so far apart, but it's only temporary. Why don't we try and work at spending long week-ends together, here or in Geneva, as we had planned. Let's at least try."

"No, Leo." No mischief in her eyes. No humor in her tone. She spoke with finality. "You see, I'm in love with another man, and I can't live a lie. I have to be totally open."

"Oh my God," Leo whispered. He looked down at the table, at his hands as they began to shake. Uri had been right. He had known beyond what Leo had told him. And he had understood. But Leo felt that old sense of betrayal again.

"Sergio Ramati and I are very much in love," Elizabeth said in a quiet tone, much like a parent would speak to calm a child. "He is married, but cannot get a divorce. I am married, and I don't particularly want a divorce. So, I'm asking you, Leo, to accept the situation. You live your life, and I'll live mine. We'll always, no matter what, stay friends. But that's how it is. Of course, if you insist on a divorce, I'll go along with that."

Beads of perspiration ran down his face. His stomach cramped, then fluttered. He stared into his empty glass, and then at Elizabeth. He leaned his elbow on the table and exhaled heavily.

"Forgive me, I'm in such a shock. Whatever I say will not make sense. I am distressed beyond measure. Hurt, angry. I don't think I can say anything. I can't even think straight."

"Well, that's how it is. There's no need to say anything," Elizabeth said in a matter-of-fact tone. "I've just told you, Leo. It's over. Get on with your life."

Leo went up to his room and looked at the flowers he had bought for Elizabeth earlier in the day. He lay down on the bed and closed his eyes. The next morning, he walked into the drawing room. Mr. and Mrs. De Sola were sitting in silence, and to their credit they looked as distraught as he.

"Leo, poor darling, how are you? Did you sleep?"

"I feel ghastly. I had no idea what was going on. Please tell me the truth. Where did I go wrong? I love her so much. I must have done something terribly wrong."

"No, you didn't, my boy," Mr. De Sola said. "To us you are a son, not a son-in-law. We are honored and privileged that you came into our family."

He glanced at his wife, and something passed between them. They must have discussed what to tell him. Leo realized that this hadn't just happened to him, but to the whole family. And Elizabeth had allowed it to happen, no matter what he could have or should have done.

"We are filled with shame by the way Elizabeth has treated you," Mr. De Sola said. "We have no words to defend her behavior. If you wanted to divorce her, you would have our blessing and total understanding. If you wanted to bide your time to see if her affair with this Italian comes to an end, then try and heal the marriage, you would have our support. This is a decision for you to make."

"Thank you." Leo dried his tears with yesterday's handkerchief. "I love you both so very much. You have been wonderful to me from the very first moment I met you that evening at the synagogue around the corner. Now I think it would be best if I were to move out and find my own apartment. But please let me ask you an honest question. Would you like me to resign from the bank?"

"I would be horrified if you did such a thing. You are a credit to the bank. You have earned the respect of my colleagues on the board. The clients like you. You have a career with us for as long as you want it. I don't want to hear any talk of resignation."

"Are you serious about wanting to move out?" Mrs. De Sola asked.

"Yes, I am." Leo stood, not meeting her eyes.

✳

Within a few months, Leo adjusted to a life he never would have chosen for himself. He ached without Elizabeth. In his innermost heart, he remained hopeful that once her affair was over, they would rekindle their love. He wrote to her with brutal regularity, and she replied with news of her job and her various trips. But she refused to return to London. She would not see Leo or anyone in her family. Leo remained close to the De Solas and dined with them as he had promised, twice every week.

Leo rapidly climbed the ladder at the bank. Through his connections in London's Zionist circles he introduced to the bank a number of new clients, who brought not only their investment portfolios for management, but their corporate needs as well. Many asked for advice on loans, mergers, and acquisitions, and Leo set up and oversaw a new department to cater to this growing clientele. In due course, he became a director of the bank.

At the next monthly board meeting, Sir Terrence Drobe, the chairman, turned to Leo and said, "Leo, we have been approached by Banque Lapis in Geneva about a possibility, and we need to discuss it with you. Though our stake in their operation is only ten percent, we want to protect that investment like any other. And because you spent a few years with them, we value your opinion in this matter. Banque Lapis wants to do more Greek shipping loans here in the City, which would be very good business for us."

"What are they offering?" Leo asked, remembering the deep vaults with art and gold for the Church.

"They'd like to send us one of their shipping experts, and have us increase our stake in their bank to thirty percent. What do you think? Leo, I'd like you to spearhead this. Hambros and Kleinworts have had a lock on this shipping business for far too long. We should break into this market. Same goes for the film industry."

"Agreed."

Leo surprised even himself with his decisiveness, given his reluctance to dive back into a business network that he knew in his heart was not for him. Yet he looked and felt at home in a boardroom.

"Now," Leo offered, "there is something that I need to bring up too. I have been invited to join the board of the Anglo Israel Bank. It's well-established and highly regarded by the Bank of England and enjoys the support of some major institutions. I believe that the association would be good for us. It could open doors for us in what is going to emerge, I believe, as a major economy. Does anybody object?"

He looked around the table. He and Mr. De Sola were the only Jewish members of the board, and the bank was not generally considered overly friendly toward members of the Jewish community. While hungry for the business that Leo had brought in, they were still not totally enamored with this new clientele.

"Why don't you bring in some of their people for lunch one day?" A fellow board member asked.

"Yes. I'll ask Sir Henry and Victor Rothschild."

"Sir Henry?" another board member asked.

"Sir Henry d'Avigdor-Goldsmid, the chairman, and Lord Rothschild is a board member."

"I see," Lord Nichols responded, reluctantly impressed. "Well, I think we've done good work today."

"Not yet." Mr. De Sola chuckled. "This may not come as a surprise, but I would like to announce my retirement as vice-chairman of the bank. I am tired, frankly. I have been with the bank now for close to fifty years. I'd like to take it easy."

"Oh come on, you're as fit as a fiddle," one of his co-directors bellowed across the table.

"Thank you, George, but believe me, it's becoming a strain. I'm happy to stay on as a director. But I want to be relieved of the additional responsibilities of vice-chairman."

"So that means we need to appoint a new vice-chairman."

"As far as I can see," Sir Terrence offered, "The perfect candidate would be you, Leo."

The idea hit him like a sniper's bullet. Leo flexed his hands under the table and kept his face steady.

"I'm flattered that you should think so, Sir Terrence, but I decline. The job of vice-chairman carries with it many social responsibilities more suited for a happily married man. Not one who is still married in the manner in which I am."

There was no audible response, which Leo took as their agreement. He sensed the state of his marriage was common knowledge. He cleared his throat and reached for his leather folio of notes, but set his hand over it instead. He was afraid it might shake.

"On another matter," Leo said, "I have a loan request to submit, but I must make full disclosure of my interest." He waited for the other bankers to switch back to business mode. "I am an investor in a private French real estate company that has expanded over the last few years and is undergoing some major construction projects in France. They're seeking a loan of ten million for an acquisition in Germany."

That night, as he helped his father-in-law out of a taxi, Leo could see how much he had aged. His brain was still as sharp as ever, but the arthritis in his legs, and the gout he had suffered for years, had become worse over recent months. He knew that someday he would recite the Kaddish for his father-in-law, as he had done for the rest of his family. His advanced age had come, it seemed to Leo, sooner than it should have.

A few weeks later at the office, Leo received a telephone call from his brother-in-law. Anthony's voice was thin and quick.

"Leo, our father-in-law fell while walking downstairs at the house. His head hit one of the steps and he was knocked out. The ambulance came and took him to St. George's Hospital. He died within an hour."

The words fell into a void. The phone nearly slipped from his fingers then Leo clutched it tighter and calmly said, "I'll be right over. Has anyone called Elizabeth?"

"Yes, I did. She said she would call her mother."

Leo hurried from the bank and jumped into a cab. He felt that if he rushed, he could somehow undo the man's death.

26

M R. DE SOLA'S FUNERAL TOOK PLACE QUICKLY AND QUIETLY. At the graveside with Mrs. De Sola, Holly, and her husband Anthony, Leo stood with his hands folded uselessly in front of him. The hole in the ground was the size of the casket and no bigger. Much smaller than a mass grave. About the same size as the opening of an oven.

Leo blinked hard and focused on the reflection of the sky in the casket's varnish. Don't think about the body inside. Or the old man's withered limbs. It was just a body. Like millions of others, his mother, his father, his cousins, his friends. Wherever his father-in-law was going, he would join all the others who had disappeared from his life.

Elizabeth did not attend the funeral, but she did come to London the following week to visit her mother for the day. Holly stayed away and advised Leo not to appear at the house while Elizabeth was in town.

The will was another story. Mr. De Sola had a comfortable estate and left Leo a major portion of his stock in the bank. His death left an empty seat at the boardroom table that Leo occupied without joy. The other men's respect and also resentment were palpable, like a faint electric current that raised the hair on the back of his neck. But Leo was ready for this responsibility.

✳

"We have been approached by Banque Lapis again," Sir Terrence said to Leo. "They're very impressed by our expansion in recent years. Especially our having been thought of as somewhat of a sleeper in the city, given that we're now one of its golden firms. In fact, they see that our success is largely a result of your efforts."

Terrence was young for a chairman, Leo's elder by only a few years, with the ego of a lifelong banking veteran. The best way to deal with him was to treat him with a combination of humor and the utmost respect.

"Thank you," Leo said, "but we're a team."

"That's true, but you've built up our corporate department from scratch, and we're all very proud of you. Indeed grateful. You've made us all a lot of money."

"Yes." Leo chuckled. "I haven't done too badly myself, either."

"Banque Lapis wants you over there to do the same for them. Their managing director wants to take it easy, and they have no immediate natural successor. The idea is that you should go over there, run the bank for a few years, then return here and take over for me when I step down as chairman and managing director."

"I know Banque Lapis, of course." Leo's hand went to his chin. "I cut my banking teeth with them years ago. I'll give it some thought. I like Geneva, but it has a sour taste for me. My wife is in Geneva."

"Yes, I know," Sir Terrence replied. "Your poor father-in-law was greatly distressed till the end of his days about how she behaved. He felt very let down by her and so sorry for you."

At the back of Leo's mind, he remained hopeful that by being in the same city as Elizabeth, reconciliation might still be a possibility. He checked his watch and gave Terrence a curt, professional nod.

"Okay, I'll do it. It's a challenge."

Leo took up residence at the Hotel de la Paix in a suite that gave him a glorious view of the lake and of the Jet d'Eau. More than simply a room and bed, the large suite included a full kitchen and separate sitting area. It was a far cry from the days when he and Elizabeth shared a dingy apartment. The location also gave Leo the opportunity of regular exercise by walking to and from the bank every day.

On his first day back at Banque Lapis, Leo sat behind his new desk and reached for the telephone. "Monsieur Ponier, please bring me the records of all our current depositors." Leo's mandate was to develop the bank's loan portfolio, so one of his first tasks was to familiarize himself with the deposits that the bank was holding for clients. He wanted to get a feel as to how many depositors the bank had, as well as the dates of the last transactions. "Let's start with just the numbered accounts and the amount of the deposits."

"Certainly, sir," the drab little man said.

A few minutes later, Monsieur Ponier came into Leo's office with a perfectly inked ledger of accounts. Ponier, a middle-aged man who had joined Banque Lapis a few years earlier, was the head of the banking department. He always wore a bowtie and had a meek and almost flinching way of accepting orders. He promised to be a reliable old cog in the wheel, making Leo's job easier.

Leo took the file back to his hotel that night. While poring over it, he noted some interesting facts. Some of the accounts had no activity since September of 1939—over thirty years before. He took a red pen and circled all those accounts. He was puzzled. There were over two hundred of them. Some of the account numbers were marked with asterisks.

The next day he detoured through the banking department on his way upstairs, and leaned into Monsieur Ponier's office.

"Come and see me, please."

The man flinched and followed on Leo's heels all the way to the executive offices. He stopped in front of Leo's desk, leaning slightly forward as though the only thing preventing him from sitting in Leo's lap was the spacious piece of furniture between them.

"Please sit down," Leo said. He cleared his throat and indicated the ledger of accounts on his desk that Ponier had brought him the day before. "I looked at this last night and saw that we have over two hundred accounts on the books with no activity since 1939. I'm puzzled by this. Also, I see a number of asterisks on each of these pages. Please, can you tell me what you know?"

"Certainly, sir. First, the asterisks. These indicate customers who also had safe-deposit boxes with us."

"You say had. What do you mean exactly?"

"Where the client had rented a box, but after non-payment of the rent for some time, the bank had the right to open the box and empty the contents."

"What did the bank do with the contents?"

"We checked our documentation to see if the client had left a will or any specific instructions. If so, we carried out the client's instructions." Ponier's face was growing flushed. He looked like he was sitting for an exam.

"And if there were no instructions?" Leo asked.

"Then we wrote one more time to advise the client that if we didn't hear from them within two months, we would sell the contents, generally at auction if they had any value. If they didn't, we destroyed them."

"And what happened with the proceeds of sale?"

"We deducted what was owed by way of rent, and the balance went into our reserve account."

"Monsieur Ponier, obviously the bank has records of what was sold and to whom. Please have someone in your department make a schedule of what went to auction from these accounts with asterisks, and how much was realized."

"Certainly, sir." Ponier nodded several times with birdlike bobs of his head. He seemed surprised by the request. "It will take a week or so."

"Also, see if there is any information on file showing what was owed by way of rent on the boxes. If so, let me have a schedule showing rent owed in one column, and in another, what the client's balance was at the time we opened the boxes and sold the contents."

"Yes, we can do that too, sir."

"Good, Monsieur Ponier. Now, there is something else."

"Yes, sir?" Ponier's eyes swept the desk. He was flushed again. His efficient memory seemed to be filling up, and he was getting nervous.

Leo tossed him a pad. "Here. Although I'm sure you don't need it. Now, please have someone give me a total of the deposits in all these inactive accounts, and let me know what the bank's policy has been regarding crediting the accounts with interest." Leo took a final look at the list and handed the pages back to Monsieur Ponier. "After all, the total balance on these accounts will be in the millions."

"I'll have all the answers and schedules for you next week, Mr. Bergner."

Leo wanted to brood about the deposits longer, but he couldn't concentrate when he left the bank that evening. In spite of himself, his step lightened, and he whistled as he reached into the closet for a fresh shirt and tie. He checked his profile in the mirror, wiped away a speck of blood from a razor cut, and hurried out into the street again, headed for a restaurant that overlooked the water.

"It's lovely to see you again, Mrs. Bergner." He smiled, then offered Elizabeth a single pink rose, its stem bare.

"And delightful to see you too, Mr. Bergner." She giggled, nervous and trying to conceal it.

They hadn't seen each other in so long and had shared few communications. Leo found himself checking his tie more than once, and in spite of a limited wine list, he couldn't make up his mind. He finally sent the waiter away to bring out whatever would pair well with Elizabeth's choice of trout.

Over dinner, they talked largely about her parents and how her mother was coping with widowhood. It was the easiest subject that was not also awkwardly superficial.

As the waiter cleared the plates, Elizabeth said, "I don't suppose Holly will ever forgive me. Have you forgiven me, Leo?"

The waiter was gone, but Leo couldn't bring himself to answer yet. He laced his knuckles under his chin and frowned at the tablecloth.

"Honestly, no. I've grown accustomed to a way of life that I never wanted. I believe we could have had far better lives if you hadn't, shall I say, sought love somewhere else. How are things with you anyway?"

"I don't know, Leo. Sergio and his wife will not get a divorce. And I have to confess, being the mistress of a married man has lost its appeal after these few years."

"You knew what you were getting into."

"Not at first," she said. "In the beginning, he told me he was single. Then there was talk about him and Francesca getting an annulment. But that takes forever. It's all so ludicrous because she has a boyfriend in Rome."

She went on, even though Leo bristled. She had the gall to give him a sob story. Why hadn't he seen this side of her, this lack of empathy, this self-centeredness before?

"It's not as if she's the poor destitute unattractive scorned wife," Elizabeth continued. "She's a beautiful woman, a member of the Agnelli family, and according to Sergio, she has an apartment in Rome next to the Hassler and a villa in Portofino. Anyway, enough of me and my woes. What about you? Is there anyone in your life?"

"If you must know, I had a very promising relationship with a lady in London," he lied. "An American. An actress. But she went back to the States. We both know that long-distance relationships are fraught, don't we? So that ended. I've had a few relationships since, but they could best be described as flings, nothing serious."

His spirit was sagging, and Elizabeth didn't have anything to say to that. The lights glittered on the water. He felt himself sinking into the blackness between the reflections.

"It seems we may both end up alone, doesn't it, Leo?"

"It doesn't have to be that way, Elizabeth. We could try again, you know."

She didn't reply. Instead she wrapped her fingers around the stem of her glass and looked at it, meditating.

"Did you hear what I said?" he asked gently, his heart skipping in hope.

"Yes, I heard, Leo. Let's just see how things work out."

"So you don't rule it out."

"No. But I'm not making any promises, either."

Leo paid their bill and helped Elizabeth into her coat. It was white and lightweight. He hadn't seen it before. He struggled for something safe to say as they walked along the street, and found nothing. Instead he said what was on his mind.

"You should know that I'm going to be in Geneva for at least two or three years. Can we do this again?"

"You mean, can we date?" She laughed.

"Yes, that's what I meant."

"Leo, just call me whenever you like. If I'm free and in the mood, the answer is yes, we can have dinner. But no promises, okay?"

"Understood."

✳

"Mr. Bergner." Monsieur Ponier and his young assistant took their seats opposite Leo. "Dealing with the safe-deposit boxes first, we have prepared various schedules. The first details those items that were sold at auction, the dates of sale, the net proceeds, and from which box they came. The second details the items that were not sold at auction but which were sold for a fixed price and then delivered to a client in Italy. The schedule shows the sale proceeds and the delivery dates."

"Who was the client in Italy?"

"Pontificio Istituto Teutonico, Mr. Bergner."

The client at the end of the train trips so many years ago. The client with the vault below the surface of the earth. The one with the amazing art.

"Now, we have two more schedules," Ponier continued. "These relate to deposits that are standing to the inactive accounts."

Leo was at the edge of his chair. He clasped the schedule tightly and studied it.

Ponier explained, "You will see in the first column the balances on the individual accounts. In the second column you will see the interest that has been credited to the accounts, and the date that interest was credited appears in column three. At the bottom you will see the totals. All the deposits have been converted, as you had requested, into dollars as of last week's exchange rates."

"Monsieur Ponier, you and your department have done a great job in assembling this information for me. I'm going to study it all over the next few days. Thank you."

"Oh, Mr. Bergner, there is one more schedule. This one shows the amount of rent the client owed on their box, and their amount on deposit with us at the time we foreclosed on the box for the unpaid rent."

If Elizabeth had been afraid of Leo calling her too often, she would have found her worries baseless. After his meeting with Ponier, Leo became absorbed in studying the records, to the exclusion of all other activities at the bank and in his life outside of it.

First, he checked the dates of the deliveries made to the Pontificio Istituto. While he didn't have his own diaries and records available for those years, he considered it a fair assumption that some of those deliveries he had made himself during his trips to Rome. Monsieur Fabre still worked at the bank. He made a note to discuss this with him over the coming days. If Fabre could confirm a specific date that he went to Rome, then Leo would have gone the week before or after.

He then checked what was delivered to Rome. In many cases, it was simply gold bars. On other occasions, it was paintings, sculpture, and items of jewelry that went by truck. He compared the schedules. His eyes opened wide when he saw that a Rembrandt had been sold at auction for eight hundred thousand, but another Rembrandt had been sold to the Istituto for a mere one hundred and fifty thousand. Was that possible? He made a note to find a contact at Sotheby's, or somewhere similar, to check the auction records for the paintings.

He then turned his attention to the schedules of the inactive accounts. The bank was sitting on deposits of close to seven million dollars, on which a total of one hundred and ten thousand dollars of interest was credited to the accounts in August 1941. There were no further interest credits. And it was now years later. Even assuming an interest rate of five per cent, the bank had avoided interest payments of more than ten million dollars over the years.

Gold was sold at market price to other banks, yet sales of gold to the Pontificio Istituto were at substantially lower prices around the same time. Leo was confused. Why would the bank have sold gold at half the market price to the Istituto? The final schedule confused him, too. If the customer owed the bank for unpaid rent, and the bank had the right to debit the customer's account with that rent, then why—if the customer had substantial funds on deposit—didn't the bank just do that, rather than foreclose on the box?

He stood outside the bank, breathing fresh air. It was nearly midnight. He was in his shirtsleeves. His mouth felt dry and he hadn't eaten anything since lunch. He hadn't eaten many good meals in weeks. He was responsible for the money of the dead, and until satisfied that he was not perched atop a great injustice, he could not abandon his post.

Rabbi Aaron would have been proud of him.

✳

Uri had agreed to extend his layover on his way to Paris, and the two men sat in Leo's kitchen.

"Come to Paris," Uri said. "Or to the fucking Arctic Circle, for God's sake. Step away from it. You look like hell."

"I have stepped away from it. That's why we're meeting here and not in my office." Leo got up to make more tea. "I need a name, if you can give it to me. Wasn't there a fellow you worked with in Israel, a Martin somebody who knew art? Anyone who could possibly tell me the value of some paintings."

"What?" Uri ground his cigarette into his saucer. "You're an aficionado now?"

Leo explained what he could of the situation. It felt good just to talk and have his friend ask questions. Uri was keeping himself fit, and his former bluntness had mellowed into a calm strength. His eyes had hardened, though. Uri grew suspicious of the story.

"Keep yourself out of it," he said.

"I can't." Leo shook his head. "I've accepted this responsibility."

"You don't have to."

"Somebody does."

Uri laid his hand on Leo's shoulder. The warm kitchen light made the hairs on his arm shine gold. "You can't bring your family back, my friend. We would all do anything to bring them back, avenge them, anything. God knows I would. But I see what you're doing to yourself, and in a very dangerous environment."

Leo scoffed.

"What, you don't think so?" Uri lifted his hand from Leo's shoulder. "You don't think that sharks don't follow the scent of blood? You think where there's money, there aren't thieves?"

Leo saw Uri to the airport and returned directly to the bank. At his desk, he removed a thin address book from his jacket pocket and dialed the number Uri had given him.

"Martin, it's Leo Bergner. Uri's friend. How are you?"

After listening to some social trivia in London, Leo turned to the reason for the call.

"Martin, we have a courier going to London tonight. Tomorrow, I'll have a schedule delivered to you that shows some rather bizarre sales that Banque Lapis handled after the war. It appears, for example, that they sold a Rembrandt at auction for eight hundred thousand, and then sold another Rembrandt to an Italian institution for one hundred and fifty thousand. I know nothing about art prices, but that strikes me as odd. You may see on the schedule other anomalies. Just let me know what you think."

"Of course," Martin replied. "But so much depends on condition and authenticity, Leo. One painting may have a wonderful provenance and may have been authenticated by the premier art experts in a specific field, whereas another could be in poor condition and may be of dubious authenticity. It's hard to be precise by merely looking at a schedule showing names of artists and prices. Do you have listed the names of the paintings?"

"Yes." Leo's gaze followed his forefinger down the list. "They all have titles."

"Good, then we may be able to reconcile the provenances with the names of the paintings. I'll wait for the list."

A knock interrupted Leo. He rolled down his sleeves and put on his jacket.

"Come in," he called, and smoothed his hair. "Oh, it's just you. Sit down, Monsieur Ponier. How long have you been at Banque Lapis?"

"Six years, sir."

"Where were you before? I've forgotten."

"Union Bank of Switzerland."

"In the same capacity?"

"Yes, sir." Ponier shifted in his seat. "Sir, are you all right? Is everything okay?"

"Monsieur Ponier. What I am going to discuss with you is extremely confidential. You are not to discuss this with any member of the staff, or any other director or auditor. This is between you and me. Do I have your word?"

"Yes, sir." He was nervous. "What is it you want to discuss?"

"If you cooperate with me, I will see that you are rewarded. I cannot be specific, but your assistance will not go unappreciated. You will be acknowledged in a tangible and quantifiable manner. Do you understand?"

"Yes, sir." He gave his full attention to Leo, as if his neck were on the block. "Tell me what I can do."

"Monsieur Ponier. In a nutshell, I believe that Banque Lapis has taken advantage, in a substantial way, of those of our clients who were victims of the Holocaust."

"Really? How?" His face flushed. "What makes you think that?"

For an instant, Leo worried that he'd made a terrible mistake, that Ponier was not loyal at all, he was an anti-Semite, a mindless beetle who didn't want to hear a sour word about his employer. But it was too late to stop.

"First, let's take the bank deposits that you had scheduled for me." He handed him the schedules. "You will see that in total, the accounts had deposits of seven million. No interest has been paid on those accounts for thirty-odd years. Taking a rate of five percent, that equates to approximately ten million that the bank has not paid in interest. Now, look at when the last transaction on each account took place. 1939. Doesn't it strike you as odd that after the war, none of the account holders, not one, contacted us to discuss their accounts or question us about interest?"

"Yes, it's odd."

"Not really. It's because these people were, in all likelihood, gassed in the concentration camps." He studied the man's reaction. "Like my parents. My parents, Monsieur Ponier."

"Oh, I see. I didn't know." Somehow this calmed the man. He met Leo's gaze and removed his reading glasses. "I'm truly sorry."

"Now you can understand why I'm committed to getting to the bottom of this."

"Yes, I do see."

"Now, Monsieur Ponier, we are a tiny Swiss bank. This cannot be a unique situation exclusive only to Banque Lapis. Think of all the other Swiss banks—Union Bank, Swiss Bank Corporation, Credit Suisse, Bank Leu, and all the others. Imagine what they are sitting on by way of unclaimed deposits, which they have had the use of for all these years, interest free. Can you imagine?"

Ponier nodded carefully, frowning at the papers. His eyes shifted side to side, absorbing details of the schedule.

"You're right, Mr. Bergner. You know, we're lucky to have these numbered accounts all listed separately. There was talk a few months ago during the annual audit about condensing these inactive accounts into one. If we would have done that, and the old records were destroyed, we would never have been able to research this."

"Who suggested that the inactive accounts should be condensed into a single account?"

"It arose just before our annual audit. A representative of the Swiss Bankers Association called to recommend that we should do that. The Association was making a general recommendation to all banks that this should be done."

"I wonder why, Monsieur Ponier." Leo's tone shifted to sarcasm. "Seems as if they wanted to avoid a possible scandal, don't you think?"

"It looks like that."

"Who has access to these accounts? Who do we need to put names and addresses to the numbers?"

"That's a very sensitive issue." Ponier sighed and replaced his glasses. "And, it's against the law. You, as managing director of the bank, should have certain rights of access to those details. I suggest you speak with Madame Risset in the Secretariat Department. She and her assistant have custody of all that information."

"I will do that."

Leo added a note of dismissal to his voice that Ponier picked up on. He rose to leave.

"One more thing," Leo said. "Why did the bank sell gold, artwork and jewelry to the Pontificio Istituto at substantially lower prices than market value?"

"I have no idea, Mr. Bergner."

"Swiss Banks are not known for their magnanimity. Was there a special relationship between Banque Lapis and the Istituto?"

"I don't know, Mr. Bergner." Ponier approached the desk again and leaned on the back of his chair. "The bank's roots are Greek, which would suggest Greek Orthodox, not Roman Catholic. Monsieur Hug and Dr. Breitman both retired a few years ago, and as you probably know, they are devout Roman Catholics. I believe they served on a lay committee at the Cathedral in Place Cornavin." His thin lips grew tighter, and he actually rolled his eyes. "You know, Monsieur Hug upset many of us because he was always collecting money for some Franciscan monastery. We felt obliged to contribute to safeguard our positions at the bank. He was quite a tyrant at times. No tears were shed when he retired, believe me."

"Thank you for your trust, Monsieur Ponier." Leo nodded. "You're my ally here."

After Ponier was gone, Leo summoned Madame Risset to his office.

The woman who stood before him was attractive, in a chilly way. She had a broad face with cheekbones and fine brows that somehow made her eyes seem bluer. They were the color of a clear winter sky, a blue that shut you out. She had a rigid posture that seemed ideal for pacing the grid of secretaries, supervising their flying fingers, and discouraging their errors.

"I'm going to give you these pages," Leo said. "I want the names and addresses for each of these accounts, and the dates of the last correspondence the bank sent or received from the account holders. This is confidential. I'd like you to get back to me on these by the end of the week, please."

"But, Mr. Bergner." She assessed the list without tilting her chin from its military set. "There are about two hundred accounts here."

"That's right, Madame Risset. I also need to set up meetings with Dr. Breitman and Monsieur Hug. Please, can you let me have their addresses and telephone numbers?"

She exited Leo's office, having no choice but assent. And to her credit, she finished early—in three days. Once again she reported to Leo's office.

"Mr. Bergner. These are the names and addresses of the account holders that you requested. And here are the telephone numbers and addresses for Dr. Breitman and Monsieur Hug." She laid the file next to his open hand. "My colleague and I have worked many hours of overtime to get you this information."

"Thank you. Make sure that the payroll department is advised."

"I will, Mr. Bergner."

"Now, I also need the date of the last item of correspondence, either from the client to us, or to the client from us."

"You will see that information in the final two columns."

"Thank you. You have done a good job."

Leo glanced at the list of two hundred account holders. The majority of names were clearly Jewish or of Jewish origin. There was no correspondence, in either direction, since 1941.

✳

Given Leo's upcoming trips, it was too late in the week to schedule meetings with either Dr. Breitman or Monsieur Hug, so Leo put that off until his return. He was due for a visit to Mrs. De Sola, and he wished to meet the art appraiser. He began with Martin.

"Leo," Martin said, seated behind the desk in his office. "I looked at the schedules you sent me. You're right. Some very strange transactions. It's good you had the names of the paintings. Our research staff was able to check on the provenances of a number of them."

"So what have you learned?"

"Follow me closely." Martin turned the sheets so they could both study them across his desk. In person, he was older than he sounded on the phone. "In the case of items that went to auction, that was easy, given that we work with all the European auction houses and share research information. These paintings all seemed to fetch the correct market prices at the dates of sale. However, it's the paintings that did not go to auction that are the most interesting. Most came from five collections. The same is true of the jewelry and the bronzes. From just five collections."

"And which collections were they?"

"The Wertheims in Berlin, the Dreyfus family in Florence, the Lavy family in Munich, the Goldsmid family in Amsterdam, and the Aaron family in Paris."

The final name made Leo's heart squeeze. "All Jews."

"That's right. These people all had large collections, and their acquisitions were well-documented and widely known in the art world. These paintings were sold to the Istituto at substantially less than market value."

"Martin, thank you."

"Stay for a drink? I'm about to leave."

"Thanks, but I can't."

Leo left Martin's office and walked blindly south, toward the Thames, understanding fully for the first time—he had unwittingly facilitated one of the largest thefts in history.

When he arrived to visit Mrs. De Sola, she informed Leo that someone had telephoned for him and left a number. This surprise put Leo on alert. Who would try reaching him at the De Sola's?

The caller was Andre, whose firm had acquired the real estate in Nice. But the caller's urgent news had nothing to do with Leo's investments. Maitre Talais had suffered a heart attack.

Leo apologized to Mrs. De Sola, and of course, she understood completely. "Go," she said. "Go immediately."

Once Leo arrived in Nice, his only focus was reaching the hospital as quickly as possible. When he entered the room, he witnessed a man beyond cognizance. Maitre Talais's body, shrunken under the hospital sheet, seemed no bigger than a child's and was reduced to a skeleton. He reacted neither to his wife's voice nor to Leo's. Under Leo's hand, the old man's skin seemed already dead.

"My husband was always so fond of you and your parents," Madame Talais said, "and of Monsieur and Madame Kaplan. He was honored that in the thirties when there were so many attorneys in Nice, and many of them were Jewish, that your father and Monsieur Kaplan came to him. He was very proud of his business association with your father and cousin."

"We all did well, Madame Talais. And the way your husband looked after my interests, even though I was far away and my family had perished, was wonderful. He never took advantage of me. That made him special."

"He is a unique man."

The conversation was stilted. The unusual familiarity with which she had greeted him on their first meeting was gone. Leo waited for a pause in their exchange, and when it came, he rose.

"Thank you for coming to visit us, Leo. You must be aware that you may never see him alive again. But I hope you and I will stay in touch."

"We will, Madame Talais. We will."

He couldn't bring himself to remain in Nice, so he rented a car and decided to stay at La Colombe d'Or in Saint-Paul de Vence. He called Elizabeth from his room.

"What's the matter, Leo? You're unusually quiet."

"I was going to say the same about you. What's wrong?"

"I'm so busy at the office, and my relationship with Sergio is fast becoming very problematic. I think it's over."

"Am I supposed to say I'm sorry?" Leo twisted the blank pad of paper on the bedspread, as if there were an answer scribbled there.

"That wouldn't be sincere. I'm just saying maybe I did make a mistake. Anyway, that's how it is. I need to get away for a few days."

"I'm in Saint-Paul de Vence. It's a long story." He thought it best to ignore her breezy tone and change the subject. "Poor Maitre Talais is dying. Why not join me in Saint-Paul? I'm here until Sunday."

"You never give up, do you?"

"That's not an answer." He smiled. "Would you like to come?"

The line was silent for almost half a minute. Leo doodled, fighting the urge to beg.

"I'll come, but on two conditions," she said. "Condition one is that we have separate rooms. Condition two is that you will not discuss *us*, or bring up the word *reconciliation*, or anything to do with that possibility. If you can handle that, it's to be just a weekend where two old friends travel together. But nothing else, okay? I just can't handle it right now. Sergio is putting pressure on me to relax and be content with the status quo. I can't have you putting pressure on me too. Is that understood?"

"Okay."

"And don't say anything to my mother or Holly, either. Now tell me why you're distracted. Is it just Maitre Talais?"

"In a nutshell, I'm discovering that the bank may have done some weird business just after the war. That's all I can say right now. Maybe I'll say more when we're together."

✳

In spite of Elizabeth's insistence on conditions, the weekend went smoothly. Leo was relaxed in Elizabeth's company, and she in his. The mood, however, was not light. Elizabeth was depressed and preferred to remain in her room. She would sit on her balcony gazing at the village below and at the scenery, the green fields, the old walls, and the church on the hill.

Leo ended up spending most of the time alone, brooding about his investigation. He'd spoken to Uri again, who believed he needed a distraction.

Maybe a mistress. Something. Leo did not tell him that Elizabeth was asleep down the hall.

On the flight back to Geneva, Leo turned to Elizabeth and abruptly asked, "Well, have you made up your mind?"

"Yes, I have," she answered. "But don't gloat. I'm going to end my relationship with Sergio this week. For sure. My mind is made up. Thank you for the weekend. It helped clear my head. And thank you for letting me be, and for not putting any pressure on me."

"No, that will come next week."

He smiled. She did not.

✳

Leo's investigation slowed down after he returned to Geneva, and he decided it was time to telephone Uri to see if he could help. His old friend seemed to have an unending list of contacts in every part of the world, and in every profession—so much that Leo teased him about being Mossad—but Uri refused to share anything else.

"Not even the name of a good attorney?" Leo asked. "You're the only person I trust completely."

"Go screw yourself."

That was Uri, his old pal, as brash as ever. Denied any help from his friend, Leo would have to find a competent attorney on his own. Over the next few days, he asked his associates in the city for recommendations and heard the same name over and over again. Louis Weill.

Leo put through a call. "Maitre Weill, I've been told that you are considered one of the top attorneys in Geneva. I have an interesting matter to discuss with you. Why not come to the bank, and we can have some lunch."

"I would be delighted, Monsieur Bergner. But you are mistaken. I am not one of the best attorneys in Geneva. I am the best attorney in all of Switzerland."

The attorney Weill wore flamboyant suits that were better matched for a New York fashion show. On their first meeting, he wore a black one with bold yellow pinstripes and an aquamarine handkerchief. His heavy-framed glasses were decorated with a few small diamond studs. The hand he offered Leo was similarly ringed and reminded Leo of an Arabian harem cushion, down to the red velvet gloves he held loosely in his other hand. Leo was embarrassed that so many heads turned in the bank's dining room.

Over lunch, in a private corner of the dining room, Leo gave Maitre Weill a full account of what he had discovered. He told him of the trips he and Monsieur Fabre had made to Rome to deliver heavy suitcases and crated artworks to the Pontificio Istituto.

"So basically," Maitre Weill said, studying the various schedules, "you are asking me to try to contact the account holders on these lists, or their heirs, and also to see what I can find out about the Istituto. Obviously, I will need to engage private investigators. It will be difficult to trace these people if most, if not all, perished in the concentration camps. Even if they survived the camps, in the time since, they may have died. But I will give it my best shot. You are embarking on a worthy cause." He lifted one eyebrow above his diamond-studded glasses. "Not one that is so worthy, however, that I will waive my right to a fee."

"I understand, Maitre Weill."

"And I will also need a deposit on account of my fees and expenses. Private investigators do not come cheap."

"I will personally take care of your fees and expenses. Just let me know what you require. And there is something else to which I must alert you."

"What's that?"

"Obviously, Banque Lapis is not unique. Every bank in Switzerland must have similar skeletons in their closets. Multiply our involvement here by whatever you wish, and take into account the big banks like Union Bank of Switzerland and Swiss Bank Corporation and so on. This could be a major scandal here in Switzerland. In fact, my assistant, Monsieur Ponier, told me that we were fortunate to have the numbered accounts listed separately. There was a discussion during the annual audit that the inactive accounts should be condensed into one account. If that would have been done, this task would be practically impossible. We need to research this quickly."

Weill scowled at his notes. Behind his façade, he was actually a rather plain-looking man, and what he'd heard clearly upset him.

"This is all interesting, Monsieur Bergner. I have got the message. I will get back to you in a few days when I know how much I will need from you. In the meantime, I will try to get some information from Rome on the Istituto."

"And I will pin down some old colleagues who have been avoiding me."

✳

"Dr. Breitman, how are you, sir?" Leo asked over the telephone.

"What do you want of me, Mr. Bergner? I have heard from Madame Risset that you have been requesting certain information, and Monsieur Hug called me a couple of hours ago to say that you have invited him for lunch. What could you possibly want to see me for? I am retired from the bank. This is my private number."

"I thought we could catch up on old times." Leo conjured a playful, friendly tone. "It would be good to see you again. I hope you're enjoying your retirement in Lausanne. May I invite you for lunch next week?"

"I will be away."

"Perhaps when you are back."

"Maybe. Call me at the end of the month, if you must."

Leo was puzzled by Dr. Breitman's response. He had always regarded him as his mentor, and they enjoyed a good professional relationship, if a gruff one. And hadn't Madame Risset betrayed bank confidentiality by speaking with Dr. Breitman? And why had Monsieur Hug been so quick to contact him?

These questions troubled Leo, but for the next few days, he had no time to ponder them. Maitre Talais finally succumbed, and Leo flew to Nice for the funeral. Another dinner with Elizabeth passed without her giving him any hope of reconciliation. The topic was taboo, and clearly she was in a depression following the breakup of her relationship with Ramati. Leo reached across the table to take her hand, but she withdrew it as quickly as he had offered his.

When the turmoil subsided, of another funeral and dinner with a wife who didn't love him, Leo returned to his office feeling that work was his only refuge. And he'd made a list of outstanding questions in his pocket notebook, which he flipped open as soon as he and Monsieur Ponier were alone.

"Tell me what you know about Madame Risset. Let's start there. Since I asked her to give me the information I needed, which she did of course, she has been surly and offhand whenever I have reason to speak with her. Also, as far as you know, is there a relationship between her and Dr. Breitman?"

"Of course she is in contact with him, Mr. Bergner. She's his niece. I thought you knew that. Everybody in the bank knows it."

The next day, Leo left the office early to drive to Montreux for his lunch appointment with Monsieur Hug. He sat at a table and Hug soon arrived. The man had only gotten balder, and brown spots covered his scalp.

Leo politely rose. "You look well, Monsieur Hug. Obviously retirement suits you."

"I dare say it does. I spent fifty years at Banque Lapis, and some of those years, particularly during the war, were extremely difficult. And now you're back at Banque Lapis as the boss, I hear. Are you making many changes?"

"No, not really. We're expanding the lending department and attracting a number of corporate clients, which is good. But no real changes."

Monsieur Hug seemed friendly enough, but there again, he had been quick off the mark to contact Dr. Breitman, who had been very much on the defensive. They paused to order. Hug showed great interest in the menu.

"Monsieur Hug, I need to ask you a number of questions. I would like your cooperation. I'm discovering some very strange transactions that took place at the bank immediately after the war. And certain things seem irregular right up to today."

"Like what?"

"First, why did we sell so much artwork and other assets to an Italian institution at a fraction of fair market value? These items were not ours to sell. They were owned by clients of the bank who had entrusted them to us for safekeeping."

Hug broke off a piece of bread, playing for time while he conjured a plausible response.

"These clients had not paid their safe storage fees. It was as simple as that. Under the terms of their agreements with the bank, we had the right to open the vaults and foreclose on what they had there. That's normal."

"But wouldn't it have been normal to take from the proceeds of sale, what was owed and credit their accounts with the balance? And if they had credit balances with us, why didn't we simply deduct what they owed for storage from their accounts?"

"I don't know about that. I only did what I was told to do."

"By whom, Monsieur Hug?"

"Dr. Breitman, of course. He was the general manager of the bank."

"As far as you know, what was the relationship between Banque Lapis and Pontificio Istituto?"

"You'll have to ask Dr. Breitman."

"Another question—why has the bank never credited the inactive accounts with interest?"

"Please, Mr. Bergner. You should discuss the matter with Dr. Breitman, not me."

"Is that why you telephoned him after I spoke with you last week? To warn him that I had questions?" Still he continued, "Is that why Dr. Breitman won't meet with me?"

"Mr. Bergner, may I remind you, I am no longer an employee of the bank. I am under no obligation to tell you anything. May I also remind you that I am old enough to be your father. When you were at the bank years ago, you were my subordinate. I demand to be treated with respect."

"And, Monsieur Hug, I demand truthful answers. Theft of a client's property is a very serious offense anywhere in the world, particularly in Switzerland, which prides itself on its banking. I repeat, I demand honest answers. Suppose I tell you that two of those inactive clients have surfaced. They are demanding to know, quite rightly, why the bank did not automatically deduct from their accounts the amount owed for the rent of their boxes. Under the terms of their box rentals, the bank is expressly authorized to deduct those quarterly charges. The bank could have done that on these two accounts to this very day and still, Monsieur Hug, those accounts would be in substantial funds. It is your signature on those agreements. It is your signature on the instructions to break open those boxes. I demand, in the name of the bank, and in the name of Swiss banking, full and truthful answers."

"I was following orders, Mr. Bergner." Hug looked down at the table and closed his eyes.

"A lot of people in Germany said the same thing at Nuremburg, Monsieur Hug. That's not good enough."

Hug sighed. "Dr. Breitman did have a special relationship with the Pontificio Istituto. The head of the Istituto was an Austrian, Bishop Alois Hudal. He was born in Graz. Dr. Breitman's mother was also born in Graz. Bishop Hudal was very controversial, passionately anti-Communist. After the war, it is well known that he was instrumental in helping Nazis escape to Latin America and seeing them get established there. That's all I want to say. You will need to speak with Dr. Breitman."

"So, putting two and two together to make four, on those trips to Rome that Monsieur Fabre and I made years ago, week after week, we were taking property that the bank had stolen from its clients, to sell to the Bishop at ludicrously low prices, and of course, the bank pocketed the proceeds. Then the good and pious Bishop sold those items at market prices to finance the escape of Nazi criminals from Europe. And, if that wasn't enough, the devout Bishop saw to it that the Nazi bastards established themselves comfortably in Latin America. Is that what you're telling me we did, Monsieur Hug?" Leo shouted, "Is that what you're telling me!"

Hug withered where he sat and said nothing. His pate had flushed a purple color that entirely concealed the brown spots. Leo stood, threw down a few bills on the table, and walked out.

✳

A few days later, Maitre Weill burst into the bank, wearing a velour ascot the same flushed-pink color of his face. He demanded to see Leo.

"Maitre Weill," Leo said, seated behind the desk in his office. "Please, sit and relax, and tell me what you've found."

"I have looked into all that you told me of your conversation with Monsieur Hug. We're onto something. My contact in Vienna has been very efficient." He took a piece of paper from his waistcoat pocket and read from it. "Alois Hudal was born in May 1885 in Graz. He died in Rome a short time ago, on May 13th. With that information, my man in Vienna was able to track down details of Bishop Hudal's parents. He had an older sister, Heidi, and a younger brother, Walter."

"Tell me more," Leo said.

"Heidi Hudal left Graz, and after university in Vienna, got a job in Zurich. She ultimately married a Swiss, Heinz Breitman. They had a son. Your former boss."

"My God, so Bishop Hudal was Breitman's uncle?"

"That's correct. That is part of the special relationship between the Istituto and Banque Lapis."

"Jesus Christ. No wonder he refuses to see me."

"That's not all. There is the question of Madame Risset."

"She is Breitman's niece."

"She is also the granddaughter of Walter Hudal, Bishop Hudal's younger brother. She is Bishop Hudal's grandniece. She must have married."

"Maitre Weill, let me check something." Leo dialed the director of the personnel department. "Monsieur Olivier, bring me Madame Risset's personnel file as quickly as possible. Make sure no one knows."

Olivier was a close friend of Ponier and seemed aware of Leo's personal interest in the Holocaust. He was quick to proceed. Monsieur Olivier tapped on the door a few minutes later, nodded to Weill, and handed the file to Leo.

"Thank you, Monsieur Olivier. Please wait, you can have it back in a moment."

Leo turned to the first item in the file. It was Madame Risset's original application to join the bank, dated 13 March, 1934. She was seventeen years old and her name was Pauline Hudal. She advised the bank of her marriage to Marcel Risset in 1943 and of her wish to be known thereafter as Madame Risset.

Leo passed the file to Maitre Weill. He quickly studied it then handed it back to Olivier.

"Thank you, Monsieur Olivier," Leo said. "That will be all."

After the door closed, Weill didn't speak right away. He cleared his throat into a handkerchief and folded it again, carefully, as if sorting his words.

"Monsieur Bergner, I am becoming very emotionally involved in this. I did not think I would. I thank you for engaging me to work on this." He tucked the handkerchief into his breast pocket and stood, unwilling to meet Leo's eyes. "I will waive my fees totally and will agree to absorb fifty percent of all the costs involved if you would be agreeable to absorb the remainder."

"Maitre Weill. That is very generous of you. I appreciate it."

"You see, Monsieur Bergner." He patted his pockets and sighed. "I too lost my family in Auschwitz."

＊

Leo met Elizabeth for dinner that evening, and afterward, watched as she drove off into the night. Then he went to find his own car in a nearby lot. His watch said half past eight. The parking lot was poorly lit, and he had parked his BMW at the back. As he approached his car, he was surprised to see that even though the parking lot was close to empty, his car was sandwiched between two large trucks.

As Leo reached in his pocket for his keys, the drivers' doors of the two trucks opened, and two men emerged.

"Who are you?" Leo demanded.

The men were hooded, and the taller of the two was the first to speak.

"Monsieur Bergner. We are not going to kill you. You're lucky that our instructions are just to teach you a lesson, not to kill. But if you don't alter your ways, we may be instructed to kill next time."

Before Leo could answer, the other man was at his side. Leo wrestled as the man secured him in a stranglehold, and his partner paralyzed Leo with a pounding blow to his stomach. Then his face, and again. Everywhere without end, the two delivered agony until Leo could take no more, leaving him slumped in the dark, beaten, silent, and unmoving.

27

LEO WAS CERTAIN THAT HE'D BEEN FIGHTING IN JERUSALEM. He'd been hit by a sniper, and the wound was infected. In his delirium, he thought he heard Hebrew pass between the doctor and nurses. Leo opened his eyes.

"Where am I?"

A nurse came to his bedside. "Good morning," she said in French. "You're in the hospital in Geneva. Now you've woken, a doctor will come see you shortly."

He tried to raise his hand to his face but let it drop. Too painful. His pain-sharpened mind began to remember. Dinner with Elizabeth. The bank.

The nurse moved along and another person took her place.

"I am your physician," he said. "Guillaume Martin."

Leo reached for his face and found his cheeks badly swollen. The light touch of his fingertips was enough to make the bruising sting.

"What happened to me?"

"You took quite a beating. A broken cheekbone, nose and two broken ribs. A security guard found you unconscious in a parking lot around midnight, and the ambulance brought you here. The police have been notified, and an officer should be here shortly to take your statement. Now try to get some rest."

Leo nodded. He passed out again, but when he awoke, he believed he was in a London hospital.

A nurse came to his bedside. "You have a visitor, a Madame Risset."

"Please show her in." The name meant little to him.

"How are you, Mr. Bergner?" Her winter-sky gaze held some meaning for him, and he felt threatened. "It seems as if you've had a bad time."

"You could say so, Madame Risset." Ah, Dr. Breitman's niece, he remembered. It all came back to him—the connections to Hug, and Breitman's connections to the Istituto.

"How are you feeling?" she asked.

"Terrible." Leo maintained his air of confusion, hoping to gain information before she realized his sharpened awareness—she could be an accomplice to last night's crime. "It is kind of you to come," he said. "So everyone in the office knows?"

"Yes, pretty much. We've had a reporter from La Suisse on the telephone, too. He just left a message to say he'd be coming to the hospital to interview you. And I've brought you some newspapers and magazines. I'll put them on your nightstand."

"Thank you. Please, would you telephone Maitre Weill and tell him to come see me as soon as possible. He's my attorney."

"I will. I suppose there's a lesson in all of this. Don't leave your car in the darkest corner of a deserted parking lot." She laughed but it wasn't funny, or she was faking her amusement. "I'd better get back to the office now. I'll call Maitre Weill the minute I'm back. Do you need anything else?"

Her face and posture had warmed to him. She even seemed maternal.

"Thank you, Madame Risset. That will be all."

If she hadn't spoken with the reporter, how could she know about the parking lot? The hospital staff, perhaps, but would they know? Only the ambulance driver. He speculated on who had hired the thugs to rough him up. Three possibilities: Dr. Breitman with the help of his niece, Madame Risset; Sergio Ramati because of his affair with Elizabeth; and the Swiss Bankers Association would want him silenced, for sure.

The next time he passed out, Leo knew he was in Geneva. He kept seeing the trucks, the shadows around his car and within the trucks, and the narrow shadows between the thug's clenched fingers—coming for him again and again.

A voice boomed in the hallway. Something about needing no visiting hours. A feral hope in him thought the voice sounded like Uri's. But when the door opened, Leo blinked at the fuzzy mass of rich colors and fine cologne.

"Maitre Weill, thank you for coming so quickly. I must have dozed off after Madame Risset left."

"My God, you look terrible. Well, I suppose you're lucky. They could have killed you." He shut the door and pulled a chair to the bedside. "Any idea who was behind it?"

"I've been thinking about that, of course. It was either my wife's ex-lover, Dr. Breitman at the bank, or the Swiss Bankers Association."

"And which is the most likely?"

"Dr. Breitman and his niece." Leo repeated her comment about where his car was parked.

"It seems suspicious to me," Maitre Weill agreed.

"I'd like you to contact Monsieur Ponier at the bank. He's on our side and can be trusted. I don't want to call him specifically. Who knows who may be watching. Also, a reporter is trying to reach me. That's not going to look too good in the paper tomorrow."

"Tell the press to call me, if you wish. I'll deal with them."

Within five minutes of Weill's departure, the reporter arrived. When he realized that Leo wasn't going to give him much information, he left on his way to see Maitre Weill.

*

"Darling, gracious," Elizabeth said as she rushed to Leo's bedside. "You've been badly beaten. I called the bank to thank you for dinner last night, and your secretary gave me the news. I came over as quickly as I could. Who did this to you?"

"A couple of thugs," Leo said. "Probably friends of Sergio Ramati."

"He wouldn't... I mean, that's not his style."

"You mean he's not mafia, and the mafia doesn't believe in roughing up a guy."

"I don't think so." She looked faintly offended. "It's plausible, but in my heart of hearts, I don't see him behind this."

Leo didn't either, but he just wanted to test her reactions. The more he thought about it, the more convinced he became that Dr. Breitman and Madame Risset had arranged the attack.

The next morning's paper carried a front line story:

Prominent Geneva Banker Badly Beaten

Leo Bergner, managing director of Banque Lapis, was found unconscious near his BMW in the parking lot of the Parc des Eaux Vivres restaurant at midnight on Wednesday evening. He was rushed to the hospital with multiple fractures and is expected to remain hospitalized for a week. The assailants are unknown and the motive is unclear. There is no evidence of robbery.

✻

Leo received a few calls from members of his staff and from Monsieur Ponier. Elizabeth came by to visit him again, and he began to feel better. But there was one visitor he had not counted on.

"Sir Terrence, how are you?" Leo said. "Have you flown all the way from London just to see me?"

Leo was not cheered by the sight of his chairman, for whom he had limited respect and affection.

"Of course." Sir Terrence had dyed his hair since Leo last saw him, and he treated Leo to a banker's oily smile. "I want you back in London. This is not good for you or for Banque Lapis. The best thing right now is for you to get out of here and spend a few days recovering in London. Then come back to the bank as my vice-chairman."

"But why? I still have a lot to do here."

"I don't want you here. Beatings in car parks do not give the bank the right image." He spread his hands, inviting Leo to see reason. "You have to get out of Geneva. Who was behind it?"

"I truly don't know, Sir Terrence. Whoever it was, their instructions were not to kill me. It was meant as a lesson. I remember that much before they beat the hell out of me."

"Leo, I know you were the innocent party in this, but nevertheless, the publicity for the bank is bad. It would have been better if you had been robbed. That would have established a motive." He leaned closer and lowered his voice. "People will speculate. Were you linked with the mafia? Was there blackmail going on? God knows, man, there will be gossip and that's not good. I want you back in London as soon as possible. Then this will die down."

"But, Sir Terrence, I have a lot of unfinished business here."

"Too bad."

Leo detected harshness in his chairman's tone that was unlike him. He was smooth. Leo might have trusted him if Mr. De Sola hadn't said once, long ago, that Terrence was not only a meticulous banker, he was a manipulative snake. He had risen from the ranks within the bank because he had a way of coercing his competitors to quit, concede, or otherwise humiliate themselves in front of the wrong person at the wrong time. He was a man of wheels and gears, not heart.

"And if I don't return to London?" Leo asked.

"Then you're out. That simple." Sir Terrence softened his voice. "It's in the best interests of the bank here, our bank in London, and you personally."

"Thank you for coming to see me, Sir Terrence. Give me time to think about this."

"All right. Take your time and look after yourself. And when you are discharged from here, I don't want you going back to Banque Lapis for any reason other than to collect your things. Is that understood?"

"So I am fired from Banque Lapis?"

"No, your secondment to Banque Lapis has come to an end. You are returning as vice-chairman to one of the most successful banks in London. Is that so bad?"

Leo never cared for Terrence, the slimy worm, but today there was little question of why. He was being brushed away. Probably because he had discovered the questionable accounts.

"Successful because of the Jewish clients I brought in," Leo pointed out. "At the very same time Banque Lapis was robbing Jewish Holocaust victims blind. There are people in Switzerland who want me out and they've got to you, haven't they?"

"You're hallucinating. Think about what we've discussed and get better. We need you in London."

Sir Terrence left. Leo could not bring himself to thank him for his visit. It had not been a pleasure.

✳

"I must see you, Maitre Weill. Can you come to the hospital today? I need to discuss something with you."

"And I with you. I will be there at seven."

At their meeting, Leo told Weill what had happened with Sir Terrence. He shared his suspicions and fears as well. And that he would most likely have little choice in what he did next.

"What do I do?" Leo asked. "Resign from the bank and tell them to go to hell, and work full-time investigating the Swiss Banks? Or do I go back to London, become vice-chairman, and leave it all to you?"

"Let me think about it for a few days. Can you afford to give up your position at the London bank?"

"I can. I have a financial interest in the bank, and they would buy me out. My investment in the French real estate company is quite substantial. I'm okay."

"Monsieur Ponier visited me yesterday. He will cooperate with us all the way. He is an honest, sincere, dedicated and totally trustworthy man. I offered him a reward but he would hear none of it. He is helping out of purely the best motives. Now, I have other news, somewhat distressing. I had a phone call early this morning from the Israeli Embassy in Berne. The ambassador came onto the phone. Very pleasant and friendly. He said he would be in Geneva next week and wants to see me. You too, if you're up to it."

"What's distressing about that?" Leo asked.

"They have heard through the grapevine what we're doing here and what we've uncovered so far. They want us to stop immediately."

"Why the hell would the Israelis, of all people, want us to stop?"

"It's very simple. They don't want to embarrass Swiss Banking or Switzerland itself in any way. Israel, the ambassador explained, needs all the friends internationally it can muster. Israel is developing excellent relations in Switzerland in all the sectors, not just banking. What we're doing may provoke tremendous hostility toward Jews, and that will mean Israel."

"Well, they can go to hell," Leo muttered. "You and I are children of Holocaust victims. We owe it to that generation. This is absurd. We have Breitman wanting to silence me, the Swiss Bankers Association wanting to silence me, my chairman basically firing me unless I move back to London, and now the Israelis want me to stop."

"I'm inclined to agree, but it's something we need to think about. There are obviously enormous ramifications to all this."

28

AFTER LEO WAS DISCHARGED FROM THE HOSPITAL, HE MOVED into Elizabeth's small apartment on Chemin des Fleurettes, within walking distance of her office. She made it a point that she would sleep on a sofa in the living room. In truth he would have been more comfortable in his own suite at the hotel, but acknowledged that to decline her hospitality would have been churlish.

Her apartment also allowed Leo to continue his confidential discussions with Weill, who was a brilliant and committed man, so Leo was willing to consider his every opinion and strategy.

"I've thought about it," Weill said. "Your instinct is to resign from the London bank. I understand that but it would be wrong. It would give the impression that somehow you are guilty of something. To be fired from the London bank and removed from Geneva at the same time puts out all the wrong signals. Going back to London as vice-chairman is a reaffirmation of the respect and support the board has for you. Simple as that. I think you should go back as soon as possible."

"You're right," Leo admitted. "Although I really want to tell them to go to hell."

"Now, I met again with Monsieur Ponier. I made him a proposal. I said to him that he must know many people at various banks around town. He should make gentle inquiries of them to see what they can uncover. You have long said that if Bank Lapis could have perpetrated such deeds, the others must have their own stories to tell. Or hide, as it were."

"I know, that's been on my mind for a long time. I'd broached that with him before."

"I also told him," Weill explained, "that if he has to wine and dine people, we'll cover him for that. If he wants to take his wife and family on a vacation to England, you'll look after him. Okay?"

"Of course," Leo agreed. "Then he knows we are here to support him in this important work."

*

Leo helped Elizabeth clear the table and take the dirty plates into the kitchen. There was hardly enough room for the two of them to stand there at the same time. She turned to open the refrigerator door and collided with him. He quickly put his arms around her and pulled her toward him. She didn't resist.

He tilted his head and kissed her on the lips. She did not pull back. He kissed her again and felt her hair tickle his cheeks. Her lips parted, and he nervously explored her mouth with his tongue. He moved his hand under her hair, deftly unhooked her blouse, and stroked her silky skin. She delighted in being touched, stroked, and desired. He felt her excitement build as her tongue aggressively danced with his.

"Come," he whispered. "Let's go to bed, darling."

He pulled back and led her to the bedroom. At the door, still holding his hand, she turned to him.

"Darling Leo, forgive me. I'm not ready yet."

"What?" he asked.

"Please don't be angry, but not tonight, Leo. Forgive me."

He shook his head in disbelief and walked into the bedroom. He stood at the window, confused and angry. A few minutes later, he heard her quiet sobs as she lay on the living room sofa.

*

"Leo, come and sit down." Elizabeth was at the dining room table, her hands wrapped around a cup of coffee. Morning light streamed in past the sheer drapes.

He pulled out a chair and sat across from her.

"I'm sorry about last night," she said, focusing anywhere but on him. "Really sorry. Don't be angry with me. I don't want you to go back to London in an angry mood. After you went to bed, I couldn't sleep. I've been up all night thinking."

His heart thudded. He would not allow himself to anticipate her point. He had learned to hide his feelings from her, agony though it was, and he knew that whatever came next would not kill him. He told himself to expect yet another disappointment.

"Leo, the idea of reconciliation is taking hold. If you're willing to forgive me, I think we could work out some of this. I do need more time to think, though. Don't rush me, but I want you to know I am coming around to the idea. Go back to London, settle in, and in a few weeks, I'll come over. I'll write to Mummy and let her know. I'll ask her to help me mend the fences with Holly. What do you say?"

"I say I love you very much, and you've made me very happy, my darling." He heard Uri in his head, calling him a fool. But in that moment he loved Elizabeth more than ever. He took her hands and kissed her.

✳

The next day, Leo arrived at the bank in London and was greeted warmly by the receptionist. His old office had been retained for him while he was in Geneva. Not only that, but someone had kept it spotless. Leo glanced around, then found Sir Terrence standing at the door.

"Welcome back." Sir Terrence shook Leo's hand warmly. "We're all thrilled that you're back. The board is having a celebration lunch for you today in the board room."

"That's very nice. I look forward to seeing everyone again."

"Leo." Terrence did not wait to be asked and sat down across from Leo. "We're going to put out a press release today that you're back and have been appointed vice-chairman. I think you should spend the first couple of weeks getting together with your clients and reconnecting with them. David Thomas did his best while you were in Geneva, but some of those relationships may be a bit shaky, and we don't want to lose them to our competitors."

"I'll get on it straight away."

"I don't want you to handle this shipping business anymore. I'll give that to Robson. And that goes for everything else that was ongoing with Banque Lapis."

"And why is that, Terrence?" Leo took the initiative of dropping *Sir* even though the privilege was not offered.

"It's better that way."

"Tell me, Terrence, while you were in Geneva a couple of weeks ago, who else did you see apart from me?"

"I popped into the bank and saw Le Clerc. Now that he's chairman of the bank, he goes in for a couple of hours every week. He's not a bad chap. How did you get on with him?"

"I had little contact with him. He left me alone. Did you see anyone else?"

"I saw the Geneva director of the Swiss Bankers Association. He was very solicitous about your welfare." Sir Terrence lit a cigarette. He drew on it and turned his swivel chair to look out the window, away from Leo. "And I had lunch with old Dr. Breitman. I always liked him." He shrugged as if relieved and turned back to face Leo. "He too was sorry that you had that unfortunate experience."

"*Sorry?* He was instrumental in arranging it."

"Nonsense. What reason would a retired Swiss banker have for wanting you beaten up, for God's sake? You're paranoid."

"There's no sense in talking about it, Terrence. I'm here now, and I'm going to devote all my energies this week to ensuring that my clients stay loyal to us. I'll see you at lunch. Thank you."

Leo was determined now. Terrence had his agenda and Leo his own. He asked his secretary Claire to assist with a special project, telling her that it had nothing to do with the bank. And that it was most confidential.

"You're going to get used to hearing from a lawyer named Louis Weill, and someone at Banque Lapis called Monsieur Ponier. If you're not busy for dinner tonight, I could explain everything to you, otherwise lunch tomorrow. The board has me booked for lunch today."

＊

A few days later, Leo was at home again, of a sort. He sat at the dinner table with Mrs. De Sola, Holly, and her husband Anthony. They were the only family he had.

"Listen," Leo began. "I'm going to share some very special news with you. It's not official, but it looks very likely that Elizabeth and I will get together again. She told me the day I left Geneva that she was very favorably inclined toward a reconciliation. I am jubilant. She has ended her affair with Ramati."

"We're thrilled for you, for both of you," Mrs. De Sola replied. "I had a letter from Elizabeth yesterday and she told me the same thing. It's wonderful news."

"Holly, what do you say?" Leo asked. "Elizabeth wants to be friends with you again. It means a lot to her."

"If you and Elizabeth get together again, that's wonderful news." Holly put down her soupspoon. "I think you have been a perfect saint to have waited for her. To take her back after all the misery and hell she put you through these past few years. I don't think Anthony would be so forgiving if I took a Latin lover, would you, Anthony?"

"It would be tough, I have to admit." Anthony gave an embarrassed grin. "Leo, I applaud your magnanimity and your ability to put all of it behind you."

The next evening, Leo took a taxi from the bank to Claridge's where he had arranged to meet Uri and Francine. Uri was in the international banking department of Bank Leumi and traveled several months throughout the year, ostensibly on bank business. Leo still suspected that Uri was a Mossad agent, but he resisted the temptation to ask. Francine was a professor in French Literature at The Hebrew University. Though their marriage was long behind them, Leo suspected that they were still companions, or at least companionable.

"How wonderful to see you both," Leo greeted them as he walked into the dining room. "Sorry I'm late. The traffic was hell."

Uri gestured for Leo to have a seat. "We have something to discuss with you, Leo. And, we want to do this over a relaxed meal."

"Sure, what is it?"

"Avram asked me to talk with you." Uri's hardened gaze focused on Leo. "He's known you for nearly as long as I have. He's very fond of you."

"We always got along well."

"While Avram is the ambassador here in London, his cousin is the ambassador to Switzerland. The Israeli Embassy in Switzerland and the Foreign Ministry back home are upset with what you and your attorney are doing. It's very detrimental to Israel's relations with Switzerland. The Governor of the Swiss Bank has had a few telephone conversations with the Governor of the Israeli Central Bank. They want you to stop forthwith. No good comes of this, believe me."

"Uri, I love you. You're my oldest friend. We sat next to each other as frightened kids on the bus all those years ago on the way to Marseilles. I wouldn't refuse you anything in the world, but how can you, you of all people, ask me to do this?"

"We've talked about this before," Uri said firmly. "This isn't the way. You've already had the brains knocked out of your head once, and I want to make sure it doesn't happen again."

"How can you ask me to turn a blind eye when I have actual knowledge of the thievery that went on? Vast sums of money and priceless artwork were stolen from people like our families. Shouldn't there be an accounting?"

Francine shuffled in her chair. "Uri, I'm with Leo on this. It is shameful for the government of Israel to turn their backs on this."

"Leo," Uri said, "it's not just the Israeli government, it's also the Jewish community in Switzerland. There's going to be a gigantic backlash against them domestically. They will run the risk of tremendous anti-Semitism if you don't stop all this immediately."

"Uri, I hear what you say. But I have to do it. I will talk with Louis Weill and see if there are things we could do differently to minimize the backlash you fear, but bottom line, we are not going to stop. It means too much to me. Let's change the subject."

"I agree," Francine said.

The waiter came for their orders, and after his departure, they sat in silence. It was awkward, the three of them each disagreeing in some way. Leo shrugged it off and focused on better news.

"Elizabeth and I are getting together again. Hopefully, she'll be here in a couple of weeks, and we'll put the past behind us. Only look forward."

"Well, let's all drink to that." Uri raised his glass. "Now, will you at least agree to have lunch later this week with Avram? He and Leila would love to see you."

"Of course, but I'm going to tell him exactly the same thing I've told you."

"You always were damned stubborn," Uri said with a smile. "You should try to see the big picture."

"I thought we changed the subject," Francine remarked.

"How long are you both here?" Leo asked.

"Francine goes back to Israel this weekend. I'm here for a month."

"On Bank Leumi business?"

"Well, sort of. I'll be working out of the Embassy. I'm managing some international public works projects the government is involved in. We've got things going on in Ghana, Kenya, Ecuador and Iran. Avram has given me an office at the Embassy, but I'll be staying here."

"Sounds like Mossad to me," Leo joked. They laughed.

✳

The following week, Uri telephoned Leo at his office.

"What are you doing this evening?" Uri asked. "There's a cocktail party at the Dorchester for the president of the World Bank. I thought we could go and then have a bite to eat afterward. Avram may join us later as well."

"Why can't we just have dinner? I'm sick of all these World Bank receptions this week. It's constant. I've been to three already. God alone knows how many Sir Terrence and my other colleagues have attended. Isn't it a farce? They're spending hundreds of thousands on entertaining these fat cats at these unnecessary receptions. They're staying at the best hotels, money no object, and they're here to solve the problems of poor, undeveloped countries. They're all too soused and overfed to discuss anything other than food, drinks, and hookers."

"Leo, I have to go. Bank Leumi expects me to attend. Come on, we'll stay half an hour and then grab a bite. Francine is back in Israel, and you're on your own too, so…"

"Okay, okay. I'll meet you in the lobby at half past six."

Leo stared at the now silent phone. On impulse, he dialed Elizabeth at her office.

"Oui, hello," she answered immediately.

"Darling, how are you? It's been a few days."

"Sorry. I intended to telephone you today but I'm swamped and I'm leaving Geneva this evening for a couple of weeks. Something cropped up."

"What's that?" he asked.

"I'm standing in for one of my colleagues whose wife gave birth prematurely the other day."

"Where are you going?"

"To India—Delhi University," she said. "I'm a speaker at a symposium on child labor. And while I'm there, I have a number of meetings with the government in Delhi, Bombay, and Calcutta. In a way it's very exciting, but I wish I had more time to prepare."

"Are you going alone?" he cautiously asked.

"Yes. Why?"

"When will you be coming to London?"

"I expect when I get back I'll have to spend a few days here. But hopefully the following weekend."

"Wonderful." A tightness in his chest released. He suddenly felt talkative. "Your mother is thrilled, and don't worry about Holly. She and Anthony are really looking forward to seeing you. You made your mother so happy when you wrote to tell her about us."

"Good. Darling, forgive me, but I have to run out to the doctor and get my vaccination for the trip. I'll call you when I get back."

He put the phone down and smiled. She sounded pressured, but for once, not by him. It would all work out in the end, he was sure. His cheerfulness boosted his spirits even further. He snapped his favorite tie off its hanger and made it into a perfect knot.

In ten minutes he was in the hotel's lobby. His cheer was short-lived. Uri was late.

"Sorry, Leo," Uri called from the doors. He rushed toward him. "It's been one of those days. Shall we go and put in our appearance at the reception? It's in the ballroom. That way."

As they approached the wide double-doors, they were obliged to stop at a table and pick up their name badges. An attractive woman was busy asking each person their name, and when she got to Leo, she hunted through the fan of alphabetically ordered badges, but she couldn't find one with his name. Leo declined a handwritten one.

"I have lots of business cards on me if anyone wants to know who I am." Leo moved away from the crowd of people at the table.

Beyond the double-doors, bankers of all ages, shapes and colors, plus their wives and girlfriends, packed a stiflingly hot and unbearably over-crowded room.

"I don't think this was such a good idea, Uri. Let's not stay too long."

"Yes, but I have to work the room a bit. There're a few people I need to schmooze."

"There must be five hundred or more people here already, and the party only began twenty minutes ago."

Pink-faced, earnest young bankers, fresh out of business school, rubbed shoulders with veterans from banks around the world. A mélange of languages at deafening volume produced a cacophony that made meaningful conversation impossible.

A jazz trio played in a corner, but only the bassist was audible. The ballroom had no bar, and waiters had to perform circus tricks to wend their way through the throngs with trays of canapés and champagne.

"It's less crowded over there, Leo. Follow me."

Uri pulled Leo into the crowd. It was a struggle to keep from bumping into people and sending their drinks flying, but Leo managed. He spotted one of his old colleagues from London and waved, but it was impossible to penetrate the mob and get within range of conversation. He gave up.

"Uri, this is murder."

"I agree, but at least it's slightly less shoulder-to-shoulder here. Let's just stand here awhile and watch the masses get drunk on free champagne and gorge themselves on the smoked salmon and caviar."

"It's really disgusting, isn't it? Have you seen the people you need to schmooze yet, or can we leave now?"

"Another twenty minutes, Leo. I'll just stand here and finish this glass. Then I'll force myself back into the fray."

Leo watched for a waiter to squeeze past so he could at least get something cold to drink. He ignored the bodies pressing against his margin of clear space and looked for a tuxedoed waiter. Then he noticed a man wearing a tan suit who did not move on.

The man approached Leo and seemed to say something, but it was lost in the noisy room. Even though he was standing just beside Leo and Uri, the man had to shout to be heard.

"You must have found the only place in the room where you have at least half a meter of space to yourselves," the man said. "Do you mind if I stand here with you until I can find my wife? She is out there somewhere in that crowd."

The man pointed to the mob that had now grown to probably seven hundred. His hair and eyes were the same unobtrusive, quiet color of his suit.

"Not at all." Uri leaned closer to the man and shouted, "It's just too crowded, isn't it?"

"Yes, and I can hardly hear a word. I lost my hearing in my right ear. Too much duck and pigeon shooting."

The man spoke English with an accent that was hard to identify. It sounded German, but some words sounded closer to Spanish.

Uri tried to introduce himself, then Leo, and the man replied with his name, but no one could hear anything.

"Can you read his badge?" Leo asked Uri.

Uri asked the man, "Did you fly in for the conference, or are you based in London?"

"What?" he replied, holding a hand to his ear.

Uri repeated the question. The man smiled, obviously still not hearing it.

"There's my wife over there," he shouted. "I'm going to get her. Please, may we occupy your space here for a minute? It really is the only place where we can talk."

Uri nodded. The man pressed toward the knot of women that contained his wife. He had a slight limp.

"He's brave to try to navigate this room," Uri said. "He's sure as hell going to bump into someone and knock a glass over."

"Did you see his name badge?" Leo asked.

"His first name is Bruno, but I couldn't read his last name."

"Never mind. Let's get the hell out of here. No waiter has had the decency to offer me a drink."

"Leo, stop kvetching, for God's sake. I have to work the room. If we bail out now, it would look very rude. Look, he's bringing his wife over here now. She's stunning." His smile became the adolescent Uri's that Leo remembered from their days in the kibbutz. "Just look at that woman. She could be Sophia Loren's twin."

Leo was too busy taking a glass of champagne from a waiter. Once he'd taken the first sip, he looked up. The stranger and his wife moved as quickly as they could through the densely packed ballroom, coming toward Leo and Uri.

"She is stunning, I have to agree, Uri. But there again, you and I always did have the same taste in women ever since the kibbutz."

"Here we go again. Francine."

"Isn't it a true test of friendship that we can now laugh at—"

Mouth open and jaw dropping, Leo stood gawking at the woman, her cleavage, and the emerald pendant cradled between her breasts. The emerald he had always known. The pendant his mother had loved and worn.

The woman's husband, glad to have reached the outer limits of the crowd, smiled and put his arm around his wife. Leo could not speak. He couldn't move. All he could do was stare at his mother's emerald. The size of the pendant would have given it away, or its antique cut, but even the setting was the same, even the chain around the woman's neck.

"Bruno Franzmann," Leo hollered. "Bruno Franzmann. Bruno Franzmann from Augsburg. It's Bruno Franzmann from Augsburg. My piano teacher. That's Bruno Franzmann from Augsburg!" Leo had gone berserk, shouting without end, "Franzmann from Augsburg! That's my mother's emerald. My mother's emerald. My mother's emerald!"

Uri looked at the man and his wife, then back at Leo, unsure of what to do. Bruno looked uncomfortable and his wife confused. Leo was a man possessed, and his face was growing pale and damp. Then, as Uri reached for Leo's arm, the glass slipped from Leo's fingers, spilling champagne across the woman's dress and shattering when it landed. Leo lost his knees and dropped to the floor.

Uri shouted at the top of his voice, "Call an ambulance!"

✳

Bruno grabbed Elena's wrist and pushed past the crowd around the fallen man. He penetrated the mob, hauling Elena alongside and aiming for the ballroom's double doors.

"What's going on?" Elena asked. "Bruno?"

"We're leaving. We're going straight up to the room."

"But that man on the floor. At least wait until the ambulance arrives. Bruno, for God's sake, what's going on?"

Medics with a stretcher passed Bruno at the door and pushed through the crowd he was frantically trying to escape. Elena stopped. Bruno forced her toward him and made her follow him to the elevators.

"Bruno, what is going on? You're practically pulling my arm out of its socket. I've never seen you like this." She twisted her arm free. "You're like a crazy man."

"Lower your voice." Bruno felt like he was under a thousand heat lamps. "People are looking."

"Of course they are," she shouted. "They want to know what's happening, just like I want to know. Will you please explain?"

An elevator opened and Bruno pulled Elena in. The doors closed. Bruno sighed and selected their floor. Privacy at last, alone with his wife.

"Bruno, I demand to know what the hell is going on."

"I'll tell you everything later. Now will you please shut up? I need time to think."

"Is that all you can do, tell me to shut up?"

He wiped his clammy hands. His heartbeat thundered in his skull. He faced the polished steel panel of the elevator car, which presented his reflection—a ghost staring back. He would be the next to collapse.

The elevator doors popped open. Bruno took Elena's hand and herded her along the hallway. At their door, he fumbled with the key, then pushed her into the room. The door slammed shut. He let go of her, went to the bar, and poured a cognac. Elena just stood there glaring at him.

Bruno took off his jacket and threw it on the bed, then loosened his tie and collapsed in an armchair. He closed his eyes and wiped his brow and started breathing deeply.

"Do you need a doctor?" Elena's tone softened, concerned for her husband.

"No, I'm okay. I just need time to think."

"Bruno, I insist on knowing what's going on. What did that man mean about Augsburg and his mother's emerald and a piano teacher? What's going on? What haven't you told me?"

"Elena, I will tell you everything, I promise. Just let me think for a while." He sat forward on the chair and cradled his glass of cognac. "Please don't bombard me with questions just now. I promise, I'll tell you everything. Trust me."

He reached out for her hand, brought it to his lips, and kissed it. She pulled away and went to the bathroom. He picked up the telephone and dialed from memory.

"Agnes, it's Señor Fernandez." He looked at his watch. It would be afternoon in New York. "Something unexpected has cropped up. My wife and I must leave London tomorrow. We need to return to Argentina as quickly as possible. Please arrange it and call me back with the details as soon as you can." He didn't wait to hear Agnes's sleepy agreement. "Thank you."

Elena had come out of the bathroom. She'd taken off her jewelry, and her neck was bare. She stopped, her hands clasped together at her neck.

"What?" she asked. "We've only been here three days, and now we're going back tomorrow? Bruno, you have to tell me what's going on. You owe it to me."

"For Christ's sake, stop. I've already promised I'll tell you everything. Now please start packing, we're leaving tomorrow. By the time we arrive back in Argentina, you'll know everything, okay? We'll have ten or eleven hours to discuss it on the plane. I repeat, on the plane. Not now, okay?"

✳

When the ambulance arrived for Leo, Uri declined to ride along and asked one of his colleagues at the conference to go instead. Uri would return to the embassy. There was no clear reason to do so, only that somehow, it wouldn't be right to ride along. Nothing was right or had a reason. This couldn't be happening.

At the embassy, Uri met with Avram, but their meeting was short. Seeing that Uri was clearly shaken, and gravely concerned himself, the ambassador summoned a car to deliver Uri to Middlesex Hospital, with instructions to call immediately with news of Leo's condition.

After talking with three nurses and two doctors, Uri gathered what he could and found a payphone in the hospital waiting room.

"They're running tests," Uri explained to the ambassador. "The doctor said he'll know more in a couple of hours. They're giving him oxygen and he's on drips. I don't have any other news at the moment."

"Is he conscious?" Avram asked.

"In and out," Uri answered. "He keeps repeating *Bruno Franzmann* and *emerald*."

"Does he recognize you?"

"I think so. He said something about Elizabeth but I couldn't make it out. The doctor said he should rest and that I shouldn't engage him in conversation. Please, call Elizabeth immediately."

"Of course. Give me the waiting room number, too."

Uri paced the hallway for a few minutes, trying to overhear any new information from the nurses, until the waiting room phone rang.

"Well that was bloody useless," Avram complained. "The stupid woman has recorded an announcement that she's traveling for a couple of weeks and will not be retrieving messages, so callers should telephone again in two week's time. Have you ever heard of anything so unhelpful?"

"It's not a problem," Uri said. "Tomorrow we can get a number for her. Our people in Geneva will have contacts at the International Labor Office. I'll call you later when the doctor tells me more."

Uri went outside for a cigarette. When he came back, he intercepted a doctor exiting Leo's room.

"What can you tell me, Doctor? I'm Uri Nusbaum, a friend of Leo's."

"He is stable for now. His heartbeat and blood pressure are all over the place, but we're steadying him with medications. He's had an x-ray and an EKG. We don't see any heart damage. He may have had a minor heart attack, but we're not sure." The doctor checked his notes. "The cardiologist will see him early tomorrow morning. We're arranging for an echocardiogram at seven o'clock, and Dr. Goodman will decide if he will have an angiogram or a stress test."

∗

As the plane approached Ezeiza Airport in Buenos Aires, Bruno stole a glance at his wife. Her face was in perfect profile, looking as smooth and placid as a piece of stone.

"Are you angry?" he asked. "You've been awfully quiet."

"I'm tired and drained," she calmly replied. "Very tired. Buenos Aires to Europe roundtrip within seventy-two hours is exhausting enough, and then to be hit with what you've told me on top of that. Jesus."

"You must believe me when I tell you that I was never, ever involved in doing anything in the camps. I give you my word that I only worked in the administrative department. There is no blood on my hands, I give you my word."

"I believe you," she said. She finally turned her head. "But why did you never mention this before?"

"I was ashamed." He looked at the back of his aging hands and the veins bulging from his skin. "Because of my foot, I wasn't able to serve in the army. I had to spend the war working in the camps."

"You should have told me before."

"Yes," Bruno said. "I probably should have."

"So what happens next? Why did we have to run away from London like criminals?"

"It was a nervous reaction." He folded his hands on the tray table and forced himself to look at her. "I didn't want any confrontation in a public place. I'm the vice-chairman of a major bank. Do you think I wanted on my first trip to London, with my wife at my side, someone yelling and screaming *Nazi, Nazi, Nazi* at me? I've been known for over thirty years as Fernandez. I've built up a major company on the New York Stock Exchange worth billions. All of a sudden, a ten million to one long shot, I bump into someone I haven't seen since the thirties, screaming *Nazi* at me."

"It still doesn't make sense that we had to leave so abruptly." She turned her profile to him again.

"You don't understand, being in Argentina during those years, what it was like in Europe in the thirties and forties. We all went through hell."

"The Jews seemed to have suffered the most."

"Yes." Bruno thought for a moment. "You're right."

The plane's engine changed pitch. For several minutes, neither of them spoke as the ground moved closer. Maybe he would take her to the estancia tomorrow. Seventy thousand acres of some of the most beautiful real estate on the planet, manicured grounds, colonnaded galleries surrounding the ranch, horses, ducks on the lake. He could do some shooting. After a few weeks of solitude and beauty, maybe he could figure out how much of his wife's trust he had lost.

"You still haven't answered the question," Elena said. "What happens next?"

"If Bergner dies or is dead already, nothing will happen. No one will make any connection between him and me. If he survives, however, then God only knows. He may come looking for me. The Jews will never let go. They came after Eichman, they're still looking for Mengele, Borman, Priebke and Rauff."

"Do you blame them?"

"No. Not really. But I'm not like the others. I was only in the administration department."

"And only following orders," she said, looking as unreadable as a sphinx.

29

"So that's the story of Bruno Franzmann," Leo said. Two hours earlier, Uri had arrived at Leo's home and settled into Leo's favorite chair. Leo had spoken of his days in Augsburg, the piano lessons in return for extra math coaching, and of course, the emerald. While Leo talked, he had placed a framed photograph on the table between them.

"But are you sure, Leo?" Uri looked upset.

"My mother wore that emerald pendant practically every day of her life until it was stolen from her. Of course I'm sure. I used to stroke that pendant when my mother would come into my bedroom at night to tuck me up in bed and read me a story. I can still feel the pressure sometimes of it biting into my chest when she would hug me. Look at that other photograph over there on the piano, the one of my parents."

Uri stood to pick up the photograph and study it.

"See the emerald pendant," Leo said. "That pendant belonged to my grandmother's grandmother. That's how long it's been in my family."

Uri shook his head. He was without words. Leo was not.

"What can you find out about Bruno Franzmann for me?" he asked.

"After your ambulance left, I went in the hotel and spoke with the girl at the reception desk. She showed me the guest list. There were three Bruno's listed. I didn't catch his last name with all the noise going on, and I couldn't read it from the badge he was wearing. So I tracked down all three. One Bruno is a Swiss banker from Zurich, another from Sweden, and a third Bruno lives in Argentina. We all know about Nazis and South America. He's got to be the guy. Bruno Fernandez, vice-chairman of a major Latin

American Bank and chairman of TIC, a multinational conglomerate."

"I want to meet with him."

"For what reason?"

"I need to talk with him. Help me. I know you're Mossad, and you know that I know. Through your connections, get me some data on Bruno Franzmann, please."

"Leo, if I do get the information you're requesting, and if you do meet with him, what then?" Uri's face softened. "You're not going to pull any stunts, are you?"

"Like what?"

"Like kill him."

"Of course not."

Silent, Uri made Leo the target of his sharpening stare. "Right, like you and your Jewish Brigade revenge squad. You weren't going to kill those Germans, either, I suppose."

"Uri, that was years ago. I'm not killing anyone. Please, Uri. I'll need as much background information as possible. Where I can reach him, address, telephone numbers and so on. I want to get through to him, talk to him."

"I'll see what I can do."

"Don't let me down, Uri. This is very important to me."

✳

Leo's private secretary Claire arrived at his apartment at half past six. He poured her a glass of wine and she gulped it like it was apple juice.

"Now," Leo asked, "what's happening with Maitre Weill?"

"He's working almost exclusively on this. Through your colleague at Banque Lapis, Monsieur Ponier, they've discovered some funny goings-on at Union Bank of Switzerland, and they're very excited about that. Maitre Weill says he may have to spend a week or two next month in Zurich, looking into even more banks."

"Good. When I get back from Argentina, I'll pop over to Geneva and meet with him. What's going on at the bank?"

"You're much missed. Sir Terrence really wants to retire, and he wants you in the hot seat as soon as possible."

"I know, I know. My heart isn't in it at the moment, with what's going on in Geneva and now Argentina."

"What is going on in Argentina?" She smiled at him with curiosity. The wine had already made dark purple creases at the corners of her mouth. "You haven't told me."

"I'll tell you when I get back from my trip." Leo set down his glass and picked up a folio of papers.

✳

The phone rang, waking Leo to morning light penetrating the living room curtains. He sat up in his chair and groped for the phone. Uri's voice greeted him.

"I've received a dossier on Bruno Fernandez in the diplomatic pouch. It arrived this morning. I've read it, and it certainly makes interesting reading. My colleague attached to the embassy in Buenos Aires has found out quite a lot about Mr. Fernandez."

"Do I have contact information? Let me find a pen." Leo pushed through the papers next to his leg.

"Don't worry," Uri said. "I'll bring these over. You not only have home and office numbers, you have his very private unlisted numbers that bypass his secretary and go direct to him and his wife."

"How the hell did you get that?"

"Well, Leo, those of us who work for you-know-who have our ways."

"So I was right all along." Leo laughed. "You're a Mossad operative through and through."

"No comment, Leo. I'll drop off the file this afternoon."

✳

CONFIDENTIAL

Bruno Fernandez is thought to be one of the most powerful civilians in Argentina. He is vice-chairman of one of the country's fastest-growing banks; its holding company, of which he is chairman, is quoted on the New York Stock Exchange. TIC is a major conglomerate with diverse interests ranging from oil exploration, television, banking, radio, airlines, import, export, construction and newspapers. The company has a representative office in Jerusalem that was established to liaise with the Ministry of Defense regarding Israeli exports of military equipment to Argentina and with the Argentinean Ministry of Agriculture relating to Israeli imports of Argentinean grain and soybeans. Mr. Fernandez has homes in Buenos Aires, Patagonia, Iguazu and New York. Married with two children (a son and daughter, twins), his wife is the daughter of a former vice president of Argentina.

Mr. Fernandez, while popular among the Argentinean community, is reviled by the country's German community. As Bruno Franzmann, he immigrated to Argentina after the war. During the war he worked in the administrative department at Dachau. He also had responsibilities at other concentration camps. It is believed that the Pontificio Istituto Teutonico in Rome and the ODESSA assisted in securing his passage from Europe to Buenos Aires and helped him establish himself in Argentina. He is known to have applied considerable pressure on other former Nazis to invest in his activities, facilitating the rapid growth of his business empire.

In recent years, he has suffered from deafness. His wife is involved in charitable work in New York and Buenos Aires and is a major influence on her husband. She is active in the Church and serves on a number of Catholic Committees.

For detailed contact information, see over...

What irony. Leo had fought in the Palmach and spent his formative years on a kibbutz. He'd taken a wound for Israel in 1948. Now he was being told by the Israelis not to fight for the rights of Holocaust victims to recover their stolen property. At the very same time, Israel was doing business with a Nazi who had an office in Jerusalem.

✳

Uri's London office overlooked a row of sycamore trees. This gave him calm. Still, he flexed his fists until his knuckles cracked. It was a bad habit, and he had been doing it all morning. He paced, then picked up the phone.

"Yossi, it's Uri in London. Thank you for the dossier on Fernandez, but your work isn't over yet. Leo is a good guy, you know that. However, on anything to do with Nazis and the Holocaust, he can be a loose canon. He's flying to Buenos Aires on Thursday. From London via Madrid. I'll get you the rest of the information. He's going to be staying at The Alvear. He may be exposed to considerable danger. He's out to get Fernandez. I want him tailed twenty-four seven."

"We have contacts at The Alvear," Yossi answered. "And we have people at TIC. After all, we do so much business with them that we need a couple of moles there. So it's no problem. But you should know that this Fernandez doesn't take a piss without his bodyguards accompanying him. Does Leo know that?"

"I told him. I asked him not to go. But he's headstrong and insists."

"We'll have him tailed, don't worry. And we can also tap his hotel telephone."

"You can do that, Yossi?"

"Sure. With all the Arab big shots who stay there, we have good people at The Alvear."

Yossi was deadpan, but Uri knew him well enough to know that Yossi was proud of his work.

Uri grinned. "Good. It seems there is nothing more to add."

30

THE FLIGHT TO BUENOS AIRES WAS TIRING. THE LAYOVER IN Madrid was longer than expected. Fortunately, Leo had an empty seat next to him and had been left alone with his thoughts. Upon arrival at his hotel, he showered and read for a while before going to bed.

After a good night's sleep and a light breakfast, he went and stood in front of the telephone. He picked up the handset, hesitated, then put it down and stared at it, contemplating whether to make the call then or later. Soon, he thought, then he resolved that time would only fuel his dread. He grabbed the phone and dialed the number.

After a few rings, a man answered, "Hello?"

"Bruno Franzmann, I need to speak with you."

Silence. Leo waited. He had a plan in mind, and he had the patience to employ it.

"Leo Bergner. I don't know what to say. I thought you might have died after that party a few weeks ago."

"Would it have been better for you had I died?"

"I don't know. Maybe. How did you get my private number? Only a handful of people have it."

"I want to meet with you."

There was a clatter in the background and crying, like children fighting over a toy. Bruno's children would have been adults. He had grandkids perhaps. After some rustling and muffled voices, it sounded like a door shut, then the line became quiet.

"Why?" Bruno asked.

"There is much we have to discuss."

"I don't think so. Augsburg is a long way away. It was all very many years ago. I don't know what you have made of your life since you left Augsburg, but I have a whole new life here in Argentina. I'm married with two children and a successful business. We do not need to look back and wallow in the past."

There was an ease and good humor in his voice, and it bore no trace of smugness. He did not sound anything like the taut, dour piano tutor of forty years ago.

"We need to live in the present," Bruno continued. "We need to hope for happy and healthy times ahead and continued prosperity."

"I think you owe me the courtesy of seeing me."

"Why? So you can kill me?"

"I have no wish to kill you. That would achieve nothing."

"Where are you calling from?"

"I'm here in Buenos Aires. I'm at The Alvear."

"You're here?" He sounded disquieted again. "I thought you were calling from London. I didn't realize you were here."

"I arrived late last night."

"Have you flown here especially to see me?"

"Yes."

"And it is your intention just to talk?"

"Yes."

"What is so important that you want to discuss with me? Who was I in your life anyway? I gave you piano lessons, your father gave me math lessons for a time, and your mother gave me slices of great cake."

"And you took her emerald pendant."

Silence. Then, "Did you come alone?"

"Yes, I'm totally alone. I am unarmed, and I don't intend to hire any bodyguards. Do you agree to a meeting?"

"I need to think about it. Call me in an hour."

"No, that's not good enough. I've come a long way and waited many years. All I'm asking for is half an hour. Just the two of us. No guns, no bodyguards, and you can be assured that I'm not planning to kill you."

"Okay, I will meet with you once."

"You set the time and place."

"I'm not in Buenos Aires at the moment. Your telephone call was redirected automatically. I'm at my estancia in Iguazu. I'm not planning on being back in Buenos Aires for a couple of weeks. Either wait in Buenos Aires until I return or fly up here."

"I'll fly to Iguazu. How about tomorrow?"

"Tomorrow it is. But I'm not going to have you at my home. My wife will be disturbed by your presence. She has been very confused and distressed since that encounter at the hotel in London. We should meet somewhere else."

"Whatever you say. You name the place and time."

"There is a hotel, the old Hotel Internacional, located in the Parque Nacional Iguazu. I will meet you in front of the hotel at five o'clock tomorrow evening."

"I will be there."

"And, if you give me your word that you will be coming unarmed and on your own, I will do likewise."

"You have my word."

"Let me ask you a question. Are you nervous about meeting me?"

"No, I am not," Leo replied. "Not about my physical safety. I'm more nervous about my emotional reaction when we come face-to-face."

"Well, at least we have that in common. Auf Wiedersehen."

Leo went to the window and drew back the curtains to look out. Consumed by his darkest thoughts and deepest fears, he could not take in the view.

31

During the rainy season, few tourists visited Iguazu Falls, a wonder of nature located on the border of Brazil and Argentina. Spread out along the rim of a crescent-shaped cliff over two miles long, hundreds of individual cascades and waterfalls plummeted nearly three hundred feet into the gorge below, producing a thunderous roar.

The ninety-minute flight from Aero Parke to Iguazu was empty. Walking from the terminal building to pick up his rental car in the adjacent parking lot, Leo buttoned up his raincoat and tightened his scarf. Trees swayed in the wind, and fallen branches littered the road to his hotel, some twenty-five minutes away.

The hotel was an eyesore, but the concierge at the Alvear had recommended it on account of its direct views and easy walking distance to the Falls. It was still only one o'clock. Leo had four hours to kill before his meeting. Once he had checked in, Leo didn't feel much like eating, nor was he in the mood for sightseeing.

The girl at the front desk suggested a restaurant close by. It was shabby and looked as if it could disappear altogether in a strong wind. The doors and windows rattled, and the only things holding it down seemed to be the two elderly locals who sat at a table in silence. Leo ordered *parrilladas*, the house specialty. While waiting, he glanced up at the ceiling and saw water dripping from a leak into a bucket on the floor. The paintings on the walls were all askew, and there were cigarette burns and holes on the leather seats. The food, however, was delicious.

Back at the hotel, Leo spent a few minutes looking at the greeting cards on a rack in the gift shop. Because a stunning girl worked at the counter, he bought a few to avoid appearing cheap. Then he checked his watch.

Four o'clock.

The concierge, in answer to Leo's request for directions to the Hotel Internacional, recommended he take one of the hotel's golf carts. The man waived the usual fee in the expectation that Leo's tip would be generous. The seat was damp, and to be doubly sure that he would be handsomely rewarded, the concierge wiped the seat and handed Leo a dry towel.

Leo started the golf cart, which lurched forward in an unexpected jerk. He followed the directions on the posts along the hotel's driveway and onto the wide stone pathways toward the park's entrance. Within a few minutes, he passed through the main entrance and into the parking lot. He followed a sign toward the Hotel Internacional and steered the cart to one side when a tour bus wanted to pass, and it continued toward the exit. It looked as if there were only two passengers.

The old hotel was now within sight. Single-story built in a U-shape, it had a red roof, doors painted green, and white walls fronting a well-manicured neon-bright lawn. Mature pine trees shot up to the sky, branches swaying heavily. The hotel had a covered veranda, also painted green inside. Steps on either side led down to the garden.

Leo looked around and felt alone. For the first time since leaving Buenos Aires, he became aware of the physical danger of being here. He felt as though he were again on the Jerusalem street. He remembered the prickling sensation along his neck that should have warned him that he was the target of a sniper's bullet.

He parked the golf cart directly in front of the hotel's entrance and remained seated. The jungle, seemingly on all sides of the hotel, was thicker than any he had ever seen—a mass of tall, dense tropical trees and ferns. Around the perimeter of the lawn was a stone path that split into different directions. Leo made out the signposts, which indicated that one led further into the jungle and another toward the Falls. He was distracted by the shrieking of a pair of squabbling, brightly-colored toucans on a nearby tree, hopping from branch to branch. Their enormous tangerine bills rapidly nodded up and down, their tongues sticking rudely out at each other.

Leo looked at his watch. Five more minutes. Suppose Bruno did not appear. Then what? Should he contact him again, or simply fly back the next day to Buenos Aires?

In the distance, someone walked along the path, then onto the lawn and toward him. The man was about two hundred yards away. Was it Bruno? It was two minutes before five. As the person got closer, Leo detected a limp. It had to be Bruno. Leo looked around. Bruno had kept his word and come alone. Now the man was before him. He had no time to consider his feelings.

"Thank you for coming to see me, Bruno."

"I suppose we could have been luckier with the weather." Bruno stopped and looked up at the sky, then at the hotel. He beat his gloved hands together. "It's miserable today, isn't it?" He removed his hat to shake off the rainwater, then put it back on. "Shall we sit in your golf cart and talk? I'd like to sit down. The walk from the park's entrance took longer than I thought it would. I left my car in the parking lot."

Leo walked in silence toward the golf cart. His heart beat fast but threatened neither to stop nor hesitate. He would be all right doing this.

Side by side, they settled into the shelter of the golf cart.

"Well, I'm here." Bruno adjusted his hearing aid. "What do you want to talk about?"

"On the one hand," Leo said, "there were so many things I wanted to discuss with you. But now that we're here after all these years, and after so much that has happened, and our different destinies, I don't know how to begin."

"Thirty-plus years," Bruno said.

"I think part of my confusion is that I don't know whether I'm meeting you as an old friend and mentor, as an enemy, or as a thief who stole from my family."

Bruno nodded. He took off his gloves, exposing hands that seemed too rough and ruddy for one of the most powerful men in Argentina. His fingers were still long and nimble-looking, though.

"Have you ever been to the Falls before?"

"No, never," Leo answered.

"They're quite something. I fell in love with them years ago. My wife and I have an estancia about twenty miles away. I'd like to retire here, but after a couple of weeks my wife nags to go back to the city. If you want to see the Falls, they're only a few minutes away along that trail. You should see them while you're here. We'd have to leave the cart here and walk."

Bruno put his gloves on again. Leo didn't know why he'd removed them in the first place. Then he realized that Bruno was as nervous as he was.

They climbed out of the golf cart and started walking.

"You know, Bruno, I first met you on my eighth birthday. I remember that day like yesterday. You came to our house and played Chopin. Do you still play the piano?"

"Not often. When I first came to Buenos Aires, I used to play in cocktail lounges to make extra money. But the bills are all paid, and in truth, it only reminds me of the past. You, do you still play?"

"Now and again. I'd like to play more, but I'm out of practice. Perhaps we both should have just stuck to music."

"If we'd had a choice." Bruno shrugged.

They arrived at a fork in the road.

"This will bring us to Devil's Throat." Bruno pointed in the direction they should take. "It's the most impressive part of the whole area. It's about five hundred feet wide and about two-thirds of a mile long. It marks the border between Brazil and Argentina. They say that Argentina has the Falls and Brazil the view. But believe me, the view you'll see in a few minutes is extraordinary."

"It's getting noisier too."

"Yes. If we want to talk some more, we should stand here for a while. Then go on. Once we're at the Falls, the roar is deafening, even terrifying."

"How's your foot? I saw you still limp." Once the words were out of his mouth, he wondered why he had asked the question. Did he really care about the answer?

"I had an operation on it in Brazil a few years ago." Bruno shrugged. "A hot-shot surgeon there thought he could do something. But it was a waste of time. Are you married?"

"Yes, to an English woman. She lives in Geneva. We've had a troubled marriage. But when I get back to England, I'm hopeful that we'll have a reconciliation. And you, how's your marriage?"

"Perfect," Bruno replied without any hesitation. "I am very fortunate. My wife is the most wonderful person. My marriage to her was the best thing that ever happened to me. She has made me into a proper person. As you would say, she's made a mensch of me." He smiled and lifted his shoulders in embarrassment. "Before I met her, well, let's face it, I wasn't such a nice person."

"But you've done very well, by all accounts."

"That's true, but the way I achieved my success wasn't always, as you people say, strictly kosher."

Leo could not resist a smile.

"Do you hate Jews?"

"No. I don't hate anyone these days. Looking back now, Hitler was crazy to turn on the Jews. Think of the talent that Hitler forced out of Germany. Imagine if that talent would have remained in Germany, Germany would be one of the superpowers today, next to the United States and Russia."

"And think of the Jews who had not yet been born, the lost next generation, what they might have contributed."

"We have an office in Israel, you know," Bruno said. "We do a lot of business with Israel."

"Have you been there?"

"I'd like to, but I'm afraid to go. Someone may recognize me. Just like you did. My wife has been very unnerved since that evening."

"Have you been back to Augsburg since the war?"

"No, never. In fact, my first trip back to Europe was when we saw each other a few weeks ago. I had no plans to visit Germany after London. Too many years have passed. Do you have children?"

"No, no children."

"We have two. They're both in the States now. Great kids. They take after their mother, thank God. Fortunately, they have her beauty and my brains. God help them if it would have been the other way round."

He laughed. The damp air muted the sound, as if it was resisting the small note of levity. Leo smiled.

"It was the Pontificio Istituto in Rome that helped you escape from Europe, wasn't it, Bruno?"

"Yes, it was. Why do you ask?"

"Because of the irony of it all. After the war, I worked for a bank in Geneva. Every week or so I acted as a courier with a security guard and a priest. We took heavy suitcases of gold to the Istituto. And later, we used to go by road in a truck and take artwork."

"You mean to tell me that you—a Jew—helped the Istituto finance the escape of Germans, people like me, from Europe." Bruno stared at Leo with a look of disbelief.

"Life is strange, don't you think?"

Bruno nodded. He patted his pants pocket and pulled out an envelope folded in half.

"I've been carrying this envelope to give you. I don't need it anymore. It may be useful to you."

"What is it?"

"Practically everything I own has resulted from the contents of this envelope." Bruno handed it to Leo. "Make whatever use you want from the list. There's no more financial juice left in those oranges. But if you can see a use for them, or if that man in Vienna—what's his name, Wiesenthal—is interested, let him have them."

Leo opened the envelope. It contained the Dachau payroll records. Every member of Unit 436. Several pages of names and more.

"Why are you giving me this?" Leo asked, looking at the list and turning the pages.

"Why not? It's a different world today. Many of the names on those sheets are dead anyway. Some I've given up on. I couldn't find them. You may have better luck. Aribert Heim—he was a doctor at Sachsenhausen and then Buchenwald and Mauthausen—is the biggest fish on the list. Brunner is in Syria. You'll never get him. Mannil is in Venezuela, but I've never had much luck in finding him."

Leo stuffed the envelope into his coat pocket. His hand trembled, to imagine he now held a roster of Nazi criminals.

"My generation of Germans was shit," Bruno spat out. "Stupid brainwashed liars."

"That's a strange thing for you to say, isn't it?"

"It's the truth. We were all brainwashed by that devil and his cronies—Goebbels, Himmler, and the others. And we were all liars, too."

"What do you mean?"

"After the war, how come there were no Nazis in Germany? Why? Because they'd all escaped to Argentina." Bruno smirked. "None of them knew what was going on? Ridiculous. Didn't they have eyes and ears? Didn't they talk to neighbors? In Augsburg, when the Jewish doctors and attorneys disappeared, didn't their clients and patients stop to think and question?"

"You surprise me. When did you become so anti-German?"

"When I saw the sniveling monster bullies cave in before me. Those big-shot SS bastards who thought they were so important back in the camps, how they groveled before me when I arrived here. Me, a penniless, snotty-nosed, young cripple. I lost all respect for them."

"But they gave you a new life."

"Only through their fear. They wouldn't have given me the time of day in Germany." He pounded his gloved hands together and adjusted his hat. "If you want to see the Falls, we'd better push on. They close the park soon. It gets dark very quickly here."

The foliage was dense and bright green. There was a bend in the trail, and the noise became deafening. After about five minutes, they came to the edge of the jungle and into a clearing.

Leo stepped closer to the edge. The Falls stretched for miles, an endless curtain of roaring white cascades, and clouds of mist floating higher. Never before had Leo witnessed Nature's power on any scale so grand.

"It is breathtaking," Leo said, his back to Bruno as he took in the amazing view. "How often do you come here?"

Bruno approached Leo's side. "Whenever I'm at our estancia, I make a point of coming here at least once. It never ceases to amaze me. I can stand and watch these Falls for hours. I find it very spiritual here—but I'm not the religious one—my wife is. Anyway, in some sort of a way, I feel a religious experience standing here. The Falls are one of the world's top wonders, you know."

"I can see what you mean."

Leo gazed at the white cataract of water. Around it, the leaves shimmered like emeralds, an uncountable number of emeralds, enough for every son of man in the world. The water's boom made the leaves and the very air shudder, like a storm in Leo's chest. The Falls drowned his voice, and his throat felt tight from shouting.

Bruno touched Leo's sleeve.

"I have something else to give you." Bruno slid a hand into his coat pocket. "My wife said she would never be happy wearing it again, knowing what she knows now."

The roar of crashing water was the only sound when Bruno dropped to his knees. He looked up at Leo, disbelieving, then his gaze became vacant. He slumped to the ground. Leo searched for a reason, then he knelt at Bruno's side. Bruno was mouthing words, blood oozed from his chest, and then his breathing stopped. His hand was still inside his coat pocket. Leo reached in to find Bruno's fingers clutching a green velvet bag, tied shut by a thin shoelace. Leo pulled it apart to see what was inside. His mother's emerald pendant.

Bruno's dead eyes stared up at him. Leo put the pendant in his coat pocket and stood, his back to the Falls, and he scanned the jungle ahead. Tree branches were shifting, then a cluster of ferns near the ground. From one of the many trails, three men emerged, bearing rifles and hurrying toward him.

Leo raised his hands, fully expecting that they would shoot him, but the lead man patted the air as he ran, palm-down, indicating that they meant him no harm.

"Relax, Mr. Bergner. Thank God you're okay."

The man was an Israeli.

"Who are you?" Leo asked.

"We're here to keep watch on you. We've been tailing you since you arrived in Buenos Aires two nights ago. We saw him about to pull that gun on you. Now, let's hurry."

"For Christ's sake, you dumb pieces of shit. He wasn't pulling any gun on me. He was giving me something. He hasn't got a gun on him. Search him, you fools. I had given him my word that I wasn't going to harm him. I had given him my word. And you idiots came and interfered. May God forgive you." Leo looked down at Bruno's body. His suffering was over, but Leo's was beginning anew. He shouted, "Do you realize what you've done?"

"Okay, David, you and Rich, take care of him," the man said. "I'll get Bergner back to his hotel. After you've taken care of Franzmann, do what we've agreed with the bastard's car. But hurry. It'll be dark in fifteen minutes."

Unable to move, Leo watched as the two men picked up Bruno's body, carried it down to the walkway, and then tossed it, like a sack of garbage, into the gorge. Leo could not turn away from the sight, though shame demanded that he shun it, and anger screamed to make it stop. In shock, he could do neither.

"I gave him my word," Leo cried. "I gave him my word!"

"Come on, Mr. Bergner," the man said. "We've got to get you back to the golf cart. I'll drive."

32

LEO WALKED INTO HIS APARTMENT AND DROPPED HIS CASE IN the foyer. He'd unpack in the morning. He wandered into the living room and poured himself a cognac. He took off his jacket and threw it on the sofa. His maid had left the mail on the piano. Thankfully, there wasn't much; he'd only been away a few days. He glanced at the time. Eight o'clock.

He flicked through the few envelopes. A letter from Elizabeth. Walking back to his favorite armchair, he caught a glance of the photograph on the piano of his mother wearing the emerald pendant. It was still in his jacket pocket. With all the drama of the last two days, he hadn't had the time to appreciate the significance of having recovered it. Leo placed his glass on the table and approached the sofa where he had tossed his jacket. He took the green velvet bag out of the pocket and removed the pendant.

It hung before him, catching the light. He felt his mother pulling him to her breast on the platform in Nice, and felt the thin airmail paper of her letters in his fingers. He felt the charge of warmth he'd felt on his eighth birthday, his family around him, everyone alive and happy. The pendant had meant so much to her. First it was stolen from her, then her life itself was stolen. He picked up the framed photograph and draped the emerald around the black wood.

"There you are, Mami, you have your pendant back again."

Leo sat back in the armchair, feeling an ache in his body that he couldn't pinpoint. He took a sip of the cognac and let it warm him. Then he opened Elizabeth's letter.

My Darling Leo:

*As you can see, I'm still in Delhi. This letter will come as a
shock, but life is never smooth sailing, you know. There is a major
change of plan.*

*I hope you will not be too devastated by my news. Sergio's
wife was killed in a road accident last month. Sergio is now free
to marry. He has proposed and I have accepted. I am very happy
and even though you will be disappointed I hope you will in time
forgive me. I'd like us to now move forward and get a divorce. I
hope you will cooperate with me on this.*

Let us try to stay friends, darling Leo.
With love,
Elizabeth

He let the letter fall to the floor. His hand drifted to the picture frame,
and to the emerald pendant. He pulled it closer and stroked the stone with
his thumb and forefinger.

"You know what," he said aloud, "I never even asked Bruno to give it back,
but he did. And he died thinking that I had broken my word to him."

✳

A few weeks later, Uri and Leo walked from the deserted airport terminal,
into the dampness of the cold, gray morning, and toward the long line of
waiting cabs. They each wore a heavy overcoat. Leo gave the driver their
destination.

✳

"I found it, over here," Uri shouted across the abandoned cemetery.

Leo pulled his hat down, dug his hands deep into his coat pockets, and
walked toward his friend who stood near a grave fifty yards away. Uri stared
solemnly at the gray, broken headstone. With a gloved hand, Uri wiped away
the moss to read more of the faded engraving. Yes, it was the right grave.
Miraculously, it had only taken them half an hour to locate it.

No one was present except for them. They'd picked a gloomy, wet November day to search for a grave they'd never visited before. The cemetery had been badly bombed during the war by either the British or the Americans, and the local Hamburg community had done little in the interest of its restoration. Damaged headstones crumbled around them. Many graves had suffered direct bomb damage and lay open, partially covered by wooden planks and corrugated metal sheets. The ground was wet and deep with drenched leaves. It was Sunday, and the office buildings around the cemetery were empty. The only sound came from the planes landing and taking off from the airport, just a few miles away.

Leo approached Uri and nodded. He stared at the headstone—Klara Bergner. He barely remembered her. He was six or seven when she died, and as she had lived in Hamburg, a long way from Augsburg, there had been little contact. She was his grandmother and had died in 1929, at the age of eighty-nine. She had lived through some interesting years, though she'd missed the carnage of the thirties. What would have been her fate? He already knew the answer. A thousand thoughts and images flashed through his mind.

Uri stepped back, not to intrude on Leo's space.

Leo looked down at the soft ground. It had been raining since early morning. He tried to clear away most of the leaves between the two graves. He reached in his coat for a garden trowel that he had bought the day before. He knelt beside the grave, oblivious to the wet dirt on his coat and trousers, and he began to dig a hole. Uri watched, but when he saw that Leo's wet cheeks were not from the rain, rather his tears, he took the trowel from Leo, coaxed him aside, and finished the job.

Minutes later, Uri stood again. The two men stared down at the small hole dug in the ground. From his coat pocket, Leo brought out the green velvet bag, loosened the drawstring, and reached inside to take out the emerald. He held it in his hand for two long minutes, raised it to his lips, then placed it back in the bag, and pulled the drawstring tight. Uri watched as Leo bent down and placed the bag at the bottom of the hole. As Leo stood, he nodded, and Uri, the trowel still in his hand, shoveled dirt over the bag and then filled the hole with pebbles. Leo turned around, picked up a broken piece of a headstone from a nearby grave, and carefully placed it on top. He watched as Uri spread soil over the last few open inches of the hole.

They stood close together, subconsciously reaching out for each other's hand, and in unison, recited the traditional Mourner's Kaddish, their eyes focused on the ground below.

Grandmama's emerald had come home.

AFTERWORD

Billions of dollars worth of Jewish property was seized by the Nazis during World War II. Beginning in 1996, several class action lawsuits were filed in United States federal courts, seeking restitution from particular Swiss banks that allegedly conspired with the Nazi regime to obstruct access to Jewish deposits and confiscate the assets of Holocaust victims. In 1998, the parties agreed to a settlement of $1.25 billion.*

To this day, the wealth stolen from Jewish citizens during the war remains to be fully recovered, and most of the perpetrators responsible for these crimes have never been brought to justice.

*Source: Holocaust Victim Assets Litigation (Swiss Banks) CV-96-4849,
www.swissbankclaims.com

ABOUT THE AUTHOR

Photograph by Nathan Sternfeld

Stephen Maitland-Lewis is a British attorney and former international investment banker. He held senior positions in the City of London, Kuwait, and on Wall Street before moving to California in 1991. He owned a luxury hotel and a world-renowned award-winning restaurant and was also the Director of Marketing of a California daily newspaper. Maitland-Lewis, who lives in Beverly Hills, is a jazz aficionado and Board Trustee of The Louis Armstrong House Museum in New York. His first novel, *Hero on Three Continents*, received numerous accolades.

www.maitland-lewis.com

CPSIA information can be obtained at www.ICGtesting.com
Printed in the USA
BVOW08s1836220114

342711BV00001B/43/P

9 780983 259633